Almost English

Charlotte Mendelson's last novel, *When We Were Bad*, was shortlisted for the Orange Prize for Fiction, and was chosen as a book of the year in the *Observer, Guardian, Sunday Times, New Statesman* and *Spectator*. She is also the author of *Love in Idleness* and *Daughters of Jerusalem*, which won both the Somerset Maugham Award and the John Llewellyn Rhys Prize. *Almost English* is her fourth novel.

www.charlottemendelson.com
@CharlotteMende1

Charlotte Mendelson

Almost English

MANTLE

First published in Great Britain 2013 by Mantle
an imprint of Pan Macmillan, a division of Macmillan Publishers Limited
Pan Macmillan, 20 New Wharf Road, London N1 9RR
Basingstoke and Oxford
Associated companies throughout the world
www.panmacmillan.com

ISBN 978-1-4472-2993-3

3 5 7 9 8 6 4 2

A CIP catalogue record for this book is available from the British Library.

Typeset by Ellipsis Digital Limited, Glasgow
Printed and bound by CPI Group (UK) Ltd, Croydon, CR0 4YY

Visit **www.panmacmillan.com** to read more about all our books
and to buy them. You will also find features, author interviews and
news of any author events, and you can sign up for e-newsletters
so that you're always first to hear about our new releases.

To my grandparents

And for my children

'We are in Transylvania and Transylvania is not England.
Our ways are not your ways, and there shall be
to you many strange things'

Bram Stoker, *Dracula*

'It is a most miserable thing to be ashamed of home'

Charles Dickens, *Great Expectations*

*There is a glossary and guide to pronunciation
at the back of the book, on page 388.*

Prologue

Thursday, 29 December 1988

They do not know it, but the wolf is already at the gate.

Seven o'clock on a moonlit night at the end of December; a terrible time for a party, and the guests are about to arrive. After the complex agony of invitations, the expense, the whipping of cream, the residents of Flat Two, Westminster Court, are almost too tired to greet their visitors, yet there is so much still to be done. They have been up since five in a fury of efficiency, wiping the underside of ornaments, Hoovering beneath the many rugs, rolling pastry, slicing cucumbers: innumerable tasks if this evening is to be perfect, as it must be. And now, while Marina's grandmother and great-aunts rest on their beds, Marina and her mother stand in front of the wardrobe in Marina's little room, pretending not to panic.

'Can't I just wear my school jumper?' asks Marina. 'Lambswool's smart.'

'Maybe not enough, sweetheart,' says Laura, her mother. 'You know they hate . . . never mind. What about that green dress?'

'Grotesque,' says Marina.

'Where's your long skirt, then? Oh Lord. What does your grandmother say?'

'I don't *know*,' says Marina, ominously wet-eyed. 'I look repulsive in everything. I—'

'*Dar*-link,' says a voice from the doorway. It is Marina's grandmother, not resting at all: Rozsi, eighty today and not a woman one disappoints. '*Vot*-apity you don't vant to look pretty. Look, I have this.'

Marina turns round and sees the blouse Rozsi is holding out to her: olive satin with a leaping gazelle motif. 'I . . .' she says. 'I think—'

'And Laura, *dar*-link,' says Rozsi. 'Tonight you also try.'

Laura's mother-in-law is not easy to ignore. One does not become a major figure in the world of ladies' underclothing if one is weak. Laura swallows. 'Yes,' she says. 'Of course I will.' She frowns at herself in the wardrobe mirror: her wet hair, her fair apologetic Midlands skin. Save me, she thinks, as the liver-spotted arm withdraws. 'Marina, love. Your kilt?'

'I could,' says Marina doubtfully. She lowers her voice. 'Mum, I . . . I wondered . . . can we talk?'

Usually, this would make Laura's heart beat faster. However, she is less vigilant than usual, thinking of all that dill still to chop. 'About what?' she asks distractedly.

'It's complicated. I—'

'*Dar*-link,' they hear again from the doorway, 'hurry. We have still to set out the *sair*-viette.'

'Coming,' says Laura. 'Sweetheart,' she whispers to her daughter, 'we'll talk later. I promise. OK?'

Part One

1

How the world loves a party, particularly one in honour of a great age attained. Some of the guests, being quite as old and impatient as their hostess, have arrived early, with enormous boxes of chocolates and expressions of defiance. Every time the intercom buzzes, Marina or her mother has to rush over to let them in. It would have been easier to have left the street doors open, but the residents of Westminster Court are security conscious, for reasons of their own. Here, in the barely respectable depths of Bayswater, some stranger tries to gain admittance once or twice a night. It is better to be sure, and so the doors are shut.

In any case, downstairs in Flat Two the noise is incredible. Everyone is eating, smoking, gossiping; they are not thinking about unwelcome visitors.

The guests who hurry in from the shabby street in the drizzle do not, at first sight, look as though they could possibly be the source of so much noise. If you had happened to come across them as they took their cold constitutionals in Hyde Park this afternoon, they would have seemed perfectly normal elderly Londoners, looking forward to a quiet night in with a cup of tea and a chop and the *Radio Times*.

At least, that is how they think they seem.

But come a little closer. '*Dar*-link' is their usual form of address. Are not their hand gestures a little more extravagant than those found in Surrey, their eyebrows more dramatic, their hair swept back like something from *Nosferatu*? They seem both more formal and more exuberant than you might expect, as if you had wandered into a theatre dressing room of the 1950s, not a cramped west London basement flat. Their bags contain poppy-seed pastries as long as your forearm; velvet-packed pralines, smuggled by fur-wrapped pensioners on the overnighter from Berne. Their perfume smells like the air in a hundred department stores. What are they speaking? Nothing you know, no rolled 'r's or recognizable sounds but either an entirely impenetrable language – *megmásíthatatlan, örökkévalóság* – or a distorted English, full of dactyls which dust familiar words – '*Pee*-codilly' or '*vosh*-ingmochine' or indeed '*Vest*-minstaircourt' – with snow and fir and darkness.

Oh. Hungarian. Now it all makes sense.

So where is little Marina, granddaughter of the house? Is she sitting humbly at the feet of a dashing octogenarian? Is she having her hand kissed by a young accountant, being complimented on her embroidered apron? She was here a minute ago, beautifully dressed for the party: not perhaps in the height of fashion, but in the circumstances . . . Besides, she is always so polite, such a credit to her relatives. Very strange: where has she gone?

'*Boldog születésnap!*' Happy birthday, cry the guests to Rozsi. '*Kezét csókolom*,' I kiss your hand. Some of them actually do it. There is also a great deal of cheek kissing: the very young led by the hand to pay homage to the elderly.

'*Yoy, dar*-link! I *rare*-member I ven you vere *so* high!'

These people make the French look reserved, the English costive. And, at the centre of this kissing, cheek-pinching maelstrom are tonight's hostesses, two of the generations resident in this little flat: three old women and an abandoned wife.

Marina, known tonight as '*Mor*-inaka' or Maza, to rhyme with 'Pots-a', is in charge of coats. Furs and sheepskin and mackintoshes already fill the hall cupboards; the twin beds in her great-aunts' room lie buried under a sea of headwear, although they are far from the Endless Steppe. Nevertheless, the piles of protective outer garments keep growing: berets and fedoras; gloves like warm leather claws.

The air stinks of tuberose, caraway and garlic: the universal scent of central European hospitality. But Marina is not hospitable. After only an hour her skin is tender with cheek pinchings; she has been matchmade, prodded and instructed beyond endurance, and the night is young. Soon they will come to find her, to admire the shape of her fingernails, the thickness of her lashes, their eyes peeling back her clothes, weighing her like fruit. This is not new. She has been brought up to accept the questions and kisses as if nothing could please her more, however much lava is boiling inside. The problem is that Marina has changed. She can bear their scrutiny no longer because her life is a disaster, and it is her fault. She betrayed them and escaped them, and now she wants to come back.

Be careful what you wish for.

This is one of the wise and inspiring precepts she has been gathering lately; she has forty-three so far, six in Latin, but they haven't helped at all. They did not save her from making the worst choice of her life: Combe Abbey. Boarding school. She had wanted to be different, to escape just for the sixth form, and now she is reaping what she sowed.

Five more terms to go.

She is sitting on the edge of the larger bed: that of Zsuzsi, the younger of her two resident great-aunts, the beautiful one, who has a silk pillow to avoid facial wrinkles. Zsuzsi would be disgusted at me, she thinks, wiping her nose and avoiding her own reflection in the three-way dressing-table mirror. Crying is ugly and so, to stop herself, she bites down on the beads inside her lower lip for the taste of courage: blood and iron. Flawed as she is, with an incorrect ratio of leg to torso and freckles everywhere, she must be courageous. Women of her family always are.

In the sitting-cum-dining-room, the party is reaching its climax. There is so much food: cold sour-cherry soup, chicken paprika, buttered noodles, stuffed cabbage, red cabbage, sweet-and-sour cucumber salad, cold *krumplisaláta*, made with gherkins and chives and hot *paprikás krumpli* with sausage. Somebody has tracked down the last carp, or pike, or perch, in London and jellied him – it looks like a him – with carrots. Although it is of dubious provenance – not from Lake Balaton but a pond near Weybridge – all agree that it is wonderful. Rozsi's sisters, virginal Ildi and beautiful Zsuzsi, beam like angels through the steam. *Schnitzel*; goose-liver pâté; Polish salami; Ildi's famous *palacsinta* stuffed with ground walnuts and rum, with lemony curd cheese and raisins or, in the unlikely event of a vegetarian guest, with spinach and only the tiniest taste of bacon. Someone has even brought a large curled ox tongue, which looks exactly as one might fear. And, alone in the darkness of the kitchen, touched with pinky-yellow haze from the fanlight in the communal stairwell, this evening's culinary highlight is waiting: *îles flottantes*, known here as *madártej* or birds' milk, bosomy islands of caramelized egg white, half-subsiding into an inland sea of vanilla custard, suspended in a Czech lead-crystal bowl.

'*Von*-darefool,' say the guests: a rare comprehensible word in an opaque wall of conversation. They are comforted to know that Ildi, although eighty-two, is cooking the food they remember: still pressing dumplings through the *nokedli* machine, chopping veal bones, melting lard. They are a wonderful family, aren't they, all things considered? Admittedly not quite as they were but then, *dar*-link, who is? They are bringing Marina up terribly well, despite everything: so respectful, so polite, and now she is at that school for English aristocrats – well, who knows what might happen?

There are many cousins here, all with mad diminutives: Pubi or Gobbi or Lotsi. The wife of one of them has trapped Laura by the window, and is cross-examining her on behalf of them all. 'So,' the cousin's wife says. '*Dar*-link. Tell me *sum*-sing—'

Despite living at close quarters with elderly Hungarians for over a decade, observing their habits like a less successful

Jane Goodall; despite the fact that she was once married to Rozsi's son and has produced Rozsi's only granddaughter, Laura does not have a diminutive. One cannot catch Hungarianness; they welcomed her and Marina into their home, have kissed and nourished them endlessly, but Laura remains a puzzling pet.

'I really,' she says. 'I mean I can't—'

'*Vot* are you doing?'

'Sorry?'

'*Pro*-fession-allyspeaking. You know I am once *mus*-e-um director? *Vair*-y big museum in Czecho,' the cousin's wife says complacently, bracelets clanking on her loose-skinned arm. 'But you? You are not still reception girl for *von*-darefool doctor?'

'Oh – the surgery? Yes, yes I am.'

The cousin's wife shakes her aged head. She is wearing Capri pants, or what Rozsi would call 'a little *troo*-sair', and a blouse and waistcoat; perfect, if alarming, lipstick; huge glamorous glasses and a bronze puff of hair. Compared to the others, she is dressed casually; it is almost a slight.

'And,' the cousin's wife continues, offering Laura a pink Balkan Sobranie, 'you are lonely, yes?'

'No!' says Laura, stepping back.

'Fortunate, to live with the others, but lonely. So. I know.' They both look down at Laura's pointless wedding ring.

'Not at—'

'Of course now little *Mor*-inaka is at *vot*-you-say board school—'

'Boarding school, yes, bu—'

'The evenings, the weekend. *Vot* are you doing with so much time? You are learning a language? Instrument?'

'Er . . .'

'Do not tell me,' stage-whispers the cousin's wife, 'you are having *boy*-friend?'

'Me? No, not . . . not at all!'

'Because of course without *Pay*-tare . . . vell.'

Laura has been expecting this all evening. Given the number of Hungarians present, their rampaging curiosity and lack of embarrassment, she knew it would come. Poor Rozsi; they can hardly ask her. The disappearance of Peter, Rozsi's younger son, and his abandonment of Laura his wife and Marina his child, is not for general discussion. Laura, however, is fair game.

'You hear from him again?'

'Peter? No, gosh, never. Not since, you know, that first time, there was a, a card he sent to—'

'Yes, yes, of course I see this. You do not know where he is, all these years – *tair*-ible. You cry and cry, don't tell me, *dar*-link,' she says, thumping her fragile-looking breastbone; she has, Laura is certain, been happily married to the cousin for many decades.

The questions keep coming. At least her inquisitor is, as she reminds herself ceaselessly, so affectionate; they all are. When Laura visits her quiet father in Kestonbridge, the Cumbrian village to which, after her quiet mother's death, he quietly retired to a bungalow, people who have known them for twenty years are still hard pressed to greet her. Here, they embrace her like a daughter, albeit a disappointing one.

Warmth, she tells herself once again, is not to be sniffed at. Since taking them into Westminster Court after Peter walked out, Rozsi has refused to let them consider leaving, even after Ildi was mugged on an Acton bus and moved in, and then widowed Zsuzsi followed. They share their food with her. It is like being raised by wolves.

The problem is that they think they know her. They do not realize that, however sweetly Laura smiles, however demurely she answers, there is somewhere she would prefer to be, something she would rather be doing. And someone, of course, which nobody else must know.

They never will. The idea that, after over a decade of chaste abandonment, Rozsi's shy daughter-in-law might have, well, needs, has not crossed their minds. However, there are no secrets here, particularly from one so observant as Marina.

Could Marina conceivably have guessed?

Please, God, not yet. Still, Laura worries. With so many inquisitors stuffed into this little flat, no corner where secrets hide, or are hidden, is safe.

'*Nev*-airmind,' the cousin's wife is saying cheerfully, putting her bony hand through Laura's arm and frog-marching her back into the throng. 'One day when you are old *vom*-an like me you understand. Men leave. Children leave. All that is left is death.'

With a roar from the crowd, Rozsi stands.

To the casual Englishman, were one present, she might appear as other grandmothers: reading glasses on a chain, worn wedding ring. Do not be deceived. Rozsi is unusually clever and fearless even by her compatriots' standards. Her younger son Peter, Laura's former husband, used to call her Attila, with reason. Laura, whose references are more prosaic, thinks of her as Boudicca dressed as Miss Marple. She has a white bun and black eyebrows, her cheeks are soft and age-spotted, but consider the cheekbones underneath; you think she forgives easily? Think again.

Her cake, as is correct and traditional, is not a birthday cake at all, but simply her favourite, a rum and walnut *dios torta*, made by her devoted elder sister Ildi last night. Rozsi, remember to blow the candles out, for luck.

Haaapy Birsday to you . . .

Rozsi looks, all agree, very well. Tonight, in her good dark red dress with gilt buttons, she could not be beautiful; she is too severe for that. But striking, handsome even, like a relatively glamorous Russian spy. Why should Rozsi care about beauty: the smartest of the sisters, a career woman for all these years? And isn't her life at eighty something to marvel at? Despite everything – that terrible business with her poor late husband and then *Pay*-tare disappearing – to be working still is remarkable. Wonderful. Look at them now, see how Marinaka loves her grandmother; Rozsi will never be lonely. Isn't that something else to be grateful for?

Haaapy Birsday to you . . .

The cameras flash at Rozsi and, to be truthful, a little more often at her younger sister Zsuzsi, the beautiful one, with her lovely skin and her good teeth and her cigaretty laugh. Those

13

who knew the famous Károlyi girls, Kitti-Ildi-Rozsi-Franci-Zsuzsi, back in Pálaszlany over fifty years ago, claim that people would stop on the street to gaze as Zsuzsi passed by. Men were known to have killed themselves for her, and marriage, then early widowhood, have not reduced her powers. Several of her suitors are here tonight, tall white-haired handsome 'boys' in beautiful suits: rich Bíró Eddie, globe-trotting André, Tibor with his duelling scar, still patiently waiting for her to choose after all these years.

Haaapy Birsday dar-*link Ro-ji,*
Haaapy Birsday to you.

Rozsi, of course, widowed almost as young as her sister and more unjustly, has no such suitors. She lifts the knife. She smiles.

2

'*Ven* you think the doctor arrives?'

Laura turns slowly. Ildi, the elder of her aunts-in-law, unmarried at eighty-two, still going to evening classes, cooking for fifty without apparent panic, is looking concerned. Of course Dr and Mrs Sudgeon are invited; all the elderly Hungarians and Czechs go to his surgery. It is worryingly easy to imagine distinguished Dr Alistair Sudgeon sitting on their hard-wearing green leather sofa, making conversation. Rozsi will be so proud.

'Hmm,' says Laura, a little too loudly. 'Well.'

Careful, says the voice of sense in her ear. Laura, however, has never mastered being careful. She was not careful when, as a hopeful would-be teacher, twenty-six and astonishingly clueless, she was impregnated by the handsome and utterly spoiled Peter Farkas behind a sweet-chestnut tree in Kensington Gardens. She was not careful for the next three years, tending baby Marina and fighting the cold in their rented flats while he pretended to paint, and borrowed from his overstretched parents and then left them entirely in the lurch.

And, well over a decade later, sharing her mother-in-law's two-and-a-half-bedroom flat with three pensioners and a sixteen-year-old, sleeping at night on their uncomfortable sofa with her clothes in the sideboard, she may be beyond carefulness entirely. Which perhaps explains why she has pledged her loins to the last person she should have chosen: Alistair Sudgeon, her very married employer.

Marina is in the kitchen, washing up cakey cutlery. It is hot in here, and she is wearing a black wool polo-neck, with a huge locket of Zsuzsi's, a kilt, black fifty-denier velvet-look tights and Edwardian ankle boots. She knows – she thinks she knows – how bad she looks, so why does she keep expecting someone's handsome grandson to turn up and fall in love?

Because, she tells herself, punishing her ugly cuticles with the washing-up brush, you always think that the next moment is when your life is going to change, and maybe it never will.

This is a recent realization, which she is struggling to accept. Before the sixth form, clothes were tricky but it hardly mattered: her Ealing Girls' friends were as scruffy as her, as styleless. It was their collective ignorance, she is coming to understand, which doomed her. While elsewhere girls were developing taste and fashion sense, crimping their hair and experimenting with coloured eyeliner, learning what would suit them, she and Katie and Katy and Ursula barely noticed what each other was wearing. Other things were more important, such as memorizing the titles of all Shakespeare's plays.

Then she came to Combe and discovered she had fallen irretrievably behind.

How did this happen? First of all, she never knows what you ought to like. Red, for example, the colour of her duvet cover at Combe and her favourite jumper, is common, and she hadn't known.

Second, what if she dares to try something new but looks stupid, without realizing? She has a terror of this. That, and having food on her teeth.

Third, she is naturally unappetizing.

The truth, which her family do not acknowledge, is that some people can look all right, while others can't. If you're pretty, it's fine to check your reflection in a mirror, or wear mascara. But what if you're not? It'll look like you think you are all right, that you can improve your appearance by smoothing your fringe, but you still have glasses, and spotty upper arms, and hideous knees, and eyebrows like a boy's. Some people are beyond improvement and, when they try, they look like fools. This Marina will not be.

She is uniquely cursed in other ways. She is shy; clumsy; short; fatherless; scared of cats, and the dark, and the future. She is going to be a doctor but knows she isn't up to it, and if she doesn't get into Cambridge her life will be over. And, unbeknownst to anyone at Combe, she lives with old people in a little bit of darkest Hungary, like a maiden in a fairy story. Or a troll.

These things are too shameful to be spoken of. She keeps them in her rotten heart. On reflection, it occurs to her now, maybe her heart is the problem. For, although technically quite innocent, Marina has a very adult love. A world away, in Dorset, the boy she longs for – Simon Flowers, senior music scholar, day boy, bound for Cambridge this very October – is attending polite little family gatherings, packing his physics notes for the new term, writing essays with the clarity of the pure of heart. Nobody knows of her passion. There are so many reasons to keep her love secret: not least that it is against the school rules. And she will be teased about it, which is insupportable. And her family do not approve of boyfriends until she is at Cambridge, '*meen*-eemoom'. And he is an active member of the Christian Union.

Yet although Simon Flowers is in the year above, she knows him well, by observation. He may even have feelings for her. He has smiled at her in Chapel, for example, which is quite unheard of for an Upper, particularly one so glamorous, so talented. Admittedly, they have not technically spoken but she has stared unwaveringly at him to convey her devotion; he can't not know how she feels. It is deafening. She thinks about him every few minutes, planning for their passionately intellectual future. She feels physical pain at the thought of their being asunder. And so she has become increasingly sure that the life-changing moment of union will happen; it has to. Thought beams should make a difference. If you want to see someone enough, they should come.

But what if he doesn't? Nothing, not even the many tragedies of her youth, has pained her as much as the mere sight of his sensitive hands, his leather briefcase, his wire-rimmed glasses. Without him her life will be ashes; besides, she will be unable to care for another. First love can never be repeated. She has read Turgenev. She knows.

'Quickly,' whispers Great-aunt Ildi. 'Where is nice ashtray for Mrs Dobos?'

Mrs Dobos, her grandmother's employer, raises her prima ballerina's head and stares at Marina, as if assessing stock. She is on the most comfortable chair; they dusted behind the radiators in case she looks.

'Here it is,' says Marina, with a lovely smile. 'All washed up specially.'

'Marinaka *dar*-link,' says Mrs Dobos. 'You still do not tell me about Combe-Abbey. You are liking it, as I say you will. You are happy there. I can tell: you eat well. Your bust grows.'

'I—'

'Of course you are happy. It is *von*-darefool school. *Von*-darefoolopportoonity.'

'Yes,' says Marina. 'I am very very lucky. Thank you, Mrs Dobos, for recommending it.'

Once Laura was reasonably intelligent. She had thoughts like: what should we do about Europe? She cared about starving children, about the decline of native woodland. As it turns out, all that concern was varnish. She is merely a collection of needs which are unfortunately not going to be met: to free herself from Dr Alistair Sudgeon, her ageing paramour; to carry her daughter's pure childhood scent around with her in a sniffable capsule, if not Marina in person, like a papoose; to slice through the knot of guilt and duty and financial embarrassment which tightens daily and find somewhere else to live: an independent adult woman with her daughter.

Until September, only four months ago, she could cope with all of this. It was so good for Marina to be brought up with the in-laws, with their culture and their love and all that food; it hardly seemed to matter that she, Laura, wasn't even related to them. When she compared Westminster Court with the bungalow in Kestonbridge, or an unaffordable studio flat beyond the M25, she knew that they were lucky.

Then Marina went away to school and none of the treats Laura had promised herself, cinema matinées, visits to friends in Bath and Bristol, had happened. She did not want them after all; she just wanted Marina back.

Her entanglement with Alistair Sudgeon is not helping. Any minute now he will appear on the doorstep with Mitzi, his wife, with whom Laura seems to be becoming obsessed.

Mitzi Sudgeon is a legend: her energy, her terrible fecund power. Unlike Laura, who has reached her forty-second year with no more to her name than a teenager, houseless, carless, husbandless, Mitzi excels. In addition to four children she has produced hundreds, probably thousands, of pastel drawings: dancing gypsies, merry vagabonds, babes in arms. Her jam is perfect, or as close to perfection as can be achieved without the legendary Nemtudom plums of Tarpa, near the River Tisza, of which Laura has frequently heard. She makes curtains and marital bedspreads. She bakes relentlessly. She organizes pensioners' aerobics sessions at Alistair's surgery.

She is, moreover, an actual Hungarian. In 1956, while the eight-year-old Laura, daughter of two irredeemably English postal workers who called each other 'Mother' and 'Father' and aimed only not to be noticed, was failing to learn to skip in a Birmingham playground, plucky Mitzi, only three years older, was stowing herself away on a tannery barge and preparing to meet her future.

The guests show no sign of leaving. There is still more cake to be eaten: a symphony in chocolate and cream; there are Sobranies still to smoke, black *kavitchka* to drink, marzipan fruits to nibble, families to be discussed. They are all dreadful gigglers; Ildi, whispering to Zsuzsi in the corner, has tears of laughter running down her pink cheeks. And the food keeps coming. Rozsi's oldest friend, Pelzer Fanni, has brought a toddler-sized box of her favourite chocolates from Austria, *Mozartkugeln*, decorated with his silly girlish face.

'*Von*-darefool,' say the shoals of interchangeable cousins. Laura smiles and nods until her cheeks ache with insincerity. She fears them all: protective, touchy, there is so much they insist on knowing, and Laura is no match for them, least of all tonight.

What if, when Alistair arrives, whose desire, or at least the thought of whose desire, so excites her, she starts glowing through her clothes? One of the in-laws will surely notice; not Ildi, too sweet and innocent for suspicion, but what about Zsuzsi, with her instinct for sex? Rozsi, whose thoughts are unreadable, like a polar bear's? My jig, she thinks, is up.

She needs somewhere to think. It will have to be the bathroom, although it will be considered a dereliction of hostessly duty. Shyly she begins to kiss her way towards the kitchen, slashing through the alien corn and, whatever her lips say, her mind is thinking: please. Please. Please.

But what is she asking for? Love, peace, privacy? Or the

opposite of peace: something that will change everything, for better or for worse?

Marina is going back to school in under a week, and another evening has been wasted. Laura has barely seen, let alone talked to her, or grabbed her and sniffed her hair, howled like a lunatic, held on. She wants to lie face down on the cold tiles and weep. But she cannot, so she tells herself to buck up, blows her nose, and washes her face like the mildly disappointed marmalade-making Women's Institute member she could so easily have been.

Water is dripping off her nose. She looks like a different species from her daughter, as if a Labrador had produced a salmon. If Alistair talks to Marina, will she talk back?

It happens all the time: people think she is just another nervous teenager, easily melted, and Laura winces to see how their teasing always turns her child to stiffness like a small strict scientist, how quickly she is offended and embarrassed, her flammable pride. Is it normal to be simultaneously so self-conscious and so prickly? Since starting at Combe it has been worse, for reasons Marina will not discuss. Show them what you really are, Laura wills her, watching her daughter's monosyllabic answers. With her big worried eyebrows and dark thick plait, she has the air of a small Russian poet about to kill herself for love.

Oh, darling, thinks her mother. One day someone will see you. Just, please, not yet.

When the intercom buzzes, Marina knows. This, you see, is how love feels: a heightened awareness, almost psychic, that the beloved is here. Like a magnet seeking metal, a stranded alien found by the mother ship, she is propelled towards him, dodging aged Hungarians with their walking sticks and their determination to pinch her youthful flesh. It is not surprising that she has sensed his approach. In a sandstorm or an avalanche she could probably detect him. Her body would thrum like an antenna, if that is what they do.

How she thrums. Given the strength of her devotion to Simon Flowers, how could it not be him? He must have relented. He has come for her.

'Hello?' someone says into the intercom box. No one answers, which is a sort of sign. Her heart is banging, and organs do not lie. She has willed him here: a hot metallic beam of longing, pulling him all the way from the house he shares with his parents and two little sisters at 29 Mill Road, Stourpaine, Blandford St Mary, Dorset, DT11 2JP, into her arms.

'I'll go,' she says, although everyone is looking. Electric blood booms beneath her skin. Could she have wished him into existence? Until now, fetching the *Evening Standard* for her great-aunt Zsuzsi, or going to the National Portrait Gallery to catch up on the Tudors, or watching the people on the up escalator as she goes down, with her better profile carefully turned their way, she has been certain that in the next minute, or the next, or next, her fortune will change. All it would take was one large aristocratic family or kindly professor. They would recognize her unusual sensitivity, her hitherto unsuspected beauty, and they would welcome her.

This holiday, in the era of Simon Flowers, it has been

different. He must come to London, after all, to visit elderly relatives, or buy madrigals. Every time she leaves the flat she is merely a surface, ready to be seen by him.

Now, at last, he will see. Her life will change tonight. She bangs her elbow on the door handle but hardly notices. The air in the basement corridor is pure oxygen. She flies over the sparkling night-blue linoleum, bypassing the lift, in whose coffin of walnut veneer and leatherette she has dreamed of kissing his chapped lips and now, after her time in the wilderness, can dream again. She will look upon his dear scholarly face and he will rescue her, transform Combe, relieve her of her virginity, set her off towards the glorious adulthood which awaits her. So what if boarding school is not what she had hoped? If the boys are scary and the girls are aliens and they call the townspeople of Combe and Melcombe peasants? She runs up the stairs and bursts into the entrance hall, the strip lighting blazing benedictions upon young love.

The pitch of the party has definitely changed; it is quieter, tenser, as if an adulterer is in their midst. They may be sensing imminent excitement: a storming out, tears, insults. When Laura was growing up, public displays of emotion would lead to lifelong polite ostracism. Her in-laws, however, can take drama in their stride.

Or maybe they are waiting for the Sudgeons, she thinks, as the telephone begins to ring.

Because of the noise, Laura hurries into the great-aunts' room to grab the phone between their beds.

'Hello?'

There is only silence.

Her mouth is dry. 'Hello?' she says again and then, softly, probably inaudibly, she whispers into the yellowing plastic: 'Is that you?'

Silence.

'Who is it?' calls her mother-in-law through the doorway. '*Viszontlátásra, dar*-link – hurry, Mrs Volf goes now.'

'I . . . I think a wrong number,' she shouts back, and the line goes dead.

Simon Flowers is not here. Nobody is. Marina leans back against the front door, trying not to be seen by the people waiting at the bus stop, and is rinsed by a cold wave of self-disgust.

Heartache spreads across her chest, telling her that she will never love again. Simon Flowers is the only boy at Combe she can imagine even liking. He has qualities the others lack: intelligence. Fineness. Beauty, even, if one is sensitive enough to see it. She would give him everything. She would even, it seems, risk letting him into the flat.

Unbeknownst to him, this was to have been a significant, almost ceremonial, moment. For Marina, most things are. She has powers, although she is not sure how they work. Perhaps a suspicion had always been there, an awareness that all that stands between her relatives and their gradual decline into poverty, starvation, diseases missed by neglectful doctors who laugh at their accents, is six years at medical school and lifelong vigilance. However, she had only been away at school a few weeks when she realized that everything she fears stems, via an osmotic process in which she is the conduit, from Combe. Combe is not her family's salvation but their nemesis, she can see that now. Everyone there is so healthy. Everyone at home is weak and flimsy, and growing more so, while she is away from them.

Perhaps, without the homesickness, she would have felt less oppressed by responsibility. Instead, as term, slowly, passed, her sadness did not retreat. She missed her elderly relatives' wrinkly elbows, the soft cords of their necks; whenever she saw a pensioner at a bus stop she would try to carry their bags. What if, as she increasingly feared, she was actually killing them long distance?

One freezing November evening, passing the ruins of Combe Abbey on her tremulous way into dinner, she saw a stone which seemed to be glinting significantly, and made a vow. Under the gas-style light of the new old-fashioned street lamps, she accepted the task of protecting her relatives from pain, sorrow and death. I alone, she swore, will do it, whatever it involves. Decontamination. Quarantine. And, obviously, ensuring that no one from Combe ever crossed the threshold.

The only exception was to be Simon Flowers: a boy of whom even her family would approve. So great was her love that she had decided he was worth the risk. But he is not here. The damage has been done by thought alone and—

'Hey,' says someone in the bus-stop queue.

'Hello?' She squints into the darkness, hoping that Simon Flowers's slender frame will materialize but, in his place, stands someone vaguely familiar: a paleish, slabby, mouse-haired boy. Her face starts to heat like a kettle element, tainting the air around her.

'Come on,' he says. 'You know. School.'

'No, I don't,' she says, although she does recognize him now, a younger boy from Combe, a Fiver, not even in her house: Guy somebody. Rain is beading on his hair, she notes, still observant despite the shipwreck of her hopes and dreams. 'What are you doing here?'

The downpour increases, as if a dial had been turned. He surveys the dry cleaner's, who have picked this moment to load clothes rails into their van. 'I know, weird, isn't it,' he says. 'Went to buy a compact disc on Queensway.'

'Really?'

'And then I'm meeting my mother in Holland Park, but I lost my cab money. They said the bus went from the corner. You don't live *here*, do you?'

Marina is not good at being insulted. She goes stiff; if anyone teases her she is frozen for days.

'Anyway,' he says, not even noticing.

She wants to turn away but he could say foul things now about her at Combe. Also, he does not seem to be mocking her. 'Good, good luck then.'

'Thanks.'

She is about to go inside. But she hesitates, as she always does, and in those few seconds the door to Westminster Court is slowly pulled open. The Combe boy looks round. Marina turns. There, silhouetted by the strip lighting like an avenger, stands an old woman in a floor-length emerald cocktail kaftan, with a cigarette, an ornamental hair clip and big round gilt clip-on earrings: her great-aunt, Zsuzsi.

'I come to find you,' says Zsuzsi. 'Everyone asks, you miss the— who is this?'

The Combe boy's eyes open very wide. Is it her eyeshadow or her golden hair or the accent? Marina barely hears it but she knows it is there. People often ask Rozsi how long she's been in London, as if she's a tourist, and are visibly shocked when she says, 'Forty years.'

Rozsi would be bad enough; Zsuzsi is a disaster. Now that Marina has started at Combe, she needs her elderly relatives to be less conspicuous. There are already rumours that she is a Kraut.

'Actually,' she says, 'I was just com—'

But Combe boys are polite to adults. He leaves the bus queue and holds out his hand. 'Guy Viney,' he says. 'I'm so sorry, I didn't realize you lived here. I'm one of your, ah, daughter's—'

'Daughter?' says Zsuzsi, beaming delightedly. '*Von*-dare-fool. Such a nice boy. One of Marina's school friends? So—' They have been asking and asking her to bring people home. They are obsessed with Combe. They do not realize.

'Well,' says Marina, 'we don't really know each other. He's only a—'

'He wait for bus?' says Zsuzsi, looking as if she is about to offer him a cigarette. 'No!'

'It's fine,' says Marina, as Guy Viney wipes his face with his sleeve.

'Not-at-all,' Zsuzsi says. 'Don't be a silly. We do not let him go like that, a boy from the boarding school. *Tair*-ible. He is wet. He is hungry. He is—'

'Zsuzsi,' says Marina, 'really. I don't . . . we don't . . .'

Her great-aunt takes Guy Viney's arm. 'A friend of Marinaka,' she breathes, as if naming a rare and precious element.

'He's not my—'

'Shh. Young man, I take you inside.'

Marina follows them, with difficulty, into the tiny lift. He takes a lungful of stairwell bleach and overheating and she visualizes the exchange of gases in his alveoli: Farkas air going in, contamination out. He will endanger them and she, Marina, is the point on which it all hinges, like the twist in a loop of DNA. He isn't even very tall and his hair is nothing like a Merchant Ivory hero's. Above the clanking gears he answers questions while Marina stares at his red right ear, thinking of what he will see when he enters Flat Two: the plate clock from Trieste; embroidered folk items; glazed pot holders; Zsuzsi's *Royalty* magazines, the numerous dictionaries and the cupboard fridge on legs.

'I . . .' she begins. Zsuzsi expects politeness, but this is an emergency. The lift is stopping. Could she just drop to the floor? 'Actually—'

He pulls open the grille. Marina hesitates, her hand on the walnut veneer. Zsuzsi gives her a little push. 'Hurry now young boy,' she says. 'We eat cake.'

And it is too late. Everyone turns as they enter the Farkas flat, smiling at him, then at her, as if—

Oh, my God. They can't think that.

They put him on the sofa. They bring him an extra-large slice of what Zsuzsi unnecessarily informs him is boyfriend cake, and coffee, which he nervously declines, and so thrilled are they by everything he says, and so eager to spot signs of love in Marina, that she cannot stand it. She sees him being made to talk to hundreds of relatives. She squirms, she blushes. She starts to sweat. He catches her eye, this infant, this Fiver, this destroyer, and he smiles.

It is the day after, New Year's Eve eve, and they have been clearing up since breakfast. There is only just room in the kitchen for two people; it is five feet wide, maybe nine feet long, so careful choreography is needed. Poor Marina, who cannot pass a door frame without crashing into it, continually hurts herself. What, wonders her mother, has she done to herself now? Is this why she is being so difficult?

The problem is that Marina could be bleeding dramatically and would not admit it. Although her face shows every emotion, pride closes her up. She has been this way since babyhood, refusing to admit to pain, or distress, or even ignorance, as if she thinks it is dishonourable. It's like having a little Hapsburg, thinks Laura vaguely, somewhat out of her depth.

'Sweetheart,' she says, when Marina bangs her hip on the oven for the second time, 'are you really all right? What is it?'

'Nothing,' says Marina, looking offended.

It cannot be normal for a teenager to be so reserved. What if living with the world's most formal pensioners has somehow over-matured her? Was it something to do with that rather lumpen boy at the party, with whom Marina was so set-faced, so gloweringly wooden that any (dear God) thought of romance on his part must have stuttered and died? Or could it be that bloody school, with its petty rules, its cheese-paring insistence on charging for every tiny 'extra', its complacency? She keeps catching herself cursing it, then remembers that Combe was Marina's choice, her ardent wish, and Marina will never admit that she was wrong.

'But—'

They eye each other over the knife drawer. Mothers are supposed to know their child instinctively: not Laura. One of her many greatest fears is that Marina might want her, need her even, and she, Laura, will fail to realize: 'If only she'd told me,' she will say afterwards. 'If only I had known.'

3

Marina never thinks of Guy Viney; she notices this quite often. Spring term, Hilary, is about to begin; only four months have passed since she started at Combe and she feels exhausted already, achy and defeated. She goes to see *Dr Zhivago* at the Czech Centre and attends a children's New Year party at the house of Mrs Dobos, with lemonade and coffee and a real gypsy violinist, embarrassing to watch, and she can't even pretend to enjoy either. A frown is settling into the skin of her almost-seventeen-year-old forehead. Packing takes days; she seems unable to make decisions about which home clothes will stand up to the astonishing cold, how many photographs she can bear to have scrutinized. It's like going off to war. What were once merely things now have special significance; her family's safety depends on identifying a hitherto unnoticed lucky scarf, her future on the crucial pen which will get her into Cambridge. Cambridge. She holds her breath when she thinks of it; it is too sacred to be spoken of. She wants it. She needs it. She is in love with it, and valueless without it. She must not be distracted now.

So passing Fivers are nothing to her. Guy will ignore her when they are back. She is another's anyway.

But Combe is interested in its pupils' social lives. They print a crested booklet, the *Register*, containing contact details. She cannot find him in it but occasionally, when rereading Simon Flowers's address, she sees herself there as others must see her: Farkas, Marina; Flat Two, Westminster Court, Pembridge Road, London W2, with her telephone number: 01 229 8753 – an open invitation.

What does madness feel like? Can you develop it quite discreetly on the bus home from Oxford Street, carrying mothballs? Can it be normal to cry in department store toilets, at advertising hoardings or thoughts of distant famine? Somebody must know.

Laura needs a trusted friend in whom to confide. But half of them have crossed to the dark side: Basingstoke, Bedford, Doncaster. St Albans. The London survivors are too sane, too married; they have bedrooms, and whole houses; they have produced charismatic scruffy children who adore them, or live sterile but sexually satisfying lives of style and beauty. She cannot ask them whether, when they stand on an Underground platform, they think of jumping. It isn't depression, obviously. She isn't catatonic in an armchair, she doesn't have time. Besides, she is not entitled to misery. Her life, compared not only with that of starving Ethiopians but also her very own in-laws, is easy; it is simply that, without Marina, a layer of resistance has started to peel away.

Did it happen in the run-up to Marina's going, or on the day she left? In either case, it is Laura's own fault; she should have stopped her. It was a test of motherhood, which she failed.

Or perhaps, she thinks, after yet another stern self-talking-to, perhaps this is how women her age are supposed

to feel. There is no way of knowing for certain. The lives of women like her, without men, away from their children, do not feature in magazines. When, on the Tube, or tidying the waiting room at work, she happens upon an advertisement for microwave ovens, sun-dried tomatoes, granite worktops, stippling, hyacinths, her soul lifts. Whisper it: this does not happen at exhibitions of German Expressionism. And it is possible, she wants to explain to the world, to be a reasonably intelligent woman – shamefully ignorant and under-educated, yes, but once attached to a modestly adequate brain – yet to long for the four-seasons duvets she will never have.

So if she is not stupid, how is it that Mitzi Sudgeon has everything, the labour-saving devices and career and Alistair Sudgeon, and she, Laura, has not? Is it for want of personal grooming? If she had concentrated properly during drawing lessons, might she now have him? Most women your age, she tells herself many times a day, do not live in a basement with two virgins and two widows and innumerable house plants. They are not told off at mealtimes for being too quiet; they have friends. Lovers, even. Is it any surprise that, after thirteen years, you are a little low?

Many times a day Marina checks that the phones are on the hook, in case Simon Flowers decides to ring her; although, when he does, it would be better if she were out. Being in would mean she is either a saddo or desperate for him, practically a slut. This is the boys' favourite subject, who is a dirty slut and who is frigid and, since discovering that this is how girls are divided, she has devoted many hours to deciding which she is. What with that, and her chemistry struggles, and trying to learn about jazz for when she and Simon Flowers do finally meet, the holidays are racing past. She feels like an old person, watching the days run out, and all her plans for the holidays – ear-piercing, daily sit-ups, reading *Ulysses*, possibly learning a bit of medicine in case of future emergencies – have failed.

This is partly a question of time. She has less of it now; her old habits of preferring certain streets to others, touching doors and her lucky ribbed tights and shampoo and pens, have expanded until they take up hours. Everything has some bearing on the future. It isn't just the street name, or the houses, or past associations which makes Bridstow Place auspicious, Pembridge Villas a source of contagion, Talbot Road a better route home than Colville Terrace. And it isn't just safety; nowhere round here feels safe. It is the combination of these which makes everything either light or dark; it promises a safe future for the relatives and Cambridge for her, or wilderness. When she thinks of last term, before she had realized the harm she could do, it makes her feel sick: all that poison, stored. Now, with less than a week to go before term starts, she is resolved to be vigilant. If anything bad happens, it will be her fault.

Only five nights later, as Rozsi is shouting answers at *Mastermind* – 'Fool. Belgrade!' – and Ildi is in the bath listening to Rimsky-Korsakov live from the Festival Hall, and Zsuzsi is speculating about the bottle of Opium, 'first-class', she was given by Eszelbad Béla while his wife was not looking, and

Laura is trying to remember her mother's recipe for Victoria sponge, the phone begins to ring.

It is exactly half past eight. Who can it be but the anonymous caller from the party, about whom Laura has had such extraordinary dreams? Fantasies, strictly speaking, even while she has known in her heart that it was almost certainly Mitzi Sudgeon. Laura's affair, love or otherwise, with Alistair will have been discovered. Men have wives.

'Oh, let's not ans—' she calls. She should be with them, doing her daughter-in-lawly duty, but there is peace in the kitchen, with the familiar soothing English labels: Tiptree, Twining's, Tate & Lyle. She recites them to herself, quietly, secretly, as a drowning explorer might murmur the National Anthem as his dug-out slowly fills.

They all ignore her. Zsuzsi, with the confidence of the much-telephoned, hurries to answer it. She is wearing towelling bath slippers embroidered with **Hotel Bristol, Baden-Baden**, a present from Mrs Dobos, which Laura suspects were not paid for.

She puts down her whisk and prepares to be exposed.

'*Ha*-llo,' says Zsuzsi. 'You vait one moment, please. Laura!'

'Actually I . . .'

'Come, *dar*-link.'

Wiping her forehead with her apron, Laura approaches. 'I don't—' she begins.

Rozsi silences her with a look. 'A fellow student,' Zsuzsi whispers, smiling as she tightens the belt of her satinette *pongyola*. It smells of cloves which she, or Hungarians in general, use by the handful as a moth repellent. 'For Mari-naka. A boy!'

Laura's stomach swoops back uphill. She edges past the sideboard and armchairs and bookshelf and dining table until she is standing in front of Marina's bedroom door. Icing sugar dusts her hands like an interesting skin disease.

'Sweetheart?'

Laura's mother-in-law suspends her viewing. Zsuzsi, watching through her gills, unwraps another marron glacé. She has been waiting all day for Laura to paint her toenails Havana Moon. A bus rumbles down Moscow Road, a black-bird whistles from the cherry on the front path. Inside Flat Two all is still.

'Marina. Darling?'

Still silence, except, perhaps, for the faintest possible sound; a drawer being shut, a pencil rolled. She's listening to jazz in there, of all things: it sounds like one of Peter's Charlie Mingus tapes, although those are boxed up in the storage room next to the caretaker's flat. Poor pet, what must they think of her at Combe?

When I have a minute, Laura decides, I'll take her to a record shop. Buy something modern.

The old women wait, in Hungarian, for Laura to knock. The problem is this: whoever designed this flat understood storage but not the emotional needs of human beings. Although, to be fair, it was probably built for a nice ordinary English couple and their child, not all these Károlyis and the endless tide of visiting cousins. Marina's bedroom is essen-tially a corridor, off which the bathroom and the toilet lead, like a boa constrictor digesting a sheep. This affords her no privacy, not that the great-aunts think this matters. Despite their absolute silence on matters sexual and the lengths to which they will go to avoid being seen entering a toilet, Rozsi and Ildi and Zsuzsi are startlingly relaxed about the female body, keeping each other company when they have baths, stumping around the flat in nothing but supportive Swiss underwear and rubber orthopaedic shoes. Marina may be young but they show her no quarter, continually whipping back shower curtains, patting her *popsi*, assessing the progress of her breasts. This must add to her terrible bodily shyness. How on earth does she cope at school?

Laura, too, believes in privacy. She is just thinking: I will count to ten, no, twenty, when Rozsi appears behind her, heaves the door open over the carpet ripples and reveals Marina, slightly pink, on the threshold.

'Why are you slow? That very nice young boy Guy, he wait on the telephone,' announces Zsuzsi from the sofa, and Marina runs past her mother and slides the hall door closed.

Laura hovers in the sitting room, trying not to look at the wavy shape of her child behind the glass, the telephone cable trapped like a sea creature's tender frond. Her daughter, about whom, until Combe intervened, she knew almost everything: the only living person who had exactly the same sense of humour. Those days have passed. Marina is in a lengthy solemn phase, which is probably perfectly normal.

I miss you, she thinks, even as her daughter is standing there.

*

What was Guy Viney's motive? He was, he said, just ringing to say thank you but, even if his mother made him, boys like him do not ring girls like Marina. It doesn't make sense. He may only be a Fiver, single sex since he was thirteen, but he must know this. Was it a dare? Was someone standing beside him while he dialled the number, egging him on: Olly Sands, who did the knickers questionnaire? The short ugly boy who won't sit next to girls because he says they have hag fleas? And, if so, why would they do it? As far as the boys are concerned, Marina does not exist.

Combe has a caste system and nicknames are the key. They started in the first week, parthenogenetic, like mushrooms, and stuck: the whole school uses them. You have one if you are famous in school, either officially Hot, with Disney eyes and long legs like Marie-Claire van Dere ('Vanderwear') and Alex 'Nips' Nash, or impressive, like Fernanda 'Queeny' Dodd. And you have one if you are ugly, like 'Fatima' Bryan, or poor Sarah Molle, who is known as Anal Mole.

Marina tries to tell herself that it is better without a nickname. She doesn't want six hundred boys making mechanical wrenching noises every morning when she walks up the Chapel aisle, like sexy Joanna 'Spanner' Aitchison, particularly now she has discovered that spanner means tool, which means penis. But the truth is that being unworthy of a nickname is a disaster. You are invisible.

She can hear the oldies getting ready for bed, talking loudly in Hungarian as if a language she doesn't understand won't wake her. Since Combe started they have stopped offering her bedtime food, grated apple or a segmented orange. It seems extraordinary that only last year she used to lie in bed idly eating and writing letters to her friends, like a White Russian before being shot.

'*Hanyszor fogsz felkelni ma éjjel?*' she hears Ildi say.

'*Ahányszor kell,*' says Zsuzsi. Is there, she wonders, any way to *engender* a nickname? No one discusses them, and girls cannot invent them. But, without one, she might as well leave.

Secretly she has dreamed of this. People do; someone called Imelda left after Marina's first week, and apparently two girls the year before. She can't stop thinking about the shame of returning to the school you left; the teachers' faces, the friends who wrote pledges of eternal friendship on your faded Green Flashes, whom you had thought you wanted to escape. She has promised herself only to consider it if her mother raises the subject; Marina has been waiting and waiting, and now it is too late.

The new term is now only two nights away. All her Ealing Girls' friends, whom she left for Combe, are back at school and, if she hadn't tried to change everything, she'd be with them.

This is the problem. It is her fault. Even a cowardly person can be brave once in their life, and then it ends in disaster. Károlyi women are always brave; that is almost the only fact she knows about the five beautiful sisters who lived in the mountains, or the forest – her knowledge is hazy – and whose father's bees made the best honey in the country.

'In Hungary, you mean?' Marina asked once.

'Yes,' said Zsuzsi.

'No,' said Rozsi.

'He was your father. You must know,' said Marina, trying to joke them into revealing something, and then the great-aunts started crying and she never found out.

Anyway, Rozsi and Ildi and Zsuzsi are Károlyi, first and last. The existence of lovely Zoltan, Marina's grandfather, of Zsuzsi's short-lived dentist husband Imré, even of Marina's own father Peter, has done nothing to weaken the matriarchal line. And so she, Marina Farkas, has striven from birth to be a true and worthy Károlyi. She has been raised on tales of their acts of daring: Cousin Panni smuggling her father's stamp collection through Customs; the time that Zsuzsi had to climb through a government minister's window; or when Great-aunt Franci met her husband, Ernö, on a broken-down tram and commanded him to marry her. Rozsi is the bravest of them all; she once hit a policeman. She could easily rule the world.

Marina is falling asleep. I am not brave, she thinks and, as she sinks through drifts of unconsciousness, she starts to imagine situations in which her courage might be called upon, and would fail her. And then, the innocent, she sleeps.

In the next room, on her sofa-cum-bed, her mother lies awake. This morning, the first day back at work, she and Alistair were almost discovered. She had been in his office, ostensibly bringing him letters to sign but actually enduring an explanation of how difficult Christmas and the New Year had been, when the door opened and in came his wife.

Alistair looked terrified. Laura accidentally said, 'Sorry.'

Mitzi coolly ignored them while producing cheesecake from her bag, trimming loose ends on his blood pressure cuff with her '*nee*-dlevorksisor'; straightening his certificates. 'I leave you now,' she said. He hardly spoke to Laura for the rest of the day.

The truth is that she doesn't care. Only two nights left of Marina; she cannot bear it. The shock does not seem to have worn off at all. She wants to creep into her room to watch her sleeping. She has done it before: the back of Marina's head, barely distinguishable from the blankets, a pale smudge which is probably a hand. Sleep, my love, my darling, she thinks, as a mother should, but what she really wants is for Marina to wake up and talk, and that is irresponsible. The girl needs rest, for when she goes back to that awful place.

My darling, she pleads silently into her forearm. Stay with me.

4

Combe began, as disasters often do, with a few small sparks. Marina had begun to fear that her chance to have fun and sexual experience was slipping away. At Ealing Girls', and home, they thought they knew her. What, she would think, walking in the drizzle from Ealing Broadway, if I want to be someone different?

'Do I have to stay at Ealing for the sixth form?' she'd asked one evening, after Urs had been reported by a stranger for eating on the Tube.

'I suppose . . . well, not necessarily,' her mother said.

Suddenly it made sense. A better school, a famous school, would change her life. They were all so determined that she should do medicine at Cambridge, and how would she manage that from scruffy Ealing, with its dark poky labs and its half-blind chemistry teacher? They ordered a range of prospectuses for London day schools, but the classrooms looked disappointingly like those at Ealing, and the girls in the photographs were much more glamorous. That ruled them out. Was she cool enough for a mixed State school? She quite liked the idea of saving her grandmother money, but Rozsi would not consider relying on the government to pay for her grandchild's education. Besides, Marina was beginning to wonder whether true sophistication was realistic in London, where every bookshop and café seemed to contain old ladies saying 'You must be Farkas Rozsi's *grand*-daughtair! *Dar*-link, you *re*-membair me?'

Then, one night, as she watched *St Trinian's* on television with her mother and Ildi, she had a brilliant idea: boarding school. Cricket pavilions, and midnight feasts, and Gothic stone. Oh yes.

The moment she started imagining it, her heart beat more quickly with dreams of reinvention. She could try anywhere, become a traditional boarding-school girl, or an arty progressive bohemian, and some time passed before she realized how stuffy an old-fashioned all girls' school would feel after Ealing; how out of her depth she would be among people who had grown up in co-education. And so it was that Marina Farkas, girl, from a girls' school, a female family, was left with only one alternative. She would investigate the venerable boys' public schools which now took girls in the sixth form.

The snowball grew larger; she was running to catch up. There was a question buried in the middle, like an aniseed ball: did her mother know her, love her, enough to refuse to be parted from her child? Apparently not. She just let it happen, flicking through prospectuses, trailing around with Marina and the great-aunts at open days, and did not once protest.

Right, thought Marina. If you don't care, if you want to be rid of me, I'll apply for them myself. Besides, the others were excited. These ancient schools were beautiful, and famous, and fantastically well equipped; practically little colleges, which surely would give her a better chance. Mrs

Dobos, her grandmother's friend, summoned them to her white-carpeted Maida Vale flat, with the prospectuses. They told her what they had seen at the open days: boathouses, cloisters, 'dormies', '*com*-putair' rooms, observatories.

'Svimming pools?' asked Mrs Dobos.

'Inside pools!' said Rozsi, who will swim in anything: black water, weedy woodland lakes.

'Very good,' said Mrs Dobos. 'But Combe Abbey, where my great-niece went, of course you look there too.'

'Of course,' said Rozsi, shooting a fierce look at Marina. 'Of course!'

So she applied to sit the exams. She had done all this research, and no one seemed worried about the money. The snowball rolled over a bump and picked up speed. She probably wouldn't get in anywhere. But it would be silly to lose courage now.

She won a place at all four schools she tried. But even though the two most genuinely famous ones offered her scholarships and Combe Abbey only a modest bursary, she found herself thinking that Combe might be the place for her. Some of the others, with their icy radiators and silent gardeners raking the drives, their school farms and yachts and clay pigeons and compulsory outdoor skills expeditions, were clearly not. Combe, however, seemed to be the perfect combination of impressive age, good results and moderate status. And it was in Dorset, near Blackmoor Vale; very healthy, agreed the great-aunts, and not too difficult by train.

And if her relatives were worrying for her about daily Chapel, or drugs, or a ratio of four boys to one girl, they didn't say. She was anxious herself, who would not be, but more about whether her constant backache meant osteoporosis, or if she could bathe her breasts in cold water often enough to firm them adequately before September. Soon fat crested envelopes began to arrive from Combe Abbey, to be read as a reward between her GCSEs until the pages softened. There were calendars of Chapel services: Matins and sung eucharists in the Choir which Marina would joyfully attend, raising her voice on high to 'Ave Verum' by Byrd (William, 1543–1623). They examined the little plan of the abbey ruins, to which the school was attached, its old walls skilfully incorporated into newer buildings by an Old Combeian architect with, suggested Marina's mother, friends in the Planning Department. They went to Rozsi's optician, where, after a lengthy examination, she was permitted to have semi-permeable contact lenses to be worn for two hours a day. She practised with them every night; it was like putting grit in her eye, but it would be worth it.

A scarlet fever questionnaire arrived; then the *Almanac*; the school rules, the supplementary rules for scholars, and the rules for what at Ealing Girls' were just called monitors and at Combe were apparently 'Sirs', even the girls. They purchased a recent copy of the school magazine, the *Combeian* (£5 from the school bursar, Colonel Perry). They were sent packing lists, details of permissible extras (scientific calculators, tuck boxes, riding boots 'if wished'; desk light [UK plug]; laundry bag; 'one [1] mug'); the addresses of approved purveyors of the boys' exciting tailcoats and girls' disappointing blazers and the school scarf in navy and pink;

a brochure of Old Combeian Association cricket jerseys, cummerbunds and decanters; a book list; and, most deliciously of all, the exact dimensions of her trunk.

She had never desired any object more. Her love for her twin-deck JVC tape recorder, even for her desk, paled in comparison. The night before her grandmother went into town to buy it, she could not sleep for excitement. But at Harrods, the only official stockist in central London, Rozsi chose black leatherette with shiny brass studs: an enormous disappointment, which Marina concealed.

Besides, there was always the *Register* for comfort: the masters, degree and alma mater noted, down to the head groundsman (Henley Agricultural Institute, Dip. Hort.); and, better still, the boys: three years' worth of Freshers and Removes and Fivers called Quentin and Hugh and then the entire Sixth, girls included: two hundred and forty-three possible friends for midnight feasts, moorland house parties and, almost certainly, marriage. It didn't seem to matter, at the time, that girls had only been admitted to the sixth form for three years. How much difference, she asked herself, could that make?

But she would have to change her old self; no doubt about that. She needed class. She spent the summer preparing. She read *Tom Brown's Schooldays* and *Billy Bunter* as if they were textbooks. She tore pages out of Mrs Dobos's old *Tatlers* and *Harpers & Queens* ('For the Smart Insider') to decorate the inside of her wardrobe: square-jawed men lounging about in libraries and beautifully dishevelled women on grouse moors; Scottish Christmases in velvet and taffeta. She was in love with tartan. There was a world out there in which people celebrated Burns Night with wild country dancing, drank sloe gin at point-to-points, bundled up for the night in cold stately homes under opossum car rugs 'like Granny wore in her Daimler'.

Oh. Please. Yes.

This was it: the future. She was at the peak of nervous happiness and thought that another, higher, peak was beyond. It would feature cheery refectory meals beside tall friendly English girls with welcoming families; stimulating lessons in well-equipped Victorian laboratories; handsome boys writing her sonnets beneath historic oak trees. Handsome boys, like, at a push, Guy Viney. Soon it would not matter that she could neither hurdle nor paint nor sing, her shyness in the showers would be irrelevant, for at Combe she would blossom and become herself. And even when she had waved her family goodbye on the terrible first day, watching their hats receding down the drive and feeling she would die of pain and fear, she had not realized how much worse it would become.

5

Rugby: Dorset and Wiltshire sevens, U18 (all day),
Salisbury; Freshers' swimming time trials, Recreation
Centre, 4.30 p.m.; squash tour to Kuala Lumpur
begins (minibus leaves Garthgate 5.10 p.m.);
Countryman Society talk by Mr Kendall: 'Forestry:
An Ancient Craft', Old Library, 7.30 p.m.

The first days back are horrible. Marina keeps expecting her
mother to come and take her away. But what if she can't?

All the fears of childhood have come back with new
vigour now that Marina is too far away to protect them from
intruders, race riots, Spanish flu, nuclear winter, IRA bombs.
Guy Viney is irrelevant, a plaster on a spurting wound, and
so the first time she sees him, muddy and laughing at lunch
with Ben L and Ben P and Rich from her year, she ignores
him. She is busy trying to think of a reason to be near the
crypt when the Combe Singers, in which Simon Flowers is a
tenor, finish practice. Guy won't speak to her now they are
back at school. She certainly won't speak to him.

Then, on Friday night, she has to queue right behind
him in the Buttery. He is extremely sure of himself for a

Fiver. He is talking to horrible Giles Yeo from Marina's year and, although Giles always ignores Marina, when Guy says, 'Wotcha,' Giles gives her a curious look.

Why is Guy so confident? Fivers usually keep to themselves but he finds a table with Giles and some of the Bens and says, 'Come on,' so she sits down with them. As she sprinkles cheese on her baked potato, grate by grate, she watches him consume mulligatawny, beans, double chips, peas, broccoli, grilled tomatoes, buttered rolls and two vast sides of breaded haddock, and listens to his silly jokes. Once or twice she laughs, accidentally, and he grins at her. She concentrates on resisting the temptation to take off her glasses; it makes the Buttery less frightening, but she is so short-sighted she will walk into a table. If only, she thinks, I were normal, like everybody else.

'Can I have your custard?' Guy says.

She won't let down her guard just because he's younger. He's still secretly laughing at her; he'd probably be one of the boys holding up score cards for the new girls, if it hadn't been banned last year. Apparently they had to; that's why Imelda someone ran away into the night and was never seen again. Even so, they still put up lists giving marks out of ten in some of the houses: maybe Macdonald, where the boys won't speak to girls at mealtimes, or Fielding, where they ambush girls with buckets of water for wet T-shirt contests, not just in the summer term as in other houses, but all year long.

She must have a score. She wants to know what it is.

What kind of girl, she thinks, wishing she hadn't eaten her crumble, would—

Then she looks up and sees Simon Flowers.

Behind him, in slow motion, the Buttery doors flap shut, open, shut. She can feel the slowing of her atrial diastole; she is barely breathing by the time he reaches the trays. He speaks kindly to the one-armed dinner lady. Why is he, a day boy, having supper at school? Probably he's been practising his jazz guitar riffs, or playing the organ alone in the Chapel, and a scene from her numerous imaginary sexual adventures catches her unawares.

Her heart booms towards him, yet he does not see her. She must practise saintly patience. How long must she wait? A week? A term? If you haven't got off with someone by the time you're seventeen, you will definitely die alone. It's a measurement, like lung capacity. Everyone here has been doing it for years; she has pretended the same.

'What's up?' says Rory Kingsly. 'You look like a flid.'

Two blonde girls from the year above giggle.

'Shut up, Kingsly,' says Clare Laker. 'You sound like a knob,' and she mouths at Marina, 'Pitiful.'

But Marina who, four and a half months in, still feels her true Combe friend is yet undiscovered, hardly notices. She is thinking: I can't go on. Simon Flowers: Simon. Come and get me. I am ripe for you.

Meanwhile, in London, Laura exists. She polishes the grill pan until it shines like pearls; she helps Ildi find her lost Italian dictionary; she feeds Rozsi's jade plant the correct quantity of vegetable water and battles the relentless London dust; she makes up her bed each night on the sofa cushions and falls asleep, eventually, to the perpetual murmur of the World Service, to the snoring and sighing of elderly immigrants and buses hissing past outside. Around and around in her tired head one thought spins, 'What should I do?' as if, with five minutes of hard thinking, she will realize that she has all the solutions already: a good man, close by and single, with whom to fall in love; somewhere affordable to live, where she can eat baked beans and listen to music befitting her age group and walk around in the nude; a professional qualification about which she had forgotten; a nearby day school which her child will consent to attend.

She goes to work and feigns interest in plans to replace the receptionists' plywood shelves with plastic-coated steel. Black or grey? Who cares? She sits on the bus and feels guilty about the Farkas-Károlyis' unlimited kindness; about her father, her daughter's father, and her daughter. Then she comes home again and tries to think about Alistair, or composes letters to Marina, which she rewrites until nothing she wants to say is left.

For the last eight months, since Marina started preparing to go away, Laura's life has been controlled by the Royal Mail. Her spirits, too, now that she thinks of it. She had been proud of how well she coped after Peter went, and through the long years of sofa-dwelling in Westminster Court. But now, whenever she is out, she looks for postcards – paintings from the endless exhibitions she attends with the in-laws and, when away from them, 'Great British Fry-Ups' or 'Piccadilly Circus by Night'. When at home she is thinking of amusing observations, timing her day around the arrival of post. She sent a card every day last term, but now she has decided she must restrict herself. Marina hardly ever commented; she just became tenser and crosser. Clearly, all Laura's careful non-expressions of love were too much.

Days pass. Life, if one can call it that, continues: a constant counting down of the hours until the end of term. Perhaps, she thinks, tidying the waiting-room magazines, I just need sex.

Sex is, however, not easily obtained. She has not touched the private flesh of Dr Alistair Sudgeon since a month last Tuesday, when they arranged for her to do an evening spring-clean while he 'worked through files'. It was not even particularly satisfactory. The effect on her of cold vinyl, antiseptic odours and, curiously, his white coat on the back of the door, to which she had so looked forward, had not been positive. But more, or elsewhere, or better, is out of the question. How can she be old enough to feel this tired, yet have no privacy whatsoever? Alistair is so busy at home, is so widely known – at least, in W2 – and also, perhaps, like Laura, has certain ambivalences (how can she ask him when they are together so rarely? How could she raise, by letter, something that would require discussion, even a row? What is a bubble burst? she sometimes says to him in her head. He does not answer).

Does this mean, she asks her reflection in the bus window, that things will never improve? In which case, might I be having not a nervous breakdown, but simply a disappointing life?

At this thought she jerks her face away and finds herself

being smiled at sympathetically by the woman opposite. She smiles back before she notices the woman's multiple badges, her rat's-tail plaits and tattooed thumbs. Now even mad people pity her. If, she thinks, trying to be matter of fact, the bus skidded now on Westbourne Grove, would that be so bad?

Every morning after First Quarter Marina and the other West Street girls rush back to the house to check for letters. West Street is just outside the school grounds, reached via a narrow passage beside Bute House. It is not a house in its own right, but a place in which female quasi-members of the boys' houses live. It was once part of a terrace, now partitioned like an experiment for mice, and Marina has failed to make the slightest sense of the labyrinth. Whenever she ventures to the upper floors, the double staircases foil her. She has endless dreams of being lost.

There are no mullioned dormitories or coats of arms here, no crested oars draped with football socks, no miasma of Paco Rabanne. West Street is clean, and vigorously air-freshened. There is a kitchenette, floral curtains, doilies. The fire doors are decorated with posters of kittens in hammocks, thoughtful bears. The carpet is dusky pink. And there is a matron, Mrs Long, whose twin passions for Benson & Hedges and her flatulent Dandie Dinmont terrier, Anthony, sit uneasily with her stringent domestic expectations. Other girls receive constant correspondence: brotherly post from agricultural colleges; cheery catch-ups from their mothers about puppies and their fathers' business trips; invitations to charity fashion shows. They all have thousands of people at other schools in common and read out bits of letters: 'Jamie – no, silly, Stowe Jamie – says we *have* to go to the Gate-crasher Ball.' The only girls who keep their correspondence private are the recipients of love letters, like the eye-linered and patchoulied Simonetta Bruce, to whom Marina has taken a fierce dislike.

And Marina herself. How could she show her post? This is her total so far: one forwarded membership reminder for the Puffin Club; one grumpy eight-page letter from Ursula Persky, her best friend at Ealing Girls', tucked inside a *Hamlet* programme from yet another school trip to Stratford; a single postcard from her mother saying not much; and one of Rozsi's brown paper packages.

How she loves these parcels. How she hates them. This one contains sponge fingers, a leaflet about childhood ill-nesses, unsolicited lo-calorie sweetener, a bank-bag of fresh ten pences for the pay phone, a *Tatler* from Mrs Dobos and a short letter: 'Hallo darling don't you want a lovly hair cut? Tell me I ask Krystof any time he helps you. Sorry you are not siting next to me. I try to send beter letter soon.' Unlike Ildi, who fills exercise books with vocabulary and old diaries with informative facts ('*Raphael died on his 37 birthday. Crucifiction* [sic] *early picture (about 20 years). A bit provincial (see fluttering ribbons). Best in the figure of Christ. Painted for a convent*'), Rozsi is not comfortable with writing, at least in English. Her handwriting suits Hungarian better. Last term she sent Marina a sewing kit which must have been hers; when Marina ran to the bathroom with it and opened the lid, an old browned piece of lined paper fell out. The smell of the flat has faded from it, but she still has the paper: a few meaningless accented words, written in pencil, too full of possible momentous secrets to throw away.

She keeps having premonitions that harm is coming to them. Since Combe, or was it before, she cannot stop expecting it, attempting to prevent it, knowing that nothing she does will be enough. The fear that she will contaminate them is much stronger this term. Simonetta 'Slutter' Bruce has the room next to Marina's, and her music and loud laughter infest everything Marina owns. Although she is an Upper, and is best friends with a girl in School House so is often elsewhere, the smell of her Players and Rive Gauche means that she always seems present: a force for bad. Apparently, she has had sex in Divvers; her mother is dead, or at least divorced. Two days into the new term Marina is using her jumper sleeves to open doors which Simonetta might have touched. She holds her breath when she comes upstairs. If someone in Marina's family dies, Simonetta will be the reason.

She cannot cry now, about to go into chemistry. All day she aches for her mother, who has not written again, but she saves her sodium chloride tears for the night.

6

Rozsi is in lingerie. Once they all were; she and her handsome husband Zoltan owned FEMINA OF KENSINGTON, as it still says on the shop front, and Ildi, when she came to London from Budapest in '56 with a chemistry degree, wrote their letters, and beautiful Zsuzsi, whom it is difficult to imagine doing anything, apparently travelled for them to Greece and Vienna and even 'Petersburg', where they understand the power of elastic. What Laura has never quite followed is – well, all of it, really. The heroic origins of Femina have often been repeated: Rozsi's discovery of some missing money when sweeping a different shop, Ginswald's on the Finchley Road, when Peter/*Pay*-tare was a babe in arms and Zoltan was fighting in the war; her honourable elevation to assistant and the small suggestions which led to her being permitted to design one perfect brassiere, then another, and then to be given a shelf, a section and, in the end, when they had saved and borrowed enough, for the Farkases to buy their own tiny shop and break free. But there is something murky at the back of it, some fell moment when Zoltan weakened, and everything was lost.

Zoltan was a lovely man: not as funny as Peter but

gentler, more chivalrous, with the same terrible steely pride. The formality, or sense of honour, which in Rozsi is so terrifying was, in Zoltan, a comfort. With a man who wears a vest to conceal his chest hair on holiday and a tie to see the dentist, who expects toddlers to stand when their mother enters a room and who eats bananas with a knife and fork, you know where you are. Laura, his mere daughter-in-law, misses him more as the years pass; he loved her, although obviously not as much as he did Marina. He cannot be mentioned at home: there will be crying. So on the bus she imagines conversations in which he offers understanding, and forgiveness.

But what did he die of? Somehow she has forgotten, and now she wants to know. It happened suddenly, and at that moment Marina was a tiny child, Peter an increasingly unreliable mess, and their fourth-floor one-bedroom flat in north Acton like something from a Pinter play. All she does know is that Femina, still revered by its loyal customers for its old-fashioned service and the firmness of its silhouette, had to be sold to Mrs Dobos, their compatriot. Rozsi, now merely the manageress, is old. Her salary is her sisters' only income, apart from a decreasing amount of what Ildi calls home-working: occasional bits of proof-reading for Czech and Hungarian business acquaintances of Rozsi's, which Ildi does on a fold-out table.

Combe Abbey is the natural home of children with well-fed hair and indulgent businessman fathers. Perhaps there is financial leeway for some families, but it is hard to imagine the bursar offering help to Marina. If Laura loses her own job, due to ineptitude or sex or its absence, what will keep the wolf from their door?

She is carrying her bedtime glass of water into the sitting room when the phone rings. She jumps like a guilty woman.

'Hello?' she says. 'Hello?'

No Marina. No anyone. The fizzing thickens into the sound of breathing, of thinking, pale granules clumping together to form a shape: almost a face. Pale, with red hair. Who else could it be but Mitzi Sudgeon? Hatred has an echo.

War has been declared.

Sunday, 22 January

Sung eucharist (Crypt Choir) or pastoral address, Divinity Hall: Canon Paul Sheath, 'Overcoming Temptation'; hockey: Pineways Tournament, 1st XI, Sholtsborough (minibus leaves 11 a.m.) (A); OC Society talk by James Pollinger: 'Constable: His Art, His Life', Combe Lodge Chamber, 5 p.m.; Wine Appreciation Society: Rioja, deputy headmaster's rooms, Cordfield; Choral Society rehearsal (open), Divinity Hall, 7.30 p.m.

It is strange, Marina observes, that once you start noticing someone you see them everywhere; in the queue for tuna crumble, or hiding under the Praecentor's Gate from a down-pour of acid rain. Now as well as Simon Flowers, and various enemies, and Wilco the feral groundsman, she begins to spot Guy Viney all the time.

'All right?' he says when he sees her, even in public. The shame of talking to someone who has read all Jane Austen's novels, even *Lady Susan*, doesn't seem to occur to him; he clearly does not know that in lessons she is the only girl who puts up her hand. Or is it because he is younger? He is lucky that she acknowledges him at all.

'*Minden jól,*' which means 'very good', says Zsuzsi on Sunday morning, when Marina rings home. 'How is that nice boy?'

At that moment Marina realizes that no one at school has referred to Guy's visit to Westminster Court. Is it possible that he hasn't told everyone, that they are not laughing and mocking behind her back?

Maybe he won't ruin her. Maybe he is nice.

But that is all. They have nothing in common, whereas Simon Flowers, scientist with a soul, is a perfect match. If he boarded like Guy, they could talk all night; instead, he goes home to his family, about whom she knows not enough, except that his mother is a librarian, which warms her heart. She would pay all her money to visit his house for a single minute. Guy Viney must have a family too, but who cares?

That evening Alexia 'Sexier' Prior says, 'Come with me, no one else is around,' when she is getting ready to go to Percy to see her crush, Jim Finn, and so Marina goes. The staircase is rich with the smell of plimsolls and what she suspects is boys' deodorant, sprayed in flammable quantities. Guy's room, Percy IV, is next door, up in the roof. His door is open. 'Hey,' he says. 'Want a chocolate biscuit?'

Percy IV has a romantically steep ceiling, a collapsing armchair, carved stone vines around the door and a glow-in-the-dark 'Stairway to Heaven' poster. For a Combe boy he is friendly, although the Fiver sitting on a beanbag, his room-mate Tosser something, ignores her. At first Marina just smiles and nods as they talk about football; if she fails to look interested they will call her a 'woman', which is a grievous insult. But Guy keeps giving her biscuits, and doesn't refer to having seen Westminster Court, or laugh when she says, 'But who is Jim Morrison?', and when his friend says, 'WSK,' which means West Street Knockers, he tells him to shut up. Guy doesn't ask her questions either, but when, almost for something to say, she starts talking about Cambridge – mocks, predictions, UCCA forms, the masters' frustrating lack of interest in helping her choose a college – he doesn't look disgusted.

'Oh, right,' he says. 'A brainy bird.'

'Honestly not,' she says. 'It's . . . actually, I'm really scared. I'm never going to make it.'

'Bollocks,' he says. 'Just give it a whirl.'

When she gives up on Alexia Prior and starts to go, he says, 'Come by any time,' and, because he is not remotely a romantic option, she does. She has never been good at Social in the West Street television room, where combinations of Allegra and Isla and Ellie and Nicky and Alex and Fleur and Vix and Belinda and Antoinette 'Toni, rhymes with Joni'

Collister and Daisy Chang and Annabelle 'Pubic' Tuft eat white toast and discuss either the First Eleven, or frequency-wash shampoo, or which boys they all know at Marlborough and Wellington, every single night.

Upstairs is worse because her bedroom contains Heidi Smith-Russell, her Hilary term room-mate, daughter of a millionaire poultry-feed manufacturer near Chichester. Heidi has a Filofax and buffs her nails twice a week; she claims that this is as important as washing your hair. Marina wants to ask Mrs Long if they were put together this term because they are equally unpopular, but fears the answer. Anyway, unlike Marina, even Heidi has friends.

Guy saves her. Because she has a boy to visit, the West Street girls don't mind if she misses Social, but their indulgent smile and references to 'happy hour' confuse her. 'It's not *that*,' she says, burning with shame and pride. Nevertheless, the next time she goes she wears her contact lenses and then just sits blinking on Guy's beanbag, feeling like a fool.

He is quite funny for a Fiver but not at all attractive: too pasty and puffy-haired for that. He likes explaining in detail why he fancies Amanda Stapleton, known as Knobule: her tennis shoulders, her long flicky hair. His maleness is irrelevant, like a dog's. Later, in her room, she thinks about Simon Flowers just as much as before. Besides, she has work to do: an assessment of Hardy's nature poetry, the respective properties of chlorophyll-*a* $C_{55}H_{72}O_5N_4Mg$ and chlorophyll-*b* $C_{55}H_{70}O_6N_4Mg$. She writes on and on in brown-black ink, past midnight, past two, and although her backache is worse, and sometimes she doesn't seem to be breathing properly, and her heart aches, she tries to keep her mind on the golden prize: Cambridge. Isn't that the point of it all? Simon Flowers will be there too. They will punt, or bowl, or play croquet, in an intellectual yet passionate union, miles away from Combe.

As she falls asleep she thinks of him chastely in bed in Stourpaine, and barely misses her mother. Or, rather, discovers that if she refuses to let herself, closes herself to even the possibility of pain, she can bear not to be with her. Besides, it is safer for the Farkases not to be thought about and, although forcing her mind away is like bending metal, she is Rozsi's grandchild. She manages.

Then everything changes.

On Saturday nights they are allowed, Within Reason, their freedom. This means alcohol. The Combe Abbey rules about alcohol are perfectly clear: never before the sixth form and, if every term a Fiver stomach or two has to be pumped, there is no need to discuss it. On returning from dinner out (never just drinking) on a Saturday night, Combe pupils must report to their housemaster. Why the housemasters never notice that everyone is completely drunk is a mystery. It has happened to Marina twice already; she remembers nothing at all of the first time, and the second she insisted on walking in a straight line and broke a chair leg. There are always awful stories: paralytic staggerings into the arms of the headmaster's wife, vomit in the Chapel, turds. Today is the birthday of Selina Knocker, the sweet but stupid child of the head of the navy who is, physically at least, in all Marina's classes. This must be why Marina is invited, but

Guy is a Fiver, too young to be in town after dark. So why is he allowed, even if their parents do know each other? She tries to ask, but he just grins and says, 'Ve haff vays.'

She is wearing contact lenses. Dust and drizzle and her own fringe keep blowing into her eyes as she walks along the dark East Combe Road, next to Selina's cousin Gypsy. No one brings coats, let alone their great-aunt's umbrella from Fenwick's, so Marina's teeth are chattering, which she is trying to disguise with conversation. Because this part of Dorset is so very flat and ringed by hillsides, she often has a feeling of being cut off from the rest of England, as if they are walking at the bottom of a meteor hole. If only, she thinks, I could see London from here, even just a bit of Esher, I would know they were safe.

Gypsy, Jippo, is unfriendly but very beautiful, with long brown legs and big blinky blue eyes. Apparently she has just been skiing and seduced an instructor. Marina is struggling to find common ground.

'Where are we going?' she asks, after an awkward silence through which Jippo sails, serene. 'I mean, I know the name, but I haven't . . . is it a, a *smart* restaurant? I mean—'

'Just Capote's.'

'Oh. Thanks.' She has already spent too much this term on inspiring postcards and impressive Penguin European Classics: *Orlando Furioso, Oblomov, The Trial*. She cannot ask her mother for more money. They pay probably hundreds every year for her fees, and then there are the train fares and the Old Combeian Society (motto: *Floreat Combeiensis*), for which Rozsi signed her up for lifetime membership, together with OCS crested lapel badge and fountain pen, before Marina's first day. Even the uniform, all those ties and tennis shoes, must cost quite a bit. I will order modestly, she thinks, and sits down, moved.

But they are cold and damp, and order hugely: onion rings, *frutti di mare*, lamb chops, steak. She eats her Margarita pizza and drinks enough house white to make the night seem glittery, the future not exactly golden, but not leaden either. She catches Guy's eye and smiles. She can even stand sitting between Giles Yeo, who has slicked-back hair and Ray-Bans, and Bill Wallis, whose shirt has bow ties and champagne bottles on the sleeves.

'Wop,' they call each other, 'flid' and 'spaz' and 'faggot'.

They lean across to talk about rugby, pretending to be very careful of her WSK but otherwise ignoring her. Bill's three brothers all came here; next year he will be captain of the rowing team, so it would be unwise to annoy him. Nevertheless, Marina refuses to make conversation, on principle. She looks towards the salad bar with an enigmatic smile, thinking of being with Simon Flowers at Cambridge, crossing the quadrangles in lab coats on their way to making discoveries.

They walk back to school in formation: popular girls at the front like Amanda 'Saddle' Collindale, who hunts, and Michaela Buonasenda the nymphomaniac; Guy in the middle, Marina at the back. The streets of Combe are deserted.

'Where are the peasants?' bellows Bill, and Saddle snorts. Marina is almost too frightened to breathe. Her lips are dry.

Townspeople really might attack them; I would, she thinks. Victoria Porritt, 'Muffster', a big-haired fat girl in Fitzgerald House, Fitz, with a Tory MP father, totters on the cobblestones and takes Marina's arm.

'You don't want to be a *doctor*, though, surely?' she says. 'I mean, really.'

'Well . . .' If she explains that it's not about wanting, Victoria Porritt might not understand. 'I, I quite *like* the sciences,' she says.

'Ugh. Biology. Chemistry! How can you stand it?'

Marina swallows. 'What do you want to be?'

'Nothing. Married.' She puts her wet mouth against Marina's ear. 'Did you know I was finger-fucked by Pete Galbraith at half-term?'

Through silent Garthgate, which usually she avoids despite the new lamp posts and illuminated night guard's hut. Victoria Porritt does not care. She eulogizes her pony and Marina joins in, the little fraud. Above the spire and ancient towers, the Plough lies upended in the cold. Her heart is clanging. Only babies are afraid of the dark. They face the blackness at the end of the passage. Then, enormous in a strip of lamplight, out of the shadows looms Guy.

'Piss off, virge,' shout the boys at the back, head-locking him and ruffling his hair.

'Oh, help!' screams Victoria Porritt and hurries off to join the others.

Guy grins at Marina. 'Bet you haven't seen this,' he says, and leads her back through the night to a little fence, easily climbed. Into the navy sky above them stretches another tower, a spray of stars, a single lit-up window. They are in a little walled garden hard up against the side of the ruins; there are flowerbeds, but no house close by.

'Like it?' he says, lowering his voice until it is just breath in the cold.

A branch of something is close to her ear; it smells sweet although it is winter. Rozsi would rip it off and take it home; she knows no shame. The bat roosts and jagged pressing leaves, the distant footsteps, are horrible. Their curfew is eleven; breaking it is punished with rustication, like sex. She smiles nervously, consolingly. He is just a Fiver, showing off. 'Shall we—'

He moves closer: not exactly a friend. Although he has never shown the slightest sign of interest, indeed has discussed further his inexplicable desire for Knobule Stapleton, an atmosphere is developing which even she cannot miss. It fills her with sadness; she had such high hopes. In all these long years when nobody has wanted to kiss her, she has been ready, memorizing Stevie Smith's 'I like to get off with people' and e.e. cummings's 'may i feel?' until she and Ursula knew them, literally, backwards. She understood passion and desire, and how they would feel when they found her.

But boys like him, she realizes, about to hatch, must need girlfriends too. And if they can't have Knobule Stapleton they will aim lower, and lower, until they end up with her.

7

Many miles away, in west London, Marina's mother sits at the dining table, making notes on the index cards she keeps in a folder labelled

LAURA'S WORK

Laura is a receptionist. Not even a good one, as Alistair, in his capacity as her employer, makes perfectly clear. She spends her working day in a morass of shame and minor disasters, not putting telephone calls through, hiding sub-standard photocopies, worrying that she has forgotten to tell someone that they are pregnant, dying, both. Her job has, however, three advantages: a constant supply of memo pads and ball point pens labelled CYNOSTEX FOR CYSTITIS and AGROLAST: THE LARGER HERNIA PATCH; proximity to Alistair, which is, she reminds herself often, the enabler and not the sole cause of their passion; and, most importantly, patient confidentiality. Even Zsuzsi respects this; most of Laura's paperwork is about verrucas, or mump vaccinations, or any of the many areas of human suffering in which she has no interest. Consequently, every day Laura lugs home a pile of non-exciting correspondence, and in the margins, in light pencil, she expresses herself:

Oh God rescue me. A: won't you ring?
Marina Marina Marina God I can't stand this.

What choice does she have? Here in her candlewick sar-cophagus, space is limited. Her bedding lives in a suitcase beside the bookshelves; forty years' worth of childhood books and over-exposed Polaroids tangle in her mother-in-law's spare drawer. If Laura kept a diary under the sofa cushions, someone would find it, yet there is much in her mind which needs an outlet. Such as, for example, her feelings about the fourth great advantage of her job: a little drawer, a little key, a cupboard in Dr Sudgeon's office containing Tramadol, Valium, Temazepam, of whose comforting existence she has been thinking more and more. Would, she wonders now, purely theoretically, twenty be enough?

This is how it begins: an ordinary teenage love story. He never, obviously, contravenes the Six Inch Rule by touching her in public, or is affectionate in private, or acknowledges their intimacy where others could hear. It is better this way, given that he is in the year below. However, everyone, from children in the Freshers to the head boy and captain of rugby, Thomas 'Tom' Thomson, seems to find her less freakish now.

It's like being married. They have a routine. Girls are not allowed in boys' rooms after Hall, but luckily Guy is helping the Freshers build a feathered gondola for *The Merchant of Venice*, in which Marina has a humiliatingly small part. Drama at Combe Abbey is spectacularly lavish, like its sport. Participation, the pupils are frequently told, 'is what makes a well-rounded Combe Man', although most of them stick to rugby. Guy, however, has been roped in by his housemaster, Pa Stenning, to help with the props. And so, three or four times a week, Marina accompanies him beneath the stage of Divinity Hall.

Although the handsome bachelor Pa Stenning is the head of drama, he never checks on Guy and his little shivering team of Removes and Freshers, tapping away in the cold. Guy says Pa Stenning trusts him. He smokes cigarettes, cupped in his hand like a workman, and issues instructions. Marina pokes among the smelly costumes, practising her formulae and the laws of chemical combination, waiting for him like his French lieutenant's woman, trying to think of conversational topics which might interest him without boring her to despair. Then they go round the corner to 'check the rig' and clinch under the cables: Guy's shirt sleeves around Marina's soft body, the smell of hot dust and sweat. She likes the way his veins stand out in his forearms, the size of his wrist bones despite his youth, and this encourages her; she is not dead to his attractions. Yet when his Doc Martens nudge her penny loafers she edges away, as she would never have done from Simon Flowers.

Perhaps because he still fancies Amanda Stapleton – he talks about her and then gets off with Marina, as if she is a spittoon – he is less pressing than she had expected. She is still splashing her bust with cool water, experimenting in private with scrunchies, regularly applying lip balm. Nothing helps. Should she be stoking his ardour? Shouldn't he be trying to ravish her? So she does nothing but let herself be kissed, and sometimes she can almost feel herself tipping over into excitement when they kiss particularly hotly, their bodies cores of fire wrapped around with cold.

When does petting start?

She is not, whatever his friends think, a prude. She has been waiting for someone to touch her breasts since she was eleven. Sex, she has always known, will be wonderful. Maybe, she thinks now, exhausted yet wide awake at three in the morning, looking across to where Heidi sleeps in a haze of vaginal deodorant and body spray, she was wrong.

'You're Mrs Farkas, aren't you?' says a voice.

Laura is shopping in Fritz Continental on the Edgware Road for the particular brand of blueberry jam the aunts-in-law prefer. It is a guilt present; this week she had hoped to buy herself a magazine, but she feels she should be making up to them.

She turns. The woman beside her, frowning at crisp-bread, is tallish too, worried-looking too, distantly familiar. 'Oh,' says Laura. 'School – I mean, Ealing. Aren't you—'

'I taught Marina history. Bridget Tyce.'

'Sorry. I'm an idiot. Miles away.'

'Mm, I'm the same.' They look at each other. 'I have a Russian mother-in-law,' she tells Laura, 'with specific crisp-bread needs. Do you happen to know—'

'That one. They like the seeds. I thought . . . Aren't you *Miss* Tyce?'

'Well, not a legal mother-in-law. Teachers have sex too, though, you know,' she says and smiles.

Laura smiles back; there is a pause as they both consider the sex Miss Tyce has been having.

'How *is* Marina?' Miss Tyce asks.

'Well—'

'We miss her, you know. Bright girl. I do hope she's happy.'

Laura's face says it. She means to come out with the usual reassurances, opportunity and facilities and privilege, but the words will not form. She feels her bottom lip beginning to betray her, and coughs. 'Well.'

'She isn't?'

'It's, well, to be honest, it's a shock. I mean, not just for me! But, but she'll settle, I'm sure. We're all very proud.'

'Boarding school and Marina: it's hard to imagine. Not one to suffer fools, is she? No. Well, we'd have her back in a second.'

Laura nods. A cloud of unknowing sinks upon her, blotting out decisions, feelings, the future. She wants to lie down and sleep.

'If you did, if *she* did change her mind,' she hears, 'we could discuss it. Definitely possible. But don't leave it, or it'll be too late.'

When Marina rings home on Sunday morning, the ten pences hot and damp in her palm, she has decided to mention, just by the by, the fact that she is a tiny bit homesick.

It doesn't work that way.

'Antibiotics,' her mother tells her, sounding distracted. 'It's her age . . . they want to be sure.'

'Poor Ildi.'

'She is eighty-two, sweetheart. They'll keep an eye on her.'

'What if it's more serious?' asks Marina. Ali Strewer canters past her in full lacrosse kit. Marina steps aside to let her pass, bangs her elbow on the pay phone and gasps, but she will not cry. Last night, with chemistry homework to finish, she had not enough sleep and too much coffee and now, despite never having been to a funeral, she can see clear as day Ildi's coffin, half open like a pope's; a sad dark chapel. A sob catches in her throat. The relatives are too vulnerable without her, yet nothing makes them happier than knowing that she is here.

'Are you positive everything's all right?' she asks her mother.

'Definitely. Why not?'

'I just thought— Never mind. I'd better go,' she says. 'I'm very busy. By the way, I've lost another lens. The left. No, the right. Hang on—'

'Oh, my love. Can't you be more careful? The insurance won't keep paying. I mean, it's fine. But just try, please?'

Now Marina feels even worse. Her problems are manifold. For a start, she isn't in love with Guy, although he is quite nice to her, so perhaps she is incapable of passion like a psychopath. It's not even because he's younger, though obviously that adds to her self-disgust. She is pining so badly for home that she can hardly sleep, but she can't worry her relatives, and Urs would gloat and say again she was wrong to leave, and there is no one else she can imagine telling. Among the many other incidents she will not think about, buried in a pit of fear and shame, is the time she rang the Samaritans last term from the pay phone out by the petrol station, and then, on their advice, went to see the school counsellor: Ma Gilbray, the chaplain's perpetually smiling wife, with her pearly lipstick and Lady Diana hair. Sitting on a patchwork cushion in the Gilbray family study, Marina remembered a story about the last Combe chaplain, who tape-recorded confessions and played them for laughs in the staffroom, and found it hard to confide.

The idea of admitting how she feels is unbearable. It is too big, too easily ripped open. Every time she thinks of Cambridge she feels as if she will burst with desire and desperation, and the fear that something will happen to upset the celestial balance, that she will fail to do the one safeguarding thing, makes her sick with fright. She has also become a tiny bit obsessed with washing her hands. So now as well as asthma, or whatever is causing this feeling that she can't take enough oxygen in, she has given herself eczema. She is the only girl in the Lowers with no idea how to make small talk or flirt; she remains unnicknamed. Doc Ventner won't let her answer a single question in biology, only the boys in his house and, whenever she asks Doc Steven how long her English essay should be, he says 'as long as a miniskirt', which is not helpful. She has never fainted or ridden a bicycle; she doubts that she could climb a tree. She is afraid to swim in case boys see her in her costume. There is no Poetry Society. She is irrelevant.

Then Guy makes a suggestion.

It is eight o'clock. Laura and her in-laws have had an early dinner (mushroom *palacsinta*, cabbage with caraway, which is *kukorica*, or is that something else? Ladybirds?). And now Rozsi, Zsuzsi and Ildi, over Danish butter biscuits and *kavitchka*, which definitely means coffee, and a performance of Mozart's *Requiem* on Radio Three, are discussing their acquaintances, laughing until they weep. It is happiness, of a sort. '*Buto*,' they say, '*chunyo*,' and Laura smiles weakly; these are words she should know by now. The in-laws take her failure to learn Hungarian very well, like a small physiological malformation. Marina has learned to count to ten, and knows certain key words such as slippers and tomato; today in the kitchen, thinking, how hard can it be, Laura looked at a cookery book over Ildi's shoulder:

Borjúláb kirántva

A borjúlábakat legelőbb megkoppasztjuk a következő módon: Veszünk sárga szurkot vagy 15–20 dekát és megtörjük egész porrá két vastag papír között. Aztán a lábakat egyenként mindenütt nagyon jól dörzsöljük be vele, fővő vízzel forrázzuk le és vegyük ki az asztalra vagy táblára és sietve gyorsan dörzsölve húzzuk . . .

Papír: paper, she guessed, and felt quite satisfied.

She has been polishing shoes: one of her manly jobs. Something about the ancient shoe-cleaning case, dusters made from Peter and Zoltan's shirts, duplicate brushes bequeathed by the dead Károlyi sisters, poor Kitti and poor Franci, is weighing upon her. Marina has a new posh accent; Penelope Leach says this is perfectly normal. Maybe she is happy there, and Combe is good for her. Maybe.

'I'm having a bath,' she says eventually. 'Unless . . . ?'

'*Vot*-apity that you don't vant to sit with us,' says Zsuzsi, addressing an envelope in loopy foreign-lady handwriting to one of her many dearest friends, Lady Renate Kennedy *née* Rivka Kroo, wife of Britain's foremost importer of Czech crystal hedgehogs. She and her sisters do not like Sir James, formerly Jenő; they refer to him contemptuously as being 'more English than the English', although everyone knows that he was born in Hódmezövásárhely. Lady Renate, however, is an authority on most things, including the inadequacies of Laura Farkas. The very envelope itself seems to be looking down on her.

'I'm sorry,' Laura says. 'I'm tired.'

A look passes between Rozsi and Zsuzsi. Slowly, sadly, Laura runs four inches of scalding water into the chalky turquoise bathtub. She takes off her clothes. She stands, naked, in front of the mirror and looks at her forty-one-year-old body: vigorously used by one or two unmemorable boys in the small Birmingham suburbs, then at teacher training college; desired by Peter Farkas but evidently not enough; utilized occasionally by Dr Alistair Sudgeon. Is that it? If one discounts all that is wrong with her, her height, her face, elephantine knees and big red hands, is it possible that anyone could ever find some of the rest of her attractive again? Look harder. Squint through the steam. Her skin is soft. Her breasts are . . . well, breasts. Gingerly, she rubs her shoulder with her thumb, her collarbone. Her nipple. Darling, she whispers to herself, and looks away.

She lowers herself into the water, back against the cold enamel, calves and thighs bright pink, the *Requiem* reaching an exciting climax two rooms away. Sadness seems to close around her. She thinks: I want more than this. I . . .

'*Qui tollis*,' she hears over the clanking of the hot-water pipes, '*peccata mundi, miserere nobis.*'

I cannot go on like this.

'*Dona nobis pacem.*'

I cannot go on.

Guy's hand is on Marina's school blouse, but he doesn't seem to know what to do with it. It floats above her sturdy bra, a Courtauld Damask Touch in oyster, which she begged Rozsi not to make her bring to Combe, while he kisses her. Her skin awaits him. Daringly she sticks out her chest a little further: still nothing. What is she doing wrong?

When Laura emerges from her bath, hot and sore-eyed and modestly belted into her towelling dressing gown, *pongyola*, with a cardigan on top, everything has changed. She does not know this. She is thinking, Oh God, not *Last Year in Marienbad* now, I want to go to bed, do I actually have to sit on the sofa and pretend to be interested or could I— when Ildi hands her her post. It is nothing, only a bank statement for £53.32, and a manila envelope with blocky biro capitals: the council about dustbins, or the library with Ildi's new card. She will deal with it later. First, she has a task.

She has made a resolution in the bath, and now she must act upon it. She sits at the dining table, pretending to watch the film and covertly nibbling at the belt of her dressing gown. She is working herself up to ask a difficult question: should they do something about Marina? They have all made sacrifices: Rozsi's income; Ildi's Post Office savings; the brooch that Zsuzsi claims she sold and, obviously, Laura's entire poxy salary, hence her having to live with people to whom she is unrelated, and inexplicable, and presumably rather a pain. That can't be enough. Rozsi and the others must be borrowing money from somewhere, one of the distant Ottos or Fülöps. They have put themselves in debt for this.

But, she imagines saying to Marina, to Rozsi, to Miss Tyce at Ealing, is it possible that we have made a mistake?

'Come home with me tomorrow,' says Guy.

They have been getting off against the backdrop for last year's *As You Like It*. As always, combining kissing with breathing is a challenge, especially when her legs are shaking. Sexual activity is punishable by immediate expulsion, and this is fairly sexual, isn't it? Yesterday she heard a story about a girl who had very drunk sex with a boy from another school at a party, and then the boy told his head, who told Dr Tree, and the Upper girl was expelled, though not the boy. And she is scared of the damp dark down here. And what if she suddenly begins to menstruate? Her cheeks are still hot; on the way here she had passed Thomas 'Tom' Thomson performing one of his many head-boy duties, commanding two Upper girls to kneel on the ground before him to have their skirt lengths checked. Marina had slowed; she still isn't used to it. 'I'm not,' Tom Thomson had said, gesturing to the older girls to stand, 'going to check *you*,' and they all laughed, Marina too. What choice did she have?

'Hey, mon, chill,' says Guy, who has been listening to a lot of Bob Marley. He thinks she is nervous about kissing in general, that she is innocent in all things. This is because of an awkward misunderstanding last time they were down here: her fault.

'Have you had any, you know?' he had asked her.

'What?' she said, her mind moving like lightning but pretending it wasn't, to buy herself time.

'Thoughts. About sex. Sexual. Fantasies. I mean, before me.'

'Um.'

'Obviously not wanking,' he said chivalrously. 'Not *that*. But general, like, thoughts?'

What could she say? He would be disgusted, and disappointed. So she said 'No!' and now he clearly thinks his job is to instruct her.

It is also important that he does not know of an incident in her past: last year, at the cinema at Notting Hill Gate. A middle-aged man in a Barbour with dark hair, a respectable man, was sitting beside her; she did not notice him at first. She was with Urs and Kate Frere; they were watching a French film about sorrow. Then she felt something, once, twice: the lightest possible tickling at her breast.

She glanced down. The man's arms were crossed. His fingers had accidentally brushed against her.

'Sorry,' she whispered, edging away. It happened again.

She moved again. The third time, it hit her like a blow to the head: he's doing it on purpose.

She was too ashamed to move. The fourth time she felt him, she said to Urs, 'I need the loo.' When she came back she kept her head down, found another seat, never said a word, or forgot the sight of his fingers, his thick gold wedding ring. Her right breast has always been darker and guiltier because of it. She is still afraid of meeting the man on the street.

Guy stops kissing her. 'Marina?'

'What?'

'Come to my house.'

'Why?'

'Why? To visit, you spack. Oh, no, don't go all weird. I've got to go anyway, and you could too. Keep me company on the way, meet my family. I don't mind.'

She rubs her finger along the edge of the Forest of Arden, too insulted to look at him, too stupid to come up with a Dorothy Parker response. 'I don't think—'

'Don't sulk. Honestly. They're cool, my parents,' he says.

'I'm not sulking. I just can't,' she says. The truth is that this weekend she has no plans at all. This is a good thing, she has been telling herself; she can make friends. Have fun. But she knows that she will be spending her Saturday evening in West Street, drinking lo-cal minty chocolate or milky tea which she does not dare refuse, and pretending to be in love with Mickey Rourke.

'Why can't you?' he says, jiggling his finger hard in his ear as if releasing pressure. 'Because of your grandparents?'

'Grandmother. Well—'

'Why's it up to her?'

Her face feels frozen. She is trapped; she wants to bite her way out. She thinks: he's going to start telling everyone about them, but she only says, 'I've got to go.'

'Anyway, your lot are all going to a party or something, aren't they? You said. So they don't even need to know. Everyone goes to each other's houses all the time. You know, discretionary exeats.'

'I, I've never even heard—'

'Just ask Pa Daventry.'

'No,' Marina says. 'I can't do that.' Her housemaster, Ronald Daventry, husband of Jonquil, father of twins, deputy senior master, is very popular. 'Oh, Davs,' the boys say at any mention of him, 'what a guy.' But he doesn't like Marina. She feels grubbily, disgustingly female in his presence. He does speak to girls, as the boys like to point out, but only the pretty, chirpy ones; never Marina. He presides over assemblies as if they are a private joke and when he has parties for the rowing squads, girls are not invited. 'He'll definitely say no.'

'Don't be stupid. Everyone does it. Anyway, honestly, you'd like it there. Hang out with my sister. You can meet my father too.'

She isn't really listening. How could he have said she was sulking?

'Hello? He . . . people usually want to meet him. He might actually quite like you.'

'Oh, really?' She is imagining his mother and father as younger too: short, playful, silly, unlike hers.

'Yes. You don't know, do you?'
'What?'
'I knew it. Fantastic. So you're not—'
'What?'
'He's Alexander Viney.'

8

Saturday, 28 January

'So,' says Laura's mother-in-law at breakfast, spooning com-
pote from its Maxwell House jar. 'You go with Ildi, or don't
you vant to come with me?'

'She does not listen,' Zsuzsi says. Does she usually wear
this much eyeshadow? 'Ildi, *dar*-link, you make this with,
what-is, *birsalma*, kvince – or apple only?'

'*Igen*, kvince,' says Ildi. 'You vont *von*-illó too, I buy it
next veek. The taste is *ursh*-sehóshernleehótótlón, *nem*?'

Laura blinks. She pretends to be thinking. She is no
genius; her mind, if anything, seems to move more slowly
than other people's. Some time after they have spotted a
problem and skirted around it, slowly into disaster she falls.
But the truth is that this morning she feels particularly
unalert, thanks to a dream in which she gave birth to triplets
unaided. She had been hoping to get through the morning
without anyone talking to her at all.

'Laura.'

'I . . .'

Rozsi's eyebrows lift. Something flashes below the surface, a volcano under the sea.

'*Tair*-ible,' Zsuzsi observes, but Rozsi says nothing. She

has always been polite, except for times when Laura deserved it, like when she referred disrespectfully to Mrs Dobos's late husband Elmer, or compared Zsuzsi to the newsagent's beautiful Afghan hound. That was years ago; Peter had to apologize for her, and even so Rozsi would not speak to her for five days. 'We are talking with Ildi for many minutes,' she says stiffly. 'Don't be funny.'

'I'm sorry,' Laura says. 'But what?'

'The Hungarian Bazaar.'

Laura mouth falls open. 'Oh God,' she says. 'It's not today?'

'*Igen, igen,* of course it is. The – what is it, *huszonnyolc*, tventy-eight. What for you think Ildi bakes *beigli*?'

'I . . . I hadn't . . .'

'We leave twenty minutes to help with set-up,' Rozsi says, rolling up her napkin. 'You change this jersey.'

There will be Mitzi Sudgeon and no Marina. After last year's Bazaar, a three-hour frenzy of personal comments and awkward questions, she promised herself that she would never go again. Who would not, in such circumstances, dream of sudden death? What a relief it would be; she cannot remember the arguments against it. Nevertheless, because she lacks the courage, she tries another way out. 'It's silly, but the funny thing is that today—'

'Of course you come. Mrs Dobos waits for us.'

'I, I thought it was next week. In fact. It's just—' Even I, thinks Laura, must have become a bit tougher over the years. I must have absorbed something. I will just refuse.

They cannot make me do it, she thinks, reaching for her post.

They make her do it.

What choice does she have? She gets ready. Or rather, while the others listen to the news she chooses her least awful skirt from the sideboard and creeps through Marina's room to look in her wardrobe mirror, breathing her smell but being careful not to pry. She tries to imagine herself presentable from the point of view of Alistair, who is in his own neat way an attractive man. She squints into the mirror; she closes one eye. From the neck down this is impossible. From the neck up, through a shivering blur of eyelash, she can almost believe that her hair is less mouse and her cheeks are less pink; that the loveliness of her dark browy daughter did not pour directly through Marina's father's side, but gained something hazier, gentler, from her. This is plainly untrue but, to support it, she begins to brush her teeth, wash her face, apply her almost invisible lipstick, bought for adultery, with a shaking hand. She does not meet her eye again.

By the time Laura has emerged the others are all waiting by the flat door. Zsuzsi looks at her outfit, bobbly, fraying, and shakes her head.

'*Vot*-apity you do not want I lend you blooze,' she says, complacently stroking her own cuff, the chocolate-brown silk with a gold stirrup motif bought in Paris when she was married, before Laura was born. Her gilt earrings are the size of plums.

'Thank you,' says Laura. 'Oh, Rozsi, no, let me take that box.'

Usually, when Laura, like a minor husband, tries to save her mother-in-law from hobbling with shopping bags, she says, 'Silly girl. Look at these legs, I live for ever,' and Laura gives a smile like cracking mud.

This morning, Rozsi lets Laura take the box.

Ildi locks the door. Zsuzsi checks her lipstick in the glossy lift wall. Laura remembers that Rozsi told her to give her brown coat to Oxfam. She should probably go shopping for a new one, except that she can't afford it and, if she could, she ought to buy something for Marina instead. Zsuzsi, naturally, is in fur, at least on her collar: black, silken, inches thick – ocelot, or man. From time to time she turns her head and her huge eyes, her pretty little nose, her profile are beautiful, like an aged doll. Rozsi is wearing her favourite suit, black bouclé, with a green and gold silk square. She looks like a Soviet minister engaging in leisure, but it agrees with her; she has an air almost of amusement, as if she expects good sport today. Even Ildi has a brooch pinned to her lapel: a nest of robins in enamel, one of the innumerable love tokens Zsuzsi receives from Gyorgy, a 'nice boy' whose costume jewellery was once reputedly worn by Princess Grace of Monaco. Ildi's bright white hair is fluffy with excitement.

'I wonder,' she confides in Laura, 'the walnut *beigli*, I should have make more? The seed is good but—'

'They're both delicious,' says Laura, as they approach Porchester Baths. They are walking slowly to keep company with Rozsi and her hip. This is a sad development. Only two years ago she could walk into Soho more quickly than it took by bus.

'You mean, er, the *diós*?'

'Vell done! *Vair*-ygood! You are nearly right, poppy-seed is *mákos*. Now tell me, what do you think?'

I think, thinks Laura, that I am losing my grip. My only child wants to be at boarding school and not with me, and Alistair will be at the Bazaar with that bloody wife, and if I have to suck up to Mrs Dobos again, or Perlmutter Sári, or Pelzer Fanni with her terrible wart, I will go mad.

'I'm sure everything will be fine,' she says, putting the box down so that Rozsi can catch up and feeling, as she does so, the crackle of paper in her pocket: an envelope, the one which arrived yesterday. Like an innocent passer-by touching a case containing a bomb, she tears it open.

The letter is from her husband, whom she had hoped was dead.

9

'Who's Alexander Viney?' asks Marina.

She has rung Ursula from the pay phone. Behind her the girls of West Street prepare for Saturday morning school, crashing up and down the stairs overhead in search of Feminax, hair-dryers, prep books covered in Laura Ashley wallpaper and synchronized-swimming nose clips.

What she needs is a dose of home, or rather Urs's home: the intellectual certainty, the unembarrassed family self-belief, which Marina loved and envied and hated her for. But Ursula is prickly on the phone. She thinks Marina abandoned their life together for Combe, but has conveniently forgotten the little put-downs, the teasing about Marina's clumsiness and forgetfulness and persistent losing of every important item. She keeps reminding her of the highlights of their youth: the notes in Latin; the minor secrets revealed. 'Your made-up friends' is what she calls everyone Marina has mentioned from Combe. 'They don't know you like we do.'

Ursula doesn't know her either. Marina, she thinks, is just like her: loyal, dutiful, devoted, sure. You can talk and talk for seven years: lessons, journeys in the third carriage of the District Line train, hours of telephoning, twenty-page letters. You can pledge eternal best friendship. Yet that doesn't mean they understand your other world, when you're not together, at dinner with your mother and three old women, in bed at night.

How Marina misses her. So she has phoned, and been fondly interrogated by Mr and Mrs P, and updated Ursula on her thoughts, if not feelings, regarding the Embryo, as Urs insists on calling Guy, and enquired about Ursula's plans for Mr Burnett from Ealing Boys', once glimpsed at a science quiz. Then Marina makes herself ask about Guy's father.

'You are joking, *n'est-ce pas?*' says Ursula. 'You must know who he is.'

'I don't. Is he that actor with no lips?'

'You know nothing. Your memory has been razed, hasn't it? Er, hello, Ursula, your best friend?'

'Stop it. You know that's not—'

'Don't you remember the Marrying Game?'

'When we had to choose which historical figure we'd most like to kiss? And I chose Peter the Great and you said the only sane choice was Gustavus Adolph—'

'No, no no. Wrong game. It was that time at Soph's – we put the names in her Laura Ashley hat, the one with the silk scarf, not the felt. We ate strawberry ice-cream, I seem to recall.'

'Oh . . .' This was during their fortune-telling phase, when despite the boys they 'knew', the example of their parents, reason and rumour and evidence, they foresaw, unequivocally, long joyous marriages ahead, and trouble-free children with artistic tendencies, and pre-eminence, or at least modest glory, in whichever job they chose: conducting at the Proms, say, or running MI5. The secret sorrows of adolescence would be rewarded. 'It's the only way to save ourselves from . . . you know,' one of them had said, and they all thought of their mothers, and were silent.

'I got Harrison Ford,' says Marina now.

'No you didn't. That was Cristina Koralik – we let her play. She kept asking about having sexual intercourse, you must remember. And I got that comedian, though sadly not Stephen Fry, to whom I am affianced. No, silly, you definitely had Alexander Viney.'

Not 'definitely'. You should say 'absolutely'. 'I'm not silly,' says Marina.

'Well, you did. Don't go all quiet on me. You know. From the telly. The *Making of Kings* fellow. Sophie chose him, she fancied him secretly. We were having that phase of mental promiscuity, you know.' Sixty-six map centimetres away as the crow flies, Marina blushes at the thought of how many boys, even now, feature nightly in her private bath-time orgies, as she breathes through her mouth to escape the reek of air freshener, and tears slide itchily down her temples and into her hair.

'You do know,' Ursula is insisting. 'We thought he was brilliant in Lower Five. Miss Covs showed *Our England* in double hist. You must remem—'

'Him? Oh my God. Seriously? I'd forgotten – of course, Viney, of course it's him. Then why wasn't he in the Combe *Register*?'

'Never mind that,' says Urs. 'You've prob even got his books. I have, *Tudors in Love*, it's fantastic. Sophie's definitely read one of them, although it is about eight hundred and ninety-two pages long. She could lend it. Or have you gone all cool, now you're in love with the Embryo?'

'Stop it. Wow. I hadn't realized. We loved him.'

'Yes, wow! By the way, remember that time Roz said—'

'I should go,' says Marina. 'Sorry, but they kill you if you're late for morning school.'

'God, you and your Saturdays. Are you still in uniform? Is it ebbing your life-blood?'

'You know I am, I have to.'

'OK, OK. So quickly, tell me, why do you want to know about Alexander Viney? Are you a swinger?'

So Marina explains.

Ursula is squeaking like a guinea pig. 'You are joking?'

'No. Honestly. I thought Guy was, well, I just didn't make the connection. He doesn't look . . . he's just ordinary. Not romantic at all.'

'You know what this means? You could actually do it. Marry him.'

'Guy? He's in the year *below*.'

'No, Guy Senior. The famous one. You could! That was the idea. Or at least you have to try. We plighted.'

'I'm sure it's pledged.'

'We'll ask Zoë. But you have to.'

'Don't be mad.'

'You're being mad. Look, you said the Embryo invited you. You could meet them. Just say yes.'

'I can't,' she says, but a strange heat is growing in her chest: an emptiness, like love or hunger. She remembers

Alexander Viney's face perfectly now: oldish, but not much more than her friends' fathers.

'You can.'

'Don't, Urs. I'd look . . . stupid.'

For a moment Ursula is silent, then: 'You promised us. Your old friends. Maybe you think we're just babyish now, but—'

'You know I don't.'

'Well. We promised each other. That's all I'm saying.'

Laura stands at the Porchester Baths entrance. The others are up the stairs ahead of her, scanning the horizon for interest; they love taking umbrage when people stay away. The letter from her husband, Rozsi's son, Marina's father, is trembling in her hand.

He is coming back to them.

This is the miracle they have longed for. To the Károlyi sisters all men are sacred; they have only to change a light bulb to be deified. Even more than dull Robert, Rozsi's elder son, the charming cavalier Peter has always been particularly revered. When Laura first visited Peter's parents, having assumed until then that calling himself 'foreign' was a pose, it felt like entering a flat in Prague or Vienna: the wall of classical LPs and art books; the extraordinary food; the photographs. *Pay*-tare the Holy Infant was everywhere: his indulged boyhood, solemn in a tiny mackintosh; his handsome adolescence, smirking next to his proud beehived mother at a wedding.

The signs were there and she missed them. When he

started drifting away for hours, then days at a time and eventually failed to return at all, it was horrible of course, but, after years of his indolence and drinking, whispered fights, promises to reform, at last Laura could breathe. I only have one infant to look after now, she told herself, and tried to feel consoled. Then she ran out of money, and accepted Rozsi's verdict that Marina needed her grandparents, and they moved, temporarily of course, into Westminster Court. And Marina has coped, if refusing to discuss it is coping. They have all managed, even poor Rozsi, who pretends that *Paytare* is simply obliged by work to be elsewhere, like Robert in Australia.

So where has he been? Unconscious? At sea? His letter, unexpectedly sane and contrite for someone in his position, refers vaguely to friends. Could that mean bigamy? She had not foreseen the humiliation of knowing that he was alive all along. Hating him, trying not to think about him, was easier. Now, much worse, there is hope.

Because, if he does come back, everything might change. She gazes blindly at the embroidered banner above the swing doors:

WELCOME
to the Magyar League for Women

| 56th |

Annual Bazaar

If he comes home, she is thinking, Marina might soften. Rozsi might forgive her for having driven her sacred son away. Laura could even act on a long-cherished fantasy, in which she rings the headmaster's secretary at Combe, dispenser of poison from her panelled castle, and instructs her to send Marina home.

Idiot. Your ex-husband, she reminds herself, is a drunk, and feckless, lazy, self-indulged. He brought us all endless grief, Marina most of all, and he must not be allowed to do that again.

'Laura.'

She looks up. Rozsi, Zsuzsi, Ildi, all more vulnerable than they know, are staring at her from the top of the stairs.

'What is it, *dar*-link?' Ildi asks.

Aren't they stable now, and coping? The last thing Marina needs is drama and that is what he'll bring. Before telling them anything, and destroying what they do have, she must read the letter properly, alone.

'I . . .'

Imagine if she announced that he was returning and he let them down: that unwashed hair, those big dangerous eyes. They have spent the last thirteen years building barricades. She cannot just open the door to let the whirlwind in.

'Laura? What is it?'

'I . . .'

She means to tell them. Of course she does. Even when her hand moves towards her pocket, entirely of its own volition, she intends to do the right thing. She just needs a little time.

10

Of course Marina is not going to Guy's parents' house. But at break, hunger and the thought of a weekend without her mother send her to the tuck shop, where everyone else spends pounds and pounds on blue fizzy drinks and a disgusting margarine-flavoured biscuit known as Slice. She is paying for her sherbet pips when he comes in.

'OK?' he says.

'Why?'

'So what are you doing later?'

'Auditions for the Choir.'

'But you said you can't sing.'

'I know,' Marina answers stiffly, looking away because she is an adulterer, who can't stop thinking about Simon Flowers's solos. 'But I should try.'

'See?' he says. 'You might as well come back with me – have some fun, not with those spazzes. Don't look all hurt, you know what I mean. If we meet in Mem at one fifteen we'd catch the twenty to.'

No, she thinks. Not your scary father, and your mother who will look down on me. I can't do it.

Then she imagines being able to tell Ursula all about it. Her family too: they believe in courage and, more than that, in famous people. Zsuzsi once bought an ice-cream next to Lady Antonia Fraser; in the retelling they have become close friends. They all expected Combe to be full of the children of eminent people, not only the kind they have met – some-one from the Czech embassy; Lady Renate's friends; George Arthur, the unconvincingly British conductor – but also the greatest excitement of all: aristocrats. Although as a child it has always embarrassed her, now that she is a woman it makes sense. They don't want her to grow up like their neighbours' grandchildren, baking Hungarian biscuits and going to folk-dancing lessons on Saturday mornings, then joining their family's business. They want her to be more than this.

Dear Lord, she thinks, please let me be adequate. Let my baseness be concealed.

'OK,' she says. 'Yes, OK.'

It is like an English church fete, deformed. One may, indeed must, buy painted napkin rings and embroidered place mats; costume jewellery donated by Zsuzsi's friend Gyorgy and discreetly folded flesh-coloured support tights from Femina; celluloid tourist dolls in Hungarian national costume; tapes of gypsy flute music; dried mushrooms, salami, garlic plaits. Someone's well-meaning English husband is manning a second-hand book stall featuring a 1973 Austin Rover users' manual, Dick Francis paperbacks, Baedeker guides to Swiss spas. The air is blue with cigarette smoke. There is a coffee stall, with porcelain cups and the brown sugar crystals they are all obsessed with and, naturally, food: stuffed *paprikás* and pancakes and chicken cooling under foil duvets, some of it in the white harvest-themed Pyrex of home. And, on an altar in the middle of the room, stands a cake stall presided over by Zsófia Dobos, Mrs Dobos to her friends: patron of the arts, owner of Femina and, in her day, proprietress of a famous delicatessen in Soho, although that day is past.

The old women flutter round her, praising Mrs Dobos's flower arrangement, her lace tablecloth and the creations of her elderly protégé Rudi, reputedly a former employee of the great Gerbeaud but now living in poverty in Holloway.

'*Nez.* Beautiful, *nem?*' says Rozsi. Obediently Laura nods. This is not enough; she must turn round to admire Rudi's pistachio *mignons*, arranged like the overlapping scales of a mighty fish. She looks in the general direction of *krinolinkies*, Wasp's Nests and Bear Paws; Cobbler's Delight; Gâteau Princess Anne; a '*my*-ladeesvims' ('Sorry? Oh, My Lady's Whims. I see'); rum and hazelnut kisses; marzipan crescents; cakelets of plum, or chestnut, or sour cherry; 'student food'; cheese medals; sweet cabbage dumplings and a monstrous praline and wafer *Pischinger*; not to mention *beigli* galore, which have been shipped from a *beiglimeister* in Budapest.

'I buy one of the necklets for Marina,' says Ildi, looking crestfallen, hurrying towards a row of padded satin jewellery cards.

How can Peter be back? Peter, who behaves as if it is reasonable to disappear and then be resurrected? Who has, since she last saw him, gone mad. His letter, crunching in Laura's pocket, really says so: 'The balance of my mind – dodgy at the best of times, as you know – was disturbed.'

What does this mean? Marijuana? Women? It has an ominously legal sound: has he been in prison? Unlikely; he was too soft for crime. Could he have moved on from wine and strange dusty liqueurs and even the terrible Unicum, Hungary's national drink, to something worse? Worse, even, than a thirteen-year hiatus, and a character change? Could the little maddening chips in his nature, the fanatical protectiveness about his mother and acceptance of his role as family god-head, have coagulated into that?

Or could it not be him? The handwriting had been like his, she thinks, but not exactly. What would an impostor want from her in-laws? Attention? Money? To worm his way into their complicated but arguably warm embrace?

Please, God, she thinks, going nicely with her in-laws to kiss a horrible powdery old woman called Borbála, let it be blackmail, extortion, anything but the return of the prodigal, entirely irresponsible yet still, apparently, perfect in the eyes of the Károlyis. And, if he is coming back, he will be alone. Because wherever he chooses to live, in his mother's flat or some revolting alternative, Laura cannot go through that pain again.

Marina has never sat next to a boy on a train before; until Combe she had hardly been on a train. A great ball of breath keeps being trapped in her throat. The scale of her unfitness to meet his parents is only just occurring to her. She is wearing all her best clothes: stone-washed jeans, maroon Marks & Spencer V-neck bought for her by Zsuzsi, in a smaller size than she likes ('*Vair*-y good. We see your bust'), the brown ankle boots which she rarely wears in case of scuffing, and her birthday green velvet jacket, of which she is so proud.

'This is great,' says Guy, nuzzling her neck like a horse.

'Is it a long journey to, you know, um—' she asks hopefully, fiddling with the paperback of Gogol's *Dead Souls* which, after long deliberation, she has decided is not too pretentious to bring: it is a comedy, after all. She has been dreaming of a lengthy Tolstoyan train ride with serfs scything the cornfields; somehow she had even envisaged a sleeper compartment, in which Guy would attempt to kiss her.

'God, I don't know,' he says, biting into a colossal cherry scone. 'Blandford then Limehurst, Winsham St Peter, Goring Water, Goring thingy, Staithe. Shaftesbury, East Knoyle, lift to Stoker . . . less than an hour. Fifty minutes? Weekend trains aren't up to much.'

The mere mention of weekends makes her stomach squelch with anxiety. He said his mother would clear this exeat with Pa Daventry, but surely it's not as easy as that. It has all happened so suddenly; when she thinks of Rozsi she feels faint, even though, she tells herself, her mother won't care, or even notice, so in a way it's her fault.

Guy keeps grinning at her. When she accidentally rests her knee against his, he does not pull away. She looks at the spots on his temples and remembers the questing way that his lips met hers in the ticket queue, as a guinea pig's might. Simon Flowers, she thinks, despite having decided to forsake all thoughts of him this weekend, Simon, I will ever be thine. She tries to remember how much money she has in her purse, in case she needs to flee.

'You won't mind if my father's not there, will you? My sisters might be, but—'

'Don't you know?'

'Why would I? One of them's married, children, everything. Only Lucy lives with us. I just meant that maybe you were expecting my dad to be there. Because you, people, seem . . .'

'I don't mind.'

'Good girl,' he says and, with a soulful expression, tucks a strand of hair behind her ear. They have stopped at a tiny station. She keeps her eyes on two big black birds, crows or ravens or rooks, near the train track, which are fighting over a stone. One wins the battle; it flies towards them with the stone in its beak, over ridges of what Dr Tree calls 'good Dorset clay' and is almost above the train when a sound outside startles it. The stone falls to the ground, so close to her window that she can see it if she cranes her neck, which she does because one day she might regret not having looked. It is not in fact a pebble but something small, furry, bloody: a baby rabbit or mouse, or something worse. She looks away quickly, appalled to find she wants to cry.

Guy is telling a story about some boys pushing a master's Vauxhall Astra into Divinity Hall. She is horribly nervous. As the rackety little train passes through Blandford Forum towards Shaftesbury, she witnesses one of those special effects for which the English countryside is famed. The raindrops racing down the glass suddenly slow. Sheets of gold pour on a distant field; the clouds tear open and the entire carriage is bright with winter sunlight. It must be significant. The train whispers 'Alexander Viney' with every rattle of the wheels. Are they wheels? She thinks of all the things she has forgotten to bring: perfume; sanitary equipment; a spare book; a rape alarm; a copy of her most impressive English essay, in case Mr Viney is interested. 'Be a good girl,' she imagines her grandmother saying. The carriage door squeaks: Viney. Viney. Alexander Viney. I, thinks Marina, am not a good girl. I am ready for love. Ready for sex. Dear God, let it start.

The Hungarian Bazaar is like being consumed by loving cannibals. Wherever she turns, old women ask her, 'So, no more children?' and shake their heads pityingly, or squeeze her upper arm or pat her bottom; 'Hodge vodge?' they ask, *hogy vagy*, 'How are you?' and she smiles and nods as if these are merely rhetorical questions. People keep giving her paper plates of veal, and she has to remember to thank them in Hungarian, 'Kusenem saipen,' *köszönöm szépen*. Her pocket feels transparent, she may be sick. She has to tell Rozsi about Peter's letter but here, in public, is not the right time. I'll do it tonight – that would be kinder, thinks Laura, looking up to see Alistair and Mitzi Sudgeon pushing through the swinging doors.

She reaches behind herself for support and finds her hand closing on a bag of paprika, squashy as a tiny corpse. Her brain is still struggling with the idea of Peter Farkas but her eyes follow the man she sort of loves. Or, rather, they follow his wife. Like a rabbit fascinated by a circling hawk, Laura gazes upon her nemesis.

Mitzi Sudgeon is pale, like something found in a cleft in a Carpathian mountainside. Her hair is dyed red; she wears lipstick but otherwise she looks fragile, naturally thin: a woman too busy doing good deeds to eat. She smokes stylishly. She has virtuous breasts. Not pretty, exactly, but beautiful, powerfully attractive both to elderly maternal Hungarians and to men, of every age. She looks like a tiny diplomat at an enemy's wedding.

Alistair, with the methodical humourlessness she tries to find touching, has confided about their marriage: the union brokered by his first employers, kindly Dr and Dr Országh-Nagy, Mitzi's guardians (or were they kindly?), the dietary control and screaming rages, the many faults she finds with him. However, Laura's rival has not only beautiful eyes and a waist but also the blessing of the holy Catholic church, which Alistair, despite not being himself a Catholic, finds unbreakable. Not that Laura wants to marry him. She just wants to be married.

Never mind, she thinks, eyeing them from behind the leather goods like a chicken with a fox. She will buy something for Marina, even though she can't afford to. She swallows hard but there is dust in her throat, or ash, or sorrow, and she cannot be rid of it.

Almost an hour passes. Laura takes a sip of hot coffee and somehow misses her mouth, dabs her breast with a napkin and spreads the stain, spills icing sugar from a little walnut pastry on to the brown patch and, hideously soiled and besprinkled, is turning to go to the toilets when she crashes full length into Mitzi Sudgeon, who is bearing teacups on a silver tray. Everything falls to the floor including, after a hesitation, Mitzi.

'*Jesus Maria!*'

'Oh God, I'm so sorry,' says Laura. 'Let me—'

The hall stills. Down on the parquet, Mitzi feels her ankle gingerly. Alistair, her medically trained lawful husband, kneels in slow motion. His eyes are on Laura's; they seem to press against her with anger, or ardour, or a plea for understanding. Despite their stolen time together, she does not know him well enough to be sure.

'It is . . . it is,' says Mitzi, as if she is trying to be reassuring but has no words. Her accent is improbable even by Hungarian standards. 'I move, I hope.'

'God, I'm so sorry,' says Laura again. 'I'm so stupid. I—'

'No, not stupid,' says Mitzi. 'But you are so much bigger than me. And . . . oh!'

Alistair, kneeling, his neat hands on her skin, has found a sore place on her ballet dancer's blue-veined instep. Laura looks down at his balding head. Breathing is strangely difficult. She watches his fingers creeping up the thin white calf of his wife.

'Can you walk?' he says to her.

'I . . . I *sink* so,' she says. Gently, professionally, he puts one of her arms over his shoulders and helps her to rise. There is murmuring all around them, mercifully not in English.

'I'm . . . this is awful,' Laura says.

'Please,' says Mitzi Sudgeon. Laura steps aside to let them by. As Alistair passes, her spirits seem to fall slowly through her chest and onto the parquet. She kneels to gather up the broken teacups and, in a broken voice, Mitzi says, 'My bag.'

'Let me,' says Laura, but Mitzi bends down, still supported by Alistair. She leans towards Laura.

'Do not touch,' she hisses. And then they are gone.

11

In the country Guy makes more sense. She sees the fields through which he will have gambolled, the cows whose milk, presumably, nourished all those big white teeth.

West Knoyle is a disappointingly ordinary station, ringed with ratty garden sheds: blue sky, the sadness of naked trees. He strides across the tarmac towards an estate car, oppressively cheery in his football jumper. Anyone could be here to meet them. Marina's family do not know where she is.

She grasps her bags as if they contain important medical supplies and follows.

The car is old and filthy and apparently partly wooden, its back windows edged with moss. The passenger seat, comprehensively ripped, contains a box of jam-jars; beside it, one finger on the steering wheel, sits a woman with longish blondish hair, smiling, thin, good-looking. She is wearing muddy grey cords and a moth-holed jumper. Wow, thinks Marina: staff.

'My mother,' says Guy, and pats her shoulder.

'So, Marina.' Mrs Viney's greeny-grey eyes meet hers in the rear-view mirror as she reverses masterfully towards the station barrier, parking voucher between her teeth. 'What a treat,' she says in her Radio Four voice, 'to meet you at last.'

'Oh!' says Marina, blushing. Shyness seems to light her

from within; her movements are clownishly magnified. 'You're welcome.'

Guy ruffles her hair. 'Isn't she sweet?'

As polite as she tries to be, Mrs Viney is even politer. 'Awfully selfish of us,' she says, 'to drag you all this way to see us,' and she praises Marina for bringing such good weather. 'We're terribly dull, I'm afraid,' she says. 'I hope we'll be worth your while.'

But when Marina tries to be gracious back, it sounds ridiculous. Mrs Viney is not wearing earrings; thank God that Marina has left Zsuzsi's old clip-on garnet pendants in her toilet bag, but what else has she got wrong? If only she could see if Mrs Viney is wearing a watch; she has a feeling that she won't be, and silently undoes her own. Guy does a rich belch, which makes her blush, but Mrs Viney only says, 'Guyie, must you?' and Marina turns her face to the window to conceal her shock. All her best items, her new green toothbrush, the Liberty shower cap from Mrs Dobos, are squashed into a carrier bag between her legs. She squeezes it between unracehorsey ankles and wonders if it looks overstuffed. Guy hasn't mentioned whether or not she is expected to stay the night.

Guy is no use. He has hot chocolate on his chin. He won't stop teasing her about the red-and-yellow station tulips she brought his mother, currently banging their heads against her knee as he gestures and winks and she furiously shakes her head at him to shut up. Now he is describing the latest escapades of Henry and Benno and Nick and Giles Yeo, whom his mother seems to know, while Marina tries to flatten her hair back down and regain the art of conversation.

The car smells of disintegrating leather and apple stalks and dead leaves. 'Are you,' she asks Mrs Viney politely, 'a plantswoman?' and Guy laughs so much he does another burp. Boys do this at school but she is appalled for them; if anyone heard her do that she could never look at them again. Why is she even here? In a stranger's car, being driven deeper and deeper into the countryside, with no coat on. She grips the handles of her carrier bag with sweating hands and—

'Oh.'

'What?'

'Nothing,' says Marina, sensing for the first time the scale of the test which awaits her.

'Silly girl, tell me.'

'Just . . . that . . . there's a dead bird on the floor.'

There is a little silence like a sucked sweet. 'Is there?' says Mrs Viney. 'What kind?'

'Chump,' says Guy. 'It's just a hawk moth. You made it sound like a, a chaffinch had flown in, or something. A blue tit! Ha.'

She turns her burning face to the glass. They drive past violently trimmed twiggy hedgerow, a trout farm and something called an Honesty Box from which Mrs Viney buys a pot of brown jam. She is telling Guy about the nephew of a Mrs Kershaw, 'You know, the Cluney char,' dead in a corn silo.

'Oh, God, how awful,' says Marina.

'Well, he was twenty-six.'

She keeps having a powerful urge to apologize. Sitting behind the thin shoulders and glossy hair of Mrs Viney, she feels sick and starving simultaneously. What if at dinner they expect forfeits or charades, or a recitation of Noël Coward? Mrs Viney is lovely, for a mother: fragile, but you can imagine her riding to hounds. Her mothy green jumper, which must be cashmere, is torn at the shoulder. Poor woman, thinks Marina kindly, as Guy, mid-anecdote, squeezes her knee a little too hard and his mother laughs. Marina directs a short but, she hopes, powerful prayer to the back of Mrs Viney's neck: oh God, she thinks. Let me be you. Let—

The car shudders dramatically.

'God!' she says. 'Is it a, a puncture?'

'Cattle-grid, thickster,' Guy says.

'I *know*,' she whispers crossly. 'Shh.'

Then the car slows. The Viney house (never 'home') has a short drive, a tall hedge, and a messy half-tarpaulined pile of logs, broken flowerpots, petrol containers, farm machinery. Mrs Viney swoops into the space beside it. As Marina climbs out of the car, she accidentally gives a little grunt of disappointment. The house is – well, modern: yellow Lego bricks with ruched blinds and pointy shrubs and a wishing well. 'Oh, lovely,' she says, projecting well in case Mr Viney is waiting to greet them. Besides, she tells herself, it must be stylish, just not in a way she yet understands. 'What a sweet bird bath!'

'Darling,' says Mrs Viney, crunching across the gravel, 'that's Barker's, the neighbour. We're over here.'

She is heading for a gap in an old wall Marina had not even noticed, green where the guttering has leaked. Beyond her lies another house entirely.

'God,' says Guy. 'You're not serious? You thought . . . ha! That's brilliant.'

It feels as if her skin is cracking. 'I didn't mean that one,' she says with dignity. 'I was joking.'

'Hilarious,' he says.

They approach the real house around its side. Marina's eyes are stinging so she registers only height, grassy leagues or hectares stretching into the distance, mist and terraces and trees. The house seems infinite, like part of a school, except that Combe is a mess, Gothically old and new and faux-old, and this is sand-coloured, beautifully regular, at least three storeys high with balconies and a castellated roof, like something from a postcard. As they approach, there is a thunderous barking, as though the hounds of hell are loose. Like a duckling, Marina follows Mrs Viney through a thicket of mackintoshes (never say 'raincoat'), outdoor garments and sporting goods. It is no warmer than outside. The air is faintly scented with rubber.

Mrs Viney says, 'I'm afraid it's a dreadful mess.'

'Oh, not really,' says Marina. 'Don't worry. I mean, God. This house is enormous. Does it have a, a name?'

'Nah,' says Guy behind her. 'Just the Old Rectum. Rectory. Or Stoker, if you're desperate to call it something.'

'Not desp—' Marina begins, but Guy is already saying, 'Dad in?'

Mrs Viney pushes open a door. There before them stands another kind of man entirely, from whom fame radiates.

'What the h—' Then his voice changes. 'Hello,' he says. 'And who are we?'

12

'Dad,' says Guy. 'Marina. Marina, my father. We, um, I—'

'Marina. Aha. Good name.' Alexander Viney looks at her thoughtfully over the top of his glasses. He is shockingly three-dimensional; escaped from the crackly school television to stand before her, live.

'Hello, darling,' says his wife.

It is impossible not to smile at him when he shakes your hand: those interested blue eyes, that short silvery hair and big imperial nose, that appearance of strength, like an intellectual stevedore. Until this moment she has thought that the perfect man, the only kind she could imagine marrying, would be tall and thin and elegantly aquiline, like Lord Peter Wimsey in daguerreotype. Mr Viney looks as though he chops logs off camera. She doesn't care. She steps aside to let Mrs Viney pass, treads on a vast navy galosh, then stumbles against something softer.

'Bloody hell!' he says.

'Oh my God. I – I'm so stupid. Are you—'

'That,' he says, 'was my bad foot.'

'Oh no. Oh, God. Sorry. Sorry.'

Mrs Viney and Guy are beyond them, in the hallway but, when she ducks her head to slip by Mr Viney, thinking comforting thoughts of death, he stops her. 'Wait.'

'Sorry. Oh, yes.' With a mighty effort she lifts her head.

He is holding out his hand. 'So, you're a friend of my son's, are you, from school?'

'I . . .'

'Of course you are. I can see, from his little red cheeks, that you are. Well, good for him.'

First, Guy says, they will go for a walk. This seems a pity. His mother is reading the Saturday papers in a room apparently reserved for the purpose, and his father has disappeared.

'We could wait and . . . he might like to chat to us,' she says.

'God no,' says Guy. 'Need to stretch my legs.'

They go first to talk to a man in a nearby field about drainage, and then to feed a colossal horse, Billy, who has cracked teeth as big as her finger and strings of drool pouring from his gums, and thence to a freezing bluebell wood, which she had always assumed was a fictional construct, like Hades. It is a horrible place, dark and probably dangerous. Trees are fine individually, essentially just big plants, but these black weeping woods make her think of Baba Yaga, crows and huntsmen and maidens walled up in towers. There is too much nature here, moving in the darkness, flying things, distant rumbling. Marina is sitting on a soggy tree stump watching Guy kick at some rotten wood, when he suddenly puts his cold hand up her jumper. At that moment, something tears through the undergrowth behind them and a tall girl, with irritatingly gamine hair and Quink-coloured jeans, appears from the shadows, escorted by a huge brindled hound.

'Hello!' says Marina, like an eager shepherdess inter-rupted with the young lord. Should she stand? She starts scrambling to her feet, sees faint amusement in the girl's expression and subsides into a wobbly kneel in the thick damp leaves, holding up her hand to be shaken.

'What *are* you doing, you mad girl?'

There is a creaking, rustling hesitation, punctuated by the sound of hungry canine sniffing centimetres from Marina's groinal area.

'Get up, you loon,' says Guy. 'This is my sister, Lucy. Lucy, Marina.'

'Hello,' says Lucy Viney with a cooler, calmer smile, while Marina struggles back on the tree stump with mud all over her knees. Like Marina, Lucy Viney is wearing a V-necked jumper, but the effect is so different. If only I'd worn navy, thinks Marina, and a shirt underneath with thick stripes, and old walking boots, and—

'You poor child,' says Lucy Viney, who is barely older than she is. 'Aren't you cold?'

Marina's heart gives a little slip of hope. She thinks: this is someone I could be friends with, if Guy stays out of the way. She could teach me. 'No,' she says, trying to stop her chattering teeth.

'You are sweet to come all this way,' Lucy says. 'For Guy.'

'Oh, no,' begins Marina.

'But,' Lucy says, with a significant glance at her brother, 'it's terribly sad that Papa's working this weekend.'

'She's not bothered about silly old Dad,' says Guy.

'I – Guy invited me, actually,' Marina says hotly. 'I'm not a, a tourist.'

'A tourist!' Lucy Viney is greatly amused. 'Er, this isn't a stately home, lovey. Not many follies and urns here.'

'I know that,' says Marina.

'Don't be touchy, sweetie,' says Lucy Viney in a bored voice, hiding her hands elegantly in the sleeves of her huge waxed jacket. 'One becomes so protective. I'm sure he'll think you're marvellous.'

Then she ignores her. If it were possible to lie down under the leaf mould and die of shame, Marina would do it. She examines a sinister-looking fungus, feeling at first so sad that her throat hurts, then more picturesquely tragic.

'Ah,' she says with a loud sigh. 'The woods make me so melancholy.'

Guy frowns.

'Rummy?' Lucy Viney says suddenly.

'Sorry?'

'Luce is mad on cards,' says Guy.

'Oh. I, I don't think th—'

'You must. What then? Racing Demon? *Vingt-et-un?*'

'Nothing,' Marina says, trying not to look shocked. 'I, I mean, not well.' She looks nervously at Guy, but he is wiping something on a tree trunk. 'Maybe,' she says brightly, thinking of the West Street girls, 'we know someone in common. You're at Hill House, aren't you?'

'Yes.'

'Well then. I think Antoinette at Combe went there. No? How about Liza Church?' Why isn't this working? In West

Street they talk like this all the time. 'Sara-Jane Brownleigh? Sorry, "Turtle"?'

'No.'

'Oh. Well, so, so you're going to Edinburgh next year.'

'This year, actually. History of Art. Yes. I hope, Guy lovey, that you're not thinking of a tedious year out when it's your turn, like some of the idiots at school. Or,' she says, smiling at Marina, 'you?'

'Definitely not,' says Marina, who had been on the verge of deciding to spend her year out in Florence. 'Your house is lovely.'

'No,' says Lucy Viney. 'Our house is amazing.'

Marina feels her smile set. 'Um, you might know a friend of mine, actually, who's an Upper at, at Combe, Simon Flowers. He's very musical. He's going to Cambridge, actually, to read, um, natural sciences. Tall and thin.'

'I'm sure,' says Lucy Viney, 'I don't know him. He doesn't sound at all like the kind of person I would know.'

Marina tries to smile while biting her lip. 'I just thought, well, you know some of the Uppers at Combe, don't you? Guy said.'

'Not really, no. Guess,' she says, turning to Guy, 'who got into dire trouble with Papa last week? You know that new chap round the corner?'

'I know where you mean,' says Marina, and is about to say Mr Barker, the bird-bath owner, when Lucy Viney asks, 'Oh, so you know them up at the Hall?'

'I, not exactly,' and Marina sees the encouraging look fall away.

The Vineys, brother and sister, begin to walk back towards the house; Marina, rehearsing a defence of Simon Flowers, hurries beside them like a page. She scans the fields for interesting local wildlife, searches for something intelligent to ask about rural pursuits, but can remember nothing beyond the maple-syrup snow in *Little House on the Prairie* and something in *Lark Rise* about sheaves. Wood pigeons, or perhaps cuckoos, sing their peculiar song as they leave the shrubbery. What can only be outbuildings cluster to the side of the house; one has what looks suspiciously like a stable door. There is even a mighty oak with a bench around it, almost as if they have stepped into a film set in an English country-house garden, not a real garden at all.

It is twilight, the hour in children's literature when the adult world comes to life. Guy's house, Stoker, has long many-paned windows, in which dimples and puddles of the dying sun reflect like fire. If I lived here, thinks Marina, I would probably become a poet.

But the truth is that she is starving, muddy and frozen and wondering how she will converse with the Viney parents at dinner. Guy's other sister, Emmy, Emster, might come by for a drink; she is married to someone called Toby. Maybe, thinks Marina, pointlessly biting a big chunk from her thumbnail, I should just go back to school now. Would anyone care? Her throat tightens. I am, she thinks, of humbler stock.

Just as she is wondering about buses to the station, they reach a stone terrace, blotted with lichen, with grey cannon-balls on every other step. 'God, I love your house,' she says, and the Viney children look at her as if surprised. Perhaps

I am, she thinks, unusually responsive to Beauty. Rather moved by her sensitivity, she looks out across the woods to a river valley just visible where the trees part, as if the scenery had arranged itself for her delight. 'Wow,' she says. 'Is that a tennis court?'

'Yup,' says Guy.

'Afraid not much of one,' says his sister. 'Bit too pitty for a really serious match. Do you play?'

Marina gives a snuffly simper. The worn edges of the stone in the gloaming, like the rosy brick wall beside it, make her chest hurt with love and envy. From inside the house comes the clinking of china. Mrs Viney will be making dinner: probably steak and kidney pudding, or partridge, or a fricassée. Into the silence Guy lets out an enormous fart.

'Oh!' says Marina.

'Stinker uno,' says Lucy Viney and, without further comment, they walk up into the house. Marina has no words. There is something about bodily emissions in her *Sloane Ranger Handbook*; you are meant to find them hilarious but she is too stunned to speak. She has barely ever done an audible one herself; at home, such things are never, ever, mentioned. What are the rules for this?

And so the moment for leaving passes. Much, much later, now a different adult from the one she might have been, she wonders if this was the moment when she chose the interesting path through the forest, where trouble lay in wait.

Guy's mother has set out food of fantasy: an entire cold roast chicken, warm wholemeal bread, floppy lettuce leaves, a huge piece of ham on a glistening bone. Together they sit, like adults, at a big square table with a blue and white checked cloth and a jug of branches and bits of leaf. Surely this can't be just a lunch room; and what meal does this count as? High tea? It is lined with what is probably blue damask and on it hang paintings of dogs, tiny-headed horses and bloodied stags. There are decanters everywhere and nutcrackers and ashtrays and pewter birds and silver candlesticks and what she hopes is a porringer. The furniture is dark and very polished; you can smell beeswax, on top of fresh air, and wood smoke, and cold iron, and what must be port or wine. Every inhalation stokes her excitement and her terror. In the fireplace, porcelain elephants bearing little Chinese figures stand guard over the bellows and toasting forks. If she hadn't come here she would never have realized that all these things are tasteful.

'Your mum's an amazing cook,' she says wistfully, hoping that he won't ask if hers is, but he only grunts. A lawn the size of a park stretches into the distance, beyond a window framed with some sort of dead vine. Where is everybody?

She takes a modest half-slice of the delicious-looking ham. He takes three. She says, 'Why are you putting jam on that?'

'It's chutney, idiot. What? You must have had chutney before.'

She looks at her plate, the crumbly mess of home-made bread on the tablecloth because she didn't know what to do about side plates, and makes herself say, 'I . . . I should ring home. Just so they—'

'Nah, don't bother,' he says. 'They'll be fine.'

'No, you don't— I really have to. And I should get something better for your mum. Chocolates?' She hears herself say 'chocklits' but he doesn't seem to notice. 'If I could run to the shops.' The tulips are still upstairs on her bag; two have lost their heads. What can she give the others? Rozsi rarely leaves the flat without a selection of gift items – boxes of handkerchiefs; stockings in plastic eggs; wooden dolls hand-carved in Prague and horrible floral notelets; beaded glasses chains; liqueur chocolates – which she distributes to every tradesperson and cashier and even the teachers at Ealing Girls', until Marina wept for her to stop.

'God, no, not presents,' he says, grasping her hand awkwardly across the table. 'Dad hates them. People usually just leave a tip for Evelyn.'

'Do you often have guests?' she asks to distract him; she needs her hand back to fold her napkin, but there are no napkin rings. He scrumples up his and chucks it at his plate. 'Does your mothe—'

'Shh,' he says, reaching out a finger to stroke the back of her hand, tracing the tendons with a sheen of ham fat. 'Come on, eat up,' and he gives her a significant look.

Laura comes home, a little earlier than the others. I have been entombed here, she thinks as she unlocks the flat door, like a prawn trapped in aspic, and now it will all fall apart. She puts on the kettle to keep herself company and listens to the straining water. By now, she thinks, sitting on the edge of the sofa like a woman in a waiting room, Mitzi Sudgeon will be lying bravely on a chaise longue in the middle of the Bazaar, having attendance danced upon her. Yet however much Laura pricks herself with this thought, she cannot feel it. The kitchen smells of smallness, secrets which would be better kept; the stoicism of old women doing their best far from home. Think, she tells herself. Think.

She has to tell them about Peter.

The light slowly fades. She must show them the letter. There is no reason to keep it secret. Only a monster would do that.

13

In Guy's room, on Guy's bed. They are kissing in a bubble of beauty, distant birdsong, the soft pluck and suck of their mouths. Marina can see past the red rim of his ear, illuminated by the setting January sun, which pours, much warmer than it feels outside, through his window. The room smells fresh: bonfire and laundry; this counteracts the whiffs of scalp from Guy's unwashed hair.

She has lied to her family and she will be expelled.

What if, overcome by lust, he presses her to the bed and takes her maidenhood? If everything is either a good or bad omen for her future, as she increasingly suspects, then wouldn't losing her maidenhood, -head, -hood, in a country house bode well? She is trying to tell whether his penis is erect; something is digging into her, but it could be his belt buckle. Far below them someone shouts. Guy pauses and so, for a moment, she is the one kissing him, as if she is the boy. Then they switch back. 'I love you,' he murmurs.

Her heart is thumping in her right ear: with fear, or passion. 'I love you too,' she says.

By dinnertime, she means it. It must be love, this pain of longing and desire. She feels it everywhere: in the Stoker vegetable garden, where she is told real cabbages grow; in a sort of coat room by the back door, lined with worn leather shoes and sun-bleached tennis plimsolls, where Guy sends her to look for his spare football boots; on the wooden staircase, sniffing up the scent of sunny dust; in the downstairs loo with its rustic door catch and cool whitewashed walls. There is a grander lavatory, but she avoids it; the chill of the tiled floor in this one, the dead wasps and daddy-long-legs in the corners move her profoundly, the luxury of having insects you forget to sweep up. It is extraordinarily cold in here and surprisingly unluxurious; old-fashioned stiff taps, a shower curtain powdery with limescale. She thinks of the Vineys, naked behind it; disgusting peasant, she tells herself, and pinches the skin of her palm.

Outside is even worse; by now she is homesick for it. If, she thinks passionately, *I* had room for an entire flower bed of lavender, I'd learn how to dry it, or distil it; I wouldn't just leave it out there, unappreciated. There are trees pinioned against walls with wire and lead pegs. Every crumbling brick, each forgotten crevice of gate and shed and wall, makes her covetous. She fills her pockets and sleeves with black conkers, skeleton leaves, pebbles, a few strands of real wool left unnoticed on a fence.

'You're not seriously pinching that stick, are you?' asks Guy, scuffling around with a forgotten tennis ball.

'No! Course not.'

'Well, it's bloody time to go,' he says. 'Getting snory.'

'I'm just off to, to get a cardigan,' she says when they go indoors, and she runs up to her room to conceal her thefts in her overnight bag. This house smells like nowhere she has ever been, full of places a child could make her own: alcoves and dusty landings, airing cupboards, tables to roll underneath; old paint on skirting boards so thick its chips have edges. She hates that child. It should be her.

Her bedroom is the best, or worst. It is a cool pale nest of ironed white bedlinen and discreet floral wallpaper. There is a silver monogrammed hairbrush, space on the bookshelves, a dressing table whose tiny wooden drawers contain nothing but a picture hook and a couple of tiddlywinks. She can feel her lungs expanding. She thinks: I'll fling open the window, the casement, for some air.

But Marina has a problem, which she always forgets. Her body never knows where it is. If someone else, for example, pulled aside the curtain, would they realize in time that the ornament on the windowsill, a green china bird-cum-nutcracker which, in another setting, she would consider hideous but obviously not here, might be knocked off? Because she does not realize, or does not quite believe it, and so the green bird jumps off the windowsill, falls on the radiator and crashes to the floor.

She has to leave, right away. Before dinner. She will take the pieces with her, all nine, no, twelve of them, and get them mended in London. She could write a letter on the train. Or should she own up, and be cast out? She dithers, then panics, and she is just gathering her possessions when her bedroom door opens.

Laura, in the kitchen, holding Peter's letter above the bin, watches her hand tremble. Has she always been so indecisive? It is hard to remember; her memory, too, seems worse. She feels extraordinarily old, better suited to a long convalescence in a rest home than to dealing with an ex, now current, husband. The thought of him is exhausting. Wouldn't it be better for us all, she thinks, if I pretended the letter had never arrived?

It is only Guy.

'Wotcha,' he says.

Marina boldly kisses him, to distract him from the bag on her bed. Unusually for a Combe boy on a Saturday night, he does not reek of deodorant and aftershave and Clearasil and anti-fungal foot lotion. He looks, she tells herself, almost attractive, doesn't he? 'I,' she says. 'Actuall—'

'You not dressing for dinner?'

'Sh, should I have?' she asks, only now noticing that he has changed into ironed chinos, a light blue shirt. 'Really? Oh God. I can. Give me a minute. Or,' she says nervously, 'maybe I should just leave—'

'Don't be a prat. And you can't change. Dinner has to be on time.'

Tears are beginning to boil their way up her throat into her nose. She follows him downstairs, feeling her palm stick to the banisters, sick with self-disgust. What if someone goes to air her bed, as they do in *Tatler*, and finds the broken china in her washbag? How could she not have thought of dressing for dinner? Breeding will out.

Mrs Viney, whom Guy mentioned in passing upstairs is the Honourable Nancy, waits for them at the bottom of the stairs with Guy's sister, who is holding the big black dog by its collar. Marina's heart gives a little jerk of terror.

'Oh, darlings,' says Mrs Viney, who looks like Katharine Hepburn in wide black trousers and a dark pink blouse. 'You look gorgeous. Marina, what lovely boots.'

'She forgot to change,' says Guy ungallantly.

'Didn't you realize?' says his sister, who is wearing a pale grey sleeveless dress, in which her collarbones and scapula and sternum are clearly visible. Thank God Rozsi isn't here; she is not, Marina suspects, wearing a bra. 'I suppose not everyone— Guyie, you oaf, you should have warned her about our strange ways.'

'You should,' says his beautiful mother. 'But it doesn't matter, not one bit. We're all scruffbags here.'

'I could lend you something,' says Lucy Viney and, although Marina looks up sharply, she doesn't see her smirk.

'You're about twice her height,' Guy tells his sister. 'And half her girth.'

'Guy. Be good and take Beckett,' says his mother.

'No, seriously,' says Marina, 'I don't think—'

'Nonsense,' says Lucy Viney briskly. 'Tell you what, you could borrow Emster's skirt, Evelyn's just mended it.'

Marina, mystified, finds her hand being taken by Lucy as she is propelled down another corridor, past yet more doors and into a little dark room full of laundry, with a sewing machine.

'There you go,' Guy's sister says, holding out a mini-skirt in bright turquoise wool, somewhere between tweed and felt.

'Perfect,' and, sitting up on a high stool, she waits for Marina to try it on.

'I,' says Marina. Her cheeks burn; she can feel sweat on the backs of her knees and in her armpits. She thinks: I cannot do this.

'Better hurry up,' says Lucy Viney. 'I heard the bell.'

This, whatever it means, shocks Marina into life. She pulls her jumper down to her thighs and starts undoing her boots with trembling hands, talking with no idea how to stop about other people the Vineys might know at Combe. She cannot bring herself to meet Lucy's eye; her mottled thighs and navy cotton Principessa Girl underpants, which Rozsi calls her 'good school knicker'– if only today she had worn her Berlei Junior Girdle – glow luminously under the over-head bulb. She thinks: I want to shoot myself. Somehow, by talking more and more quickly, she forces herself to remove her jeans and grab the skirt, which has a difficult fabric-covered belt with buttons and a zip and a hook. She shuts her eyes as she pulls it on, over her thighs. It is tight on her bum. It will not do up.

'God, was that another mouse?' says Guy's sister, kicking a clothes basket with her toe and Marina seizes the chance to breathe in far enough to pull up the zip, feeling the pulling of stitches as she tugs it round to the back. 'Let's go,' Lucy says impatiently. 'Not really your build, Emster, but at least she's bigger than me,' and she gives Marina a smile crossed with a wince. 'She won't mind a bit.'

'I, I need tights,' whispers Marina. 'Sorry.'

'No, you'll be fine,' says Lucy, jumping off her stool. She

is wearing oddly broken-down ballet pumps, which would horrify Rozsi; her feet are long and bony, like her hands. 'I never do.'

'Please.'

Guy's sister sighs. 'Hang on,' she says and she goes out of the room, leaving the door wide open, and comes back with a pair of bobbly mid-brown tights, damp and longer than Marina's legs. 'Just washed,' she says, and Marina bends to put them on.

As they emerge into the hallway, Marina turns to ask a polite question and finds that she has been abandoned. Her throat is tight; don't cry, peasant girl, she thinks. There is a strong smell of flowers: Turkish delight, she thinks stupidly; attar of roses. I need perfume. No, scent.

'There you are, we'd quite lost you. You must think us dreadfully rude,' says a voice. When Mrs Viney puts her arm around her and walks on down the corridor, Marina's face is pressed against the rose-coloured silk, in the region of her lower shoulder, or upper breast. Held as she is against Guy's mother's side, like a dwarf in a three-legged race, she can see her jawline, the soft pale skin under her chin. She is, for a mother, startlingly lovely. Turkish delight: she breathes it in.

Here it is at last, the heart of the house: a room the size of a normal school hall, with chintzy sofas and dark forbidding chairs and a round polished table in the big bay window covered with *Country Life*. There is no trace of their host's profession here; one does not enter a drawing room in order to be educated. There is an immense fireplace, in which most of a tree is half-heartedly burning; above it on a notably ugly marble mantelpiece, cream and green and yellow like candied vomit, stand invitations, and silver christening mugs, and fat candlesticks, and photographs of people on horses.

So comfortingly old-fashioned, so cheerfully Philistine. What does it matter if there are generations of dog fur in the corners and moths deep in the velvet curtains; if the wiring, with one further mouse nibble, will plunge the house into darkness, or flames? Stoker belonged to Mrs Viney's mother; perhaps, thinks Marina, she has only just died. The parquet is coming up in the corners, and the window frames are quite obviously plugged with newspaper; if you slept in here alone you would wake up with chilblains, at best. This room says: you see, we are too grand to care.

'We're awfully quiet here,' says Mrs Viney. 'Just a few friends – can you bear it?'

'It's fine,' says Marina. Her voice is croaky with shyness; there is a strong chance of sudden dramatic fainting, or being sick. 'We never have people to din . . . I mean, not much.'

There are cold miles between the sofas; the hearth alone is bathroom sized. At home only Zsuzsi smokes; Rozsi, as everyone keeps telling her, gave up smoking sixty a day the minute Marina and her mother moved in. But all their guests do. Here, at Stoker, they are concentrating on drinking. 'I expect you know Jerry,' she says, indicating a familiar-looking grey-haired man just emptying his glass.

'Er . . . yes, maybe, I—' Marina says, tentatively putting out her hand but Mrs Viney steers her onward, saying, 'and Immo, of course, and Horatia,' smiling at a woman with big horn-rimmed glasses and hair piled up like a blonde cottage loaf. 'Olly, darling, you'll get young Marina a drink, won't you? He's a poppet,' she whispers to Marina, nodding at a man in red trousers. 'He'll love you. Now, will you excuse me? I must just . . .' and she drifts away. Guy is dealing with the dog; it is lying on its back in a basket by the fire, violently exposing itself. The red trouser man gives her a glass of fizzy wine; she nods and blushes at him like an idiot and, understandably disgusted, he wanders off. She sits down on a little old-fashioned chair, fat with tapestried cushions, but they prickle so that she stands clumsily and twists her ankle. Lucy Viney is talking to a thin dark clever-looking woman, who flicks a glance at Marina; then she, too, ignores her.

If only Marina had social graces. If only she had courage, like her relatives, or Nancy Mitford. Guy's house must be full of linen cupboards in which to hide, or helpful stableboys who, for a generous tip, might drive—

That man in a dark jacket, on a spindly-looking sofa leagues away, is Alexander Viney.

His hair is silver velvet in the firelight; with his shaven chin and mighty nose he reminds her of a mature and war-like god. To her disappointment, Marina sees that he is talking to the woman with glasses and silly hair, to whom she has taken a dislike. His hand seems to drop behind and then rise up her back, as if he is pattering his fingers along her spine. Marina lowers her eyes in confusion. She has a sudden longing to be at home, stuffing cabbage-leaf parcels with minced pork and veal, or discussing the correct age to read *Middlemarch*. She wants to ring Urs, 229 5104, and report to her: I am here in the halls of greatness, *et tout va bien. Non, je blague. Avec tristesse, comme toujours je suis dégueulasse.*

She is small and primitive, like someone in a Brueghel. No one is talking to her, with her stiff smile and stupid hands. Like a girl in a fairy story, she thinks in wishes:

Please.

Please.

Please.

But nothing happens. She smiles unattractively, walks over to a table and pretends to be admiring an ashtray made of a hoof or a horn. If she were at Simon Flowers's house she could be reading poetry aloud to his younger sisters, or watching his parents play string quartets. She could join in on the cello. Her foot touches something: a blood-smudged bone, half-gnawed, and in her shock she knocks into a dog bowl under the table. Water sloshes on the rug and the parquet beneath it; at home she would rush to wipe it up. Here she can only pray to the God of Evaporation.

'Young person,' says a voice.

All other sound seems to leave the room, as if someone had pressed their lips to it and sucked the flavour out.

Alexander Viney lifts his energetic eyebrows. His forehead crinkles in four straight lines, as if he is amused.

'So you are . . .'

'I'm Guy's er,' she says stupidly, aglow like a fiery radish. Mr Viney lifts his eyebrows again: one, two. 'I mean,' she begins. 'I— we met.'

'I know *who* you are. You said. I'm not quite geriatr—'

'Yes,' she says without thinking, 'I saw your age in *Who's Who.*'

'Indeed. Don't interrupt. Rather, the question is: *what* are you? That's the aspect which interests me.'

'Sorry?'

'Good Lord. It's quite straightforward: are you whatever it is you people say now . . . his girlfriend? Do people *have* girlfriends these days?'

She can feel everyone watching. There is a strange silence, curdy and dense. She says, 'I think, er, maybe some do. But not at Combe.'

'Oh really. What happens at Combe?'

'We . . . that's not allowed. We . . . toil, instead. Some of us.'

'Do you now?' His eyebrows rise even higher. 'Toil,' he says thoughtfully, his eyes still on her. 'D'you know, that's a good word. So you're not his girlfriend.'

'I—'

'No need to answer,' he says, smilingly. 'Now tell me. What else are you? Don't look so nonplussed: that dark plait like a squaw, those impressive eyebrows. You look like you should be ululating at Mafia funerals. Spanish? I don't know. Not Greek?'

At Combe not one person has gone this far. If they think 'foreign', they mean pale noblemen in Kensington, shooting themselves over gambling debts, but her family do not bet, or drink, or kill themselves. 'English,' she says.

'Is that so?'

She swallows her shame, like a bullfrog: *ug*. 'But my father's, well, my grandparents were, are—'

'Spies?'

It's not funny, she wants to say, but she answers, with as much dignity as she can: 'No. Actually they love the queen, and the Labour Party. They're very patriotic. The English welcomed them.'

'I see.'

'They are very loyal.'

Now he is not laughing. 'Of course they are,' he says. 'Fascinating. I shall have to guess. Not German. Polish? You have that Russian doll loo—'

'They were born,' she says, blushing all over her body, 'in the Austro-Hungarian Empire.'

'Good Lord.'

'I know.'

'Interesting.'

'Do you think so?'

'I do.'

'Actually,' she confides, 'so do I. But I don't normally tell—'

'Yes, quite,' he smiles. 'Just that phrase, Austro-Hungarian – it always makes me think of pointy helmets.'

'I know. Exactly. In fact,' she admits, 'they used to ski to school. Not that they've said. I've just seen mittens.'

'So, out of interest, where was this, precisely?'

'The thing is,' she says, 'I don't know. It seems mad. But it's not discussed. I mean, I try to, you know, ask things, all the time. But they just cry.'

'Your grandparents?'

'All of them,' she says, glossing over the true shame of her domestic arrangements. 'Instantly. In fact just the other day' – actually a year or more ago, why is she lying? – 'I wanted to know if they'd grown up on a farm, or . . . it was about pets, actually, because I'd like . . .' Change the subject. 'Or a garden. We all love gardens,' she says, gesturing sycophantically and banging her hand hard on a table corner. 'No, it's fine, ha ha! It's fine. Um . . . so, I asked, and . . . tears. Immediately. Blubbing,' which is a word she has been longing to try. 'So I never find out anything. Look, are you sure you want to talk to me? You've got guests.'

'It's fine,' he says. 'You're amusing me.'

'Am I?'

'Yes, but don't go on,' he says, grinning, and he folds his arms behind his head and stretches backwards. His chest looks very . . . virile, she decides, which is a disgusting thing to think about someone's father.

'I don't usually talk about this,' she admits. 'In public. I don't know why. I mean, about being . . .' She drops her voice. 'Foreign.'

'So you don't even know where they're from?'

'Were . . . or are, for my grandmother, yes. Maybe I've heard, but I can't remember the actual place name. It kept changing around, I think, the barriers. Boundaries. They did their sums and reading in Russian and spoke Hungarian to their parents but the town was Czech, or no, that was my grandfather. Roz— my grandmother was the other way round . . . I think. And they speak Hungarian now, amongst themselves, but they *say* they're from Cz— the Czech Republic. They call it Czecho. How can that be?' Shut up now, she tells herself, but he makes her too nervous. 'They're weirdly loyal to it. We're only allowed Czech mustard.'

'D'you know, it's rather good stuff.'

She looks at him with new admiration. 'I suppose it is. But now their town is in Russia. The Ukraine. No, Ruthen— Ruritania. Somewhere like that.'

'Good God. Tell me you're joking.'

'Me? No . . . sorry, why—'

'Never mind. So, Hungarian, eh? The world's most impossible language.'

'Everyone says that. I mean,' she says quickly, 'it's amazing that you knew. Do you . . . speak it?'

'Certainly not.'

'I don't,' she reassures him. 'Well, I know forty words. Central heating is, well it *sounds* like *kers*-pontifootaish. Seriously.' She has lowered her voice again, as if saying a dirty word. 'Tomato is, well, *porr*-odichom. See? *Mee*-krohulam is microwave, *raa*-gogoomy is chewing gum, not that I'm allow— I mean, that's how you say them, God knows how they're spelled. We laugh at them, it sounds so ridiculous,' she says. 'At the words, obviously, not my grandmother. My mother and I. At least, we used . . .' Her cheeks are burning again. 'Even Tokaj, that wine, it's all done in satchel loads, did you realize? Like *három puttonyos* means three, I think,' she says, counting on her fingers. 'Hang on, *egy ketö három*, yes, three satchels. Of grapes, I suppose. Sorry, where was I?'

'God knows,' he says, but he is smiling. 'Would you like another drink?'

'Please. Nothing sounds sensible. They even say *Hongarion*,' she confides. 'And you can't work anything out, because it's so, well, unLatinate—'

'Only marginally Finno-Ugric, is it, although—'

'Exactly! Wow. That is so, so right. So if I want to know what they're on about I have to extrapolate.'

'Extrapolate? Interesting,' says Alexander Viney, inclining his head as if towards a respected colleague.

'So why,' she persists, 'do you know all this?'

'You are very direct. Well, I had an acquaintance from that general area.'

'Oh! Really? I'd love to meet him, her . . . them. I mean—'

'Why? Don't be ridiculous.'

Marina was going to explain that she misses her Hungarians; that she thinks certain words in their accent, for comfort; that in term time she so longs for their voices that her heart leaps when she hears a foreigner on the streets of Combe, and is always disappointed. But he is laughing at her, so he doesn't deserve it. He'll go off now to talk to his more impressive guests and she will guard her grandparents' privacy.

He doesn't go anywhere. Alexander Viney is still smiling, his eyes narrowed, as if he is trying to deduce something from her face. 'So,' he says, 'the mountains – the Carpathians, as you'll know . . . or you don't know.'

'Not . . . no.'

'Well, you should.'

'I—'

'Forests, castles, goose-girls, wolves. Princes. Mountain lions.'

'Really?'

'Not really.'

'Sorry. God I'm so dim, I—'

'So they're from there? Anywhere I might have heard of?'

She narrows her eyes. Is it possible that he could be thinking that her relatives were princes? She wants to be honourable and honest; all the same, she can hardly admit that they were probably gnawing old potatoes and sleeping in pigstyes. She will not betray them. 'I don't think so. I mean, I don't *know* of any, you know, castles, or whatever. Or maybe only very small ones.'

He looks at her. 'You're probably right,' he says, and she blinks. 'Interesting. I don't know if you've found that those places tend to breed a certain sort of person. Very formal. Very archaic. Endless hand-kissing, apparently, and—'

'Oh, we don't do that,' she reassures him. 'Hardly ever. But the rest is so right. You *do* know.'

'And of course they're proud. Are you proud? And easily insulted, nursing grudges, ferocious about the family's honour . . .'

'Well,' she says. 'I'm not like *that*.'

'Of course not. Have you read George Mikes?'

She stands straight. He should know the kind of person he is dealing with. 'My great-aunt *knows* George Mikes,' she says.

'He's dead,' he says.

'Oh. Sorry. Oh.'

'Hierarchical too. Keeping things from the children.'

'What do you . . . oh, I see. Yes, they do. Completely. Wow – I've never thought before it's a sort of, you know, a *racial* thing. I thought it was only mine.'

'Just a guess.'

'No, honestly, this is so exciting. You can't imagine. I've never met someone who knows anything about them before. I mean, in real life. It's like being given instructions.'

'Really?'

'It's amazing. I just didn't know it was normal. So your friend comes from exactly where?'

'There, where you're talking about. Transylvania. What? You must know this, surely.'

'Tran . . . you're teasing me.'

'I assure you I'm not. Look, if you can't stomach that, you can say Transcarpathia or Ruthenia even. Child, it's basic central European geography. Don't look so insulted.'

'I'm not,' she says. 'Transylvania, seriously? I, I—'

'Hey!' says Guy, appearing at her side and nudging her hard with his elbow. 'You OK?'

'Perfectly fine, thank you,' says his father, but he looks annoyed. The fire heats her fiercely from one side. 'I'm interested in my new friend's roots,' he says. 'Aren't you?'

Guy hesitates.

'Although you'll need to be careful.'

'What do you mean?'

Alexander Viney keeps his eyes on her. 'Scimitars. Pet bears. Vlad the Impaler. Hungarian women are a handful.'

'She's not Hungarian. Is she?'

'Marina?'

'You don't *sound* Hungarian,' Guy says.

'Trust me. Blood of the Hun. This one may look like Frieda Kahlo in a filthy mood, but . . .'

Guy is pulling her away. His father is still watching her.

'We will talk further, my little friend,' he says, and then he winks.

14

'Zsuzsi, *dar*-link, do you vant a *kavitchka?*'

'*Nem.*'

'Rozsi *dar*-link, do you vant a *kavitchka?*'

'*Igen, köszönöm.*'

'*Szívesen*. Laura,' says sweet kind trusting Ildi, who thinks her evening holds no more than coffee and *Murder on the Nile*, 'do *you* vant a . . .'

But Laura sits in a welter of panic; Peter is coming back. In the past, if ever she missed him, she would remind herself that in his absence Marina was safe. Now that she has become unmistakably fully grown, he will want to introduce his daughter to his grim friends: renegade French teachers; embittered driftwood carvers; professional life-class models; *poets*. Laura has met these disgusting men already, knows about their numberless tragic girlfriends, their cigarette-rolling habits, their arrogant attitude to hygiene. The thought of them anywhere near Marina makes her grip her chair until her knuckles whiten.

Never, she thinks. No way. Life is bad enough without him in it. If I measure the damage his return would do against his absence, it is better for us all if he stays away.

It is like being on television: *An Adult Dinner Party*. Every-one murmurs politely. The room is full of candlelight, magnified by silver and glass and mirrors, so that it is impossible to tell how much is actual flame. They eat the food of yesteryear: smoked salmon mousse, parsnips and roast potatoes, rib of beef. Nobody comments, although it is all delicious. There doesn't seem to be quite enough.

'This is lovely, gorgeous, thank you,' she says, to fill in the silence after she has dropped her knife, and the heat of the room falls upon her. Alexander Viney sits far away across a pool of mahogany, hair glinting like fur as he bends his head to the blonde woman beside him. 'Horatia,' she hears him say; Marina nods knowledgeably, prepared to murmur Admiral Lord Nelson's dates, but he does not notice. On his other side is Lucy Viney, which seems a terrible waste. He puts his arm over her shoulder, and she leans against him.

'Family,' he says, pouring more wine into their glasses. 'Nothing like it. Aren't they beautiful?'

Marina catches Mrs Viney's eye and smiles. 'Yes,' she says, and her voice sounds like a choirboy's, pre-pubescent.

She is sitting, like a squatting slave child, on a chair slightly lower than the others, next to Olly, a student in land management, who asks if she knows Minty or Ivan, then concentrates on his food. On her right is Jerry, who is, she now realizes, familiar only because he is a famous politician; he understandably ignores her. The interesting-looking dark woman, Janey Dalrymple, has not once turned in her direction either, despite Marina's hopeful smiles. Pressed between strangers, an awareness of nearby adult bodies – the radiant heat burning from the politician's arm, the small private movements Mrs Viney makes with her hand – is forced upon her. Her nervous breathing is crude in comparison, her tongue moves too loudly. Mr Viney, she suspects, would understand this. Although her head is so hot, beneath the table she is frozen, like a mermaid. And her leg is shaking. She has only just discovered that she is terrified of dogs. Whenever smelly Beckett comes near her, a limping barrel of hair and drool, she has to grip the sides of her seat.

This, however, is the least of her problems. Zsuzsi and the others are so keen on manners but, she wants to tell them, they have left her ill-prepared. What use was their training if all she can do is hold open doors and give up seats and defer respectfully to old foreign ladies? Here it is quite different: she is an adult, with no idea how to behave among her kind. She has already made a mess of hand-shaking. Timing is difficult. Who was meant to sit first at the table, all women, or just older women, or men older than her and who serves whom, and when do you start eating? She brought her champagne to the table and had to pour it into a wine glass to avoid rebuke, which then ruined her chances of working out the right ones for anything else. Also, she has too much cutlery; she considers trying to use a knife and fork to eat her bread, just to use some of it, mercifully sees sense and then is shocked to see Mrs Viney using her fingers to wipe up the sauce on her plate. She keeps getting her compliments wrong; her spindly little chair creaked when she sat on it and, to cover her embarrassment, she said how pretty it was, and Lucy Viney said, oh God, that one, urgh, hideous, and Mrs Viney said, 'It's mostly plarstic, anyway.'

Whenever Alexander Viney glances her way, Marina tries

to look intellectual, yet remote. Mrs Viney, on the other hand, keeps giving her reassuring smiles. Once she even winks. By the time they are on their rhubarb fool and brandy snaps, Marina has stopped trying to join in her neighbours' conversation. She has forgotten Guy. She looks at Mrs Viney and thinks again: Please.

Olly the student has been growing ever sleepier and stranger. Gradually, something shocking occurs to her: could he be *drunk*? She blushes with shame for him, and disgust. Thank God Rozsi isn't here, she thinks, then she realizes that this is exactly the kind of error the Fates are waiting for. If she rings home tomorrow and finds that her entire family has been slaughtered, we all know whose fault it would be.

At last, after brandy and port and sloe gin, and Bath Oliver biscuits, which are an enormous disappointment, the dinner ends. Is it possible that she is a tiny bit drunk too? She knows what should happen now, but no one is doing it. 'Do we adjourn?' she whispers to the politician, who reels back in theatrical amazement. Her toes are wet with Beckett's slobber. Bed, she thinks: my cottony room, my dressing table, my rural views.

But Guy has other plans.

'Don't put on the light,' Marina says. 'I need to sleep.' The smell of so much fresh air is like being inside his childhood; it almost cancels out her worry that he will suddenly decide to look in her washbag and find her crime. Hungry for her bed, she wanders round in the moonlight, touching a fossil on the windowsill, thinking about castles and dark fir forests, which merge in her mind with the soft brown deciduous haze outside, the terrace and infinite little rooms. Now, able for once to overcome her terror of *The Turn of the Screw*, Peter Quint's pug face behind the curtain, she stands close to the window, her nose leaving a greasy mark on the glass, and looks out for hedgehogs on the dewy lawn.

It is so easy to imagine where she should have come from: the turrets, the merry woodcutters among the palace birches, all in silhouette against an oily rainbow sky. She wants to be proud of the family peasant-cot, but the dirty crouching truth is that she is ashamed. She would not have been a beautiful simple maiden. She would have been the witch.

'Come here,' Guy says, but she hesitates.

He walks up to her, takes her hand and puts it on the front of his chinos, where he is hard.

That, she thinks, is an erection.

Night. It is almost twelve, an hour at which, in London, nothing good can happen: only violence, suffering, furtive struggles in alleyways. There is too much fear and danger in the world for a parent to bear.

Laura walks on tiny stepping stones across a rushing torrent, picking her way between the terrors of daily life. Midnight is one of the worst times: a shameful childhood blight which, disappointingly, she has not grown out of. At home, worrying in her semi-bed, she survives it by avoidance, closing her eyes to the china clock on the opposite wall, her ears to the swishing past of cars in the rain. She awaits the telephone, the knock at the door until, at last, it is twelve-thirty, and Marina can be judged to have survived another day.

How funny, she thinks now, that Alistair Sudgeon, object of so much longing and hope, does not know this about her, yet Peter, with whom the later years were mostly endurance, used to tease her about it, which she hated, until the fear had almost gone.

Idiot, she thinks. He'll have forgotten it now. Things were better as they were, without false hope, which is why, as the church on Pembridge Villas strikes the fatal hour, Laura is crouching by the communal bins of Westminster Court in the frost, wearing a nightdress, coat, mittens and substantial knickers, teeth chattering like a child's as she fails to burn her former husband's letter in an empty tin of plum tomatoes.

One after another, the matches blow out. She is shivering dramatically. London roars at her back. All evening the letter has lain concealed in her spurious work folder, in an envelope from the milkman until, with the others at last in bed, she reread it by the glow of the street lamp where the curtain gapes, looking for clues.

There were no clues. He sounded surprisingly sane. He knew she must hate him; he referred to his many friends who abandoned wives, children, babies and, as she pursed her lips, he wrote, 'I always thought they were pricks, and they were, and now I'm one too.'

Which is, of course, exactly the sort of Peterish comment she has edited from her thoughts of him. Keeping her face averted from five floors of nets and proud window boxes, she scans the street. Was it even love, given the quantity of her crying? Hadn't his selfishness always shown beneath the skin? She thinks of never seeing his handwriting again, his allegedly good intentions, the predictable fact that he is living on someone's houseboat, and waits to feel purged, renewed. If she doesn't write back he will leave them alone, which is what she wants, and she can decide what to tell the others in due course: his mother and daughter, whom he has so horribly hurt.

But the tomato can, which had seemed, at the time, an uncharacteristically practical solution to the gratelessness of Westminster Court, contains not enough oxygen, or too much liquid vegetable, to be quite the furnace she had hoped. Burning the letter had seemed the right thing to do when it was ticking away inside the flat: a stupid idea, she can see that now. Six matches left. Five. Four. She could, she realizes now, have flushed it down the toilet, thrown it out with the potato peelings, but burning seemed better.

It is the only way; severing the last tie with this man whom she loved, or thought she loved, to the point of idiocy. This is definitely the right thing to do: a final act of revenge.

But what if she has to contact him?

She needs time alone to think what to do, how to contain him and preserve what little peace she has. The worst thing, she is absolutely certain, would be for the old ladies and Marina to come across the letter before she has prepared them, and she is not ready to tell them quite yet. Anyway, if he is desperate to see them again, which his letter did not mention, he will phone them. He—

Now, too late, she realizes that she has just watched the

last match go out. There is nothing to do but haul open the fire door; she is about to creep back inside to her lair when she sees a man crossing the road in front of the building. Her stomach slips. It is Peter. And although in the next moment she knows that it is someone else entirely – the real Peter has bigger eyes, bigger nose, bigger gut and voice and ego – after she has hurried down the cold concrete steps to the basement flat, she is telling herself that this racing heart is fear, of course it is. What else could it be?

15

'What the hell time is it?' says Guy.

'Half eight. Sorry, sorry. Shouldn't you be getting up?'

It has not been a restful night. She had brought her most country-house nightdress, green tartan brushed cotton from Marks & Spencer, but was so cold that she had to sleep in the brown tights and a cardigan too. Now she stinks of sweat.

Also, there has been an incident: only a couple of hours ago, when the sun was coming up. The unnaturally loud birds of Wiltshire had woken her at 06.44 and as she lay on her back in her cool linen coffin, alert for footsteps outside her door, she slowly came to realize that nature was calling to her in other ways. She needed the loo.

By the time she had risen, performed her five morning press-ups and tried every possible clothing combination, her need was urgent. She crept out into the corridor. She opened the lavatory door, tried to pull it shut, found that it stuck. There was no lock.

In her distress she made what was meant to be a little groan but came out as something louder, more bodily, which could be misinterpreted. Self-consciousness bloomed in the quiet: she knew she should turn round and go back to bed, but she was more desperate than she had ever been before. She had been dismissing her faint stomach ache as nervousness, and hunger: now she realized that she needed to . . . to . . . empty her bowels. The loo itself was in the bathroom, which Rozsi would consider uncivilized, and the room looked as if Mrs Viney had forgotten to have it decorated. Its walls were made of planks like a boat; it had a green-stained bath in the middle of the room connected to the wall with wobbly pipes; a broken wicker chair with a cushion; a spooky old picture made of dried flowers behind spotty glass; and, for the greater magnification of noise, floorboards instead of carpet. Everything would be audible, to everyone. She sat down on the cold toilet, no, lavatory seat and saw herself reflected in the mottled mirror by the door, frowning like a gargoyle, her knickers by her ankles, her face the colour of shame.

And, oh dear God, what to do about flushing?

Since childhood she has known never to alert others to one's night-time wee, let alone wake them, by using the chain. Never: not at home and certainly not anywhere else. One simply disguises it with extra paper, washes one's hands silently, and scarpers.

Here, now, this was not an option. The house lay in perfect silence. A passing Viney would hear her; thanks to the carpeted hallway she might not even hear them. She closed her eyes. A pipe gurgled; someone might think it was her.

Then she realized that it was.

Her stomach gave another gurgle, then a loud growl. She sat back sharply, whacking her elbow extraordinarily hard against a metal pipe which protruded from the wall. It was too dark to see but there must be blood; now she felt sick too. And meanwhile the noise in her stomach began again, more loudly than ever and nothing, not even prayer, or leaning forward to hold her ankles, could squash it into silence. The sweat smell grew stronger. Could she could find somewhere else to go, a downstairs bathroom, the woods?

It was too late. Her need was pressing. Tears rolled down her cheeks as she gave in to her fate.

Who could have slept after that? She thinks now, standing just inside the doorway of Guy's fuggy bedroom, that she probably never will. If he refers to hearing sounds in the night, or, dear God, having gone in after her, she will pass out. But he is still only half awake, indistinct in the furry darkness. To the level of his strange boy-nipples, if not lower, he is bare.

'Oi you, come here.' he says.

'I can't. I, I have to ring my home.'

'Get a grip.'

'No, seriously. I do. They, I, honestly. Please. I can pay—'

'They'll be fine,' he says irritably and, when she still resists him, sends her off with the vaguest of directions.

Her jumper smells of wood smoke and armpits. The ground floor is cold; no one is about. She keeps looking over her shoulder as she searches for the telephone. There is a reassuring pile of logs outside the back door, innumerable spare wellingtons and woolly jumpers. Last night, it occurred to her that if a war began this weekend and the Vineys offered to give her family sanctuary, she'd have to explain all about them. She has spent so many hours thinking of how she'd save them during an unspecified apocalypse – which foods in the looted shops of Queensway might be more sustaining, for example, or whether they know anyone in Scotland. What if the coast is invaded by, well, invaders? It is bad enough in London, where they are at constant risk of kidnap, murder, accident, of junkies, muggers, stalkers, flashers, gropers, rape or worse, if there is worse. Of course Mrs Viney would welcome Rozsi and her mother and the others, but it would be awkward.

A good, moral person would not think in this way. She deserves what she will get.

By the time they answer, her teeth are chattering.

'*Ha*-llo.'

'It's me,' she says. 'But I can't really tal—'

'*Dar*-link, *von*-darefool,' says Zsuzsi, sounding faintly disappointed. 'But how so early? No matter. Tell me all about those lovely boys.'

Her breath stops. Then she understands: 'Oh!' she says. 'You mean—'

'The aristocrat Lord Charles, how is he?'

Zsuzsi is obsessed with the Hon. Charlie: a sweet dullard in Bute who was polite to her on Marina's first day. Bute is, nominally, Marina's house; she sees him several times a week there at House Prayers and House Meeting and Ronald and Jonquil ('Ron and Jon') Daventry's weekly teas. He has a special bond with Pa Daventry. Thanks to his floppy fringe and noble profile, for a week or two Marina had imagined they might be friends, or possibly marry.

148

'Charlie's fine,' she says. 'I think. Actually, could I—'

'Or that young boy, for example. Gay.'

'Guy.'

'Yes, yes. So good-looking. He is not a lord?'

'No.'

'*Nev*-airmind. To me, he is so romantic. A girl has to live a little. *Igen*. Wait one second, *dar*-link. Rozsi speaks.'

'But . . . hello, Rozsi,' says Marina, pressing her dramatically bruised elbow against the wall. 'Yes. Yes. No. Not at all. How pleased? I think . . . Yes, always, very hard. Yes, the top, or near. OK, the top. *Yes*, honestly, you don't need to . . . every night. Yes, plenty. And I'm in the Current Affairs Society now, did I tell you? The only girl, and mostly younger boys but . . . No, Thursday. Yes, lots of friends. In fact,' she says, clenching her jaw to control her shivering, 'actually I'm ringing because . . . well, you know the pay phone at West Street? It's sadly broken.'

'*Tair*-ible. You must tell your master that he will help you. It is *ri*-dicoolos.' Rozsi switches into Hungarian: ongy-bongy, ongy-bongy, explaining to the others Marina's little lie.

There is a stack of cards and paper by the telephone: The Old Rectory, Stoker, West Knoyle, nr Shaftesbury. They are engraved, she is certain, not thermographed, which is reassuring. New red pencils too; unlike the little green crocodile stumps at home, the wood dark with frugality, this is unbitten, rubberless, a smooth cylinder with a perfect point: the Platonic ideal of pencils. The gulf, she thinks, between us is unbridgeable.

Then Rozsi is back. 'How can the little children telephone?'

'We're not little, exactly,' she says. 'Someone in my English class is eighteen.'

'Well, he must be a very stupid boy.'

'Yes, he is.'

'There we are. So what do they do with this bloomy phone?'

'Oh,' says Marina vaguely. 'Improve it probably. Something digital.'

'Digital? Very good.'

'So . . . the thing is, you see, I had to go to one of the other phones and ring for our Sunday chat, but I d—'

'Where?'

'The New Lodge. Actually near the Buttery. That's why it's so quiet. Don't worry.' She doesn't quite know how to stop. 'There's nothing to worry about.'

'And you are being good?'

'Sorry? Oh, right, sorry, yes, right. Sorry.'

'*Dar*-link, please, I must talk to your houseman, master, put him on.'

'But that's not . . . I, you can't. He's teaching. Rozsi, I've really got to go.'

'I worry, *dar*-link,' Rozsi says.

'Oh. Do you?'

'Yes. Of course. Soon Fenyvesi Ernö and Bözsi are here, we go for little walk, so we talk about it later. I send money.'

'No, no. No need. I've got lots. Honestly.'

'I send food then. Easy-peasy. We see you soon. Now I fetch your mother. Be good, *dar*-link.'

*

'I just, it was easier to ring early,' Laura hears her daughter say. 'Today. Or did you not want me to?'

'Of course I did. It's— Sweetheart, where are you?' Her heart is still thumping; an early-morning phone call is never good news. 'You're all echoey. Was that a dog's bark?'

'Oh. Yes. I'm, I'm at school, obviously – obviously! – but not actually . . . not in West Street. I'm in, in, you know that corridor between the Undercroft and the Praecentor's—'

'So early,' comments Rozsi at Laura's elbow, as if the phone is permeable. 'Why, tell us?'

'Is the West Street one not working?' asks Laura, closing her eyes. She can't even visualize where her daughter is standing. Why has she allowed her to live two hours away? How, she would like to know, can anyone stand mother-hood? Do other women not live as she does, trying to ready themselves for the phone call which will bring their life to an end?

I can't go on like this, she thinks, with the sudden clarity of the half-awake. Even apart from bloody Peter, this is un-endurable. All this worrying has to stop.

'Yes,' Marina is saying. 'I mean, no, no, it's completely broken. That's why—'

'Are you sure,' says Laura, sounding strict to keep the wobble out of her voice, 'that everything's OK?'

'Yes. I said.'

'There's that dog again. It does sound very close. You hate dogs, sweetheart, ever since Mrs Kroo's—'

'I don't. I mean, I don't now. You can't just assume—'

And that is how their conversation ends, with Marina an

inch or two further away, and Laura not having dared to say, 'Come home. I want you. I miss you. I can't wait another hour.'

Anyway, how could she have said it? There was no way, with Rozsi right here, to raise the subject of leaving Combe. It has to be private, and Westminster Court is never private.

She thinks to herself: you could write to her and ask.

But after a term of scouring the emotions out of her post-cards, could Laura send a letter like that?

The only way to live apart from one's child is to shut up one's heart in a metal box with chains and rust and padlocks, and not open it. She cannot bear to. She has no picture of Marina on her desk. She cannot breathe when she thinks of her.

If Marina is homesick, Laura's heart will break open. So she cannot entertain the idea. If Marina wants to leave Combe, surely she will say so.

Marina goes into breakfast. Her throat aches as an orphan's might. She rubs her frozen hands together and smiles shyly at the other guests, at Guy's sister.

'Um . . .'

'What?'

'Sorry. I . . . is there any coffee?'

There is a short silence, solid, like a pineapple cube. 'We have *tea*,' says Lucy Viney. 'We don't bother Evelyn for other things.'

'Oh. Sorry,' says Marina.

'Anyway, this is the perfect breakfast. Though, actually, do you mind, the *fresh* orange juice is Daddy's.'

'Sorry.' Biting her lip, she inspects the alien foodstuffs: porridge on a little burner; thick Salisbury honey and Dorset butter; marmalade in a bowl. If, she thinks, anyone mentions the loo last night, anything, sounds, or . . . odours, I will have to bolt. Or die.

'Shut the door, can't you,' says the politician. 'Were you born in a barn?'

Marina sits with salty porridge and milky tea, resisting the tears which are forcing themselves down her nostrils. She looks out of the window and imagines being shown around the garden in summer, the bee-loud glades thick with honeysuckle and what her grandmother calls *fuk*-sio, tall spinach waving in the breeze, all planted by someone with whom she has a bond. Does Mrs Viney's beauty conceal a secret sadness? Is she out there now, wandering alone?

I'll ask Guy about her on the train, she thinks. Though, please, God, don't let him come downstairs yet. Something else happened last night, after dinner, before the other . . . the toilet incident and the wounding, which she has been trying even harder to forget. But Guy will not have forgotten. It concerned, in part, his manhood.

It was quite interesting: an uncomfortable-feeling gristly knobble. Having never seen a real one, except once on a drunk man peeing behind a phone box near Regent's Park, Marina has only imagined penises dimly, almost dutifully. Simon Flowers seemed unlikely to have one, the masters too old, boys her age too young. Besides, no one has properly explained the hydraulics: how something soft enough to need the protection of a cricket box can become hard and presumably beautiful, an object of desire. And surely something that sticks out at right angles can't enter something, well, vertical? She could not imagine what to expect.

Yet here one was, separated from her by the thinnest layer of chino. Guy was moving his lips silently. She listened to his breathing, her hand exactly where he put it, on his loins.

'Sit down?' he said in a frightened voice.

'All right.' Was it growing? Isn't that what they do? She must be excited, she told herself, only less than she had expected; more as a scientist might be, in the field. If anything she felt almost motherly towards him, puzzled, as if he was a problem to be solved.

She pressed down a millimetre further. In the nick of time she remembered something she heard in the West Street kitchen; apparently if a stiffened member is bent for any reason at all, it will be terribly damaged. Blood vessels burst. Poor boys, to be so vulnerable. Minutely, she lifted her hand.

'Nnnm,' said Guy. They stared at each other, owl eyes in the darkness. Her ignorance crouched behind her on the bed. 'Please,' he said. She put her hand back down.

Now, like a coordination exercise, they were kissing too, while she kept her fingertips lightly on his manhood. This was not how she had imagined the beginning of sex, the swoon of joyous reciprocal love in, ideally, an Italian meadow. Guy Viney's tongue was in her mouth, but her mind kept drifting from his trousers and back to the adults downstairs. Why wasn't she enjoying this more? Although there definitely was something delicious about this womanly feeling of control; she was thinking she might even slightly increase the pressure, experimentally, when his hand bumped against hers. Then it bumped again.

There was a crackling, sliding sound. He was unzipped.

Could she pretend not to have noticed? It is dangerous, apparently, as well as morally wrong, to deny them release. And she was curious, and in danger of being officially frigid, despite spending every single night of her adolescence hot and restless and full of desire. She looked down carefully, past his neck, shirt buttons, belt, to where, in his lap, floated something pale.

She had tried to do the correct thing. She really had. He felt silky, like a toy as she began, cautiously, to investigate and, although her fingers were shaking, it was at least experience. Then there was a noise.

'Christ.'

She jerked her hand away. He gave a little grunt. There was a strange doughy smell, wetness warm as blood. What had she done? 'Oh,' she said. 'I'm sorry.' He would not look at her. 'Are you OK?'

'God,' he said and cleared his throat. Semen, she thought. Squirmy tadpoles all over her hand; she could get pregnant.

'Tissue?'

'It's fine, I'll go the bathroom. Don't worry,' she said kindly, holding her hand out stiffly like a piece of rotten meat.

The big upstairs hallway was dark, the carpet soft, and she did not see his father until they were face to face.

'Oh!' she said, jumping. She hid the hand behind her back. 'Sorry.'

'Bit late to be exploring, isn't it?' His voice was so quiet that she had to lean closer to hear him. Closed doors on either side; she listened hard, but all was still. Which one had he come out of? Perhaps the Vineys sleep separately. Was he going for a marital visit?

'I didn't mean—'

'Don't apologize. Was something keeping you up?' He smiled at her in the half-light. Could he smell it? 'It's terrific to have you here.'

'Really?'

'Oh yes. In the bosom. My family is everything to me, you know, but I cannot be *limited*. The enthusiasms of young people make life more liveable. You understand.'

'Yes,' she said. When he touched her forearm, she gave a little jump. She looked up at him. A thread seemed to shoot between them. 'You must come again,' he murmured. 'I insist that you do,' and he turned and left her standing there, the thread pulled tight.

16

'The thing is,' Laura says. 'I know it's late. But I have to go out.'

Rozsi is visiting invalids; Zsuzsi is in bed with the Combe *Almanac*, reading out difficult words – 'Vot is this "Dibbers"?' – in a carrying voice through the open door. Only Ildi is in the living room, packing up knitted dolls for the poor children of Romania. '*Vair*-y sweet,' she says, waving the hand of a soldier doll. '*Ha*-llo.'

The Tube will be fastest, to Earls Court on the District Line. If only there was a quicker way. 'Hello,' says Laura politely to the soldier. 'Ildi, is that all right? I'm a bit late . . .'

Ildi, pulling down the skirt on a reversible princess homunculus, takes a breath. 'I don't know,' she says. 'They—'

'I know,' says Laura. 'But I won't be long.'

London at night. Why is her stomach fluttering? She stands in the roaring glare of the Underground, as if queuing to enter hell, and the pulse in her throat seems audible. Is it the heady fumes of strangers' alcohol, the fact that nobody knows where she is? Or the thought of an accident: fear, pain, blood loss in public, but a solution of sorts? Which would be worse for Marina, in the long term: losing or keeping a mother like Laura?

*

However, when she emerges at Stamford Brook and crosses King Street towards the Great West Road, her daughter is forgotten. Laura is wishing she had put on different clothes. Not that she will see anyone she knows, let alone have a conversation. She is only going to look.

I am burying your ghost, she thinks, you . . . you bastard, and that will be the end of you.

The boat on which Peter is staying is parked in something called Eyot's Boatyard, on the north bank of one of the confusing loops of the river. You simply open the wooden gate and walk through, along a rickety platform, above a glistening surface of soft grey mud. No one questions or molests her. To her left are huge slimy stakes, a fence for giants. To her right is creaking, splashing, the muddy tide of the Thames. She had imagined gin palaces, technology, not this almost rural calm.

Beau Geste, she reads on the side of the first boat, which is much bigger than she had expected, solidly built of grey riveted metal. *Mirabelle, Basinger, Fidelity, Scheherazade*. She does not expect to find *Vivian*. It would be better for all of them if she did not. She should turn around. She could still do it. This is where her future divides: happiness or sorrow. Life or death. Heart pounding like a dying thing, she walks on.

The problem with co-education is that you are trapped. Marina has been unsuccessfully avoiding Guy since Sunday, which makes her either frigid or a prick tease. She keeps worrying that Simon Flowers will detect the odour of sin upon her, or even actual spermatozoa – she keeps seeming to smell something similar, on the Buttery stairs or crossing Founder's Court under the trees. Oh, sperm, she can now think to herself airily. This is some comfort.

She has drawn a plan of her place setting at dinner and written down every single book she saw at Stoker; it makes her feel like a criminal whenever she bumps into Guy. He keeps trying to entice her to his room.

'I can't,' she always tells him. 'We'll be *expelled*.' Neither of them has referred to what happened in his bedroom at home; the awkwardness has turned into abruptness, as if she has done something wrong. Perhaps she has. Her elbow is still stiff and sore, which is not helping. At least when they're below stage at Divvers, with infants around the corner painting papier mâché and Pa Stenning likely to appear at any moment, there is a limit to what he expects her to do, or have done unto her. But Guy is ingenious. Shutting the prop-room door is forbidden, but he has found a place behind Costumes 4: Heralds/Mummers/Slaves, where they can lean against a packing case and not be seen.

He is very pressing.

'Aren't you scared of being caught?' she says when he undoes the top two buttons of her blouse. She has developed a habit of checking them frequently with her fingers; she has a terrible fear of accidentally coming unbuttoned in public and not noticing. Her chest in the cool air feels extremely nude. She keeps her eyes well above his waist.

'We'll be fine,' he says. 'Stenning won't say a word.'

As he feels her, she thinks this over. Next time he takes his mouth away, she says, 'Why not?'

'God, you're chatty,' he says.

'No, really, tell me.'

'Friend of my parents,' he says, trying to unpeel her fingers from the edge of the crate. She knows what he wants her to do.

'By, by the way,' she says. 'I need your address.'

'No, you don't.'

'I do,' she says, holding her head away from him. 'It's not in the *Register*, for some reason.'

'Yeah,' says Guy. 'Stenning did Dad a favour.'

Marina nods knowledgeably. 'Because of confidentiality, probably. I have to write your mother a thank-you card.'

'Not too gushy.'

'I wouldn't,' she says. 'But to be polite . . .'

'Come on, babe. Just let me—'

'OK,' she says. 'You can, if you're quick. But then will you give me their address?' It could, she thinks, be the beginning of a correspondence.

Here it is.

It looks like a home-made bath toy: a square white cabin, a stumpy dark body with a single pale stripe. Other boats have foliage outside in pots, and bright windows and fences; they might be on land, with seagulls for squirrels, were it not for the gangplanks and the smell of the river, sloshing and pulsing out of sight. *Vivian* has nothing: black wood, dangerous-looking loops of wires. She had expected luxurious bohemianism, not rot, not squalor. It looks more like a prison ship than a houseboat.

She is two gangplanks away, by *Second Childhood*. Provided that nobody comes past she can see *Vivian* quite easily. The portholes are not completely dark; there is a dim glow in one or possibly two, muted by curtains and dirt.

Surely nothing so ordinary could contain Peter? After living in her head for thirteen years, how is it possible that he could be here?

It is cold but not yet raining. She could stand here for an hour or more, just watching; contemplating how much she hates him. Damn you, she thinks experimentally and imagines how, if she had any strength of character, she would stride up to the deck and knock and shout until he emerged.

At that moment there is a sound from the boat, as if it had belched, and a splash, and a light illuminates one of the blind portholes by the door. Someone is coming out; it is him, it must be and, if he sees her here, her last grains of self-respect will crumble completely. He is coming; she can almost hear him at the door. She must get away.

Yet she hesitates. What would I do, she thinks: shout at him? Rub his face in that lost horrible time, those wasted years?

Ten o'clock. Marina lies in the bath, washing with an extraordinarily expensive Crabtree & Evelyn rose glycerine soap which she bought herself last term and has not yet dared to use. Every one of her possessions is wrong: she can see that now. She will throw out all her toiletries, her London clothes, and start again.

It feels like the beginning of a new life. She has drafted

several thank-you letters to Mrs Viney, including one – 'Thank you for your kindness, your understanding, your friendship' – which rather moved her, and then has written up the best one on a special Italian note card, adding a reference to Mrs Viney's graciousness, asking for the return of her forgotten blue flannel, hinting, lightly yet heavily, about a return visit. She has also said, which isn't strictly a lie, that during her stay she possibly had a temperature, which would explain any strange-seeming behaviour. 'My real character, you might say, is much more refined!!'

But as soon as the envelope went into the porter's bag, she realized that something about the tone was wrong. Should she have enclosed money for Evelyn, or somehow paid for her meals? Why did she say, 'If ever there is anything I can do for you, please do ~~be get~~ be in touch'?

Then Guy told her that his parents hate thank-you cards. 'And Christmas cards. And when people write actual comments in the visitors' book. It's just so . . . you know. Naff.'

'God, I know. Exactly,' Marina lied, wishing she could commit fell . . . fel . . . or no, what's that other thing? *Felo de se.* If she writes again to apologize for having written, is that correct, or will it make things worse?

Somebody shouts in the corridor outside the bathroom and she jumps horizontally, creating waves. In her first week the girls had to be measured and checked for rubella vaccinations in the San, arms crossed over their bras as they were herded towards the school doctor's office. She was still excited about Combe, and this was fuel: a genuine sanatorium; barley water. Quarantine. She was admitted into the presence of Dr Slater: 'Lie down there,' he said to her, nodding at a camp bed. But it was lower than she expected and somehow she lay down too soon, and dropped a foot through the air to the mattress.

That, she thinks, was when she should have left.

Any reasonable person would have waited to see if Peter emerged on the deck, but not Laura. Instead, in her fright she bit her lip; licking the wound, tasting blood or poisonous river mud, she stumbled on until she reached the road.

I hate you, she thinks, only partly to him. She should go home. She is going more slowly now, past big houses with gardens stretching down to the water, displaying the warm coppery rooms of families and couples, or of people as lonely as her. She walks back along the pavement, hopelessly bedraggled: the woman who missed her chance. The damp cold air stings her ringing lip, which, however, seems to lack the energy to bleed. What do I do? she asks the paving stones. What do I dowhat doIdo – but, realistically, who will answer? If only she believed in God, or there was a helpline: somebody who could decide, quite objectively, whether pining like this for one's child is proof of bad or good mothering; whether it would be better for someone in her position to stay, or dispose of herself; and, if the latter, how to do it so that her absence will be barely noticed.

She could live in a cave, a wild-haired keeper of chickens, but it would embarrass Marina.

An accident would be simpler. Don't forget you're a coward, she reminds herself; it would have to involve no pain. So, considering the comparative advantages of Tube crashes, gas explosions, IRA bombs and falling anvils, she turns a corner and there is the river, just for her.

She seems to have run out of breath. It is so cold. She has taken a wrong turning somewhere and ended up here, on a concrete bank with only spindly railings to keep her from the water.

The railings themselves are just a foot's width or so apart, connected along the top by a horizontal bar at the perfect height for unsatisfactory people, such as a short man or a too-tall embarrassingly weeping woman, to wedge their elbows uncomfortably upon it if they wished or, indeed, their foot. No one is around. She looks down at her ugly black court shoe from Debenhams, the toe scuffed because she is an inelegant walker, the heel beginning to loosen. It would fit.

No. She closes her eyes and lifts her face towards the grey scent and sound of water. People do do this, she tells herself, all the time. Virginia Woolf and . . . no, think of women with children. There was one the other day, a mother, in Zsuzsi's paper: 'So selfish, those poor babies,' she had said, and Laura had agreed. It is almost half-term and, if she does it now, Marina might think it was because Laura didn't want to spend the holiday with her daughter, which is quite wrong. But wouldn't this way be kinder, more open to interpretation, than some of the alternatives? No one passes, as perhaps she hopes they might. She wipes her nose on her sleeve; it does not matter, she reminds herself, resting her cheek for comfort on a railing tip, if her tears are obvious when she goes back to the flat because she won't be going. She almost believes it, even as she loathes her own self-pity. She could pull herself up and jump down to the bank; she is strong. But someone might see. Even now, the thought of a stranger smirking at her awkward climbing, the skirt tangled around her ugly tights or pulled across her bottom, is shameful.

Yet there is no one here. Now she could do it. Now. Now.

17

Tuesday, 31 January

Swimming: Dorset and Devon Schools'
Championship Gala, Senior Boys, Junior Girls,
Yeovil College, 1 p.m. and 5 p.m.; Lowers (geog.)
trip to Galapagos Islands begins; Shaftesbury
Historical Association and Percy Society talk by
Dr Bill Reed (Southampton Further Education
College): 'Desolation, Persecution, Rebirth:
Christianity During the Late Middle Ages', Old
Library, 7 p.m.

Why is it so difficult to think about anything else? When netball practice ends, Marina dashes to the library to look for
Alexander Viney's books. They have almost all of them: not,
as she might have assumed, dry as death, but full of human
stories, sympathetic to his characters, their desperation, their
angry pride. Better still, she is allowed to look through the
archive, the shelves labelled Alumni and Friends of Combe,
where in a yellowed Sunday supplement she finds an inter-
view: The Old Rectory, Stoker, as seen from the lawn; Guy
and Lucy in fat blond infancy; their beautiful mother.

There are notices on the library walls:

SPEECH IS SILVERN BUT SILENCE IS GOLDEN.

EATING WILL RESULT IN EXPULSION.

VHS VIDEO TAPES ON REQUEST.

Ten minutes later, after a lecture from Mrs Iredale, the notoriously sex-hungry deputy librarian, she is sitting in a windowless storage room, listening to Alexander Viney's voice. It warms his listeners: clever, seductive, certain. She has turned off the light. He is only a metre away. 'The man of letters must ignore what others require of him,' he says, 'a political agenda, say, or faith. God forbid.'

He is younger here; his hair is darker. It looks as if they have filmed this on the terrace at Stoker. Are they happy, he and Mrs Viney? Marina creeps closer to the television. Was she sitting near him, just off camera? Or wandering in the herb garden alone, thinking sad thoughts of—

'No,' said Alexander Viney, unexpectedly loudly. 'For history to reach us, it must concern its protagonists' private lives. It must speak of their hopes, their secrets: it must speak of their dark hearts.'

He seems to be addressing her. Does he mean that everyone, not just Marina, has desires which cannot be talked about?

Laura, disappointingly, is still alive. It takes courage to throw oneself into a river, to be fished out by the Thames police and written about in the *Notting Hill Gazette* so, because she is cowardly, she stared at the water a little longer, went home, woke up the next morning and left for work. Which is why, four days later, apparently unchanged except for a slight escalation of self-loathing, she is sitting at her desk at the surgery, about to make everything worse.

It would be very easy to reach Peter, now that he has decided she may. As his letter thoughtfully explained, if Laura wanted to she could leave a message on the answer phone of Suze, who is 'a' girlfriend of Jensen, who owns that grim boat, *Vivian*. The letter, still stubbornly unburnt, is stuffed at the back of the sideboard, hidden in a copy of *The L-Shaped Room*. Admittedly Laura, although increasingly unable to retain the smallest work-related fact, has remembered Suze's number perfectly, but she doesn't have to act on it. She doesn't have to ring.

In which case, why is she sitting here, phone in hand, about to dial? Because she is stupid. You stupid fool: even if his half-baked system worked, he'd hardly be able to ring you back, either here or at home, scene of so many lives he has ruined.

So she writes. Just a plain office slip, asking him to meet her so that she can say what she needs to, and establish some facts. Then it will be over.

She puts it in the surgery postbag, takes it out, runs round the corner to the Post Office under the unlikely pretext of needing an aerogramme, and only when she has returned to her desk does she realize that she is about to ruin her life, again. She can't see Peter. What was she thinking? Was there something in her harmless helpful solitary childhood, or her mother's painful sinking into death, which so weakened her that she attracts disaster? It cannot be sane to live like this, lurching between catastrophes, moving ever further from the world of normal people who live the life they choose.

The rest of the day is a daze of regret. The evening is no better. Mrs Dobos has honoured them by coming 'for a little coffee', in order to discuss the possibility that Combe might be good enough for her own granddaughter, spoilt Natalya. Laura keeps forgetting to smile sufficiently. She is concentrating on hiding the fact that, only a millimetre or two below the surface of the woman they think they see, she has been whittled out entirely, and replaced with something black and hidden.

Or is she deluding herself? Is it truly hidden? Sometimes one of the aunts will look at her even more piercingly than usual and she thinks: they must suspect. Could Zsuzsi have followed her to the boatyard, ducking behind lamp posts in a fog of Je Reviens and rain-sparkled fur?

Has Marina detected something? Is that why she was so strange on the phone?

She passes Mrs Dobos the crystal sugar. You, she tells herself, are an abomination. You are thinking of Peter and his first letter, hidden not a yard from where Mrs Dobos is sitting on the sofa, while you wait for his next.

A great furrow of longing has opened in Marina's chest for no particular reason. It starts off with her mother, which is ridiculous because her mother seems to have forgotten about her entirely. She has not had a postcard from her for four days. It grows deeper, a split, a crevasse, until she feels broken in half with loneliness and hunger. It is a dismally grey afternoon. She trails out of chemistry, which has not gone well, and walks sadly towards Garthgate. Someone familiar is climbing out of a car on the chained-off tarmac outside Percy, and her blood gives a little leap. A strange cold feeling, like escaping unset jelly, spreads over her arm and chest.

'Um, hi. Hello, hi.' She is wearing her glasses, a blouse with covered buttons from Rozsi's wardrobe, scuffed shoes, and a friendship bracelet Urs gave her in Form Four. She can feel a blush spreading across her neck like an infection. 'I . . . was looking for something,' she tells Mrs Viney. 'Someone. Hello!'

'Marvellous,' says Mrs Viney vaguely.

'Yes! Ha ha ha,' Marina says. 'Are you . . . will you . . . so, you're going back? To your, you know, residence?'

'Well—'

'Oh, by the way . . .' Should she mention the thank-you card débâcle? She looks at Mrs Viney helplessly, and receives a little smile in return.

'OK, Ma,' says Guy. 'Stagger off now. Come on, Marina, let's see if there's anything to eat.'

'Might see you tonight, darlings,' says Mrs Viney airily, 'on the way to Jasper.'

'She means Stenning,' Guy says. 'They're having, I don't know, medieval fondues with him or something later.'

Later means when? After dinner she and Guy will go to Evensong to give thanks. Chapel looks beautiful at night; they light the lamps, and the babies from the Choir School sing anthems of salvation, masses and motets and 'Let All

Mortal Flesh'. Pa Stenning, Mrs Viney's friend. *Dominus, salva me.*

'Don't forget to leave my jockstrap,' Guy instructs his mother and nods at Marina. 'Come on. Getting malnutrition.'

In childhood, Marina read comics. She always looks out for five-pound notes on the pavement; kicks aside dropped banana skins to protect old ladies; passes building sites expecting falling cans of paint. Lamp posts, however, have escaped her. She has forgotten to be alert.

And so, following Guy while trying to look meaningfully at Mrs Viney – a distress flare, only for her – she turns her head and walks slap into ten foot of antique-effect metalwork.

'Ha!' bellows Guy. 'Brilliant!'

The pain is astonishing. She must have broken her nose. She will be covered in gore. Jesus. Jesus. She touches her face, licks her upper lip; is this blood she can taste, or snot, or tears?

'Darling, are you all right?'

More dreadful than blood is death by embarrassment; worse even than this colossal pain. 'Er—'

'You can't be.'

She blows out through pursed lips like an athlete. Then she adds, 'Phew.' The agony is unabated. She needs to hide like a wounded animal, feel her skull and howl. 'Ab, absolutely.'

'Idiot!' says Guy joyfully. 'Do it again!'

'Shut up, Guy. Are you sure? It looked awfully painful.'

'Fine. Golly. Yes. Really. I'm fine.'

Mrs Viney looks quizzical. Is she worried? Is she *amused*?

'Didn't hurt at all!' says Marina desperately. Now, unmistakably, Mrs Viney smiles. Marina takes a deep miserable breath. 'But I'd better . . .'

'Yeah,' says Guy. 'Come on. She's fine.'

And he takes Marina off to the Buttery for cream of broccoli soup, mince Mexicana, potato croquettes and syrup pudding, and Mrs Viney does not attempt to stop her.

Where did it all go wrong for Laura? Was it her doing? Was she weak? Doomed by her parents' mild genes: too apologetic to escape the lower middle classes, let alone to get ahead? Or just distracted by her half-cocked consumerist hopes? Because wrong it has gone, quite clearly. Surely there is time to stop it? If she is very strong and sensible, can't her life still change?

Every time the phone rings, she thinks: it's him.

'It's me,' says Alistair Sudgeon in a hoarse whisper. 'I know the rule was no contact, domestically speaking. But I have news.'

Laura backs into the entrance hallway, away from where Rozsi and Zsuzsi and their dear friend Perlmutter Sári, just returned from a very satisfying funeral, are whispering on the sofa like members of the Resistance. There is definitely an atmosphere. When Laura arrived home from work, cold and sad, Sári kissed her, patted her dismissively on the left haunch and said, '*Tair*-ible,' lightly. They are keeping their voices low, as if Laura could have recently learned Hungarian and failed to mention it. Every second or so they shake their heads.

'I,' Laura says into the telephone, leaning against the coat cupboard, 'I thought you were someone else.'

'Who? Let's not be foolish; I'm me. Do you think Farkas Rozsi recognized my voice?' He likes saying names backwards in the Hungarian way, sometimes with accents.

'This . . . it's not a good moment.' Her palms are sticky. She has been waiting all day for word from Peter, and time has concentrated; every minute making the next more likely, like Russian roulette. 'I can't really talk.'

'Well, we have to. Might I pop round?'

Sári's perfect amber hair is only three feet away. '*Byoo*-tifool,' she hears her say. '*Igen. Nagyon szép ház. Vim*-bledon-park.'

'*Yoy*,' says Zsuzsi.

'No!' says Laura. 'Christ. I . . . don't think that would be wise.'

'I thought maybe they'd be out.'

'They never are.' Is it her imagination, or have the murmurings from the sofa died away? 'I'm sure you know that, "Jenny".'

'What? Oh, I see, they're listening. Anyway, look, everything's become rather difficult. Mitzi's being tricky. I think she may have rumbled us.'

Her mouth has filled with powder. 'Hang on,' she says slowly. 'What do you—'

Alistair says, 'I think I may have to spill the beans.'

'What? No. No, no, no. You can't. Don't, please, hon-estly, not for me, or, I mean—'

'Actually, it would be a relief, asking for her forgiveness. All this creeping around and secrecy isn't what it was.'

Even now, with a future being handed to her, she is craning to see if there is anything from Peter on the side-board. 'Isn't it?'

'Of course not. It's probably for the best, anyway. She's a very powerful woman, you know, my wife. Time to make a clean swee—'

'No! God, no, Julie, *Jenny*, it's, no, definitely not. Definitely not a good time. For that. Think of your . . . little children. Seriously, you mustn't. You need to think—'

'*Kivel beszél?*' mutters Zsuzsi.

'*Dar*-link,' Sári says reproachfully in English, 'you said she has no friends.'

Marina is leaning against the War Memorial, watched over by the fallen servants of Combe Abbey, as she waits to spot Mrs Viney through the gap in Pa Stenning's curtains. Her urge to touch walls and windows is stronger than ever; she knows that whatever happens next, whether the first person she sees emits lucky or unlucky vibrations, will determine whether or not she sees Mrs Viney, but the people walking through the Percy entrance aren't particularly helpful: Liza Church; a Fresher whose name she doesn't know. She has just witnessed Pa Jenkin, the Head of the CCF, who is putting the troops through their paces, shouting at Una 'Fats' Squire to take the long route round to the Science Block for no good reason. The entire CCF, hundreds of boys, all laughed and jeered too. I should do something, Marina thinks, be friendly to her, but she knows she doesn't dare.

Something, call it instinct, makes her glance at Percy's front door. A man in a suit is coming down the steps towards her. He clears his throat loudly, frowns, looks around.

There is, she has discovered, a painting of Mr and Mrs Viney in the Tate, from when they were young. He has just become famous; his hair is longer, as in photographs of Marina's own father. In this painting Mr Viney sits on the green green grass and Nancy Viney lies beside him, framed by a house-height hedge painted in minute detail. Marina has gazed at that painting until she is lying with them, the grass under their hands.

Turn. Please. See me.

And he does.

'You're that girl,' says Alexander Viney. 'Remind me . . . Oh yes, you.'

The shoutings and belches and slamming doors are quieter now; the courtyard dark and still. Marina has been out here for longer than she had realized and, unless she hurries, she will be late for curfew, for the first time in her life.

'I was just passing,' she says. 'I mean—'

'Goodnight then,' he says, feeling in his pockets. 'Where's my buggering key?'

Out here, unfiltered, you hear the depth of his voice, its intimacy. It makes her want to close her eyes. 'I don't know,' she says. The air between them sparkles with alcohol. He may be drunk. Now, Marina, go inside. Instead she asks, 'Have you been having dinner?'

'Yes.'

'So . . . why . . .'

'It's a complicated and dull story, involving my sentimental wife and a friend of her youth. I shan't trouble you.'

'Are you joking?'

'Why would I joke?' he says as he heads in the direction of the Old Laboratories. 'I have to get something from the car.'

She is losing him. In her confusion, she says the first thing that comes into her mind. 'It's very exciting to meet you again.'

What is wrong with her? Why is she such a freak of nature that she cannot play it cool? In her voice she can hear the great-aunts and Rozsi when they hover around horrible Mrs Dobos, their nervous flattery of doctors, the great excitement in the shop when a politician's wife once bought popsocks. But Alexander Viney does not seem to mind. He lowers his head and his stare is like a lighthouse beam brushing her face.

'Is it, indeed?' he says. 'Excellent. Tell me more.'

'I used to watch you on television. We all did. You were fantastic,' she adds politely, although in truth she barely remembers.

'Do you think so?' he says. 'I am delighted to hear that. Because my peers, I don't know if you're aware of them, the one with the bow tie and the bald one, ugh—'

She summons up Guy's way of speaking, his confident disdain. 'Oh,' she says. 'Them. They're just idiots.'

They are standing quite close together now. She can feel him: large, hot, like a temporarily tame bear. He folds his arms across his big chest. It is surprising, given how short and distinguishedly grey his head-hair is, to see dark wires at the open neck of his shirt: the infinite hairiness of men.

In the presence of greatness it is easy to forget curfews and matrons. She crosses her arms to conceal the points of her Bellissima Sally-Anne bra in whisper blue, whose Parisienne lace is showing through her school blouse, and tries to look intelligent and brave.

'You're cold,' he says, 'in that ridiculous milk-maidy garment. Here.' And he takes off his jacket and gives it to her. It is warm; it smells of male hormones. She drapes it gratefully over her shoulders. 'But let me ask,' he says. 'When you say *all* of you—'

'Oh, I see – I mean, all of us at my old school watched you. Here they're Philistines. They like game shows.'

'You're not a Philistine, though, I trust.' Something seems to ping in her chest. 'Civilizing influence on my oaf of a son, are you? I'll tell you what,' he says, touches her back with his hand. 'Come and help me with the car.'

Photographs do not make enough of his profile; he looks like something in the National Gallery made of marble. The lines around his very blue eyes suggest kindness, experience. Under the cover of darkness, she slips one arm into his jacket, its lining silky against her bare forearm like the inside of his skin and, very slowly, begins to pull the other sleeve closer around her back.

His car is big and silver. 'When's your next, you know, show?' she asks politely, as he unlocks the boot. In its mysterious depths are tentacles, tools, a bottle of blue liquid. Rope.

'We air the new series in January.'

'What do—'

She stops suddenly. A group of Uppers are coming towards them. They have music cases; one of them, a fantastically square day-girl called Tansy Edwards, is singing scales. Next to her is Simon Flowers.

Marina decides to laugh, merrily, as if she is having a wonderful time without him.

'What are you giggling about?'

She watches them walking up Garthgate; how could Simon Flowers not have noticed her, when she spotted him almost before he turned the corner? He is quite close now. She tries to smile at him as he passes, to encompass his thin shoulders and smudged glasses with interest and love. 'Well,' she says loudly, to draw his attention to her escort, 'some of us here will be watching it, I promise. Those of us who are a bit more civilized.'

Mr Viney looks over his shoulder at her. 'Fuck that.'

She smiles, to conceal her shock. 'But it's one of the finest schools in—'

'Rubbish,' he says. 'This place? If it wasn't so close, which my wife wanted – well, and if Guy wasn't a dunderhead – we wouldn't have bothered. There are many better schools.'

'Oh,' she says. 'So you think—'

'That lot,' he says, jerking his head towards the musicians' backs. Simon Flowers has not turned round; he has ignored her. Hope leaks from her like sand. 'Not much alternative to the beefy ones, is there? Just a few limp physics day boys to keep the grades up, and tedious well-behaved happy clappies. I have often noticed,' he says, 'that Jesus is bad for the skin.'

Then he bends into the car again, unaware of the mortal blow he has dealt her. Mr Viney is right; Simon Flowers is not only a day boy but he also has spots – just a few, around his mouth, which she has been trying to find beautiful. They are not.

Mr Viney is lifting out a wooden wine box. 'Plants,' he says. 'Stenning's keen on flowers. My wife supplies him. Or rather my gardener does. Hellebores and dahlias and God knows. Peonies. You're not interested in crap like that, are you?'

'No way,' she says. 'I hate gardening,' and then, because she can remember every word she has ever said to him or his wife, has analysed and prodded and spat upon it and examined it again, she blushes ferociously.

'Really,' he says coolly. 'Then we shall get on. Now tell me,' he says, locking the boot and turning to face her. He looks as though he can read her mind. 'What are you interested in? History? Historians? Like Stenning?' He grins. 'Or my kind?'

She gives a silly nervous laugh – ahaHA! 'In fact,' she says, accidentally glancing at his trousers, 'I don't, well, do history. Sorry. I just . . . don't.'

'Why on earth not?'

'I loved it. I really did. But . . . I had to drop it for A level.'

'So?'

'To do the sciences. Well, biol and chem. But I kept English. I love,' she confides, 'the Arts.'

'Science, though. Oh dear,' he says. 'Well, if chemistry is the sort of thing you like . . .'

'It's not. I mean, I had to do it. I'm meant to be reading medicine at Cambridge.' For the first time, these words do not thrill her. 'It's more . . .'

'Don't tell me. *Useful.*'

'I . . . I suppose for careers,' she says.

'Careers? What are you, forty? Surgery, I trust, at least?'

Marina winces. That is what everyone expects, what at Ealing Girls' she had always imagined. Lately she has realized how little her family understands of what she's up against. Marina Farkas, trying to hold her own among all those brilliant confident arrogant men? It's impossible. 'I . . . I'm not sure,' she says.

'But what about enriching the mind? You'll know about some crappy little atom but will you be civilized, eh? Is that how you want to live?'

'I know,' says Marina, inconveniently close to tears. 'I want to be civilized, of course I do. God, I think about it all the time, you know, books, and things. But—'

'And don't tell me it's doing good. You look like a girl who'd rather sit in a garret writing great works, not changing pensioners' nappies on an NHS gastro ward.'

She swallows. All her fantasies had involved her in a lab coat, frowning but beautiful: no secretions of any kind. 'I could do research.'

'Trust me, sweetheart. I have teams of slaves, fact-checking, photocopying: it's like the salt mines. Graduate students, mostly. Research is grim as buggery. Grimmer.'

'I thought—'

'You'd be better off dropping the lot and doing something interesting. You'll be fine, if you're reasonably clever.'

Maybe he is right. Vistas stretch out before her in which she is an aesthete, living a cultured life of Latin and sonnets and plovers: a gentleman. 'I think I *am* clever,' she says, and feels blood beating up from her heart.

'I dare say.'

He could be her mentor, her patron. People have them, the ones picked for greatness; she has read so many books about Helen Keller and Jeanne d'Arc, *Girls and Boys of History*, *Lives of the Artists*, that it seems inconceivable that she will not be chosen. But what will she be famous *for*? Time is running out. If it doesn't happen very soon, it never will.

It is too late; he is turning away from her. She says it without thinking: 'I need you to help me.'

He starts laughing. 'Forgive me. I'm not usually asked quite so directly. Certainly not by a child like you. Help how?'

'I . . . I don't know.'

'Look, I've got to get back. They'll think I've died or something. I know,' he says, giving her upper arm a little squeeze, 'we're bloody back here on Sunday, one of Nancy's tedious godchildren needs to be taken out.' Marina rolls her eyes humorously. 'Why don't you come along to that and I'll see if there's a moment to talk.'

'Oh, could I? Really? I'd love to. Just instruct me,' she says. 'Whatever you think I should do.'

18

Matins (Chapel Choir) or Pastoral Address, Divinity
Hall, Dr Malling: 'Appreciating Nature's Bounty';
lacrosse v Our Lady's Convent: U17, U18 1st and
2nd Xs (A), 1.15 p.m.; netball v the OCs: 1st and
2nd VIIs, Greer's; OC Society Banquet, Summoner's
Court, 7.30 p.m.

There has been an unpleasant scene. Apparently earlier today,
just before Marina made her Sunday morning phone call, she
received a visit at West Street. It was Mrs Dobos, unannounced,
with her repulsive grandchild Natalya, intending to spend the
morning with Marina and then to take her out for lunch.

Marina said no.

There must have been some misunderstanding. Rozsi's
ear for English is good, despite her accent, but every now and
then . . .

No. No mistake. Laura is brought to the phone; Marina
really has refused Mrs Dobos. It is grandmatricide. 'I mean,
how could I?' says Marina. 'I can't, um, not do my homework. I mean, straight, after the Address. That's when we do
it. I'd get into trouble.'

'Oh, sweetheart, I'm sure Mr Daventry would under-stand.'

'He wouldn't.' She sounds tearful. 'And, anyway, I hate Natalya. You do too. That Christmas violin concert of peasant music, last year you said you'd never ever—'

'But you can't not go out for lunch with them, sweet-heart. You, really, you should. Can you, I don't know, track her down?'

'I can't.'

'Why not?'

'I have, well, a lunch, um, plan. Already.'

'They won't care if you skip the Bakery—'

'Buttery.'

'Whatever it is. It's all, well, it makes no difference.'

'No,' says Marina. 'Anyway, it's not there.'

'Where then?'

'It's, um, a lunch for, for, biology.'

Laura hesitates. Her mouth tastes of coins. Marina is a hopeless liar – unlike, Laura thinks, her father. Unlike me. 'I see,' she says eventually, pretending not to notice Zsuzsi's disgusted frown. 'You have to go. I see. And you explained, politely? I . . . of course. Well, there it is.'

Zsuzsi sniffs. '*Rid*-iculos,' she says and turns back to her newspaper. Rozsi crashes about in the kitchen; she will be frantic. Only Ildi will catch Laura's eye; in fact, as the morning grinds slowly on, Laura begins to wonder if her aunt-in-law is trying to communicate something, with nowhere private to say it. She, too, has something increas-ingly pressing to tell the relatives. The note she received yesterday, which she claimed was from a wholly imaginary school friend, was in fact from Peter. She is meeting him near, of all places, the Elephant and Castle, this very night.

During Dr Malling's address on the dangers of personal stereos, Marina tries to locate Guy. She is feeling on edge. She overheard a story yesterday about an Upper girl who last summer, Trinity term, was having actual sex with her boyfriend – she was wearing a long skirt, sitting somehow on top of him – when the Randolph housemaster came in and started chatting to them both, with her still sitting there, her skirt spread out. Is this technically possible? Afterwards she could not stop thinking about it and, later, she had a sexual dream of impressive vividness; the content and participants are blurry now, but a certain stickiness remains. Guilt, too: Guy wasn't in it. She turns again in her chair, but a pillar is blocking most of her view of the Fivers: no sign of his unwashed sub-blond curls, his cheery expression. What if he forgets to pass on a message from his mother, with details about the lunch today? Would Pa Stenning help? She runs as quickly as she can back to West Street, looking for an embossed card saying where to meet. There is nothing for her on the hall table. Hannah North, the only Upper she likes, grins and lifts her eyebrows. Marina has no time to talk.

'Looking for something?' asks Isla Clewin pretend-sympathetically, picking chocolate off her kitten-paw slippers. Her damp hair is being plaited by Gemma Alcock, whose own is in a purpose-made towel turban. The television room smells of soapy green apples. 'Letter from home?'

'No,' says Marina. It must be on her desk. However, her bedroom contains only limply creeping Heidi, squeezing something called Primula from a tube onto her finger and licking it off. 'Has someone been up?' she asks.

'When?' Heidi loves other people's problems. 'What sort of person?'

'Never mind, just tell me. Quickly.'

'Are you late? What for? Where are you going?'

They face each other over her desk chair. Marina unclenches her fists. 'Just tell me.'

'If you say,' says Heidi, 'who you were expecting, I can say if they've been.'

'Forget it.'

She storms back downstairs. Hannah North and Isla Clewin stop talking. 'Oh poor Marina, I hope everything's OK,' says Hannah sweetly. Might the Vineys have changed their minds? I'm still not bloody having lunch with Mrs Dobos, she tells herself, making today's fifth piece of white toast and changing into her velvet jacket again, just in case. She will have to race up to Guy's room to leave him a note. Earlier, on the phone from home, Rozsi told her, 'Cambridge would not want a naughty girl,' but she can't possibly have guessed.

Can she?

Marina loves Rozsi. She does not want to upset her. May I be smited, smitten, smited, she thinks, if I ever do.

'But *dar*-link,' says Rozsi in puzzlement, '*vot* are you doing for dinner?'

Laura has told her that she is going to see the wholly

imaginary school friend, come from nowhere to meet her in central London. 'I'll eat with h— her, probably,' she says, like a murderer setting up alibis.

Eight hours to go – 'I'll be there from six,' Peter's note said, but he can wait. She looks at the sisters as they drink their coffee, as they settle down with the papers: their downy faces, their trembling hands. '*Dar*-link, you vant a *vorl*-nutvirl?' asks Ildi. 'From daughter of Lotte, she is coming yesterday from *Om*-erica, Kveens or Harlem, somevere, her husband is doctor, she is coming straight to see us from hospital. Poor Lotte, she knows no one now.'

Laura's hand hovers over the box. How can she tell what she wants? Would it be better to have one? She is unable to make even the smallest decision. She looks out of the window at the passing feet on Pembridge Road and screams help me, help me, incredibly loudly, in her head.

Marina heads for the Chapel. This is permitted, for those seeking succour. Does God really tolerate people who, despite ardent efforts, have not yet managed to believe in Him? It seems doubtful, like taking too many samples at a cheese counter, but perhaps He can tell that she is trying.

The Chapel smells of history, or decay, and is dimly lit; the chaplain considers candlelight more suitable for prayer-fulness. Yet, even here, God has so far declined to reveal His presence to Marina; unlike Heidi, who claims that Jesus came to her in the night. And where is the succour? Shouldn't His servants, curates and things, at least make an effort? Approach her in the pews and offer guidance? She cries quietly but enough to be noticed, yet none of them, not even the chaplain, seems to see. There isn't a single lost tourist to befriend. She smiles kindly at an old woman, imagining a rewarding May-to-September friendship, but too late realizes that the woman's lips are moving not in prayer but in angry mutterings, and she backs away.

By the time she has returned to find a scrappy note with instructions in Guy's handwriting, rather backward, she is already late. She reaches the Oak, Combe's smartest restaurant, at twenty past one. She sits down a little too far from the table, so that a waiter has to shuffle her chair in, like a hospital porter wheeling a big fat patient to a bed. There are medallions of venison and a pudding trolley; Mrs Viney is sitting at the opposite end of the table, talking sweetly to a family of darkly tanned blond boys who are all Combe pupils, past and present. Guy's father is in the middle of a complicated conversation about an American trip with Lucy Viney, who again has managed to ensure that she's next to him. Now they are eating their main courses, in her case roast lamb with an embarrassing amount of fat. Guy is telling one of the tanned sons about snowboarding when Mrs Viney calls across to them: 'Poor old Digby broke his – what was it, ulna? – skiing. What *is* an ulna – Guy? Marina, darling, do you know?'

'She is going to be a doctor,' says Mr Viney. The conversation stops. 'So, if she doesn't, God help us.'

'How sweet,' says Mrs Viney, looking at her.

'Dear God,' says Lucy Viney. 'Really?'

'Where is it, then?' says Guy. 'Leg?'

'Arm,' Marina mumbles.

Oddly, this improves things. Mrs Viney, who is only two people away, starts graciously drawing her into the conversation with the Blythes and asking her questions: her siblings, her UCCA plans. Her people.

'My grandmother,' Marina says, 'is a businessman.'

'*Is* she? Marvellous. What sort?'

'Er . . . lingerie. You know, underwear.'

'I do know,' agrees Mrs Viney. 'There's nothing so marvellous as really good silk underthings. Any particular kind, I wonder?'

'I . . . I don't think so,' Marina says. 'I mean, there is a bit of silk and . . . satin, but it's . . . you know, very good makes, Bella Figura and Castell, like you can buy in Selfridges and I think Fenwick's, but, well, mostly it's made of nylon and . . . cotton.'

'Of course,' murmurs Mrs Viney comfortingly. 'Cotton's the only kind anyone wears nowadays,' and Marina nods energetically. 'And of course you must carry, or stock, or whatever you call it, Aston. For their belts and gloves, at least.'

'Sorry?'

'Don't you know it? Golly, I am surprised.' Dimly, Marina recognizes the name: a grand old English firm which makes very smart hosiery and nightwear and also woollen Argyle-patterned socks, occasionally shown off by girls in West Street. 'It's Al's parents' firm, didn't you know? Oh yes, we're all shopkeepers here. Are—'

'I'm sure,' Alexander Viney says firmly, 'that the children don't need to hear about all this.'

He is smiling at them all, but Mrs Viney stops explaining. 'Bread, darling?' she says and he takes a big piece and
turns away. Embarrassment grows, like a forest fire; my God,
thinks Marina, are they getting divorced? For some reason,
possibly loyalty, she can't quite look at him; she gazes instead
at the dark panelling of the Oak, its engraved glass, its—

Mrs Dobos.

Mrs Dobos is sitting by the big palm tree in the middle
of the room. Although she is at an angle to Marina, her
granddaughter, Natalya, is not. Marina's mouth goes dry.
Mrs Dobos is eating; could she possibly have spotted Marina
without turning right round? Maybe not. However, although
they are far away, across three tables and a portable wine
stand, there is something about the set of Natalya's evil face
which suggests that she has seen her.

It is impossible to move. She thinks: I might faint.
Another girl, less sturdy, certainly would, but instead she sits
here, solid, graceless, blushing like a pig.

'I . . . excuse me,' she says.

She sits in the toilet stall, not daring to urinate in case Mrs
Viney comes by to ask her softly, urgently, if she is all right.
But Mrs Viney does not appear. When eventually Marina
emerges, it is Mr Viney who stands in the corridor, waiting.

'Hello,' he says.

Only an idiot would start crying at this, but it is as if a
wave has roared up her body and into her head; she can't
help it. He steers her past the telephone booth to the far end
of the corridor, where it is darker and more quiet. 'What is

it, silly girl?' he asks, but kindly, paternally, and her tears come faster and freer like rain, until her earlobes, even her cuffs, are soaked. He passes her a handkerchief.

'Keep it,' he says. 'Now, are you going to tell me what's wrong?'

His hands are on her shoulders. 'Look at me,' he says but, red and wet like this, how could she explain? She can just see the flat wide fingernail, the muscle at the base of his thumb, the hair on the lower section of each finger and the back of his hand. The hand moves up to lift her chin. 'I know,' he says.

She looks into his eyes: such a surprising blue, such dark lower lashes. The pores and bristles of his skin are like a secret between them.

'Enough crying,' he says. His fingers are cool, near her lips. 'I know, it's difficult. It is.'

'What is?'

'Teenage life. Life, generally. Isn't it? Not at all as it's cracked up to be.'

'Exactly! And I don't know . . . oh, all of it. Were you like that when you were a boy?'

'No.'

'No one understands . . . don't laugh.'

'I'm not. Truly. I think you're very . . . affecting.'

'I know that everyone says calm down, don't care about things like, oh, Cambridge, and love, and stuff, but I can't not. I want everything too much.'

'I do know,' he says. 'Not many would, but I do.'

'Yes,' she says. 'I can see that.' Why does she say this? It is Mrs Viney who understands, but she wants to be nice.

'I've been giving you some thought,' he says.

'Honestly?'

'And you're obviously bright, for a Combe girl.'

'Do you think? Oh thank you, that's so—'

'Don't interrupt. Which made me wonder why on earth you're doing those drab subjects. Eh? Why?'

'Sorry? Oh, you mean not history.'

'Not-history, precisely. A little life of lab technicians and glands and researching follicles: is that what you want?'

'I, I suppose not.'

'Of course not. Whereas history—'

'I honestly did want to do history,' she says. 'Don't you remember, I said?'

'No.'

'Well, I did, but my family wanted something, you know. Useful. I mean, oh God—'

'I see.'

'Well, and my best friend, Ursula, her whole family, too, think the Arts are a waste of, I mean, not practical. I only just got them to agree to English. And, well, I suppose—'

'What?'

'I, I didn't think I was clever enough.'

'Well, enough is relat—'

'No, I mean it. To do it at university, I thought you had to be brilliant. Definitely at Cambridge, anyway.'

'Now you're being absurd.'

'No, it's true. To get on in science you just have to work hard enough to learn everything, stuff it all into your head, although that's obviously . . . I'm terrified, actually. But history and English are completely different. Only boys try for history from here, and you should see them: they're so confident. That they're clever enough.'

'I thought everyone here's a thicko.'

This reveals what he really thinks of her. Her sinuses tighten, ready for more tears. 'You . . . you don't think Guy is, though,' she says. 'You didn't mean it last night, when you said—'

'Oh,' says his father vaguely. 'He isn't the sharpest knife in the block. That's why they have you lot, bright girls to up the A-level results, the league tables. Don't look so staggered. It's true.' But before she can probe this dazzling concept further, discover exactly which end of the thicko/bright continuum she inhabits, he says disappointingly, 'You're quite simply wrong. Nothing to do with brilliance – of course you can do history if you want.'

'How?'

'What are you, a what d'you call it, Lower? Isn't that what Guy—?'

'No, he's a Fiver,' she says, ashamed for them both. 'The, the year below.'

'Well, still plenty of time to change. Easy. Just tell them, and then work like a demon to catch up.'

'Really?'

'Really.'

It is strangely difficult to stop looking into his eyes. Her chest feels tender, between warmth and pain. She lifts up her face to tell him so and he kisses her, gently, almost as a father might, then leads her back into the restaurant.

19

At twelve minutes to seven, Laura arrives at the Hercules off the New Kent Road. It is, as she expected, a grotty old-man's pub, which is good; he's not even bothering to make an effort, other than to ensure they are miles from anyone who could possibly recognize him. And, knowing Peter, he has probably already left. She is feeling sick: anger, obviously. I won't even talk, she decides. I'll just listen to him writhing and squirming and justifying himself, and then I'll go.

At a table near the bar sits a man. He is tall, like Peter, broad, like Peter, but sadder, thinner faced, the paunch disappeared, and with all that dark thick hair replaced by half an inch of faded bristle. They do not touch. He does not smile. The past flows grey and fetid between them. 'Hey,' he says. 'It's you.'

'It is inconceivable,' says Rozsi, at home in Westminster Court, 'that Marina will not have seen sense. That silly school lunch; she'll have abandoned the very idea the moment she put the phone down. All this trying to be independent. Besides, she loves Mrs Dobos and little Natalya. Shall we telephone and ask how it went?'

'Wholly unnecessary,' says Ildi, listening to Jacqueline du Pré with her eyes shut.

'Of course we should ring her,' says Zsuzsi. 'All sorts of

excitements must be happening at that wonderful school, and we should be the first to know. She is absurdly old for such things, but there we go. Oh, how I envy her: that first flush of romance, the kisses under the cherry trees . . . do you remember, Rozsi, when I crept out of the ski lodge to meet Kís Istvan by the bridge and his—'

'Enough,' says Rozsi, switching from Hungarian into English.

Kisses can grow. They spread over your skin like lichen while, inside, you change too. You can't stop thinking: what did it mean?

'And another thing—'

Laura is getting into her stride. Peter has bought her red wine, then water, then a bigger glass of wine, and whenever self-pity threatens to make her cry, which would give him satisfaction, the big baby, the pretend artist, she lifts up her chin and takes a fierce gulp, and the tears recede.

She is doing so well. It is not difficult, given the brief scope of their marriage, from the banqueting suite of the Bayswater Royal Excelsior Hotel to its bitter end west of the Westway, to furnish him with details of his husbandly failings. The aftermath is an even richer source: financial indignity, gossip, guilt, uncertainty, primal infant pain. She has rehearsed and polished her hoard of resentments; she has taken them out to show him so many times in her head and, in these scenarios, his response is always either abject grovelling, or continued uselessness, both of which make her feel much better.

But the real Peter does neither. It is maddening. He just keeps saying, 'I'm sorry,' which isn't nearly enough. Unlike the one she used to know, he neither drinks so much that he starts shouting and crashing into bar stools, nor sidles off, hands in his pockets, with one of his unsanitary friends. He still dresses like an idiot in huge boots, pretentiously scruffy work clothes: an artisan hero of the Spanish Civil War. But these days they are older, shabbier. His nails are clean.

What's more, he is calm. He nods, he grimaces, as if they are friends – ha! – and he is just sympathizing about another man's crimes. He wants more details of Marina's character, his mother's health, than he deserves; it shouldn't be so easy to find out but he almost seems to want to feel as bad as possible. Fine: let him. She piles on evidence of his failings: the day when Marina stopped inventing excursions with him for her primary school weekend diary; his mother's silent maintenance of her photographic shrine. The fact that he used to laugh at his family's idiosyncrasies, and then just abandoned her to them.

And what does he have to say for himself? That he wanted to write, or send messages, but was afraid to. It was complicated. He didn't know what to do, and the longer he left it the harder it became. So bravely he did . . . nothing.

Yes, she admits when she has recovered from this outrage, they are all reasonably well, in the circumstances. Yes, they manage. No, hardly anything has happened in the last thirteen years, only the premature end of Laura's teaching career;

the temporary-permanent move to his mother's flat; the deaths of his fond aunts, poor Kitti in Detroit and Franci in Edmonton; the reign of Mrs Dobos; the transformation of their daughter – 'sorry,' Laura corrects herself, '*my* daughter' – into a public schoolgirl.

How unsettling, now that his hair is so short, to be able to see his big handsome skull, his vulnerable temples. She wants to wound them. 'There's administration when someone buggers off, you know,' she points out. 'Letters from your bank. Not bills, obviously, because you never did those. But having to tell them over and over again that I had no . . . idea where . . . What? Where are you going?'

He is gathering his matches, his pouch of 'baccy', his cigarette papers with, as usual, half a cover. 'Relax,' he says.

'How can you . . . Right, that's it.'

'Drinking-up time,' he says. 'Didn't you notice?'

'But . . .' So many nights preparing speeches; she has only just begun. Can she ask him to meet again for further shouting? 'I haven't . . . I need . . .'

'I wasn't dumping the whole thing on you,' he says. 'I mean, it's not your job to tell the others. I'm going to do it.'

'Well. Ha. You shouldn't have landed me in it then, should you? I've *lied* to them because of you.'

'OK. But.'

'But what?'

'Writing seemed better than doing nothing. A first step. You can't imagine what it's like to hate yourself for so long, you know?'

Idiot. She won't lie for him again. Anyway, shouldn't he

first answer the question of what he has been doing, and where, and how often? I have, she thinks, a right to know. Besides, there has not yet been a moment to mention Alistair Sudgeon, which is important. Peter should know that his deserted wife is in demand.

'Let's go,' he says.

An old man with perilously fastened trousers chooses this moment to begin shuffling into the Hercules. Laura and Peter have just entered the vestibule and so they have to stand aside to let him, slowly, pass. The area between front door and inner door is tiny, a box of glossy maroon anaglypta; she is trapped just behind Peter, close enough to feel his heat. Why does he never wear a jacket? His creased grey shirt, the back three inches from Laura's eye line, is unbearably irritating: his untied bootlace, his grubby trousers, yet he doesn't look as bad as he deserves. How dare his cells have renewed themselves while she suffered? And Rozsi, and Marina: whatever you say about missing them, she thinks, you chose to leave.

Her heart is beating too quickly, right through her body, as if at any moment it will reach the point when it shatters. His hormones or endorphins, that familiar Peter smell, are reactivating poisonous spores, undisturbed for all these years.

Oh God, she thinks. Don't let it all start again.

Then the cold air hits her face. No. Absolutely sodding not. It's just sweat and dirt; he probably exudes it on purpose. And it is possible that, for the first time in years, she is faintly drunk. They walk side by side past shuttered greasy spoons and flower stalls. He is properly tall, unlike her shrunken in-laws, or neat Alistair Sudgeon. He is still the only man who makes her feel normal, not a giraffe. Something floats between them: the ghost of congress past.

Do not turn. He does not deserve to be looked at. She starts to walk more quickly, furiously, to make him hurry, but he hardly lengthens his army-surplus stride, and she remembers being with him in a crowd – was it New Year's Eve? God, 1971 – surrounded by everyone they knew, and he had whispered in her ear something she has never forgotten: that the only thing they all had in common was sex. 'We've all done it,' he said. 'We all know.' And he was right; this embarrassing hilarious knowledge still amazes her: the sticky secrets of the night.

Stop it. How many New Years did he spend with you?

'So,' he says. 'They really are all all right?'

'I told you. Why are you off alcohol?' she asks.

'Packed it in.'

'No. Honestly? Just like that?'

'It was screwing me up,' he says mildly.

'I *know*. Christ, Pete, anyone would think . . . I was there. Not just you, either. I—'

'Well, I have now.'

'God. I mean good. You do . . . you look different.'

'Yoga, too. Veggie. Worked on a farm in Wales, went pure. I'm a new man.'

Liar. If it were true, which it isn't, he would have wept and prostrated himself. He would damn well have begged for forgiveness all night. And, by telling no one that he is alive and in London, she is now a co-conspirator.

She must tell them. She looks at the side of his face. She will do it as soon as she's home.

'Tube's just down here,' he says. She follows him down a short cobbled alleyway. At the other end, behind concrete bollards, flow buses and ambulances, a whirl of light. When we reach those, she tells herself, I'll tell him to leave us alone for ever. That is what I will do.

'What?' he says over his shoulder.

Without meaning to, she has sat down on one of the bollards.

'I . . .' she says. 'It's just been . . . it's been . . . When the hell *are* you going to tell them?'

Peter bends right down and looks her in the eye. Something seems to dislodge inside her, melt and fall away like an iceberg losing its grip on the land.

'Christ,' he says. 'I know I . . . it's just . . . not easy. Does she talk about me a lot?'

'Your ego! Jesus.' It is almost funny enough to stop her crying. 'Sorry, are we talking about your abandoned child or your mother?'

'Rozsi, I meant. God, I didn't—'

'No, if you must know, she hardly ever mentions you. Because then she'd cry. What did you expect? Think how humiliating it's been for her, on top of everything else. Divorce is bad enough, but . . . but . . .'

'Poor Rozsi,' he says. 'What a fucker I've been. And to you, old girl.'

Her last coverings of self-control and dignity disintegrate.

Down she sinks into the seas of self-pity, bitter waves of misery whacking her on the head. She is alone.

No, she is not. From somewhere outside the shameful swamp, a hand appears. It approaches her face, reaches out a finger to unstick the strands of hair which have stuck attractively to her lip. She closes her eyes.

Then she opens them. What the hell is Peter doing? She lifts her head to tell him so, to say leave me alone, and how dare he even presume—

He kisses her.

20

Monday, 6 February

Netball v Southampton College: U18 VIIs (A),
3.15 p.m.; Fivers art history trip begins (Florence);
careers talk by Hilary Burtenshaw, OC: 'The Civil
Service', 6 p.m.

Marina gets up on Monday morning, world-weary after a torrid
and confusing night, and finds a message from the matron:

FARKISS M. (Lwr):- ring Mother

She is almost too frightened to make the telephone work. It
is the week of her birthday and she has been orphaned. When
Zsuzsi answers, she says, 'What is it? Who rang? What's happened to Mum?'

'Don't be funny,' says Zsuzsi.

'So—'

But Zsuzsi has so many questions about Combe that
some time passes before she reaches the point. 'Your lovely
Mrs Dobos lunch yesterday,' she says, 'you do not tell us.'

'Mrs— oh, God.'

'Marinaka.'

'But I said . . .'

'Marina. I do not realize you are so stupid.'

Rozsi comes to the phone but is very quiet, which is worse. Marina's mother is not even there – 'She goes early to her surgery,' Ildi tells her when she takes over, 'she work so hard,' – so when Zsuzsi comes back the phone to ask, 'But *vy* must you go to silly science lunch?' there is no one to help her. Should she tell them about the Oak, in case Mrs Dobos saw her? But if she didn't?

'I,' she begins. 'I—'

Zsuzsi lowers her voice; it buzzes in her ear. '*Dar*-link,' she says. 'I don't believe it. Tell me, it is a boy?'

Alexander Viney's kiss is still upon her, as real, or realer, than yesterday. She can't keep it in. She suddenly says, 'Remember Guy?'

'Of course.'

'Turns out he's the son of someone famous.'

'Really? *Von*-darefool. Very-good.'

'It's that historian,' Marina persists. 'Alexander Viney. Do you know of him—'

A pause. Then '*Hihetetlen*,' says Zsuzsi in her fiercest whisper. '*Nem értem*. But this is not right.'

'No, honestly,' says Marina, but her voice wavers. 'Why? It's good. Isn't it?'

Zsuzsi will not tell her. She won't even stay on the phone. Afterwards, Marina decides that it must be one of their mad grudges, like the sisters' lifelong refusal to listen to Brahms or visit Surrey.

It is peculiar, though.

*

Laura's mind is thick with death. When she wakes up, she knows exactly what she must do.

On Monday mornings the surgery is closed, in order for Alistair to catch up on paperwork in the tiny back room where they keep the old scales and the records of the dead. This gives Laura and Marg, the senior receptionist, what Alistair calls 'ample time for administrative necessities', all of which must be completed weekly, without fail. This week Laura is even more behind than usual. Marg is not speaking to her because, as well as having forgotten to clean the toilet two days in a row, Laura accidentally ordered thirty-six non-returnable executive desk tidies in tortoiseshell plastic. If Laura asks her for help, Marg will not answer. Her immense purple-flowered back is turned away as she flirts simultaneously with the couriers and scratches her thigh with a biro. She does no work, despite her quasi-medical omniscience; why does Alistair not fire her? Fear, sexual thrall, blackmail, or his own, greater, ignorance?

So, while she listens to Marg giving pensioners made-up advice about granular ulcers, Laura types letters, quickly and inaccurately (on applying for this job she had pretended she could touch-type), to brave widows and harried fathers, giving them terrible news. She fails to obtain a replacement for the faulty ear thermometer; she telephones a specialist in parasitic diseases and is told that he is on compassionate leave, due to the death of his pregnant wife.

By eleven o'clock she has had enough. She stares in hopelessness at the last word she typed, 'Sudgerorn', and thinks: I am beyond Tippex, even retyping. She pushes back her chair. She needs to stop thinking about Peter for a start.

Maybe if she has a quick think about him first, she will succeed. She goes to the loo and is sitting, knickers round her ankles for authenticity, resting her head against the toilet paper, breathing in the perfume of old men's urine, when into her mind drifts the solution to all of this, clear as truth. She does not need a river, or an Underground train. It could be done more easily, more ambiguously and before she can do any further damage. She should do it soon.

Quickly and fairly quietly, she creeps back to reception. Marg is still on the telephone and so does not notice Laura approaching the metal cabinet where they keep bulldog clips and document ties and finger protectors and sliding open the drawer.

There is the key.

As soon as she holds it in her palm, she feels calmer. Still, she holds her breath as she walks out into the corridor and stands before the door of Alistair's office. She does not dare look back at Marg, who is saying, 'So I said, "I hope it *was* a mango."' At any moment, Alistair could come out of the back room seeking tea. Mitzi could drop in for a tidy. Act quickly, Laura instructs herself, like a commander of men. She turns the handle of his office door, closes it behind her and stands alone in the Elastoplast-scented air.

It is like being inside his skull. The light is dim; he always keeps the blinds closed, as if his framed certificates and National Trust castle plans need protection. Her ears crackle with the effort of listening. She runs a trembly finger along his windowsill, over the end of the examination couch and down the cubbyholes. Marg alone is authorized to refill them with fresh surgical tweezers; wooden tongue-depressors; KY Jelly; a fat roll of condoms; small-to-medium disposable gloves. She feels oddly sexy. She wants to steal them. What has she become?

She knows his little cupboard well; she has never been permitted to unlock it, merely to stand by while Marg does. It is, like most of their equipment, not in a state of which the General Medical Council would approve. She could jemmy it open with Alistair's Tudor paper knife. Nevertheless, the key is here, waiting to be used.

She unlocks the cupboard. Two narrow metal shelves; three rows of brown bottles. They must have been inventoried; she had not thought of that. Would Alistair, or Marg, be less likely to notice if different kinds were missing? Would just one type of pill be, well, more effective? Quicker? Or might it be better to take several, to eliminate the possibility of doubt? She dithers, picks up a bottle, puts it back in such a way that it knocks all its fellows out of line. Maybe—

There is a sound in the corridor. Quickly, clumsily, she grabs three bottles of Dalmane from the top shelf, slams the cupboard shut and, stuffing the bottles up her top, runs for the door.

21

Tuesday, 7 February

Netball v Queen's School, Taunton, 1st and 2nd
VIIs (H), 4.30 p.m.; Combe Abbey Rifle Corps
Annual Dinner: Guest of Honour Lt Col Stevens
DSO of the Welsh Guards, SCR, Basil Pilkington
Room, 8 p.m.

Marina's needs are few. All she has hoped for is an *Officer and a Gentleman*-style rescue from Chapel by Mr Viney, or a friendly letter from his wife. But although, in the daytime, her desires are all quite straightforward, the moment she is horizontal they seem to shift, sliding out of her brain like marbles, rearranging themselves in perplexing combinations.

This may be partly a question of caffeine. The kitchen is out of bounds once prep has started, so she survives on instant coffee made with water from the hot tap, liquorice, dried apricots. She cannot endure being watched so she reads until Heidi turns off her desk light, then starts to work. Or not only work. She is becoming more alert to signs. Her family is scathing about superstition; at home she tries to force it away from herself like a dog but lately, at Combe, it has been creeping back. So even as she learns the properties of liquefied gases and writes her essay on irony in *Othello*, she is constantly on the alert for indications of imminent tragedy.

This term she has discovered that, with the help of the two-volume *Shorter Oxford English Dictionary* given by her proud relatives, she can control, or at least guess, the future. Random words are full of meaning, mostly about health or illness in Westminster Court, or other clues: what Mrs Viney thinks of her; if she'll get into Cambridge; whether she will ever be invited to join the netball team, even the B team. Even the Cs.

Once started, it is difficult to stop. She makes it an additional rule to check the etymology of every four-syllable word, then three, then a few of the twos and, as almost every Greek or Anglo-Saxon word can mean something bad, if you look at it a certain way, she then has to find others to counteract it.

This evening it has gone on for even longer than usual. When at last she makes herself close the dictionary, stiff and cold and scared at two o'clock, she cannot sleep. She wants to be at home. She wants her mother. Her skin aches for her. She thinks: let me come back.

Then she catches her breath. In the rosy darkness of her room in West Street, Mr Viney has just materialized before her, saying 'a little life'. Is that what she wants? Laboratories? Hospital beds? In his voice was an implication – no, more than that – that science is somehow . . . unseemly. Base. Maybe he's right. If she thinks of the smells of formaldehyde and the ugly textbooks, even the pictures in the Cambridge medicine prospectus, do they excite her? Or does her heart skip instead at the thought of the panelled history classroom at Combe, Mr Viney giving her extra help with the Tudors? If he could really help her change—

But she can't drop biology; Pa Pond won't allow it.

Chemistry?

She thinks: you don't even like it. Pa Kendall is practically dead. Imagine doing Elizabeth I instead of nuclear fission, being part of that world, the Vineys' world, where everything is old and beautiful. What are you now? Small and ugly and cheap. And Pa Stenning—

Her heart seems to stop, then start again, more urgently. Pa Stenning, head of history: the Vineys', Mrs Viney's, friend.

Laura has been extraordinarily lucky. No one has noticed her theft. Every day she has waited for Marg's face to show more than the usual combination of bored contempt, mild digestive discomfort and irritation at the many demands of the seriously sick upon the well.

'If only,' she is fond of saying, 'they'd bloody listen to an expert,' and Laura nods and smiles and wonders what Marg's advice would be to her.

Soon, Laura reassures herself, looking abstractedly at Marg's neck hump, you could be beyond guilt, let alone punishment. Nevertheless, every time Marg stands up – she is a great fan of tea-breaks – Laura's heart judders to a halt. She sweats, and frets, and fidgets, like a normal person who wants to carry on living, unincarcerated. At least she is definitely not thinking about Peter, who has not contacted her again. Not remotely. He is absolutely the last person on her mind.

How do people find the time or privacy in which to kill themselves? This cannot go on. I, Laura thinks, cannot. Tomorrow, Thursday, she has the day off work to go with the family to Combe; it is Marina's birthday. And then it is half-term, when they will be together. Perhaps after that, time could be found.

On Wednesday evening, when she is wrapping Marina's presents, Zsuzsi, *pongyola*-ed, appears.

'Darling,' she whispers hoarsely. 'We must talk.'

Laura takes a deep breath. 'Actually,' she says. 'I was thinking . . . those clip-on earrings are lovely, but I don't know . . . I mean, they might hurt her—'

'Don't be *rid*-iculos,' says Zsuzsi. 'No, it is the boy.'

Her arms are folded. She is frowning fiercely, but there is something else in her expression: triumph? Interest?

'Boy?' says Laura. 'Which one?'

'There is another one?'

'No! I mean . . . sorry, can we start again?'

What emerges makes no sense at all. There seems to be a problem about that boy who came to Rozsi's party; Zsuzsi, it seems, no longer approves of him. 'You tell her,' says Zsuzsi. 'It is not allowed.'

Why not? She won't say. This is, for Farkases and Károlyis, not unusual, but what is Laura supposed to do?

For her birthday, Marina is hoping for: an ear-piercing token; moisturizer; slightly tight jeans; cassette tapes; a bicycle; stationery; a dark pink blouse; Argyle socks from Aston; a pet; a nickname; Simon Flowers; her old life back.

They have turned up early, to surprise Marina. On this day seventeen years ago, on a Nightingale ward at Queen Charlotte's Hospital, Laura's daughter was born.

It is shiveringly cold when the Farkases leave London, but there is spring sunshine in Combe. 'Vot a vether,' says Rozsi.

'Beautiful.'

Laura, in too many clothes and laden like a donkey, hurries around the edge of the quadrangle, or pitch, or whatever they call it, in Rozsi's wake. The skin of her forehead aches. The huge tail-coated man-boys ignore her, as do the girls, golden-maned racehorses in nasty acrylic blazers. Last night, when the others were in bed, Laura did several minutes of miscellaneous exercises on the living-room floor, stretching her blue limbs in the dark. What was the point? Look at the skin of the young, their faces. She might as well be dead.

'Marina must be in lessons,' she says. 'We're not really allowed to find . . . she might not like—'

'Don't be a silly,' Rozsi says, unbuttoning her checked raincoat swiftly, like a huntsman flaying a boar.

However, Marina is not to be found. The teachers and children they ask are not helpful: anyone would think, Laura starts telling Peter in her head, that we were just tourists inspecting the ruins, not payers of thousands of pounds in fees.

Rozsi is beginning to hobble; Ildi does not look well,

Zsuzsi, resplendent in golden faux-fox, starts saying, '*Tair-ible*,' loudly. She is quite capable of bursting into a lesson.

Oh, God, thinks Laura. But I want Marina. I need my daughter back.

'I'll tell you what,' she says. 'I'll run and find her. You . . . why don't you sit here, and I'll bring her to you?'

Leaving the others complaining in Hungarian on a bench, she hurries through a stone archway into a dead end; is squashed against the outside wall of Bute while two pensioners stagger past her with blue sacks of bedlinen; sees a herd of tiny boys marching across a courtyard dressed like army officers; and at last, hot and ruffled, arrives at West Street, where the smirking girls in the television room claim not to have seen Marina.

'But what shall I do?' she says desperately. 'I need to know—'

'I can take you to her room,' says a colourless girl with bad skin. 'We share.' And she leads Laura through an infinitely complicated series of fire doors while comparing the workers' cottage origins of West Street with her own happy home in Sussex, which features a paddock, a double garage and something called a plunge pool.

The bedroom she shares with Laura's daughter is horrible. It has three doors: one leading to the corridor, one to a fire escape and one to 'Billie and Simonetta's room. I dare say you know about *them*.' Laura nods. The girl, Heidi, will not take her hungry eyes off her face. Half of this room is Marina: the new dressing gown and Laura Ashley deckchair-striped duvet cover they bought together, the pillow she longs to sniff, a good luck wooden spoon from Ursula; postcards on the section of wall half-hidden by her desk.

Then she notices something. Photographs surround the end of her bed, of Ursula and various Kates on holiday, the beloved Miss Coverdale of Ealing Girls' accepting flowers when she emigrated to be married in Canada, before she came back. But where are the photographs of her family?

Although Marina has been too embarrassed to admit to her birthday, the arrival of her great-aunts' card – tray-sized and in a special padded envelope – two days early has helped the news to escape. It feels blasphemous to be here at all on this her sacred day, even though some of West Street are being nice; Hannah North has actually made her a card, and Jennifer de los Santos insisted that today she should be the guardian of the West Street mascot, Toffee: a pale blue boy kitten in a little T-shirt.

But this is not how birthdays should be. She is seventeen, still a virgin, still a scientist. Her family is coming later for lunch, after double biology and this term's new torture, lacrosse, which is not archaically jolly after all but involves hard muddy balls rocketing about at face height. It seems possible that she will not survive until then; I'm not even sure, she thinks, tears starting to her eyes, that I want to. And every time she walks past Tom Thomson making girls kneel she feels violently upset, which proves how badly she fits in. And her birthday letter from Ursula is mainly a paean to elegant-minded Miss Tyce: the fun they have in her early modern history lessons, the tea at her house in Ravenscourt

Park, and the story she told them there about a girl they never even knew, someone's big sister, who streaked on her last-ever day of school, through Prize Assembly. 'She must be a Sapphist,' Urs wrote.

She has just survived First Quarter, and is on her way to the tuck shop for a consoling sherbet dib-dab when she suddenly looks behind her: a woman's instinct. Just coming out of North Gate is Simon Flowers, carrying his music case, his shoulders movingly thin. He is with a girl from his year, throwing Marina into such despair that some moments pass before she notices the person behind them: it is Laura, her mother.

Zsuzsi is reapplying her lipstick when Laura returns. 'Estée Lauder,' she announces to passing schoolboys. 'Also from Hungary.'

Laura nods, distracted by her own stupidity. Marina will be furious with her for letting them turn up like this. 'Maybe we should—' she begins and then her heart seems to bound out of her chest at the sight of her daughter, her beloved, running self-consciously towards them around the grass.

She manages not to drop her bags and race to meet her, this semi-stranger in uniform. She tries to pretend that Marina looks happy to see them: so much lovelier and more worthy of life than anything else in the world.

'Now she come,' says Rozsi. 'Laura, you buy her that skirt? *Tair*-ible. *Dar*-link,' she calls piercingly across the grass. 'We wait for you.'

Marina's blush deepens, like a sponge filling up. 'I —

gosh,' she says. 'What's happened? Why are you here already? Is everyone OK?'

'Funny,' says Ildi. 'Happy Birsday!'

Marina kisses the others and then her mother. Laura bends awkwardly, trying with one hand on Marina's shoulder to convey reassurance, her huge unmanageable love, and thereby missing her chance to breathe in the scent of her daughter's hair, to which she has been looking forward since Reading.

'But why—'

Laura says, 'We . . . Rozsi . . . it just seemed a good idea to come up early. They thought. That's all right, darling, isn't it? If it isn't, we could easily go—'

'*Von*-darefool,' beams Ildi, holding up supplementary offerings one by one: a week's supply of peeled carrots, a first-aid manual, a jar of creamed spinach and a signed copy of *An Interesting Life* by Lady Renate Kennedy, of crystal hedgehog fame.

'The thing is,' Marina says to Rozsi, 'I can't—'

'*Dar*-link. We come from London with Zsuzsi and Ildi and Laura. Now we go to town and we find a nice café and eat a little something and then.'

'But,' Marina tells her, 'I'm not allowed. I'm really not. I've got lots . . . Spanish, I'm doing that now, isn't that great, and lessons and rehearsing for the play and so much prep.'

Laura's bag twists in her hands. Why doesn't she want to see us? That strange business about the Dobos lunch—

Marina has always been painfully trustworthy. Laura has

never doubted this before. Besides, in Westminster Court children respect adults; they never, never lie. She looks hard at Marina, whose face tells her that she knows Laura knows. But what *do* I know? thinks Laura. And what happens next?

Surely it isn't that she knows about me. Or is it? Jesus Christ almighty. Could she somehow have seen her mother with her father?

'I thought I was meeting you at Mario's,' Marina says. 'Should I ask Pa Daventry if I can go now?'

Laura frowns. 'I don't want you getting into trouble.'

'Don't be funny,' says Rozsi. 'I tell him.'

'No!' Marina says.

'You know,' says Laura, 'we would love to see you. But if you don't think—' It is not so easy to occupy the moral high ground when you have been rolling in a muddy morass; when, less than a week ago, you got drunk with your former – legally, current – husband and betrayed everyone you know and love by . . .

'Mum,' says Marina.

By . . .

Here it is again, that sinking sensation, as quicksand or a bog might feel, a fate she has always found particularly easy to imagine. Everything is hopeless. Nothing will be all right. Sinking lower, and I—

Then she stops. What, she wonders, is Peter doing now?

Lunch is, as usual, far from restful, but the worst moment is not when Zsuzsi confides loudly that their waiter is an idiot, or when they sing 'Happy Birthday', or Marina's lip wobbles at the sight of her book token. It is right at the end, when Laura passes her her pink-and-navy scarf and sees, written on the label: *VINEY.*

So, just before they leave to catch the London train, she pretends that she left her gloves in West Street and goes with Marina to find them. It is like walking next to a firework; Marina seethes and smoulders, but it is too dangerous to investigate. It is only when they are passing Bute that she dares to say, 'How are things?'

'You know. We said.'

'And Guy?'

'What about him?'

'Noth— nothing. He seems a lovely chap. But—'

'What?'

'Well.' She hesitates, then follows her into the television room, smiling shyly at the girls watching an Australian soap, who look away.

'Can we talk somewhere?' asks Laura.

'I have nowhere,' Marina says in a tragic monotone. 'Nowhere of my own.'

'Right. Well, maybe just through here,' Laura suggests, opening the door at the other end to where the pay phone sits, under the stairs. 'Have they fixed – oh. It doesn't look broken.'

'Why should it be?' snaps Marina. Then she stops. 'I mean, it was, the other weekend . . .'

Cold little fingers of dread and panic clutch at Laura's stomach. 'But . . . oh, sweetheart. Is something going on?'

'No, it's not. Why would it be?'

And so begins one of the worst and, thanks to their household arrangements, only rows of their life. Laura fails to find out anything, and achieves even less. Given that she has no idea why Zsuzsi disapproves of Guy, and the boy is at the same school, she can't very well forbid Marina to see him. When she tries again to discover something, anything, about this father of his, the historian, Marina's outrage intensifies. She says, 'You want to destroy your only child's chance—'

'Chance?' says Laura. 'Of what?'

But Marina will not explain and, what with the waiting Farkas party, and West Street girls bounding up and down stairs in tracksuits, and a complete lack of maternal authority, Laura cannot make her. This has become the worst possible moment to ask about Combe itself, whether she's happy here and, with Marina's dark hints about not being wanted at home, 'So you sent me away,' and some confusing references to Philistines and Science versus Art, the moment passes. Besides, it is difficult to concentrate fully when Marina's expression is so like Peter's and, really, is there much point in trying to control her child when Laura herself is being so deceitful?

'I might not even *want* to be a doctor,' Marina is saying. 'Medicine isn't everything. In fact, if you must know, it was Mr Viney who—'

'Hold on,' Laura says. 'You've been talking to him?'

'I'm allowed.'

Marina is crimson; Laura marches on. 'Alone?' Marina's silence makes it clear that she has gone too far. 'If you were, that would be fine. I mean, fine with me. Not with Rozsi, obviously.'

'But—'

'The problem is, look, can't you just avoid this man, Alis— Alexander Viney.'

'But why?'

'I, I'm not sure,' says Laura weakly. 'It's probably nothing. You know how they are.'

22

Saturday, 11 February

Cross country: 23rd Boys' Dangerhurst Run and
1st Girls' Dangerhurst Run, Petersbridge, 2.30 p.m.;
netball v Epsom College: 1st VII (Greer's), 2.30 p.m.;
Dorset/Somerset Schools' Indoor Rowing
Championships, St Steven's College, Bournemouth,
3 p.m.; Fitzgerald House Concert, Divinity Hall,
7.30 p.m.; Film Club: *Kind Hearts and Coronets*

When Ildi comes into the living room, Laura is just hanging up.

'Oh!' she says. 'I didn't realize you were heard. Here. Er.'

She could say it right now. 'That was Peter on the phone.' There is no excuse. For three whole weeks Laura has known that Ildi's nephew is alive and said nothing. If they think he is dead, she has been murdering him, over and over again.

'But, Sir,' says Marina, gripping the door handle a little harder. It is just after morning school, when Pa Daventry is usually blowing whistles on the rugby pitch. She had wanted to leave a note. 'Do I really need permission, just for one A level? It's quite diff—'

Pa Daventry is sitting in his naval captain's chair, tapping his fountain pen against a big brass inkstand: the kind of object an enraged admiral might throw. Photographs of the rugby team, group and solo portraits, muscular action shots, surround him like the angelic host. 'That's as maybe,' he says, 'but you are not an exception to the rules, Miss Farkas. Albeit that you think you are.'

He thinks girls are uneducable; he told Lucinda Prentice's brother so. Maybe he is right. She does feel stupid. Perhaps if she shows an interest in his naval models . . . 'What, what's this boat?'

'The *Ark Royal*. And it's a ship. Don't touch.'

Only a fool would cry in front of Pa Daventry, but she can't stop worrying about the row with her mother.

'A ship, of course,' she says, examining an oil painting of a naval battle. 'Yes, it does look more . . . shippy in this one.'

'That's the Battle of Trafalgar; you're pointing at the *Redoubtable*. Good God, is this some sort of joke?'

'No, no, not at all. I'm just . . . sorry.' She looks around for further talking points: that big barometer, or possibly clock? The sailing ship in its enormous bottle? It doesn't look fragile, but . . . just in time, she snatches her hand away. 'Oh great, binoculars,' she says. 'I'm always trying to spot constellations. Can I have a look? Can you just see the playing-fields from here, or—'

'Will that be all?' he says, putting them in his drawer. 'I am a busy man.'

'But,' she says. 'So if I can't ask my m— parents, I can't swap subjects?'

'Of course not. I thought I'd made that clear.'

She can hardly ring home and explain, when they have taken against Mr Viney anyway, and she is already such a disappointment. She is going to do medicine; there is no choice. If she doesn't dare admit to her recent spate of β++s and even a straight β, how will she convince them she wants to change? Being a doctor, she tells herself sternly, is what all this was for.

But.

What if she surprised them?

What if Mr Viney is right? You can't really be civilized and well rounded without knowing history; Rozsi and Ildi care about Art and Culture, they always have. Even Zsuzsi is always talking about Rome in her youth and the stupid old Musée d'Orsay.

Whereas no one at Combe is civilized, least of all the ones who do science. Last week in both biology and chemistry she made a brilliant joke about Felix Holt the Cotyledon, and not even the masters laughed. Yet Mr Viney understood her. He said she was clever; she has potential. And, anyway, it was her father – she has decided not to think of him as 'Dad', or Peter – who wanted her to be a doctor, she's sure it was, and although when she was young she did worship him a bit, and tried to imagine making him proud, lately she's been thinking less about him. Maybe it's Mr Viney whom she should be trusting.

*

This is all Peter's fault. She doesn't even want to see him again, let alone in Bloomsbury Square, like a Regency prostitute exchanging hand jobs for gin. 'We need to talk,' he'd said, but what about?

As she hurries along Bedford Place on Sunday afternoon, past the Cresta Hotel and the Selway Alhambra, her fury grows, not only at him but at men in general, the way they assume they can summon you and you will come. I need, she thinks sternly, to be concentrating on other things. My daughter's well-being, for example.

At last, a gate, closed, and a black wooden sign saying: PRIVATE GARDENS. Typical.

She gives it a shove. It opens wide.

Mrs Viney has nothing to do with it. She is the last person on Marina's mind when, heart pounding to a medically alarming extent for a person of her age, she climbs the stairs to Pa Stenning's rooms. Anyone who saw her from West Street would be astonished; you don't just approach masters like this, uninvited. But she is answering a higher call.

When Pa Stenning opens the door, without a tie and his hair very slightly rumpled, she thinks: sex. Then, at the sight of his sitting room, she forgets. There is too much to take in with mortal eye alone. It is beautiful, for one thing: mostly cream-coloured, including the carpet, so you cannot imagine Bill Salter's rugby thighs or Pa Daventry's twins anywhere near. There are real paintings and a million art books. Poor Pa Stenning, she thinks. What a waste, with no wife – only Mrs Viney, his friend, whom he is probably in love with. If she weren't already so busy, Marina could develop a crush on Pa Stenning herself.

The second she can, she will draw a plan of his rooms, to help her remember. The thought that Mrs Viney is regularly sitting on his white sofa, or the chair by the piano, while Marina mopes about in West Street, is almost too much to bear.

Pa Stenning helps her. When she reminds him that she knows the Vineys, that this is Mr Viney's idea, he looks surprised – she feels surprised – but he agrees. 'I'll probably,' he says, 'just speak to Clive.'

'Sorry, who?'

'Clive. Templar. The deputy head. Remember?'

'Sorry, yes. But—'

'If Alexander Viney recommends you, he won't refuse. I'll have a word with him, too.'

Here is the secret garden, the Vineys' world; a place she has only dreamed of. 'Will you? Would you? Oh please.'

'Yes, yes. If I remember.'

'I . . . could . . . will you tell me what he says? I'd love to know.'

'I dare say,' he says, giving her an adult look. 'And you've told your parents this, I suppose.' He is looking out of the window. She makes a sound. 'What were you going to do: medicine?'

'Yes. I mean, I still can . . .'

'Hardly. Need chemistry A level for that. Didn't you realize?'

'But—'

'It's fine. Old Kendall won't care, let's be frank.'

Marina is gaping at him. Hastily, she shuts her mouth. 'No,' she says, swallowing. 'He probably won't.'

'So. 'Tis done. Congratulations, Miss Farkas. You'll start tomorrow.'

'Hey.'

Laura says, 'This was a big mistake. No, really. If you had a bloody phone on that boat I'd have cancelled.'

He is grinning. 'You could have just not shown up.'

'Well, I—' Why is she here? To cancel out the events of last time; to punish him? To make him face the thought of telling his mother?

'Hang on a sec,' he says, bending down to examine a bit of gravel. He was always doing that, she remembers now; this must be where Marina's fossil obsession came from. Laura looks at the top of his head, thinking of the hours she spent while her daughter sifted through the sandpit in Kensington Gardens. At that moment an ill wind, gusting through the rose bushes, picks up a whiff of his pheromones and delivers it to her.

No. Definitely not. He is still a bastard. She will not fall for that. Never mind their last meeting, when she was clearly demented. This time, and for ever and ever, he is meaningless to her. Surely even chemistry dies.

'This is quartz, I reckon,' he says. 'But you never know. Mate of mine once found a diamond in Preston Park.'

'Don't be an idiot,' she says. There is the back of his neck with a new crease, the soft pale skin. Just the thought of the smell of it, like the inside of an empty wardrobe, makes her contract. She gives a small winded noise.

He looks up. No, no, she thinks: this is what she had absolutely promised herself would not happen. She is not a blancmange; she will not let it. This man has devastated every woman who knew him. Their daughter, for Christ's sake. Right, she thinks, standing up and walking off towards a leprous rose bush. That's it.

'Turn around,' he says.

She pulls at a dead-looking twig. 'No.' She seals herself against him, inhaling through her mouth, eyelids lowered. The light is thick, like primeval soup. If she could just escape—

'Come on,' he says.

It is hopeless. She can smell him over here; the air is oily with capsules of sex. He must not come over. Please, she thinks. Save me.

His footsteps crunch on the gravel. She presses her fingers into her eyes until the orange-grey shadows and softenings ache; she takes a shuddery breath, full of loathing. The pheromones are still doing their dirty work. He puts his hands on her shoulders.

'Laura,' he says.

23

I have, thinks Marina in biology, made a grievous error.

She can't stop worrying about what her grandmother will say. Tomorrow at lunchtime she is going home for half-term, by herself.

The moment Rozsi or any of the others see her they will guess the terrible thing she has done. Not only has she betrayed them and their medical dreams, but she has no idea how to do history. What madness was this? What on earth should she do?

She will have to tell Pa Stenning that she has changed her stupid mind.

No, she can't do it. Nothing, not even Rozsi's outrage, could be worse than embarrassment. Mr Viney will find out, and tell his wife, maybe his daughter. The thought of being discussed – a puzzle, a failure – makes her toes clench with shame.

And, worse still: if she can't bear the thought of that reversal, how can she possibly leave and go back to Ealing Girls'?

This is the dark seed, her greatest secret. The idea of escape has been creeping up on her as half-term approaches. She cannot imagine how she will make herself go back to Combe after spending a week at home.

They are supposed to be finishing today's dissection but

she can't identify the pig's hepatic artery, let alone its inferior vena cava. It is only the afternoon but she feels so tired, as if she has been saving lives after dark. She never sleeps before two these days; there is much too much to do even apart from the fourteen-page essays, which take longer now that the dictionary's dire predictions have to be found and counteracted, Combe's pollution neutralized. She seems to spend hours wading around in the darkest pits of the night; there are now so many rituals to observe, proliferating infinitely like a new religion only she understands.

And then in the morning, wide-eyed and jumpy, the self-disgust and worry begin again.

'Sir,' says Ivo Williams, known as Mammoth, from the back of the lab. 'There's mucus in my pocket.'

The class convulses, but Marina stands still, the scalpel frozen in her hand. She has had a realization. She *could* leave, if Combe burned down, or there was some sort of scandal. If there was no alternative. But what kind of scandal would it have to be?

Unlike last time, no one kisses anyone else. It's for the best. Laura's hands do not accidentally hold, then clutch, the small of his back, or his shoulders; he does not press her to his chest. He just puts his arms around her and they stand together, like two survivors watching the last lifeboat go down.

When it stops, she finds herself standing in a flowerbed. A tree is pressing its rough bark against her back like a big hopeless beast. 'What are we doing?'

Peter grins.

'I missed you,' he says. 'A lot. I thought you'd hate me too much to—'

'I did.'

'Marina won't want to see me, will she?'

'No,' says Laura, digging her nails into her palm.

'And I don't know what to do about Mum. I'm useless really, aren't I?'

Her brain seems to hover, like a racehorse refusing at a fence. All she can think of to say is, 'Please. We really can't.'

'What?'

'Today. Us. Ever meet like this. Peter, please. I need you to think.'

'Why? It's fine.'

'It's *not*. How can you even say that? I—'

'I don't mean . . . no, no, not more crying. Come here.'

'No! No, I will not. And I'm not upset, I'm, I'm angry, actually.'

'Fair dos.'

'And why do you *say* these stupid things?'

'Look, I hadn't— When I came back to London I didn't know what to do. If, how, to see you.'

'What? You weren't going to? That's—'

'I didn't know what to do. I just thought, being miles from Mum, well, London's big enough, I thought.'

'I didn't come looking for *you*.'

'I know. But I suddenly thought I could just, well, say hello. If I wrote to you at Mum's you'd get it. I'd heard you were there, you see.'

'How? You *knew?* What else did you know?'

'Not much. Stuff reached me.'

'Who told you? Jesus. What, spies?'

'Course not. Just guys. From London, from the past, you know. Heard the odd report. Anyway, I knew it was a bit of a . . . well. But I just missed you.'

'Then why did you leave?' He must, she thinks, be insane. Has he suffered? That's when it comes to her, one phrase: a broken man.

No, no: pity must be resisted. He doesn't deserve it. 'I suppose,' she says crossly, 'you had lots of girlfriends out there.'

'Yeah,' he says, and another piece rips off her heart and lands, steaming, on the gravel. 'But—' he shrugs. She gives an encouraging lift of her eyebrows. 'You know how it is.'

She has a sudden vivid image of shooting herself in the head. 'Well, no, not really,' she says. 'I didn't have time for all that. I was raising our child. Anyway, you got sick of *me*, remember? Remember? You called me Bore-a.'

'Bloody hell. Did I?'

'*Yes.* God. How can you—'

'What an arse,' he says.

'That doesn't even . . . oh, never mind.'

'Well, exactly. When I think about it I just want to run back there, so, well, this is the best I can do. Be here. Try to be Zen. In fact I was going to ask you. What should I, you know, do now?'

Laura sighs. 'I'm hardly . . . I don't have a clue,' she says. 'I suppose earn money? What are you living on?'

'Spot of cash I saved in Wales. I was,' he says, grinning, 'a gardener.'

'Blimey. Well, be one again. That would be a start. Or, I don't know, go back there. Whatever you wanted here, it's—'

'No, I meant with the others. I've got to see them. Rozsi and the others. I just thought of, you know, saying sorry. But it might screw them up even more.'

'Christ. Peter. I—'

'I'm serious. I'm not proud of myself. But I'm trying to change. I think. Since giving up the booze I, well. I've been doing workshops.'

'You're joking. Car maintenance? No.'

'Seriously. Oh, and therapy too. I knew you'd laugh. Male bonding. Shamanism, tantra, meditating; most of it was complete cobblers, I'll give you that, excuse for lots of stinky egos to feel sorry for themselves and sleep around.'

'Please.'

'But it helped.'

'With what? What's been so difficult? What—'

'Don't shout.'

'This is like a dream of bonkersness.'

'Yeah. Thing is, now I *hrrhrm* myself.'

'Sorry?'

'Hrrm.'

'I can't hear you. You what yourself?'

He lifts his eyes to hers. 'I own myself,' he says, and the faintest pinkness suffuses his skin.

'You . . .'

'I know what I am.'

She has a pressing desire to hit him. She is hugging herself already; now she grips herself more tightly, like a referee. 'Do you? At last. Well, I don't think that you have the faintest understanding of how—'

'Irresponsible, selfish, blah, blah. OK, yeah. It's completely true. And, thing is, I still am.'

'Are you *proud* of it? Is that what they taught you? God. You are unbearable.'

'I know,' he says. 'But being married, sorry, being a good son, a dad after what happened with, you know, my dad, all of that. I couldn't do it. And the worse I got the more I hated— well, it's obvious. So bailing just seemed the best— and then it got harder. Oh screw it. I got what I deserved. But, you know what? I still think it was better.'

A thrill of anger rolls up through her. 'What?'

'I know it's been tight. But I'd have cocked you up some other way if I'd stayed. You . . . both.'

'Hah.'

'I meant to keep away from you. I shouldn't have written.'

'Right,' says Laura. She thinks: I've had enough of this self-indulgent lunacy, this rooster of a man. She picks up her bag. Merely the thought of her pills in their dim bottles, the sugar coating, soothes her.

'There's one more thing,' he says.

Another woman. Probably dozens. You fool, she thinks, returning from the land of the dead, to nothing. 'What?'

'Maybe not.' He looks, by his standards, almost serious. 'Tell you next time.'

'There won't *be* a next time. This is the worst, stupidest, thing I've ever done. I'm not just . . . I . . .' She thinks: I could tell him how bad a mother I've been, and maybe he'd step in. How much worse could he be?

'I'm not sure.' He gives an awkward cough. 'No, let's leave it. Better not.'

'Oh, for God's sake,' she says, 'you've started.' She wants to be alone with her hoard of misery. 'Pete, enough drama. Just tell me.'

He pulls a strange downwards smile. 'Bit of cancer,' he says.

Part Two

24

The alumni of Combe have always been a disappointment. Thanks to its faintly liberal leanings, a modest endowment by a relative of fat Queen Anne, the notable ugliness of its original buildings and its belated introduction of everything from laboratories to girls, the school has never attracted pupils of quite the calibre of Rugby and Marlborough. The prospectus makes much of those Old Combeians it can claim: a spy, an unpopular post-war deputy prime minister; a racing driver expelled from the Remove; and, curiously, several authors of second-rate and now morally ambiguous children's books.

Schools, however, need history. They need money even more. Three headmasters ago, the financially suspect Captain Porteous invented most of its ancient traditions, climaxing at the end of the Hilary term, close to his own birthday in mid-March, with Founder's Day: a week-long spectacular of concerts, rugby matches, Evensong, fund-raising, feasts and, on the final day, an embarrassing pageant of Combe boys dressed as famous historical characters, processing around the Founder's Lawn to a marching band. On Founder's Day rests Combe's reputation in the school guides as 'tremendously arty'. 'Participation is a hallowed Combe tradition,' the pupils are frequently reminded; whether or not they can act or sing, they must join in. It is, the Uppers will tell you, an almighty snore. But the Lowers, Marina's year, and the younger boys still have high hopes for Founder's Day week, currently a month away. Their parents and godparents stay near by; it is a chance to show off. And there is, to an extent, misrule. Things might happen. Virginities might be lost.

Sunday, 12 February

Matins: Chapel, 9 a.m., the Rev. Jonathan Hitch, vicar of Melcombe, hymns: 285, 57, 297; half-term exeat begins

Marina is home at last. She has survived another half-term of Combe, despite being practically deranged with homesickness. Now she is ready to fall into her mother's arms, climb inside her pocket, be swallowed alive like a baby catfish. I will, she vows, never be irritated with any of my family, or the burning radiators, or nosy Hungarians asking about my periods, ever again.

How long does that last? Ten minutes? Five?

On her very first evening home, the oldies start making suggestions: a haircut; tea at Lady Renate's; coming in to Femina to be shown off. Everything makes her feel guilty; if one of them asks the slightest question about chemistry, she thinks, it will all come out.

But they do not ask.

There is nothing to do. The Ealing Girls' half-term isn't until next week. Toiling beside her mother in the tiny kitchen, every single maternal feature – her floury hair, her sugary hands, her parsleyed apron – is unbearable. She looks at the back of her head, looks at the frying pan, sighs regretfully. Her hopes for a correspondence with Guy's mother have been fruitless but, she thinks, I could write again. She might invite me. Maybe she's already decided that she will.

'Are you sure,' Marina asks, 'that no one has rung for me?'

'No, sweetheart.'

'Because I'm expecting, um, someone, a friend, to ring about homework. Just a friend. She's called Nancy.'

She knows that she sounds ridiculous, that she is stirring the pan of tomato sauce much too quickly. But her mother seems satisfied. Really, anyone would think she wanted to be deceived.

On Monday her mother and grandmother go to work. Ildi is off to the library; Zsuzsi is meeting Perlmutter Sári at the swimming pool: 'Marinaka, don't you vant to get slim?' They have left her bean-and-sausage soup, meatloaf and sliced-up oranges for lunch, money for the new Picasso exhibition and the instruction to stop biting her lip, 'because,' Rozsi says, 'it make you look like mad girl.' And, most horribly of all, tomorrow is Valentine's Day. Is it possible that someone could be at a mixed, in fact largely a boys', school, and receive nothing? She fears it is. She never has had a real one. If Guy's mother or sister asks what she had this year, she is going to lie.

Waiting for the post, in case a card has come early, is maddening. She has a furtive look at Hungary in her atlas, but instead of Pálaszlany in the Carpathian mountains, where Mr Viney said, she can only find somewhere called Polslav in Russia. What if they ask her back to Stoker and he mentions it again?

What is Mr Viney doing right now? And Mrs Viney? Are they thinking of her?

Many doctors nowadays believe that an informed patient is a happy patient. They have helpful charts and anatomical models, purchased from the pharmaceutical reps. It isn't hard to do.

But Alistair is not one of these.

How then can Laura find out what she needs to know? Marina's biology textbooks have told her nothing; they seem to edit disease from them, as if it is more important to understand pond weed than human weakness. Somewhere in this surgery may be information which could save Peter, or at least answer the questions she did not dare to ask.

So Laura leafs furtively through out-of-date drugs manuals. She pays more attention than usual to the ailments of patients waiting to be seen. At last, as the surgery is about to close, she finds a small plastic model of the human torso at the back of a filing cabinet.

'You finished the referral yet for Mrs Trent?' calls Marg. 'Only He's asking.'

'Hold on,' says Laura. 'I'm just . . . I . . .'

After all these years, how can she be so confused about

organs? These little red beans must be kidneys. She touches one with her finger; in truth, she strokes it. If only, Laura thinks, one could simply stare at them, like those metal hearts and legs in Mexican churches, and they would heal. In desperate circumstances it should be possible; but what if you did, and it used up your miracle allowance, and then your child needed healing too?

On the bus home she gives herself a talking-to. You can't spend five weeks longing for half-term, then spend the whole time in a daze, dreading the day your daughter goes back but trying to avoid her. Did you fill up on her last night, while you had the chance? Were you patient, indulgent, gripped by all those stories of tedious Pa Kendall and cruel Pa Pond? You were not.

It is only when she is walking down Moscow Road that she realizes that she has failed to send Marina a Valentine's card. She has never forgotten before, through all those years when simple mother love, and embossed kittens, were all her daughter needed; through teenagerhood, agonizing about how, with a simple signature, to convey faith in future romance without giving false hope that it was either from some spotty Ealing boy or, worse still, her father. But this year, Laura senses, her usual unsatisfactory compromise:

? *[Mum]*

will not do. It is so easy to outrage Marina; she is becoming more, not less, prickly with age. Well, Laura thinks, letting herself in through the flat door; too late. I can't start faking postmarks now.

'Hello,' she calls.

Then she sees the flowers.

There is a bunch of roses on the dining table: at least ten, big fat creamy ones. She breathes in sweetness. Marina is looking at her over the top of them, like a suspicious hare. Laura's mouth is dry; she hardly dares to ask.

'What are these?'

Marina swallows audibly, then flushes. 'I don't . . . I, do you know it's Valentine's Day tomorrow?'

Laura nods.

'But I ran after the man from the florist,' Marina says. 'And he just smirked. It was so *rude*, as if I didn't need to know. I, you didn't, um, expect something?'

'Of course not,' her mother says a little sharply.

Would it be strange to touch them? Their petals are curved like tiny breasts. When she first saw them and thought 'Peter', she was being stupid; she can see that now. What she has to do is refuse to think of him.

'Come on, sweetheart,' she says, brightly ridiculous. 'You must know who sent them to you.'

Marina's face cracks into an enormous smile. She looks down. 'So you think they're for me?' she says.

'Who else could they be for?'

'Well, no one,' says Marina.

Laura pretends to look delighted. 'Well, how fantastic,' she says. 'But it's that chap, Guy, surely?'

'Oh, do you think?' Marina looks oddly downcast.

'Well, darling, who else could it be, if they're for you? Although, well, let's see before we worry about that.'

'I don't—'

'Wait a minute. Wasn't there a card?'

'A what?'

'You mad girl,' Laura says. 'Look, that little white envelope.'

'Oh, that,' Marina says, 'I thought that was the bill,' and grabs it. Her hands seem slippery; she has to tear it with her teeth. 'Hang on,' she says. Then her face falls further. 'Oh.'

Laura looks away, to preserve her modesty, but can it truthfully be said that, in her own heart, a tiny spark of hope does not sputter back into life? Let us assume not; she is a mother. She takes the card.

Édes Zsuzsi,

she reads.

Virág virágnak.
Imré.

Behind her, Marina's bedroom door slams shut. Laura simply closes up her heart.

25

Tuesday, 14 February

Nothing from Peter. He said that he would be in touch when he had news, which could mean anything. Laura's imaginings grow more fanciful: ghostly messages during the *Six O'Clock News*, envelopes dropped by passing doves on to her type-writer keys. She decides to go back to the boat, or write a letter, hundreds of times a day. In the meantime he is always with her, breathing into her ear as she strap-hangs on the bus to Baker Street, or squashed beside her in the bath, sweat and steam on his forehead, their sternums together, mouth to mouth.

Yet every morning, when she wakes on her sofa, itching with the dust of ages, she is coshed again on the head by the fact of his disease. Or is it a fact? Could there be a mistake, or a chance of salvation? It is impossible to concentrate at work, what with the constant flow of rival medical crises: consultants' details, urology reports, investigations into cataclysmic tumours of the bowel and larynx and tongue, about which once she would have shed private tears, and now is almost immune.

Can kidney cancer really be so much better? Peter said it is. Remission: in his case is that permanent, or merely retreating? She could hardly have asked Peter himself. He says that, now that they have removed 'the bugger', he will be fine, 'if they got all of it,' which any day his surgeon will reveal.

And how in God's name does she tell Rozsi and the others about this?

For almost the first time in her life she cannot eat. She is distracted, even with Marina. Mitzi Sudgeon comes to work with nourishing beef and barley soup for her husband and Laura cannot even be bothered to hate her. Soon she will be fired, in any case, for poor administration if not for the pills, and then how will the family manage?

Marina is standing in the phone box outside Queensway Tube, trying to summon her nerve to dial. It has not been easy to escape. Rozsi has been increasingly determined to take her out with Mrs Dobos and the Dobos grandchild; Marina has only just managed to postpone it until this afternoon.

She has planned this for days. Her shaking fingers hold a bus ticket on which she has listed some conversational subjects in case Mr Viney answers, or Mrs.

However, by the time Guy answers the phone, Marina has forgotten even the most basic pleasantries. 'Christ,' he says. 'You're always so stroppy.'

'I'm *not*,' says Marina. 'It's just how my voice comes out.' But she can't talk to him any more; since the kissing she has forgotten how. She has gone socially backwards. When she hangs up, the chill wind of splitting up is whistling around the telephone booth. Please, no, she thinks. Don't chuck me. How will I ever see your parents again?

'It's Laura,' Laura is saying into the surgery telephone, with an eye on the door. 'Peter's, well, his— I really do need him to ring.'

'I do not know,' says Suze, Jensen's girlfriend. She has the kind of American accent favoured by beautiful Scandinavians with relaxed attitudes towards sex. 'I will see him later. Maybe you will try then.'

'But . . . no. No.' The word sits between them on the telephone line, a grey unit of power. 'I mean, I need to speak to him now. I've only got ten minutes; it's my lunch break and, well, I can't usually talk. Please. He said I could leave him messages with you and he'd ring. He said.'

'What can I do? I am performing my yoga now. I cannot go into the garden and ask—'

'Hang on. He's in the garden?'

'No. Of course not. He is at the end of the garden. In the boat.'

'I don't understand. His boat is at the end of your garden? You mean, parked?'

'It is moored on the water, yes. My yoga—'

'So. Sorry. You live right next to the river?'

'Yes,' she says simply. 'A very big house. My ex-husband is a record producer.'

Laura is well aware that other people, through sheer force of will, persuade strangers to obey them. Rozsi can do it. One day Marina will. 'Look,' Laura says. 'I know about Peter's, you know. His cancer. And I need to find out what his consultant said. Please. I do. So is there any way you could – ' her voice catches, but she trudges on – 'you could go and ask him now, very quickly, if he would come to the phone? Please?'

And Suze says, 'OK.'

People, thinks Marina dreamily, are like napkin rings. You either have a hallmark or you don't.

There must be moments in a person's life when they can be assessed and their value discovered. It is probably measurable scientifically: if you have reached a specified age, say seventeen, and not reached a certain height, or been able to run a mile in under eight minutes, or received any Valentine's cards at all, doesn't that make it officially, probably medically, unlikely that things will improve?

First post: nothing. Second post, on which she has always counted to bring her a life-changing letter: nothing either. The others are all out; she is threading a needle through the skin of her palm, thinking: I am epically bored. Heroically bored. Cataclysmically . . .

This is not helping. She has been for a nice walk in Kensington Gardens with Ildi, and made Zsuzsi a beautiful cup of coffee, and been forced to take stuffed cabbage to the 'poor girls' in Flat Seven, the bristly chinned Mrs and Miss Fisch, for which she was rewarded with a hard New Berry Fruit and nearly an hour of questions. Now Marina lies sadly on the sofa like Elizabeth Barrett Browning. Whenever she thinks of Combe she feels sick. But she cannot distract herself with rereading *The Snoopy Compendium* or ringing Ursula; these youthful pleasures are lost to her. Now that she is beginning to understand the scale of her social inadequacy, not a moment can be wasted. Last night she tried to read *Brideshead Revisited*, which made her weepy with disappointment at herself, and it. Maybe she should try something Mrs Viney would like; a cloth-bound *Winnie the Pooh* was on the bedside table at Stoker, softened by several generations of little Hons' hands. There is an old paperback of *The Wind in the Willows* somewhere, probably in the sideboard behind her, where Marina's mother keeps old letters and baby shoes. In a minute, Marina thinks, unless someone comes to the door to propose to me, I'll look.

But the smell of Zsuzsi's roses distracts her. The flat is full of noises usually too familiar to hear – the ticking of the plate clock, the rattling of the clothes racks in the dry cleaners' on the corner, the terminal decline of the Farkas fridge – which do not comfort her as once they might. Her family is immune to her suffering.

Meanwhile, in Stourpaine, Blandford St Mary, Simon Flowers is in the bosom of his family, having scones made for him and little posies of country flowers, practising on a grand piano in black tie. Imagining herself beside him, turning the pages, even miraculously accompanying him on another grand piano, perhaps shiny white, her throat aches with thwarted love. But why is it that, since knowing the Vineys, she feels even more confused? She is starting to realize quite how misguided, how style-less, how vulgar, she was before. If people like Mrs Viney do not see the point of people like

Simon Flowers, his inner beauty, is it possible that they are right? Maybe, she thinks dozily, musicians are less glamorous than she had realized.

Maybe she should give him up.

On Thursday, at the end of a long foul day, Ildi approaches Laura with a book in her hand. Rozsi is at a charity meeting; Zsuzsi and Marina are in their rooms. Laura thinks: Christ, she wants me to read to her. This afternoon at the surgery, Marg answered the phone: 'Sodding ring-offs,' she said, loudly enough for the waiting room to hear, but Laura has a feeling that it was Peter, trying to speak to her. The situation is impossible. He says it's his job to tell the others that he is in London but, until he does, the lie is growing; isn't she going to have to tell them soon?

And, covering everything like ash, in four days Marina is going back to school.

Ildi holds out the book. 'What is this, *dar*-link?'

'Sorry, no idea. Was there any post for me?' Other people who have done wrong either repent and stop, or are blind to their sin and carry on sinning. How do they do this, leading themselves by the hand to the next crime and the next, as if through a meadow, trampling daisies underfoot? She, Laura, knows that seeing Peter secretly is terrible, yet she has not stopped.

Ildi seems not to hear her. 'It is important,' she says, looking nervously towards Marina's bedroom door. 'I find it earlier on Marinaka's shelf, I am looking for dictionary. And I do not know what to do, so I wait for you.'

Laura flops down into a chair. Radiotherapy radiotherapy: it rings in her brain like the name of a beloved. Despite her patchy receptionist's knowledge, it is strangely difficult to remember the scanty facts he told her: what exactly they did to him before the surgery or might do now, if the news is bad. She can imagine Peter bald and sickly, can visualize his grave, but it has become muddled with the time when her mother was dying; when, if either the Aston Park hospital or Laura had been vigilant, she might have recovered. Why, Laura wonders now, am I so sleepy? I could put my head down on the table—

'*Dar*-link,' says Ildi. 'Please.'

To humour her, Laura takes the book. She reads the jacket. 'Oh, Alexander Viney. Well, that's educational, isn't it? Isn't he the one who— God, Ildi, what's wrong?'

Sweet soft-cheeked Ildi is sobbing, quietly, politely, like a Jane Austen character given tragic news. Nothing Laura can say will soothe her.

'But I don't understand. What has Marina done?' She can't remember what she is supposed to know; should she tell Ildi that Zsuzsi has already spoken to her? 'It's not . . . unsuitable, is it?' He is quite attractive, at least in his photograph, but how could a history book offend them? 'It's not, well, unsuitable, is it? Actually, I've been—'

'*Nem, nem*,' says Ildi, searching her cardigan pockets for a handkerchief. '*Nem tu dom*. It is just . . . it is just . . .'

'It's not that the wars will upset her, is it?' she asks. 'And you don't know him, do you?'

'No!' Ildi says, as if grievously insulted. 'I? No, not at all.'

'But honestly,' says Laura, turning the pages. 'I don't see the— oh, there's something written. Look, it's signed for her. See? How nice: "To Marina, my fiercest fan." He's spelled it right too. "Until," I can't read that bit. "Very best, Alexander Viney".'

'*Dis*-gusting,' says sweet Ildi.

'Look, unless someone tells me what the problem is— Is it a, a personal thing?' That must be it, she is thinking: the past. Her brain is flinching from the very idea. This is another of her weaknesses. Over the years she has heard fragments, censored for the ears of children and Englishwomen but still too awful to bear. She knows what she should have done: approached the subject rationally, researched, asked diplomatic questions, then carefully informed her child, with a mixture of fact and reassurance, of the essential facts about her family's past. She has not done this. So great is her cowardice, her selfishness, that instead she has buried the little she knows in her mind, like an inexpert grave-robber shoving the unspeakable, pale and wet and soft, back into the pit.

In Rozsi's room, the radio flicks off. 'Quickly, take it,' Ildi whispers. 'You throw in dustbin, outside. And you tell Marina—'

'I can't! I don't understand—'

'Never, ever, in this house. Nothing about him. You must tell her. But Rozsi, it will kill her. We never let her know.'

Marina is writing Guy an extremely tricky letter. Everything has to be right, guaranteed not to betray the slightest trace of what the Vineys call naffness, from the colour of her ink to the licking of the stamp. Unfortunately, the available materials disappoint. Nothing is watermarked. She considers using the Femina notepaper; she forgets to maintain her Greek ε in three separate places. Guy might not notice, but Mrs Viney will.

The content has been long in the planning but the tone is hard to gauge. Mrs Viney will be interested to hear that Marina recently visited the horticulture exhibition at the V&A; Guy will call her a ponce. Similarly, he will not be impressed with her thoughts on *Leave it to Psmith* or the lesser works of E.F. Benson. Guy won't even discuss whether his father should accept the professorship at Exeter, which Marina heard him talking about with lucky Horatia that evening at Stoker.

How, she worries, absent-mindedly tearing off half of her toenail, will she find out what Mr Viney has decided? It has clear implications for Marina's educational future; Cambridge, she has been thinking, might not be right for history. Too far; besides, Mr Viney does not approve of it: 'Too full of striving grammar-school boys.' And they hate him there, he says; someone else was given his rightful Chair. And Oxford is antiquated. This was his very word.

Marina feels tearful, almost bruised, as if someone has been shouting at her. She pretends to be very tired and spends a lot of time in bed with her eyes closed, so that she can worry in private. Every time she thinks of Combe, the contamination she is spreading, the thought of her return, the tears well up. She runs a bath and decides that, if her mother comes to check on her well-being, she'll tell her everything.

But she does not come. She does not notice that her only child is weeping quietly underwater for nearly an hour and a half.

So Marina goes for a walk in the park, as Rozsi tells her to. This is good, she thinks, tearing up a curl of plane-tree bark. I like fresh air. I like the country. Then, right by the Peter Pan statue, she sees Mrs Zagussy out with her grand-children and, to avoid questions, has to dodge behind a tree until they pass. That evening, halfway through dinner, she starts crying.

'Vot is, you miss *Top*-ofzePops?' says Zsuzsi.

'N-no.'

'Oh, *dar*-link,' says Ildi, 'I make you something different? A little soupie?' but Marina, giving her a watery smile, squeezes past her, around the dining table to where her mother sits.

'Yes, darling?'

'I—'

She stands beside her. Then she leans her body against her mother's arm and, although her mother puts up a hand to stroke Marina's cheek, she does not understand. She cannot possibly. *Sunt lacrimae rerum*, thinks Marina, as the tears roll down.

When everyone else is in bed, Laura, the Lady Macbeth of Bayswater in sprigged polycotton, knocks softly on her daughter's door.

There is a flurrying sound, a cupboard door shutting. 'Come,' Marina says, like a headmaster and Laura creeps in.

She sits on the edge of the bed, smiling fearfully at what must be, given the intensity of darkness, her daughter's hair. Whenever she kisses her sleeping child she imagines her murdered, the pillow black with blood. Marina is silent. Tentatively, like one reaching out to touch a corpse, Laura lowers her hand.

'What?' says Marina. Her skin is disconcertingly warm; her open eyes catch a glint of street light, like oil. 'You forgot you've got to buy me a different tennis racquet; no one has the old-fashioned kind any more.'

'We'll go to Lillywhites,' whispers Laura. 'I didn't mean to wake you. I just wanted to check.'

Why is she awake? Is she sad? Does she doubt her mother's devotion? Laura imagines telling her the truth about love, what it means. She could say: I can hardly bear to think about you. It hurts everywhere, my knuckles, my shoulders: a permanent ache. When you're away I sometimes have to wear sunglasses on the bus to hide my eyes. And letting you go away to Combe was the worst thing I have ever done. Almost. And, when you hear about your father, I'm going to lose you all over again.

'Mum— Mummy, I really need to go to sleep,' Marina says.

'Of course, sorry. Sorry. Have you got lots of work to do?' Are you happy? Happy enough to stay there?

'You know I have. I said.'

'Yes.' Shyly she strokes the arm beneath the blanket. Most of Laura's actions are dictated by the thought of how she'd feel if she didn't do them and Marina were to die: extra kisses, extra warnings. Peter once called it a provisional life, this constant gingerish prodding at the unthinkable. Helpfully, he left before revealing how she might change. The worst *can* happen; Marina could be hit by a bus tomorrow. Or – because Laura has always had a dread of teenage runaways, because she fears her daughter's ferocious little soul – what if Marina creeps out at night and disappears? Laura has been watching her closely for signs of unbearable homesickness but Marina confides nothing. The only clue seems to be that she wants Laura near her but this must not be pushed or relied upon. If anything, thinks Laura, I should keep my distance. That must be what she wants.

Stay, thinks Marina. Please, please stay. Her mother is wearing the torn nightdress which Rozsi wants for dusters. Marina thinks: I will save it. She moves her finger closer to the stroking hand. Closer, closer. Stay with me.

'By the way,' says Laura, clumsily, like an inept social worker. 'There's, there's a new history book on your shelf, and I wondered where it's from.' She feels Marina stiffen. 'I mean,' she says, 'don't tell me if you—'

'Hang on,' says Marina. 'Have you been poking round my stuff?'

'Of course not! No, not at all. I—'

'What then?'

'One of the others found it,' Laura says. 'I think there's s—'

'That's my private property!'

'Shh-shh. Yes, I know. But—'

'Which one? It was Zsuzsi, wasn't it?'

'I don't— Look, the thing is, where did it come from? I do need to know.'

With a great rush of falling blankets, Marina sits up. 'Why do you care?' she hisses. 'It's private, my private business. Why do I have to tell you everything?'

'But—'

'You have no idea,' Marina says, beginning to cry, 'what my life is like. You just do not know.'

'Oh darling,' Laura says, trying to pat her again, but the foot jerks away. 'It's not that. I just promised—'

'What? Have you been talking about me?'

'Just—'

'Well, don't.'

'Please, sweetheart. They seem, it, I don't know why they're so worked up, to be honest,' she says disloyally. 'And I'm sure it's nothing much. But the point is that they don't like the book, or the author, you know we did talk about it, at school. This Alexander Viney—'

'He's a brilliant man.'

'All right. Don't push my hand away. Look, did you write to him? There's nothing wrong with that. I once practically stalked Christopher Robin. I kept phoning his booksh—'

'What do you mean, they don't like him?'

'Don't be cross. And maybe it's not a good idea, you know, getting into, well, correspondences with famous authors. Men. Though I'm not sure that's it. Rozsi, I mean

256

they just don't approve . . . well. So better not. Or was it when you, when you met?'

'I can't believe,' says Marina, 'that you care about this. God. I can talk to who I like. I'm an adult! There's no reason not to, so I will. I have enough problems without this.'

Laura feels her compassion falter. Has Marina truly not noticed, she wonders, that I look even worse than usual? Is this what becomes of the only child of an only child: self-absorption, the assumption that no one has anything else to think about or do? For almost the first time in their life together, she feels herself retract. 'Darling—'

'Look, can you just stop asking me things?'

So Laura does.

26

Saturday, 18 February

'Milk?'

The situation is almost funny, in the way it might be if, for example, you were so afraid of sharks that you swam only in hotel pools, and then looked down and saw a fin.

On this, the last day of the half-term holiday, which Laura has largely spent battling the urge to ring Peter, Dr Alistair and Mitzi Sudgeon have come for coffee. The Farkases, on the way back from their end-of-holiday trip to the Dürer exhibition, met them at Bayswater Tube; they invited them back to Westminster Court. What a lovely surprise. Now Alistair is awkwardly reclining in the corner of the green sofa. Elegant Mitzi sits on one of the dining chairs. 'I do not eat cake,' she is saying, looking down at her little blue jacket, little high heels. 'So rich. I am keeping my figure after so many children, *nem?*'

Laura presses her hands hard down on her thighs to contain her murderous urges. Killing Mitzi wouldn't even be very difficult. She could just take her waist in both hands and snap her, like a wasp.

'Ah,' says Alistair Sudgeon. 'Lowra, so kind.' The great tragedy of his life is that he is not European. He pronounces her name like this in every possible circumstance. 'Just a touch of cream, if I may.'

'So.' Mitzi turns over the saucer with her sensitive painter's hands. She always makes Laura think of the Siege of Leningrad: she would sell you food, or eat you, with the same indifference. 'It is like the Herend, the *Batthyány* pattern with the gold leafs, we had, my poor family, until—' She shrugs. The eyes of the Farkases fill.

Alistair gazes upon Laura soulfully. She looks at her feet. She considers him, this person whose *membrum virile*, as he likes to call it, she has held, and thinks: if you try to have a word with me in the kitchen, I will run screaming from this flat.

'By chance you have *svee*-tenair? Sugar, not so good. And young Marina is going to be a little doctor, I hear? *Yoy de édes,*' says Mitzi. What I would give, thinks Laura, to know if she sounded this Hungarian when she arrived in London, or a little less.

'*Von*-darefool. Is a noble profession.'

'Yes, yes,' says Ildi. 'She is a good girl. *Nagyon édes*. A very sweet girl.'

Marina gives a sickly smile. She can't still be grumpy about the history book, can she? The child's infinite reserves of wounded pride are a marvel to Laura: a lesson in just how powerful, and one-sided, genetics can be.

'I'll just look for the saccharin,' says Laura, and escapes.

Marina has had a revelation. She is justifiably furious with all of them, about the book, their prying into her life. She is curious too. Their obsession with Guy and his father seems beyond the usual oldies' grudges; it seems, she thinks with a little excited mental gasp, more personal than that. Could it be something to do with the past? Lost in the mists? It could be anything: cruel jilting at an altar, land-girl love letters.

Or could it be something much more horrible than that?

I'd know, wouldn't I, she thinks nervously, if it was to do with, well, the *war*?

It is remarkable how naïve, even in middle age, Laura can be. Escaping to the kitchen was never going to work, for long. She has underestimated Alistair.

'Can I help you fill the kettle?' he says from the doorway.

'Thank you, but . . . there's really no room.'

'Nonsense,' he says. 'Allow me.'

She backs towards the Formica. He reaches across her, presses against her. He looks old and tired: a perfect match for Laura, if not his wife.

'We must meet again soon,' he whispers.

Laura shakes her head.

'We have to talk,' he hisses into her ear.

Jesus, she thinks: not the Dalmane. There is nothing between them and five pairs of Hungarian ears but vinyl tile-effect wallpaper, and a calendar of the masterpieces of Buckingham Palace.

'Please, not now. But—'

'It is important,' he says. 'Quickly, a word, if I may.'

His hands are clasped behind his back, like a television

detective with horrors to reveal. She looks around for a receptacle into which to vomit or a surface on which to sit. She thinks: I'll just confess, sack myself, and is opening her mouth to say so when he clears his throat.

'Darling.'

'What?'

'Darl—' he begins again.

'No, I heard, but, Jesus, Alistair, she's next door.'

He frowns. 'Are you avoiding me?' he says.

'How could I?'

'You know what I mean. What we had before. Stolen moments. Simple pleasures.'

'I've just,' she says stiffly, 'been trying to do my work.'

'That's all well and good. But it's been well over a fortnight since our conversation and—'

'Which conversation?'

'What? Laura, please. I must ask you not to toy with me.'

She has brought the crook of her arm up to her face and is sniffing it for comfort, like an idiot child. She tries to remember when, in the past weeks of grief and Peter, she and Alistair have talked about anything more rousing than cervical smears.

'I telephoned you,' he tells her. 'Here, in your house.'

'Flat. And it's not my—'

'Honestly, I'd have thought it would make more of an impact. I poured out my heart to you. I told you that—'

'Oh, yes, then. Sorry.'

'—that I couldn't go on in this fashion. I was minded to do something hasty. I was considering, if you recall,' he lowers his voice, but not quite enough, 'leaving Mrs Sudgeon.'

'Yes! Yes, I remember,' she whispers, patting the air between them soothingly. 'Oh, my God. Don't tell me you have.'

'Certainly not. I needed to be sure. But I had assumed that you were at least contemplating it.'

Laura takes a deep breath and sees the mess she is about to create. She has dreamed of saying: it is over. Or: Alistair, there is someone else. Stay with your wife. I never loved you. I want whatever I can have with Peter and after, or without, him I want no one at all. But how could she do it? He will fire her; he, or Mitzi. The Farkases will starve.

As she stands there, palpitating, something happens. A little spring of pragmatism rises through the London clay, past rusted pipes and oyster shells. It seeps through the foundations of Westminster Court, up into the concrete floor, the tired linoleum, until it touches her shoes, enters her skin. She realizes that if she simply says, 'I will,' she could change her fate entirely, make a home for Marina, be Peter's ex-wife and supporter only, save her in-laws from sorrow and want. This is where she can take the saner, better choice.

He is waiting. That is what she should say. Her future pours from her fingers. Choose, say the Dalmane, the diaphragms, the scalpel blades.

27

Sunday, 19 February

Half-term exeat ends; boarders must report to their
housemaster by 2 p.m.

They sit on the train back to Combe, not speaking. It is
grey outside and grey within. Laura, wiping up apple
purée from an insufficiently closed pickle jar, tries to guess
what Marina wants her to say. Neither of them has eaten
the salami sandwiches lovingly made by Rozsi, the soft
oranges and rejected chocolates, runts of the litter, pale
with neglect. I want, thinks Laura, a ginger-nut. They race
past rain-whipped climbing frames and buddleia, thickets
of leafless silver birches, the sort of scruffy sidings where
crimes are hidden. The thought of a child, a runaway lost
out there, makes her want to cry. This is England, which
the Farkases so love. She slides down a little further in her
seat and watches the rails whizz by, wishing for a merciful
accident. She thinks: I should have worn something different. She will be ashamed of me. She should be. I have
to ask about Combe now but how can I, on the way? And
after last night, when I did everything wrong. I can't exactly
ring Bridget Tyce and tell her I haven't had the courage to

say a thing, to any of them. It's too late, isn't it? I've left it all too late.

Marina is in a state of outrage. They treat me like a child, she thinks. I am old enough to have sex, and they try to confiscate my goods. Because even if *Threads of Gold: Tudor and Stuart Finance* is not strictly confiscated, the very fact that she has had to hide it in her holdall is proof of their practically criminal attitude to private property. How could any family which believes in culture not want her to read history books?

She looks out of the window, hoping to spot a rabbit but there is, as ever, nothing: no foxes, no wild boar. A badger would be good, she thinks, about to say so to her mother. Then she remembers: I am ignoring her.

If only I could have told her about chemistry. I should have said something over half-term.

And now it creeps upon her like terror: she has frittered the holidays away. The days felt wasted before they had even begun; it was impossible to wring enough intensity out of them. She had anticipated making many cups of coffee for the oldies and being kind; why has this not happened? In fact, her only attempt to be a good granddaughter involved squatting at the feet of Ildi, wishing for a convenient footstool and encouraging her to tell tales of her childhood. She had imagined taping her with her Sony Walkman but Ildi got the giggles while telling a story about Zsuzsi and a bicycle, and then the others came in.

They are in Dorset already; the train shoots through Blandford station. The sky is blue and crisp this morning, prospectus-worthy in the sunshine.

She is pretending to be asleep so that she can gaze on her mother, gorging herself on thoughts of imminent loss and crushing regret. Have her mother's hands always looked so old?

And here they are already, back in West Street. Her mother says, 'Shall I settle you in?'

'No, no need,' says Marina from inside her block of ice. Anyway, Heidi is watching, like a sperm whale trawling for plankton. The place is full of other people's families: Liza Church's mother in caramel leather, Ali's pretty twin sisters, heading like sacrificial lambkins for Combe next year. So her mother leaves; she doesn't seem to care one bit that Marina is suffering. Marina starts unpacking her clean nightie and tangerines and embarrassing tub of *körözött* and new contact lenses and bag of ten pences and, by the time she has changed her mind and run after her mother, it is too late and she has to stand there, watching her shrink to the size of her hand, then her thumb, then her fingernail, striding further and further away.

In Westminster Court time moves slowly. Ildi discovers decaffeinated coffee. Rozsi is invited by Mrs Dobos to see *La Fille mal gardée* at Sadler's Wells and ends up paying for a taxi all the way home. However, beneath the surface a current of excitement is gaining strength. Founder's Day is only twenty-one days away and the Farkases are making plans.

Laura tries to look interested. She longs to see Marina, of course she does, but Alistair is waiting for his answer. Mitzi keeps bringing him Thermoses of coffee and collecting him in the car after work. And, down in Chiswick, a little boat sways gently with the river, while Peter grows iller or stronger without her.

She tries to forget him, or drag her mind away, or focus on her own life, to which, arguably, she ought to be hanging on. It does not work. She resorts to torture.

Other people starve themselves or self-flagellate. Laura has London. At some point during most of her conversations with patients, they will refer to one of the many landmarks where, during her brief marriage to Peter Farkas, she was let down by him. She takes it out, this shame, inspects it, rolls it around in her mouth. She lets herself luxuriate in her own stupidity: a salutary lesson. You once fell in love with a prick; she tells herself this until it sounds like poetry. It sticks as a pop song might in other brains less at risk. Some people, the most depraved, come to love their punishment. She wallows in her humiliation and anger until she has remembered every detail of each shoddy betrayal, for which only a fool could forgive him.

Suze telephones her at work. Laura and Peter have agreed that he must stop ringing her himself, since the last time he tried the phone was answered by a suspicious-sounding Dr Sudgeon, looking for paper clips. 'He says you must come on Thursday,' Suze says.

'Where?' Laura asks wildly, imagining a wonderful party, or running away with him to Wales: reverse elopement.

'The boat,' says Suze witheringly. 'My boat. Where else can he go?'

*

Yet, despite extensive planning and anticipation, on Thursday Laura manages to reach Stamford Brook Tube rather late. Last time she was here it was dark; there were no trees in tentative leaf, no church bells. Now the air is, for February, warmish on her face, and on the lipstick she wears inexpertly, like a scarlet letter.

In the dusky light she can see more of Eyot's Boatyard: still creaking with danger and slimy life but marginally less frightening. Every boat she passes, whether painted like a fool's fantasy of a gypsy caravan or army grey or assembled from bits of junk, suggests other worlds: unhappy ones, obviously, but interesting.

Only *Vivian* is better suited to the dark. It, he, she, seems to be on the verge of sinking, or dissolving, kept above water level by a skirt of tangled plastic bags and willow leaves. Festooned as it is with cables and bits of rope, it looks temporary, as if built by a giant toddler with the minimum of glue. Why does this upset her? Cancer doesn't make him saintly, or more deserving. She gnaws off the last trace of lipstick and steps on the deck.

Left foot. Right. Tonight, she reminds herself, gripping the handrail, they must decide what to tell his mother; he wants her to advise him. That is why she is here. There is no reason to be excited; only a pervert would have, well, designs on a man as gravely ill as Peter.

Knock. You ridiculous woman, knock. Count, then: three, tw—

But what will she find? It is almost a fortnight since

Bloomsbury Square; he might be thinner, paler. Get on with it: five, four, three . . .

When people are dying, do they clutch onto the past, or race into the future? What will Peter want?

She closes her eyes. She breathes jerkily through her nostrils: mud, weeds, rot, sewage, slime. Ten nine eight five four—

She knocks on the door.

28

'And every-day we have a little lunch with you. You tell us where.'

'Actually,' says Marina, once again at the West Street pay phone, 'I think, well, we do have lessons during Founder's Day when we're not actually performing. Rozsi, it is still term time. We can't be with our family all day.'

Although the elders will never admit it, Founder's Day week is badly timed. There are always rumours that, in line with other members of the Headmasters' Conference, it will be moved to the end of the summer term, so that Combe mothers can be decorative in sun hats and heels, not shivering in their navy quilted gilets. However, the sixteenth of March is officially, albeit fictionally, the Founder's birthday and, in the words of Captain Porteous, 'Without Tradition, What is Man?'

So this year the pageantry climaxes on the Thursday, the day that the Hilary term ends. Rozsi has decreed that the Farkas/Károlyi party will go for two nights, the most they can afford given the mid-week closure of Femina; they will return to London on Thursday morning and then Laura will bring Marina home later that day, after Prize-Giving. This schedule means missing Monday night's Freshers' performance of *The Mikado*; on the bright side, they will be in time for *The Merchant of Venice*.

'Don't be funny,' says Rozsi in Marina's ear. 'Of course you eat with us.'

'The thing is—'

'I do not hear you.'

'The thing is, are, are you sure about coming? I don't know how, well, interesting it will be.'

'Why?'

Marina sighs. It's not just the Vineys, although she hasn't yet worked out whether to bring them all together and prove to her family how marvellous they are, or to keep them apart, for slightly baser reasons. She also has a duty to protect her loved ones. Combe is a plague pit. With every dark sad bitter-coffee night she understands more about unseen connections, the ways in which every single object, person, even thought, is either a contaminant or a protector, with her family in the middle, perpetually at risk. 'You like London things,' she says desperately. Recently in history she heard about ceintures, and the idea has stuck. If monks have their penances, their hair shirts and prickling belts to stave off vice, why shouldn't she? Having a constant reminder of her own badness seemed at first intriguing, then advisable, and it's hardly as if she's using thorns, just a Sixties belt of Zsuzsi's which any normal seventeen-year-old ought to be able to fit into. She pokes a finger inside for a moment's relief. 'Galleries,' she says, 'and plays and, honestly, I don't think you'll enjoy it. I really, I mean, I won't be offended, you see, if you stay at ho—'

'What a nonsense,' Rozsi says. 'It is lovely, *What-not of Venice*. We see you.'

'Only I'm an orange seller. I don't actually speak.'

'Never-mind. You sit with us and run on for your little talking. Anyway, we pay the hotel already, so it is done.'

'Oh. Were they . . . nice?'

'Don't be funny. Not at all. Stupid people. It does not matter. We are there. We cheer for you. Now, I bring Zsuzsi. I love you, *dar*-link.'

'I, I love you too.'

You little traitor. What happens when they find out you have given up chemistry, that you will never be a doctor, that you have lied to them? The most recent parcel from home contained not only toilet soap and a Boots guide to Symptoms but also a proper doctors' white coat, with *Marina Farkas* embroidered on the pocket. She can't possibly wear it; she bundled it under her bed, with an ossified *beigli* and other items of shame and now when she tries to sleep she can feel it through the sheets.

The panicky feeling builds. It's not as if she's even good at history. In the term and a half she has missed, a great deal has happened, as Pa Jenner, who does Europe, likes to point out: the Age of Reason, for example. Victorian England is with Mrs Tree, the headmaster's wife, who is not officially qualified so mainly reads aloud from textbooks. It is not at all like being taught by Alexander Viney. Why had she not anticipated this?

'*Von*-darefool you act,' says Zsuzsi loudly in her ear. 'Is like me at *conservatoire*, I am Boris Godunov. I tell Mrs Dobos already, she wants photograph. But *vot*-apity we don't stay nearer.' Zsuzsi resents the fact that they, or at least she, has not been invited to stay within the very walls of Combe itself, in a gracious guest suite, if not in the private apartments of Dr Tree. 'Maybe, who knows, we will be lucky.' She gives a sniff. 'Tell me, *dar*-link. You do well? How are the boys?'

'You mean—'

'Not that *tair*-ible boy, Gab, Gib, Gob—'

'Guy?'

'Of course, but other ones. You meet them?'

'Wel—'

'Very good. Ildi thinks you should not see so many, but she is old-fashioned. I say, yes. *Von*-darefool.' Zsuzsi sounds as if she means it. 'So, we see them then? We will learn all about them. And now we meet the families too.'

First, there is the smell. Laura had expected a certain level of manly chaos, socks on the floor and a shortage of clean mugs, but not this insinuating mildewed reek, as if every constituent part of *Vivian*'s godforsaken interior, rotting wood and peeling cork tiles, leaking Calor gas, lame ugly cats, has been repeatedly soaked in river water and never allowed to dry. Silverfish are in the corners. If you look through the floorboards, which is easy to do, you see them moving.

'Oh,' says Peter, 'no, that's probably earrings, and keys and such.' There are still traces of Rozsi under his London accent; this feels more comforting than it should. 'Nowhere to keep anything, you know, storage. You lose things in the bilges all the sodding time.'

There is a wounded duck in a washing-up bowl by the

sink, presumably drying, and laundry strung before dim portholes, to catch the sun. There is no sun. It starts to rain and the smell intensifies: yes, definitely sewage. It is very cold. And still they talk.

She tries to edge around the subject of the surviving Farkas-Károlyis, whom he has left behind. He starts crying: not undignified sobbing, or self-regarding wails. He simply closes his eyes, leans his head against the back of his chair and allows small tears to roll down his cheeks and fall discreetly on his ANC sweatshirt. He says, 'I just don't know how I can. I feel like a bloody murderer.'

'Well, so bloody do I. But you have to.'

'How? Tell me how. And Marina, God, I'm terrified of seeing her. Wouldn't it be worse for them to find out I was alive? All that time?'

'What, worse than you dead? Worse than that?'

He passes the test. She can see him increasingly pained at the thought of Marina; she thinks: I'll give him that. She says, 'I suppose with you being ill . . .'

'Yes.'

'Yes.'

She needs to know more about cancer. Is this boat even suitable for someone in his condition: the discomfort, the ancient mould? The cold intensifies. The lights keep flickering; it seems that he, or the fabled Jensen, has connected it up to Suze's electricity supply, illegally, lethally. 'What, running through the flowerbeds?' she says, peering out of a porthole full of spiders and flies. 'Not seriously. What about rain?'

'It's fine,' he says. 'Gaffer tape.'

She is watching something in a carrier bag floating down-river.

'But—'

'Bit soon to be sorting me out, don't you think?' he says, smiling, which could mean anything.

'Who is bloody Jensen anyway?' she says. 'Do you actually know how to sail this thing?' He looks as if he's about to cry again. All the questions she needs to ask him, such as 'Is this a good or a bad kind of cancer?', or 'How long might you have?', or 'Is it genetic?', or 'Will you let me see where they cut you?', are unbroachable, and he keeps trying to change the subject, as if he fears her reaction, or she is not important enough to be told. It all happened last summer, even the surgery, in a place and among friends she will never know. He is here not to escape Pontypridd General but because he 'wanted' to 'come back'.

'But why? I mean, why now? Not before?' And, when he is silent, she tells him, 'You could have, you know,' and he looks at her. She tells him about her job and, almost, about Alistair, and the answer she must give him. She wants to ask Peter what to do. If, thanks to her enormous reserves of patience and forgiveness, or victimhood, she is now going to be friends with her abandoning husband, as appears likely, she should be able to discuss it. She has technically only twenty-four hours in which to make up her mind.

Yet she can't say the words. 'What . . . will there be radio-therapy?' she asks instead. Apparently not, which seems odd, probably wrong. Could he be dying and no one have noticed?

'Don't be mad,' he says, rolling another cigarette on the sticky coffee table. 'I'm really fine.'

'I'm not mad,' she says. 'Just so worried.'

'Laur—'

'I know. I shouldn't be. You don't deserve it.'

'Too right.'

Yet every time their conversation ought to stop, when he could take offence or she should storm out in disgust, they keep on talking. I just, she tells herself, need to find out certain things. At last, when it is completely dark and, in Westminster Court along the river, the worrying will have started because she has no life of her own and never goes out, she dares to touch on his future.

'I've still got one,' he says. 'It's just sort of stopped. I mean, I'm not getting iller. The doc says I'm likely to—'

'Recover?'

He looks away. 'Not . . . well. You know that's not how they talk. Live.'

'Oh. Well. Good.' Although her throat tightens, she is not going to cry for him. Get a grip, she snaps at herself and, oddly, it works. 'So—'

'For, probably, a year.'

'Oh! Oh God.'

'No, not, you know. It's then, like, two. Then five. You know, probability.'

But it's like being hooded, put into a diving helmet:

nothing to see or hear or even smell, only the roar of her breathing. He might still die. He might still live.

'I don't know what to do,' she says. Her voice is too plaintive; it would irritate me, she thinks, if I were him. 'What do you want me to do?'

She knows what she would say in this position: 'Be with me.' But he does not. 'I don't bloody know,' he says.

'Oh.'

He doesn't respond. Dust and flies and death are settling over everything; the tide has turned. 'Well, so what do— maybe I should . . . let you get on with it.'

'You mean, leave?'

'Yes.'

He is frowning, isn't he? In the darkness it is difficult to be sure, but he doesn't say, 'Please, don't,' or 'I need you.' He says nothing at all.

'Pete?' she says.

'I don't want to be . . .' he begins and she thinks she hears him swallow.

'Do you want me to go?'

'If you think you should,' he says, 'then yes. In fact, definitely, yes. Please. Go.'

29

Wednesday, 1 March

Fresher trip to Rome; Fivers community workshop:
Combe Pensioners' Friendship Circle; cross country:
Dorset and Somerset Schools' League at Dorchester
College, Senior and Junior Boys, Open Girls,
2.30 p.m.; Fencing: Public Schools' Championships,
Crystal Palace (all day)

The second half of Hilary term is even worse than the first
and more confusing. Perhaps it has been blighted by bad
omens but, already, Marina is cast down by homesickness
and worry: no time to sleep, and the gnawing of her conscience. And now she seems to be homesick for Guy's house
too. Her mind keeps sneaking back there as to a love object,
towards the sunlight in the upstairs hall, the peace, and Mrs
Viney, the repository of all worthwhile knowledge, if only
Marina had another chance to ask her.

Rozsi would find a way. She has nerve. While this is not
an option for her base and cowardly grandchild, in the dark
reaches of the night Marina has started to wonder if she too,
like so many heroines, will be called upon to prove herself:
to show what she is made of. She will screw her courage to

the sticking place, although it feels more like trying to nail jelly to a rock. When it happens, whether she is saving a small child from injury or performing an act of political martyrdom, she will think of her forebears, who walked across borders and forged visas and stood up to famous men. She will be strong.

There might be a chance during Founder's Day week. Yes, she thinks, trying to whip herself into confidence, that's the answer. Less than a fortnight to go; I'll make it happen and, before I know it, I'll be staying at Stoker in the Easter holidays. I can find out then what Rozsi's objection is. Were the Tudors particularly xenophobic?

But what if it really is something to do with the war?

She has now remembered several occasions when, cello practice done, vocabulary memorized, Rozsi allowed, even encouraged, her to watch history programmes. This leads her to one rather exciting conclusion: it must be personal. The only problem is timing. Mr Viney is older than his wife but, say he is as old as fifty, he can't ever have fallen in love with Rozsi. Can he? Or – he is an attractive man – was it she who fell for him?

At night, when she is too nervy to sleep, worn out by hours of dictionary flicking and a physically demanding, albeit imaginary, sex life, she tries to imagine alternative scenarios. Are there any love-free circumstances in which Rozsi and Mr Viney could conceivably have met? Her mind aches with trying to force it. Might he have pushed ahead of her in the queue at Selfridges' Food Hall? Or slighted Mrs Dobos?

Then on Monday evening, very late, as she is writing an

essay on the majesty of Peter the Great, Charlie Mingus turned so low that all she can hear is occasional plucking, her mind, as it wanders along snowy mountain passes, suddenly stumbles upon the truth.

Rozsi, according to cousin Fülöp, used to be a Communist. He also claimed she was a student, somewhere like Vienna or Budapest; this seems less likely, but Rozsi was always clever, a fact of which they are all very proud. At least with the Communism there is evidence. Marina has heard a story about her great-grandfather, who owned a factory – no, that can't be right. He might have been the foreman. In any case, the workers, or possibly serfs, went on strike, much like the miners. Rozsi was a daring young woman, probably about Marina's age, so although she was only the second or third oldest she was sent by their father to talk to the rebels. She was meant to explain to them why they should behave. But when she came back, she told her father, 'They are right.'

This proves it. Doesn't it? So let's say that in, roughly, 1938, Rozsi was the cleverest and most charismatic of the Károlyi girls. War had not yet come to their Transylvanian village of cow bells and merry milkmaids, and neither had any English people. Which is fine, because she was in Budapest, being the kind of student Marina intends to be. And a fine-boned English officer (Mr Viney, hence his mastery of the area) on a Grand Tour stopped there to feed his horses and . . . here she is hazy, but Love must have been involved. She has the setting but not the story: a station platform. Lipstick. Snow. The romance of war but not the sorrow, because that is something she is too scared to think about.

Yes, Rozsi fell in love with him but was jilted because of her unusual intelligence and then . . . then . . . consoled herself with Zoltan. Poor Zoltan. All Marina knows about her grandfather's side of the family is that his father was a manufacturer of saddlery. Presumably, therefore, Zoltan in those days was quite rich, and glamorous, and he chivalrously rescued her.

This is all perfectly possible, provided that the ages, of which she is uncertain, match up. *Threads of Gold* is secreted under her mattress. When Heidi goes for her nightly hair-wash, she pulls it out. 'Alexander Viney,' it informs her, 'born in 1944, is a scholar of Westminster and Oxford.'

Hang on.

So if it wasn't him, who was it? Did he have brothers? Was it his father, or something to do with the First World War? That is the problem: finding out. She needs a conven-ient attic filled with caches of letters, or an elderly nursemaid with a tale to tell. Ildi might explain, but she doesn't want to make her cry. Rozsi? Too scary. Zsuzsi?

I wish *you* could tell me, she thinks at her dear grand-father, but his face is indistinct. I am, she tells herself, caught between warring families. But I will be true to the Montagues. Or is it the Capulets? Anyway, one of the two.

Laura's secret pills are calling her name. When she is at the flat the sideboard seems to throb; every time one of the aunts-in-law needs a napkin, she has to leap up and fetch it herself. Their presence makes her queasy. Might it help if she just took one?

Peter would know. Well, yes, Peter; back she goes, like an itch, a tic, to Thursday. One minute she was all ready to pledge herself to a life of nursing; the next she was cast out. What did she do? It has just ended, snap, leaving her standing like an idiot on half of a bridge, while the bit she was meant to travel across lies foaming below in the water.

Fool, she thinks. You should have known.

She is updating addresses at the surgery: who has died a lonely bedsitter death, who has wisely left for another practice. Every word is a second wasted, when Peter may now have so few. She thinks: Wilfred Bunting, I resent you. Were you the one with the wart? What's happened to my memory? Hello, Margret O'Reilly, the baldest woman I ever knew. Oh, Irene Saxle (Dcd) of Queensford Gardens W8, poor Mrs Saxle, I love Peter Farkas, again.

My God.

She stares down at the point of her pencil: the soft wood, the metallic gleam. Is that what this is? She knew already. Love was always there.

Why, Marina wants to know, is the Lower School so excited about Founder's Day? Every time Dr Tree announces a lighting run-through, or tells them to warn their parents that *Mikado* tickets are selling quickly, excitement ripples through Chapel like a wave, starting with the babies at the altar, cresting among the Fivers and subsiding towards the back. Is it because half of them don't see their parents from one month to the next?

This cannot be said for the Farkases. They have been

planning their trip to Combe since the Michaelmas term, if not before. Last night Marina had to have a discussion about whether Zsuzsi should bring her manicure set. In under a fortnight they will be booking into their rooms in Braegarrold, a bed and breakfast near the station recommended by Mrs Long, the matron, when everywhere else proved beyond their means. A full programme of fun awaits them: in addition to the ceramics exhibitions and percussion medleys and strolling mummers and an Uppers' debate ('This House Believes that Success Is Its Own Reward') and display by the Combined Cadet Force, they have bought tickets (£4 each, non-refundable) for *The Merchant of Venice*, the Founder's Society's chamber performance of *Cyrano de Bergerac*, and the orchestral spectacular, 'All About Jazz', featuring Simon Flowers on the classical guitar. There is some confusion over whether parents must buy pupils' tickets; to avoid difficulty, Rozsi has bought extra. Founder's Day, Marina is afraid, will bring the Farkases finally to their knees.

In fact, the more she thinks about it, the more desperate she begins to feel. There are so many potential disasters: her relatives are too free-range and stubborn to be controllable in the Notting Hill Gate supermarket, let alone in the grounds of Combe. They'll walk on the Founder's Lawn to rip off a branch of *mog*-nolia for the bed and breakfast, or insist on sitting with her in the Buttery and cutting up her chicken leg. Anyway, Combe is dangerous for them. What if they breathe air emitted by Simonetta? Or meet the Vineys? Marina is leading them to their death. Every night, full of caffeinated yearning, she lies in bed, her essays written, another day of Combe survived, and brambles of panic seem to creep into her mind. Could she forge a letter announcing that Founder's Day week is cancelled? She has to do something. She has to act.

Laura is going to have to start making decisions. Founder's Day is coming nearer, like a train, and she is tied unprettily to the tracks. Alistair awaits. Peter is dying; or, perhaps, recovering, and falling for somebody else. And Laura, meanwhile, a woman in love, will be spending three days escorting pensioners around an extremely minor Dorset market town.

Today in her lunch break she found herself in Boots, where she walked past unfamiliar beautifying inventions, podiatry aids, baby bottles and, at last, still trying to look like a respectable woman lost on her way to shampoo, the family planning aisle. It was appalling. She was a slut. She returned to the surgery, unsandwiched, as her punishment.

At least in eight nights she will see Marina. Marina is all right. Isn't she?

Eight nights. Seven. Then she snaps.

'It's normal,' says Guy.

It is Tuesday evening, in his bedroom. He has assured her that, if his bin is outside in the corridor, no one, not even Pa Stenning, will come in.

'But it's not allowed,' she says. 'Everyone says so. Not shutting the door when, when there's, you know, a girl in here. That's the rule.'

'Not for me,' he says, 'babe. So, what about it? Monday

night? Tues? I can guarantee at least an hour. Maybe two. We might need longer. We might go for it all night.'

'Please. That's mad.'

'Other people do.'

'But I thought—'

'It's not the same in Founder's Day week, dopey. Teachers are drunk, mostly, and parents.'

'Not mine.'

'It's not an insult, you wally. Everyone's a bit drunk.'

'I,' says Marina with dignity, 'have never seen any of my family drunk in my *life*.'

'Fine,' Guy says. 'But everyone else will be. So we can just, like, sneak off and I'll burst your cherry.'

She is now subsisting on four or five hours of sleep, shored up with Pro-Plus, which at Ealing Girls' was considered almost heroin, and pounds of apples and handfuls of raisins and dry muesli every night. She hates herself. Like the crocodile in Peter Pan, something is ticking inside her.

'Guy,' she says, only slightly wincing as he slides his hand into her knickers, 'are your parents coming to Founder's Day?'

'Sorry,' says Laura. She is hunched over the phone in Zsuzsi's bedroom. 'I, I don't know if he, if I—'

'This is Laura?' asks Suze.

'I— yes. How is he? I mean, Peter?'

'I know Peter,' Suze says, needlessly. 'He is very well.'

'Oh good! I, you see, we haven't, I've been wondering. But, sorry, you mean, well or well-well?'

'Well.'

'But . . . OK. OK. So—'

'You can speak to him now. He is here, beside me.'

'What? Right there? But—'

'Laura?'

'Yes! It's me. Where, how—'

'I thought you'd given up on me,' he says.

'Me?'

'Tell you what,' he says. 'Come over.'

'But—'

'To the boat. Tomorrow. Please. Just come.'

30

Wednesday, 8 March

During Chapel, despite the discomfort of her contact lenses, Marina makes two important decisions. First, if during Founder's Day she manages to resist Guy's accelerating sexual hopes, in the holidays she will let him do what he wants. She should be grateful to have found somebody willing to remove her maidenhood. The previous generation, she once read in a very sexy article in *Harpers & Queen*, lost their virginity much earlier, at hunt balls.

Second, she will do some investigating. Old ladies, at least her old ladies, are always wound up about something and, if some misunderstanding is keeping Marina from seeing the Vineys, it must be stopped. All she needs is evidence and she will solve everything; she'll even be able to tell her mother that she is going out with Guy. The likeliest, if least romantic, explanation is that Rozsi has mixed up Mr Viney with someone else. It has happened before. Or she might be being overprotective. Or, if there *was* a wartime romance, shouldn't they be over it now? Maybe Guy's grandfather is widowed; he might meet Ildi, and find love.

The only possible problem is technical. No one tells her anything about her family; it's ridiculous how little she knows. She can't even remember the name of Rozsi's town, so she can't look it up and, if you ask the littlest thing about where they came from, their father's factory or whatever it was, bee farm, let alone mention their parents or the other sisters, they start crying instantly, like turning on a tap. Nevertheless, she has had a brilliant idea. If her mother brings whatever she can find to Founder's Day, diaries, say, or family documents, she could show them to Mr Viney. It will be worth the embarrassment; he'll know what to look for, and then the two warring households will be united. Why didn't she think of it before?

From now on she will be happy. She'll stop all these fantasies about running away, being welcomed back to Ealing Girls'. Rozsi would never let her leave here, not in a million years and, if she did, everyone would know she was going, and the embarrassment, the mockery, would be unbearable. She must tell no one she has even thought of coming home; it would worry her mother. It might be the death of her. Marina sits a little straighter, partly to make her ceinture more bearable. Suffering is good, but she is still weak.

Obviously she has to tell her family that she is now an historian. That Cambridge is overrated: she has chosen a different future. They love famous people; when they meet Mr Viney, her mentor, how could they not be thrilled? And also – she resolves this suddenly, in the middle of 'O, Jesus I have promised' – she will cure herself completely of Simon Flowers. Everything Mr Viney said was right; day boys are different. She grips her seat to stop herself looking for him in the row behind. Now that she has given up medicine, maybe even Cambridge, what does she have in common with him? Nothing at all.

Her timing is unfortunate. Whichever God she is currently most frightened of is not looking kindly upon her; perhaps she has backed the wrong one. For, when she trails out of the Chapel porch, feeling as if she is leaving her heart behind her on the Lowers' pew, she feels a tap on her shoulder.

Vivian's door is open, as Suze had claimed. How much easier, and less terrifying, it would have been to have conducted the whole visit in theory, on the telephone. Life, equally: one could just spend a weekend planning it in childhood, all the highlights – the husband, the house and dog and garden, the children returning lovingly from the grammar school down the road – and skip the reality. Do all women, wonders Laura, spend their lives reconciling themselves, or is it that her life has been more unsuccessful than most?

A woman is sitting on the sofa. She is Nordic, tanned, sexually confident: the sort of woman all men like. It can only be Suze.

'Oh,' says Laura. 'Ah.'

A cigarette burns idly between Suze's fingers. Laura looks down at her own sausagey hands. She is shaking.

'Sit, please,' says the woman. Laura sits.

Time passes. The reek of drains and decaying wood is worse than she had remembered, joss sticks and curry, with a rich ammonia undertow. The duck sanctuary has gone; in its place sits a brindled cat on a dishcloth, eating something.

Suze leafs through a magazine, not, as far as Laura can tell, something comfortable like *Good Housekeeping* but German fashion. As if the pack ice is melting, the boat creaks and gushes, pops, drips. Laura waits with a smile of idiocy, pretending she is at ease.

'You're Marina Farkas, aren't you?'

Close up, Simon Flowers is beautiful. Think of chess grandmasters or concert pianists: imagine how they ought to look, not how they are. That is Simon Flowers, here, now, before her in the cool stone porch, smiling.

It is her moment to dazzle. Her mouth is dry; she exhales and then again, a little more raggedy-sounding, like a sheep. There is a faint smell of incense, or resin; is his skin alabaster? Or simply porcelain? He is going to ask her to marry him. She wants to be out on the far side of this moment already, analysing. Being here, inside it, is too much.

Face to face, her determination to forget him falters. Come on, she thinks. Be strong.

She has to say something. People are waiting. 'Why?' she says. Someone behind her sniggers. 'I mean,' she begins. 'What did you—'

He is thin, with a tiny chip on one glasses-lens. Her heart is racing like a rabbit's. If she could faint, or tragically die, she could avoid the disappointment which must lie ahead. A different area of her brain is reminding her that she is nobody and a fool to live in hope. And another part says: you and he are the only people alike in the school. Do something now; show him. This is your chance for joy.

But instinct has not been a friend to Marina. She followed it and left her mother; went to Combe; resisted Guy's physical urges; tried to be herself. And look how she has ended up: worse than before. Clearly some people, such as the Vineys, understand life better. She is lucky to have their example; she will follow it, like a religion. And she knows what Guy's parents think about boys like Simon Flowers.

He takes a step back. He bites his lower lip; she has devoted hours to considering its cushioniness, its pressing need for lip balm but now she looks away. He starts explaining something complicated involving Tuesday nights and a club; she can't really listen. She is concentrating on breathing through her nostrils, as though lifting a great weight. No, she tells herself, though her body is screaming yes, please, yes, like iron filings leaping upon a magnet. She inhales his manly aroma and, gritting her teeth, shakes her head.

'I—' She clears her throat. Her tongue tastes like wool; she licks her lip before she remembers that this is a powerful sexual signal. 'I don't really have, you know, much time left, for, for extracurricular . . . stuff.'

'Sure?' he says. 'Monty thought you'd like it.'

'Sorry, but—'

'And he thought you'd be good at general knowledge. But don't worry,' he says. 'It's fine.'

'Hang on. You mean, oh, my God. You, the, you mean the team? You, you're in it?'

He smiles at her kindly. 'Actually,' he admits, 'I'm the captain.'

'Wow.' In the deepest part of Combe, down a hidden

corridor reached by a secret stair, there has been a place for people like her all this time. Somewhere she could know the meaning of synecdoche or Cole Porter's middle name without being mocked. She could make friends there. She could go mad with happiness.

'You, you mean next term?' she says. 'Not now, obviously—'

'Seriously, you should come. Just for a trial.'

So this is it, here, now: one of those life-changing moments for which she has lived in constant readiness, knowing that the interim was just an unpleasant practice session, a series of trials and warm-ups designed to hone and strengthen. The future is unrolling like a carpet. Then into her mind comes an image: she and Simon Flowers, holding hands in the Vineys' entrance hall among the boots as she introduces him to Mrs Viney.

Her ceinture burns at her left side. It serves to remind her that adulthood is not about self-indulgence; that the life worth living – tempered, civilized, ascetic, like Montaigne in his tower of books – requires sacrifice.

She straightens her back. Isn't her longing to say, 'Take me,' to be accepted into the briefcase-carrying Sellotaped-glasses day-boy world, proof that she must resist? This baseness lies within her. The Vineys will show her the way out.

'When,' Laura asks Suze, 'do, do you think Peter might be back?'

She has been feeling more and more peculiar. At first she

assumed it was sea-sickness but gradually, as the minutes have passed, she tried harder to identify this simmering in her stomach, the heat which is building on her neck and back. Is it anger, righteous and refreshing? Fury that he has just turned up in the middle of London, expecting her to take charge?

Just as she is summoning the nerve to tell Suze that she is leaving, Peter appears. He looks smelly. His donkey jacket has been rained on, although no weather has been visible through the smeary portholes; his interesting head-stubble has become faintly threatening, like that of an unstable soldier from the former Soviet Union. He is with a tall fair man, presumably Jensen, who nods at her, as if she is here to swab the decks. Peter is holding a carrier bag from which he proudly unpacks two bananas, a loaf of white sliced and a bag of what looks like gravel.

'Aduki beans,' he says to Suze. 'Amino acids.'

'You said,' Laura tells him, 'to be here before twelve.'

'Oh God, sorry, so.'

'No,' says Suze. 'It was *after* twelve. I heard him.'

'Why,' Laura asks her, 'didn't you say? I've just been waiting—'

Only a wicked woman would complain about time in the presence of the sick. They all look at her with surprise, as if a stuffed animal had spoken.

'Never mind,' says Laura. 'Sorry.'

Peter smiles at her and, inadvertently, she smiles back. As the others roam about, making themselves individual hippy teas and rinsing the sprouter, she describes her farcical efforts to slip out of Westminster Court this morning and then, without meaning to, she begins to tell him about Founder's Day.

'What?' he says. 'Three days? Fuck. How are you going to stand it?'

'I know. Oh God, I know. It, it's a weird place, Combe. Combe Abbey. Horrible, to be honest. '

'And it's in Dorset?'

'Yes.'

'Christ, I hate the countryside. The way the hills follow you. Cowshit everywhere. Is it awful?'

'Yes. It is.' She does not stint. She rubs his face hard in the detail, watching the words solidify as she speaks: how much she hates it, her reservations.

'So this was whose idea?' he asks, waving offhandedly as Suze and Jensen go off with face paints to a children's party; this is, apparently, Jensen's job. It is almost impossible for Laura to be polite to them, but she makes herself say good-bye. After all, she reminds herself maturely, they have looked after him, while I have not. They have bathed him; seen his scar—

'Babe?' says Peter.

'Her idea, Marina's,' says Laura. 'Completely hers. Though the others joined in. You know. It's just—'

'What?'

She gives a wet ugly sniff. 'I, I, I didn't dare—'

'Tell them no? I don't blame you. What a bloody scary idea.'

'You're still such an interrupter. No.' She needs a tissue.

Gingerly she reaches out for a dishcloth on the counter behind her, snatches her hand away and wipes her face uselessly with her palm. 'I didn't dare, oh, I don't know. Tell her that I wanted her to stay.'

'Hey. Hey.'

'Go away.'

'I'm not. I'm going to perch here.'

'Stop it. Stop *stroking*—'

'Laura. I've been such a shit.'

'You have.'

'A fucker.'

'Yes, but—'

'A fucking fucker.'

'God, I miss hearing someone swear. Apart from me.'

'A cunt.'

'Well—'

'I have.'

'You have.'

'I wish—'

'What I just want to know,' she says, unwisely, 'is have you— Oh, never mind. Of course you have.'

'What?'

'You know bloody what.'

'I don't. Ow.'

'Just look at me. No, you don't even need to say it.'

'*What?*'

'That you had lots of girlfriends. Bet you have, millions of, of floaty sodding girls called Daisy and Saffron.'

'You don't want to know.'

'I do. I bloody do. I want to hate you.'

So he tells her, and the answer is not what she had expected; not at all.

Somehow she is naked.

Well, near enough. What is wrong with her? The door could open right now; anyone could walk in. Even apart from the repercussions, the thought of being seen in all her squashiness, the pale expanses of hideous skin, is unbearable. She would have to leave, at once and for ever.

And what is he thinking? He looks better than her, which isn't difficult; was he horrified and politely not commenting, or too busy to notice? She had not expected this. Had he?

Or had she? Her legs are shaved. She is wearing her only faintly attractive bra, a Principessa Duchesse Splendide with nylon broderie anglaise edging. He is considerably less washed than her, but this is perversely exciting; reassuring, too, because it means he had not planned this either. She is not in a trap but has chosen this, and that makes all the difference.

How extraordinary to see him, his soft hidden skin and secret hair, unclothed.

They are lying on top of his bed, his arm across her throat. She swallows hard; she is starting to feel crushed. Need male limbs be quite so heavy? He is not asleep, yet; just very, very relaxed. Laura, on the other hand, is rigid, eyes open wide as she gazes over his shoulder at the extraordinary fact of what they have just done.

31

Saturday, 11 March

Two days pass: a sexual desert. They are both so afraid of being discovered before finding a way to tell the others, that they have agreed not to be in contact. In any case, Peter rarely leaves the boat. Then it is the middle of March, the time she dreads all year, when she is obliged to help with Femina's spring stock take.

What is so dreadful about it? Everything. The smell of the back room: old perfume, Ildi's Polish *svee*-ties, Zsuzsi's cigarettes, and the dusty scent lingering in every cardboard box and polythene wrapping. The brown luggage tags and tiny paper labels on which elaborate price codes are written by hand; the typewriter for letters to customers; the card index for every single order since time began. The pictures of Marina in childhood, before whatever it was that went wrong between them happened, and the school photograph of Mrs Dobos's granddaughter, like a plaited pig. The trade brochures and kettle; the sewing tin, because customers expect Mrs Farkas to alter their purchases and, irrespective of arthritis, Mrs Farkas does it. Her ladies are not fond of change. And, worst of all, the yellowing packets of unsellable items, knee-length demi-knickers and Spirella Femme corselettes and Berlei Elastomerics, kept because of Rozsi's firm belief that 'Von day, someone vants'.

There is no choice: Laura has to do it. Rozsi writes dates as '976 and '989; she speaks Russian and Czech and German and God knows what else but cannot spell 'tights'. So here stands Laura, ticking off an unsold Gossard Long-line Thermal Camisole in Illusion, not thinking about Peter.

'I suppose . . .' says Laura a little later.

'What?'

'Nothing. This is your fault,' she says. 'If you'd just, I don't know, gone to see them, independently, like you should have, I wouldn't have had to ring you to tell you to do it. And then I wouldn't have ended up round here.'

It isn't true. She could not stop thinking about his shaved head, whether the bristle felt velvety or rough. And his skin so pale, his cheeks thinner: who could help wanting to dis-cover what else has changed? She has spent so many years energetically resisting all memory of his body, its muscles and enormous bones, its touching flaws, and what has that achieved? Nothing. Here it all was, as she unwrapped it, exactly as she had known it would be.

They are lying on what remains of a sofa. A candle, inevitably, flickers on the seat of a chair nearby, and a blow heater blasts from a suspended home-made socket, warming her right instep and two or three toes.

'I am very uncomfortable,' she says.

'Me too.'

Still they lie there. She is cold and needs the toilet and

can see her numberless physical flaws as he must, violently magnified. She thinks: I must hide myself. I want to go. But, if she stands, the delicious loinal heat, the ache, the melting in her wrists and knees, will pour out of her and leave her with nothing. She had not forgotten this feeling; she had only thought it would not happen again.

'This is all wrong.'

'I know.'

'We're bad.'

'So bad.'

'Wrong.'

'Yep.'

'Practically criminal,' she says and, an inch from her ear, he gives a snort. 'What? I mean it.'

He is laughing: at her; at them.

'Don't,' she says. 'Seriously. Don't. I'm going to ask you one more time. When are you going to tell them?'

32

Tuesday, 14 March

Founder's Day Week

10 a.m.–12 p.m. ceramics exhibition (also 10 a.m.–
12 p.m., Wednesday), Radcliffe Library (free)

12 p.m. Uppers' debate ('Europe: Friend or Foe'),
Old Library, £3

4.30 p.m. 'Hooked on Bossa': percussion medley
featuring the Combe Players, Founder's Court
marquee, cash bar, £4

6 p.m. *The Merchant of Venice*, Combe Abbey
Cloisters, £4

At five o'clock, overdressed and skittish, the Farkas party
assembles. It is almost time for headmaster's drinks, to which
the parents of the many participants in *The Merchant of
Venice* have been invited. The assistant registrar, distressed
by Marina's family circumstances, still sends everything to
'Mr and Mrs Farkas' but, with pleading, Laura has managed
to persuade her to extend Dr Tree's invitation to Marina's
grandmother and great-aunts too.

Most mothers, she suspects, drive over from Salisbury or Yeovil daily, or treat the whole week as an amusing conjugal mini-break, booking into the Oak or the Regency and consorting with friends in the evenings, while their young go to Melcombe for pizzas in rowdy groups. No one else stays at the disappointingly tartan Braegarrold; they will have the breakfast room to themselves.

But in Rozsi and Zsuzsi's marginally larger room, sitting on the Black Watch bedspreads to giggle and drink instant coffee from home, they are having a fabulous time. The atmosphere is heady, as if they are about to go into battle. 'We attend,' announces Zsuzsi, still in her huge sunglasses, 'even though I am invited to the ballet with Klein Pali tonight, he beg me. It is *Nutcracker*, such a pity. But *vondarefool*, the whole family here. For Marinaka's sake.'

Rozsi writes to Mrs Dobos on a postcard of Combe Abbey by floodlight, updating her on events so far. Zsuzsi and Ildi are pink-cheeked with hilarity; the beds are shaking. Laura smiles as if she is made of wood. Peter was meeting his consultant today for yet more results; she hasn't quite understood from his vague description which ones, but they are important. She has, with difficulty, obtained for him the number at Braegarrold; he has agreed that 'maybe me, maybe Suze' will leave a message if there is news, but will they? What would silence mean? And meanwhile, at work, where Alistair only decided last night that he could spare her for this little trip, they will be discovering misfiled lab reports; counting Dalmane bottles with puzzled expressions.

When Zsuzsi decides that it is time to open the sponge fingers, Laura dares to act.

'I'm just going to find my, er,' she says, and hurries down-stairs to explain to the landlady that if she is contacted by a woman called Suze, who is leaving a message on behalf of a mutual friend, it should be passed straight to Laura herself.

Mrs Cousins is not impressed. Having already scented impropriety in the Farkas set-up, she has visited them twice to warn against over-flushing and excessive soap use. 'This is a respectable house,' she says. 'Other guests consider our facilities more than sufficient.'

'Yes, it's wonderful, absolutely. But I'm— sorry, it's the only way my friend can reach me. It's about, well, some medical results,' she says, and her eyes begin to burn. 'Due today.'

There is a long pause. 'Well, it's highly irregular. I don't like it. I'll have to speak to Mr Cousins. And naturally if for these medical reasons you decide to take off early, there'll be no refund.'

'Thank you,' Laura says.

'Hmm.'

'Oh,' she makes herself add, 'just one more thing. If my friend does ring, please please don't tell my, you know. Just tell me. Really. It's a sort of surprise.'

She walks back upstairs with the sense that she is watched. Her legs are slow and heavy. She passes the dark doorway marked Private, the hidden telephone. What if Peter needs her?

What if he doesn't?

*

Headmaster's drinks are precisely that. 'Not a biscuit,' Laura thinks in Rozsi's voice, 'not a nut,' but the real Rozsi doesn't say a word. Laura fishes fizzy apple out of her Pimms; Zsuzsi distributes Droste chocolate pastilles. Although the light is fading and it is far from warm, the party is in the gardens of Dr Tree's house, a Victorian Gothic keep behind a very disciplined twenty-foot hedge. The windows which overlook the lawn are extensively leaded, affording only glimpses of floor-length curtains, a grand piano glinting with silver frames. Mrs Tree, apparently also a teacher, glides amongst them like a sprigged and piecrust-collared priestess, dodging the merrier fathers, greeting favoured mothers with a kiss. Faintly, in a distant rehearsal, a hundred voices are raised in song.

'*Von*-darefool,' agree the old ladies, huddling together by the drinks table. Laura searches for signs of life; yes, Zsuzsi is shaking her head, eyes following a particularly wide-hipped woman in Madras check and another in a denim shirtwaister. She looks disappointed. Her gaze moves to the men's gilt-buttoned blazers, their racy mustard-yellow trousers and brown suede brogues. Laura watches, and thinks: she is right. I should not criticize, dressing as I do, but Combe parents are hideous.

The patriarchs, waving impressive cameras, have staked out tables with hip flasks and fully rollable Panama hats. Old Combeian fathers beget Combe sons, like child abusers; they cuff each other violently on the shoulder, bellowing about 'Stanters' and something called 'jams'.

Where are the children? The play is starting in half an

hour. The other parents seem perfectly happy without them, but Laura's hands twitch with Marina-hunger: the back of her neck, the smell of her cheek. There is nowhere left to sit. Ildi picks shyly at a cement griffin. Rozsi has forgotten her Kodak Disc camera. In London, Peter is finding out if he has a future.

'Beautiful,' the Farkases say and Laura runtishly agrees. At long last, after a painful speech about fundraising golf tournaments and Lincoln's Inn old boy dinners, they are instructed to raise their glasses and toast the school 'and all who sail in her', and then, when the hilarity has died down, a side door opens and their children start to drift in.

At least, other people's children, in gold brocade and alarming make-up. Marina's family waits.

'Hello,' says a voice. 'Aren't you Mrs Farkas?'

Standing at Laura's elbow is a pale powdery girl, turned into an old woman with wobbly eye-liner wrinkles and a hair comb.

'Heidi,' the girl informs Laura, like someone at a conference. 'Marina's friend from West Street. We have met.'

The girl updates her on her slight netball injury, her inter-house debating near triumph, her progress in inorganic chemistry.

'Oh, so you're in the same class as Marina?' Laura says. 'How is . . . is she doing OK, do you know?'

'Marina?'

'Yes!'

'Um.'

'What? What's wrong?'

'*Dar*-link!' Laura hears behind her and, with relief, turns to see her in-laws swoop upon a short dark girl in an unfortunate toga. It takes a moment to recognize her daughter. Laura waits until the great-aunts have stopped their cheek-pinching before asking, 'Are you all right?'

'Yes,' says Marina, and her mother knows she lies.

She waits, trembling, in the wings for her only cue. In two minutes, just before the embarrassingly unnecessary sword fight, Marina will enter stage left, right, no left to sell oranges to the populace, before exiting, screaming, stage left. No, stage right. She keeps imagining herself running in the wrong direction; lately her brain has been full of unsquashable thoughts, like a miniature horror film. And she is so tired. There is hardly time to sleep these days. When she tries, her worries multiply in an endlessly branching hell: tree trunks into twigs, leaves, leaf veins; bronchiole, alveoli, capillaries, cells.

There on the dark lawn is her family. It does not calm her; if anything it makes her want to do something rash, run out across the stage, jump down and pull them to their feet, swatting at the Combe grass and Combe insects which are infecting them while they sit there, in blithe ignorance. Only two more nights, she keeps telling herself; that's nothing. Stop this weakness. Harden your heart.

However, she can't help noticing, even as she pines and yearns, that they seem to be taking up more room than other people. Rozsi's stretched-out legs and Zsuzsi's ancient metal-framed Harrods handbag: they just don't think. Everyone is looking at them, the oldest, strangest-looking group, in furry coats like bears who have strayed into a picnic.

Sweating like a fat pig in her costume, a grass stain already on her simple espadrilles, she glances once again at the far side of the lawn, where Mrs Viney is still sitting on the bench beside Pa Stenning and, despite Mr Viney's absence, an image comes to her: the meeting of the tribes.

Dear God. I would, she thinks, do anything to stop it happening.

What, though? How far would I go?

Anything. Hurt myself. Run amok. Even—

There is a gap on the blanket between the fuzzy outlines of her relatives. Where the hell is her mother?

One minute Laura is sitting on the grass surrounded by Combe families, lolling in self-satisfaction like basking seals. The next she is getting to her feet.

'What are you doing?' hisses Zsuzsi.

'Sorry,' Laura whispers. She blunders across the grass, dodging between picnic rugs until she finds the dangerously unsignposted fire exit at the other side of the cloisters, is waved away by a man in shorts, rushes back until she finds another opening and bursts out into the unforgiving chill of Martyrs' Lodge.

She is alone. Close by a bell is tolling. Peter will have his results by now; she must speak to him. Tears have begun to pour from her like a nosebleed. She must find out. She wipes her face on her sleeve. Marina will forgive me, she thinks, if she even notices that I've gone. One day I'll explain it, I definitely will.

She hurries across the cobbles and through an archway into Founder's Court. A few stray schoolboys, inexplicably dressed as squaddies, are setting out chairs on the grass. 'Cockcheese,' she hears one of them shout, to which another answers, 'You wish!' She keeps walking, blushing, apologetic and, although they grow quiet at her footfall, there is a definite recalibration of respectfulness as she passes: laughter again, and louder voices. She clearly hears one of them say, 'Knob.'

There is no way for a lay person to distinguish between the surrounding buildings. It feels wrong to be wandering unsupervised. What, she thinks, would be the worst thing I could find?

At last she locates a telephone, in the entrance to what appears to be a rudimentary pub: jars of penny sweets, file paper, taps for beer. Ringing to hear the verdict on Peter, death or life, is not easy; she has to replace the receiver twice before she dials correctly. Eventually, she reaches Suze.

'I am very busy,' Suze says. 'He is due in five.'

'You mean at your house? He's coming there?' Laura burns with a pure white hatred. 'Could you tell him to ring me then, the moment that he arrives? I'm at, I can't really hang around, I'm at a pay phone. Do you honestly not know what the doctor said?'

Two older boys stare openly as she waits to be rung back. She slips into a dark flinty place between noticeboards, and closes her eyes.

He is about to find out if he has a future. Who are you, she asks herself, to think he would even want you? He didn't before. You weren't enough, even then. And if you—

She snatches up the telephone as if it could bolt away from her. 'Hello?' It is Peter, and her heartbeat pounds in her ear. 'Tell me. What did they say?'

It is complicated, and made more so by his failure to ask the consultant any of the right questions. If he 'gets to' six months, as he puts it, then he has double the chance of living to a year than if he'd only got to three months, which he already has.

'Are you sure?' she asks. 'What about now? What do they know?'

Very little. He still claims that it's a good kind of cancer, the 'right' kind. 'Because a kidney's removable,' he says, as if people have perforated lines. 'Not like a liver, or brain, or, I don't know, a pen—'

'OK. Enough. And what if the other one . . .'

They listen together to what she doesn't say; it rushes in their ears like the air in a baked-bean can, like the sea. No one on the face of the earth cares as much about you as I do, she tells him silently, except—

'Pete,' she says. 'What are we going to do?'

33

It is the dead of night. At Combe Abbey, in Dorset, probably in the whole of England Marina is the only person awake.

She has written a poem:

> No more the sun
> No more the moon
> Now more the owlet's cry.
> I know not what I am to you
> Nor why I long to die.

It is moving and impressive: a genuine reflection of her suffering. Since turning down Simon Flowers's overture, for it can have been nothing else, she has been desolate. Everything is going wrong. How could her mother have missed her stage appearance? The lights were too bright to see much once she was out there, selling her oranges, but she could hear loud whispering coming from the Farkases' general area; they were probably offering their neighbours dumplings, or saying terrible things about their footwear. Everyone will know that they belong to Marina; she should not think like this, but it is true.

Also, what if someone mentions chemistry? It's probably best if she doesn't spend too much time with her family, in case of blurting it out. But then the Vineys and the Farkases may meet unsupervised. How had she even thought this was a situation she could control?

During the long night which follows, sweating against the radiator on burgundy brushed-nylon sheets, Laura tries to imagine gathering the relatives together over their All-Bran to tell them . . . what, exactly? The thing is, Peter might die; oh yes, and he's alive after all?

Then what? Would they go together to find Marina in West Street and explain the whole mess to her, in the god-awful beige television room in front of dozens of gaping girls? Must they inform Dr Tree?

Control yourself, she whispers. You cannot cry in bed beside another woman. A man might not notice but, if Ildi wakes, she will. And she would try to understand why I've kept it from them, which would make it worse. Oh, Laura imagines saying airily, I've only known he was in London since the twenty-eighth of bloody January. Yes, nearly two months. Yes, once I knew he was ill I was afraid it might be worse for you but, mainly, I was scared.

Peter wants them to know.

Maybe, she thinks, turning her head cautiously to look at her bed-mate, open-mouthed and lightly snoring on her poor aching back. Maybe I could start this off myself, tell Ildi right now, to help him. Something I could do for him.

'Ildi,' she whispers cautiously. But what if she has a stroke from the shock?

Tomorrow, thinks Laura. I'll find a time to tell her then; well, actually today. It is after four. She cannot sleep, or think; her brain clangs like a fire alarm. She has brought nothing to read; how can she, when the others have a *Life of Picasso*, and a parallel text of Lampedusa's *Il Gattopardo*? And, when she isn't fretting, her mind drifts dangerously close to sex, its warm lapping shallows, its sharp rocks.

Then she has an idea. Slowly, gritting her teeth at every sound, now that she must not wake Ildi, Laura pulls back the blankets and goose-steps amusingly over her aunt-in-law's fragile limbs to reach the floor. Her nightdress, clinging to her back and stomach with sweat, cools her skin as she moves. She feels herself clench with lust.

Her foot touches the carpet. Ildi is still snoring. She pulls her case out from under the bed, wincing at the sound of sky-blue leatherette on nylon carpet, and feels around for the box.

Why did Marina want her to bring letters? Even if the family wasn't so protective, so convinced that most things must be kept from a child, it was a silly idea. Nineteen-fifties blocks of flats do not contain secret archives behind book-cases. Had she expected a forgotten will?

The truth is that Laura's search for letters was fleeting, at best. It felt like exhumation, breathing in the sad smell of crumbled cheap paper, trying not to notice the blurred post-marks which would reveal information she is too cowardly to face. Families like Rozsi's always have horrible stories in the background, betrayals on snowy mountain passes, little children led trustingly into forests. On this, Laura finds herself agreeing with her in-laws. If she could, she would keep Marina from knowing any of it. Other people's sadness doesn't inoculate; it isn't good for you. It just makes life more difficult to bear.

So instead she has brought photographs. She found them by accident, looking in the sideboard drawer for the corn-cob forks. No, that is a lie. She was looking for pictures of Peter. And she found this instead: a red tin advertising Rademaker's Haagsche Hopjes, Zsuzsi's *svee*-tie of choice, posted to London at enormous cost by a devoted admirer in Rotterdam. There was a label with *Francia* on the lid, and a rattle of foreign coins; she almost didn't look. But then she did and inside the tin, smelling of treacle and orphaned keys, she found these.

There are thirty or so, mostly pictures of her daughter in gingham sun bonnets and rick-rack braid and startling knitwear; the fat-cheeked infancy of which Marina, knowing her, will always be ashamed. Laura opens the door a little to let corridor light in, looks out cautiously for passing in-laws: nothing. She kneels before the case again.

Here is Zoltan: grey-haired but ridiculously handsome in a raincoat on holiday; executing one of his perfect dives, side-parting intact, into black water. They make her throat close up, but it is silly to be surprised by family photographs. Other people have them; why shouldn't the Farkases? Nevertheless, it feels as if she should not be here. Poor Zoltan, she thinks, I love you. I do. I think you even loved me.

What did happen to you?

The other photographs are tiny, monochrome, frilly edged: a bowler-hatted moustachioed man walking with a woman in furs and a beautiful girl between them, like the last days of the Romanovs; another perfect dive; eleven men and women in all-in-one swimwear from crotch to collar-bone, grinning on a beach like Olympians. Someone has written '935 on the back in fountain-pen; Rozsi would have been, what, twenty-six, Zoltan roughly twenty-seven? Neither of them is in the picture. There are groups of laughing skiers in shirts and ties, even the women – *Skotarska 937 II.28* – and much merriment: a plain happy woman smoking, knee-deep in a river banked with silver birches; four tiny figures doing the cancan in front of a castle. Everyone is smiling. The sun always shines.

Laura looks more closely. She gropes behind her and pushes open the door a little more. This is Zsuzsi, definitely, standing on a rock in a sailor top, and again with two beaming younger women: they look like more Károlyi sisters, but wasn't she the youngest? Unless . . . oh God.

One of the youthful swimming-costume photographs is shot in deep grass, with long waving wheat or corn behind and a mountain; a blonde woman, a dark man sitting chastely, seriously, with hands around their knees. The man is Zoltan; the woman is not Rozsi, although Rozsi swims at every opportunity. She might be just off-camera, or behind it, except for the fact that these two look so . . . alone. Here is Rozsi in a short woollen jacket and mittens, skiing; who is the girl next to her, faintly similar, prettier? These women look so alike: wide gleaming cheekbones, radiant smiles, flat lightly waved hair like floppy berets. The man with his arms around them, not Zoltan, looks richer, older, with very white teeth and combed-back hair thinning at the temples;

he wears a buttoned-up thick shirt and pleated-front trousers and, as in one of the snowy hillside photographs, no skis. Familiar writing on the back says *34* and an illegible word; somebody else has written *English for Foreigners, L.C.C. Evening Institute.*

She sits back to think. Wasn't there someone they used to visit: Zoltan's best friend? There was, she is almost sure of it. When Laura first knew them, Rozsi and Zoltan used to see the other man, and his wife, all the time. And then they stopped.

34

Wednesday, 15 March

Founder's Day Week

10.30 a.m. water polo demonstration match,
Greer's (free)

12 p.m. lunchtime music: Military Band,
Founder's Court marquee, £3

1.30 p.m. 'Music for a Nightingale': music and song
in celebration of the English countryside by Elgar
and Vaughan Williams, and a sprinkling of Baroque
classics, with Mrs Susan James and the Crypt Choir,
Combe Abbey Crypt, £5

3–5 p.m. visual arts private view: a cocktail of
painting, drawing and sculpture, Moore Studios, £3

7 p.m. 'All About Jazz': a spectacular featuring the
hits of Fats Waller, Cole Porter, Herbie Hancock
and others, with the Combe Rock Combo and the
Combe Players, soloists Gemma Alcock (Lower,
Fitzgerald), Ben Blake-Charles (Upper, Daneford),
Tony Lemon and Mrs Deborah Tree, Divinity
Hall, £10

Last night Marina could not sleep. She is jumpy and wide-eyed; at breakfast the porridge does not anchor her. Her family are attending the Lowers' debate in the Buttery; even the thought of them makes her eyes fill. When she said good-bye after the play last night, before she trudged back to West Street alone, she dared, for once, to ignore the risk of divine retribution and tell them that she loved them. Her mother, distracted, did not say it back.

Although Laura tries to claim a headache, they are up and cerealed and standing shyly outside Garthgate by nine o'clock ('Vot a vether') discussing how to spend their day. There are limited opportunities for cultural enrichment in Combe. Marina will be working all day, she has told them; she won't see them until just before tonight's jazz spectacular begins. So, with the aid of a tourist brochure from the rack at Combe station, Laura plots today's activities: a tour of the alleged birthplace of a poet she has never heard of; a trip to the wood-turning demonstration being held at the local library; and a visit to the Combe Art Block, where they view an exhibition of awful sculpture and several studies of reflections on sunglasses.

And, pretending to need the loo yet again when they're eating ham sandwiches (salad 10p extra) at the Olde Copper Kettle ('Very nice,' says Rozsi bravely), she goes downstairs to the public phone. Suze won't like her ringing again but she has an excuse; she wants to ask Peter about this mysterious former friend – Rudi? Sándor? Possibly a Tibor – whom she is increasingly sure is the ski-less man in the photograph.

Yet the human libido is an extraordinary— what? Weakness? Delusion? Even in the least erotic circumstances, such as standing in a phone booth surrounded by amateur dramatics posters and a mop, one can be having thoughts. Urgencies. She cannot stop thinking about his hands.

He may not want to talk to her. I could always try later, she thinks, listening to the dialling tone, it's not urgent; at least this bit, the Zoltan part of it, isn't. She knows where that story will end.

Then Suze picks up the telephone.

Marina, in history, struggling with the War of Jenkins' Ear, makes a new decision. She will confront her mother. If she can't even be bothered to watch her only child (Marina) sell oranges, that's the end, isn't it? Something has died.

It occurs to her now, staring out of the window to make her tears retract, that all this could have been avoided if she'd never left home in the first place. Which means that it is her fault. Which means that no one will save her.

It sounds as if there is a party: Peter, it turns out, is already in Suze's house. 'What's going on?' asks Laura.

'It's just Jens and a couple of mates,' he is saying. 'So, hang about, what are you asking?'

'I know it seems stupid. And you, you've got other things to think about. But I need to know about Zoltan's friend.'

'Which one?'

'I can't — wasn't there someone they used to see all the time? Maybe a Tibor, or a Sándor?'

'Oh, Szőllőssy Tibor, that the one?'

'Maybe. I think so.'

'Yep. They were best friends. You definitely would have met him. Why?'

She is not going to tell him about the photographs; she decided last night. 'I saw these photos,' she hears herself saying. 'At home, you know, West—'

'*Vest*-minstaircourt,' he says, and something scrapes in her chest.

'Yes, and he was there.'

'So, right, yep. So they were best mates and then, I don't know, something happened. End of story. Let's talk about something else.'

This is what she fears. Either he won't know a thing, or he'll tell her a war story so horrible that: what? The world will crumble and melt around them because nothing will be able to bear the truth?

'What?' she says in a small voice. 'Tell me. If you can.'

'I don't know.'

'Why not?'

'I just don't. You know what they're like, they'd die before they said, well, that they were dying. For example. It was something, God, hang on, let me think. Business, I think.'

'What? You mean as in Swiss banks with stolen paintings?'

'Course not. They, it was before I was born. In Pálaszlany. You'd have to ask Rozsi.'

'How can I, Pete? Think.'

'OK. OK. I do know, I just don't like talk— Never mind. So Zoltan, my Zoltan, was meant to inherit his dad's estate.'

'Did he have one? I didn't know.'

'Course. In the country somewhere. Pink house, horses everywhere. He told me,' he says, and she hears him swallow, 'they used to take off their shoes at the beginning of the summer and not put them on until they went back to town. So, yeah, he was meant to get the business, all of it. What-ever you need to make saddles for the Austro-Hungarian army. Lasts? Saddle moulds? I don't know. Anyway, Tibor got it.'

'What?'

'He, I don't know, lied about something. He was, I think he was working for my grandfather, Zoltan's dad, managing it. The steward or something, and he—'

'Hang on. He *lied*? About his friend? Where was Zoltan, anyway?'

'At college, wasn't he? Doing doctor training. They trusted Tibor, you know, he was local. Poor. His brothers and sisters took it in turns to wear one pair of boots to school apparently. And my grandfather loved him: his son's best friend. So he believed Tibor when he said Zoltan was morally . . . what's that word? Well, dodgy, anyway.'

'You're joking.'

'Nope.'

'But why?'

Peter gives a mighty sigh. 'Because, because before Rozsi,

so I suppose just before the war, when all this happened, Zoltan had a girlfriend. And she was, wait for it. Divorced.'

'Oh.'

'So that was obviously a big deal. She had a child, I think; there was some story about crossing borders in a diplomatic car. Anyway. So, after the, whatever, cheating, disinheritance, Zoltan came to England to make a new life with various people including Rozsi, who was the divorced woman's best friend from university. You must know about this . . .'

'No I don't,' Laura says. 'They never told me.'

'Well, they did, just when the war was starting, and there was a whole palaver about Rozsi getting forged passports and visas and things. You do know that bit?'

'No. Honestly. How do you—'

'Just things I've picked up. In any case, while they were risking their lives on a train to wherever, Belgium maybe, or Amsterdam, although there'd be all those canals . . . anyway, wherever, bloody Tibor, Zoltan's great friend, was copping off with, get this, the divorced woman!'

'No!'

'Oh yes. I suppose they'd split, in the chaos, but still: after all that fuss. Tibor just took over. He even married her. Bastard.'

'So it wasn't actually to do with the war? The falling out. The . . . betrayal.'

'Nope. Why would you think it was?'

'I, I just assumed. Never mind. Oh, poor Zoltan.'

'I know. And that's not all, bec—'

'Oh Christ,' says Laura. 'I forgot. They're waiting for me upstairs.'

35

Marina, feeling bleak and black, has just entered the dark passageway between the War Memorial and the Science Block. The stone is overgrown with creepers, which bodes ill but, she is thinking, if she holds her breath she will be half-protected. So, for once in her life, she is not expecting an unexpected meeting.

But here are Guy, and Mrs Viney.

Marina lets out a breath. Her mouth is dry; she can't think of anything worth saying, only frantic prayers: *Dear God in Heaven, if Thou has not forsaken me due to unbelief, please keep my family far away at this moment.* Her uniform grows itchy; she starts scratching her neck like a village idiot, then snatches her hand away and grips it behind her back. Now she looks like Prince Charles.

'How nice,' says Mrs Viney. She lowers her cheek to be kissed and, despite everything, a little flame of joy burns in Marina's heart.

'Oh,' she says. 'Golly.'

Guy smirks at her. 'Wotcha.'

But this chance conversation, on which so many hopes are pinned, does not go well. Marina seems to be becoming more, not less, shy; every movement she makes disgusts her. Mrs Viney seems bored. Or is it annoyance? Is she about to reveal that the ornament Marina broke at Stoker has been discovered? Just when she is wondering whether to confess right now, Guy says, 'Guess who's doing Prize-Giving tomorrow? Dad! Oh look, isn't that your mother?'

And there she is, wandering happily through the Memorial Quad in her old brown coat. She kisses Marina, says a vague hello to Guy, says, 'Pleased to meet you,' in a frankly unfriendly tone to Mrs Viney. Guy is explaining how the person meant to be giving the prizes, a Commonwealth Games rowing champion who was in Bute House a million years ago yet was still taught by Pa Kendall, has had to cancel, so they asked his father at the very last minute.

Marina can't concentrate on what he is saying. Mrs Viney must be annoyed with *her*, but why? She is so polite; it is hard to tell. Marina takes a tentative step towards the mothers, one in beautiful brown leather boots, the other not.

'Oh, sweetheart,' says her mother. 'Have you seen Rozsi and Co?'

'Me?' says Marina, making warning eye gestures. 'No!'

'They were going shopping,' she says. 'There's that little boutique on the High Street and Zsuzsi—'

'Mum—'

'Don't interrupt, sweetheart. Rozsi and Ildi and Zsuzsi: are you sure?'

'Good Lord,' says Mrs Viney. 'What interesting n—'

'Mum, you remember Guy, don't you?' says Marina. 'Of course you do.'

'Sorry,' her mother says, frowning more than she needs to in the circumstances. A group of beefy men in Old Combeian blazers and long cricket jumpers stride past the entrance to the passage. 'Yes, Guy, I do remember. Are you in Marina's class too?'

'Not really,' says Marina. She is cold with sweat; her back feels oily.

'You . . . you're doing other A levels?'

'If only,' says Guy's mother. 'Actually Guy's only a Fiver. Though revoltingly precocious. They do get like that, don't they?'

'We-ell,' Laura says.

'But despite the vast age gap we've come to know and love Marina, haven't we, darling?'

'Have you?' asks Laura, frowning. 'When?'

'Oh!' says Marina. 'I've just remembered something. Pa Stenning. I mean, Daventry, Pa Daventry! He wanted to talk to you.'

'We'll let you get on,' says Mrs Viney. 'You sound terribly busy.'

'Oh yes,' says Laura offhandedly. She has, Marina realizes, no grasp of how to talk to these people. 'We are.'

'Of course you'll be at Al's speech tomorrow, won't you. You must come. I unfortunately will miss it but, er . . .'

'Laura,' says Marina's mother.

'Of course. Laura. Anyway, you must be there.'

'See ya later,' says Guy. 'Oh, by the way, wanna come out tonight?'

'Yes!' says Marina, glancing at her mother, who is now just standing there, not making conversation. 'I'd love to. Brilliant.' Her mother puts her hand on her arm. Marina pretends not to notice. 'Defi— absolutely. If you're sure? I mean, I'd love to. Yes, please. What time?'

'Dunno. I'll check. Crown and Mitre.'

'Oh yes, do,' says Mrs Viney, who clearly does not mean it.

Marina's heart thumps hard outside her body. The Crown and Mitre is a forbidden pub; where the House Sirs go, and masters. 'Mum, Mummy. We'll . . . we'd better find Pa Daventry. We can decide later. Really. Now.'

'In a—'

'No!' says Marina. 'And in fact I suddenly feel ill. Please. Sorry, um, sorry,' she mumbles, barely able to look at Mrs Viney. 'I, um—' and she pulls at her mother's arm like a rude child, a hunchback, a beast until, with the least possible grace and dignity, she leads her away.

'But what about "All About Jazz"?' asks Laura. She is irritable, and overwhelmed; what I need, she thinks, is a diagram of how everyone connects.

'I don't need to go to that, do I?'

'Marina,' Laura says, more sharply than she had intended, and they both look up, surprised. 'Of course you do. We bought tickets. You can't just . . . forget.'

'Well, I did,' says Marina petulantly. 'And it's too late now. I accepted.'

Laura can feel herself frowning. She irons out her forehead and tries to sound nice.

'Sweetheart,' she says, 'Rozsi will want you there. Don't be silly. Oh, my love, why are you crying?'

324

'I'm so embarrassed.'

'Why? How? You're so strange, pickle.'

'Don't say that!'

'I didn't mean—'

'No, you're right. I am. I am I am I am, and I just can't—'

'Oh no, you're not. You're wonderful.'

'You have,' sobs Marina, 'no idea.'

'Shh, darling.'

'I can't shh! I just wish I sodding— I wish I was dead.'

Laura steps back. She takes her hand off her daughter's shoulder. 'You don't mean it.'

'I do.'

'Don't say that.'

'Why not? I do! I mean, I don't, but sometimes—'

'Shh. Shh, my love. I know.'

They stand for a moment below the War Memorial, awkwardly embracing. You have to tell her about her father, Laura commands herself, now. Right now. But how is poor Marina to deal with that? When she is clearly so . . .

Unhappy. Now she sees it, unmistakably clear, as if a cloth has been whipped off a cage, revealing a poor suffering bird. As if she, Laura, had simply opened her eyes.

Marina has ruined everything. Now that it is too late, she can see perfectly that giving up on chemistry and medicine and her future was an act of madness, and not admitting it to her family makes it so much worse. History has not brought her happiness. Before she at least knew what she wanted; now all that ambition has been replaced by fear.

Yet if she tells her mother any of this, she'll think that the Vineys were the problem, not a source of wisdom and hope. Even if they make Marina feel lowly, which they sometimes do, they have shown her how not to be base. They matter. The unhappiness is a sign that she's improving and changing, like steel turning blue in a flame.

'We could go out for tea,' says Marina now, but neither of them can think of anywhere. It is almost a relief when she hears the familiar cry of '*Dar*-link!' and turns to see three dressed-up old Hungarians noisily crossing the Quad towards them.

It grows later and later, and the difficulty about this evening, the Crown and Mitre and all it entails, does not go away. Mrs Viney will be waiting for her, and Mr Viney, expecting to be amused. Only at the last conceivable moment, when her family are all in their seats in Divvers and Simon Flowers is probably about to come on stage to play 'My Funny Valentine', which Marina has always imagined him singing to her, does she manage to think of an excuse.

'Um,' she whispers to Rozsi, who is passing around a small bar of Swiss marzipan. Everyone else has packets of Revels from the stall in the foyer; in the raised seats on the platform along Divvers' right-hand wall, where the less important masters sit in Assembly, several connected families are toasting each other with rosé in plastic goblets. 'About later. The second half. There's a bit of a problem.'

Zsuzsi leans forward interestedly. The scarf she is wearing was a gift from Mrs Dobos: turquoise zebras cavorting on a mustard-yellow tundra: '*Ja*-jare,' she confides frequently which, after a surreptitious look at the label, Laura translates as Jaeger. She is also wearing what she calls her '*ev*-ening-troo-sair', bronze-coloured slip-on shoes and a very long gilt and green-glass necklace. 'Vot is this problem?' she asks, with no attempt to lower her voice. 'You menstruate?'

'No,' hisses Marina.

'Vot? Vot?'

'I've got . . . to go to this thing,' she says. 'A . . . a concert.'

'Ve are at a concert, *dar*-link,' says Rozsi. 'Vot a silly.'

'No, it's more classical. Classical music. Do you, I mean, sorry, I know it's a bit odd. I mean, in the interval,' she adds. 'About then. Really. I was inv— I mean, asked to help. They need help, just round the back. In the wings.'

There is, isn't there, a slight possibility that Simon Flowers, gazing wistfully out over the audience as he plucks his jazz guitar, will look for her? Will he abandon his secret plan to woo her once he sees that she has gone?

They sit through 'In a Groovin' Mood' and 'Mello Madness' in awful silence. Laura fixes her eyes on the velvet Alice band worn by a woman in the next row until the woman's husband, with the radar of the sexually undiscerning, turns around and smiles. She is going to have to speak to Marina; this is unavoidable. Could she lead her outside?

She doesn't dare. Ten minutes later they are still trapped. Zsuzsi leans across her.

'What do you say is programme of your little concert?'

Marina rips at her cuticle with her teeth. 'I can't remember. Maybe . . . Liszt?' Blood is seeping through the culvert. Laura, to stop herself from gripping Marina's hand, sits on her own.

'Better you wait until this concert finish,' says Zsuzsi firmly. 'Then we go together.'

'But,' whispers Marina, 'I have to run back to, to change. Into work clothes. It'll be dusty,' she says, giving her mother a desperate look.

'Peh,' says Zsuzsi.

A better mother would make Marina stay. Laura is too busy; she is thinking of the enormous gaps in what Peter told her, the story of his parents. Would Ildi explain, if shown the photographs?

So when, in the interval, Marina says, 'Sorry, sorry,' already on her feet, her eyes wet, what can Laura do but move her knees aside to let her pass?

'*Tair*-ible,' says Rozsi, shaking her head.

Laura touches her hand: veiny, vulnerable. She has never stood up to her in-laws but now she says, 'Could we maybe let her go, just this once?'

36

Now that Marina has escaped, she should be triumphant, not ridiculously nervous. She rushes into the Ladies' toilet and instructs herself to be calm.

With a shaking hand, she takes her first-ever lipstick, Barely Berry, from her coat and begins to apply it using her reflection in the toilet-paper dispenser. Is the colour meant to be that dark? She needs to check in a normal mirror but people's mothers are talking outside now, and girls whose voices she knows. She cannot face them. And she is already late for the Crown and Mitre.

She dashes out of the cubicle, head down, sidesteps clumsily around the queue and realizes a little too late that she has come face to face with Zsuzsi, weakly pushing open the doors with her Harrods handbag.

'Oh my God,' she says.

Zsuzsi lifts both her eyebrows. She lowers her handbag. This should be the moment when her great-aunt, always such a fan of romance, twinkles at her and sends her on her way.

But her face is stony, like a pharaoh. 'So,' she says. 'Lipstick you are wearing.'

'I—'

'Where do you go?' Zsuzsi asks.

Marina lowers her eyes. Combe girls, some from West

Street itself, are staring, and Zsuzsi's voice is not at all muffled by the sounds of banging doors and flushing.

'No,' she begins, 'really—'

'*Nev*-airmind,' Zsuzsi says, waving her hand dismissively: a pope granting a day's reprieve. 'Tomorrow you tell us the story.'

Laura, after a fruitless search for yet another pay phone, hurries back across the courtyard to Divinity Hall just as the interval bell is ringing. However, there seems to have been a misunderstanding. Rozsi, Ildi and Zsuzsi are waiting impatiently in the foyer, whispering noisily in Hungarian. From inside the hall comes a taste of what they are missing: an electric guitar solo loosely tethered to 'Young, Gifted and Black'.

'I am tired,' says Rozsi, looking thunderous. 'It is *tair*-ible. We go,' and, before Laura can appease her, she finds herself being herded back down the stairs. It is only when they are standing on the tarmac outside Divinity Hall that Rozsi announces their real motive. They are going to look for Marina. Marina is missing; she has lied.

Combe, mildly picturesque by day, becomes at night a labyrinth of dark terraces, Chinese fish-and-chip shops, boarded-up old buildings papered with advertisements for Thin Lizzy tribute acts and the World Wrestling Federation. Laura marches ahead, trying to give the impression of firmness, questions nipping at the edges of her worry. Arm in arm, the others mutter incomprehensibly behind her.

'Isn't she just, you know,' begins Laura, 'doing what she

said? Helping at a concert? With, maybe, friends?'

'Friends,' scoffs Rozsi. 'Don't be funny.'

They send her into the Indian restaurant on the High Street, full of flocking and copper urns and Combe families demanding poppadums. Then a wine bar, 42nd Street, although Marina doesn't drink so could not possibly be there, and an Italian restaurant apparently trapped in the Fifties, where spaghetti is served with lamb chops and steak, like a vegetable.

'Would it not be easier just to go back and ask at that place, West Street?' she says, trying to think even more quickly than Rozsi.

'*Hihetetlen*,' she hears behind her, which is never a good sign.

She turns. Zsuzsi and Rozsi are arguing in Hungarian. Ildi, helpfully in English, says, '*Dar*-link. Rozsi think we go back toward the what-you-call-it, *cot*-edrol, maybe we see her then.'

'There isn't a cath— oh, you mean the ruins?' says Laura.

'We are looking halfway towards London for this concert,' says Zsuzsi, 'but no. *Tair*-ible, what she do to us.'

'Oh. Well, can't we just— you could go back to the bed and breakfast,' Laura says, 'and I'll keep looking for her. She can't be far.'

'Don't be *rid*-iculos,' says Zsuzsi. 'You do not have my sharp eyes.'

'Well, true. Aren't you hungry? We could go into town for a baked potato.' Rozsi loves baked potatoes. 'There's a vegetarian café, it looked quite cheap,' Laura says and, as she glances over Zsuzsi's shoulder, trying to remember where they passed it, she sees a pub over the road, a big glass window, a sign swinging in the cold Combe wind: the Crown and Mitre. She had forgotten.

Marina's evening in the Crown is not quite as she had imagined. Mrs Viney is not at the pub after all. No one talks to her. She finishes her first half of cider very quickly. Two beer-mats are lying in peeled layers in front of her, and several crushed crisps; she accidentally knocked most of them on the floor, which made everyone groan in disgust. Simon Vass, a Dene House Upper with enormous rugby shoulders, has bought another round of beers and, for Marina, a vodka and lime. Guy, talking football, ignores her.

The evening she had in mind had featured red wine and intellectual conversation, a certain relaxing of sexual mores. Cornucopiae. And if she is, well, bored, shouldn't she be doing something better with her time, such as applying her historian's mind to the mysterious Farkas–Viney connection? Like the young Queen Elizabeth on the eve of accession, she is willing to take up a hallowed burden. She wants to start.

God, what if it *is* to do with the war?

She can see herself quite clearly, on the watered-silk sofa in the drawing room at Stoker, leafing through a photo album and spotting Guy's parents at a Mosley garden party, or marching on Belgium. Could she ask Mr Viney about it? Perhaps, if she can dare herself. She reaches for her now empty glass and, as she does so, Mr Viney changes seats.

'So, young Hun,' he says. 'We meet again, again. How nice.'

'Yes,' says Marina, her resolve evaporating. His eyes are so pale that you can't help staring at them and then you're trapped there, gazing into his soul. I need alcohol, she thinks. There should be a way of buying a drink just for yourself and a specified other: a half-round. A crescent.

'What are you smiling about?'

'Nothing.'

'You are.'

'I'm not. I— you shouldn't be on that stool,' she says. 'Don't you want the bench?' and she shuffles up.

'You're very kind,' he says.

'I'm just being polite,' she explains. 'I believe in it for old, I mean—'

'I see,' and, as he stands, something over her shoulder seems to catch his eye. He goes still. Marina, hoping for bank robbers, twists round to look at the street outside. A little group of people is standing on the opposite kerb. She turns away, only ninety degrees, then turns back.

It is her grandmother, her great-aunts. And, looking straight at her, her mother, her beloved, who will ruin everything.

Their eyes meet.

At that moment, Ildi touches her mother's arm.

Marina thinks: this is her Judas moment. She will tell Ildi now about Guy; she will betray me. Slowly, not breathing, she looks again at Mr Viney, who is still standing above her, staring into the road. He seems puzzled, as if he is thinking hard. Then he lowers his gaze to hers. They stare at each other, seriously, adultly, almost, you might think, nakedly.

She sees the questions he could ask her, suspended in those cool pale irises. She holds his gaze until he snaps his eyes away and his expression clears.

'Well, well,' he says thoughtfully. 'I hadn't—'

Guy leans over. 'What are you doing, you weirdo? With your neck all twisted, you look like the Loch Ness Monster.'

'Enough, Guy,' says his father.

She has begun to sweat. 'I'm just, you know, a bit stiff,' she says.

Any moment now Guy will say, 'Hey, Reen, isn't that your mother again?' but it hardly matters any more when a pack of furious geriatrics is about to burst into the pub. Rozsi will hit him, as she once hit that policeman. Where are they? Outside, a yard or two beyond the glass, her fate is being silently decided. Don't look. Don't look.

She looks.

The street outside is empty.

They have left her here. She is still staring, mystified, out of the window when a big hand falls lightly on the nape of her neck. 'I know what the matter is,' she hears Guy's father say. 'It's bloody freezing by this window. Your muscles must be seizing up,' and he begins to massage her: her neck, the top of her back. 'Were those women outside looking for you?'

'No,' she says. 'Well—'

'No matter. You're here now,' he says, squeezing her shoulders. 'Don't be prudish. I do it all the time to my children. Come on, submit.'

*

What makes Laura pretend not to have seen her daughter? Not sensitivity, not quick thinking but a sort of dumb defiance, creeping up her spine. Everyone needs privacy occasionally, a bit of leeway. She licks her lips, clears her throat, asks herself what harm it can do for her daughter to be in a mixed group like that, fathers and schoolboys in a public place: not with a stranger, alone. Then, when she has summoned her nerve, she says to the in-laws, 'You know, I'm sure I did see a sign about a Liszt concert, in the, the Underhall, Underthing. That does explain it: even the lipstick, Zsuzsi. It's good if she's trying, isn't it?' Then, 'Oh look, isn't that the wife of the cabinet minister who went to prison?'

Miraculously, it seems to work. Besides, her in-laws need an early night. They are leaving for Femina early tomorrow morning, just after the historical pageant but before the Founder's birthday champagne reception and Prize-Giving ('They do not give Marina presents. Why do we care?'). So it makes perfect sense to send them back in the miraculous taxi at the rank right by the school, while she waits for her daughter's return.

But what to do? Every shop and restaurant in Dorset will be shut by now; it is too late to drug herself with tea and cake, or the mild provincial shopping she secretly longs for: mead-based cordials, tea cosies, imitation gargoyles. She finds her slow way back to West Street, her legs aching brutishly as if she has been poisoned. It is a bright cold night: a night for endings. When Marina comes back from whatever she was doing in that pub, Laura will take her somewhere, to an appropriate place for this sort of conversation. She will face their troubles, speak frankly, and sort everything out.

But at West Street stringent Founder's Day safety measures are in force. Without a Blue, whatever that is, she can't even enter the building, let alone retrieve her own child. She has no choice but to leave a short inarticulate note and wander off, deeper into Combe, where she does what anyone in her position would do. She sits on a cold wall under a dripping tree outside the Combe Conservative Association, with Peter and Marina and Alistair Sudgeon and now poor Zoltan, and weeps quietly for an hour.

Having only sat in the front of a car once or twice before, Marina is not an accomplished strapper-inner. Now she burns with a fierce hot humiliation. Maybe she shouldn't have tried to hide the open buckle under her arm, but he shouldn't have told her off like a child. And she is not drunk, hardly at all, just a little bit spinny. In fact, should he even be driving? It is very kind of him to offer her a lift to West Street but, she wants to reassure him, she's often walked back drunker than this on Saturday nights, everyone does. It isn't far.

She can't think of anything to say. She watches his hands on the steering wheel; she can see, despite the darkness, the flat wide fingernail, the muscle at the base of his thumb, the hair on the lower section of each finger and the backs of his hands. She wants to be in bed but, when he suggests the scenic route, where they could look down on Combe from a Roman bridge or something, she says, 'Yes.' Maybe it's being away from school but he seems funnier and cleverer with every passing minute. They feel like equals, or something close.

'Tell me about yourself,' he says, with a smile in his voice. 'What *interests* you, Marina?' and she starts to talk, not so much about her vestigial hobbies, the neglected fossils and star charts, the practically first edition of William Golding she found in a charity bookshop in Fulham Broadway, but about, for some reason, school. And he helps her, guiding her into deeper revelations as if he is strewing breadcrumbs, leading her through – presumably, out of – the woods. He is particularly understanding about how girls like Marina are coping with Combe life. She finds herself going into more detail than she had intended, as, she imagines, a woman confiding in a man friend might feel, if the friend was powerful and clever and had a silver car and hair on his forearms. It is enjoyable. It should not be, but there it is.

'And so there's a certain amount of . . . association?'

She glances sideways. Although he is driving fast he turns to grin at her, and it is quite a sexy feeling, knowing that this man, her friend, will tomorrow be standing in front of the entire school handing out prizes. He genuinely wants to know what she thinks. 'Er, yes. I think so. Yes.'

'And is that what you expected?'

'I—'

'I mean, before you arrived at Combe. Sex, of course. I'm sure I didn't need to tell you that.'

Once she would have been too tense, too virginal, to talk

like this but that has passed. 'Well, it's funny,' she says. 'But, well, I was quite . . . hopeful. I just didn't think that, that I—'

'What?'

'Well, I was at a girls' school. And I didn't know any, you know, boys. So the thought of—'

'Of coming here.'

'Yes. And, well, meeting some . . . I was ready to. If you know what I mean. I wanted to get, get going.'

'Go on.'

'No, that's it.'

'So,' he says, smiling, 'would you say most of the girls have boyfriends?'

'Well—'

'And, even apart from parks, and cinemas and what have you, the boys have study bedrooms?'

'Some of them. But—'

'Because one might think, if they do, the masters are being a little naïve.'

'How, how—'

'I expect they're at it like rabbits.'

When he says that she feels it all over her body; her skin seems to ruffle with excitement. Everything about this conversation is exciting; it is what she has dreamed of, over and over again.

'Forgive me, but it's true,' he says.

'It's not—'

'Oh, believe me, it is. I've been a seventeen-year-old boy,' he says. She bites her lip, looks at him quickly, puts her hand to her neck to cool down the spreading flush. 'And let me assure you, it would have taken a great deal more than a closed door and an incompetent headmaster—'

'But—'

'Don't interrupt. To have kept me from fulfilling my, well, baser urges. Of which I had many. Still have, in fact.'

There is too much here to comprehend. Marina sits in silence, staring out of the window. Then he stops the car. They are on a paved platform beside a big stone bridge, looking down on the twinkling lights and inky countryside of Blackmoor Vale. An urge to confess, to seek help, overwhelms her. 'I just didn't think that I, I'd get a chance.'

'Why not?'

'Well.' These are deeper waters than she had anticipated. She swallows hard but tears still spring to her eyes. 'I, I'm not, not the type that they want. The boys.'

'Oh?'

'It's true. I'm not, not blonde, or thin, or pretty.' She gulps audibly.

'Come now.'

'No, it's true.' And then, because she fears she has insulted his son, she says, 'I mean, Guy is lovely. But we don't have that much . . . I mean, he's younger than me, and I like books—'

'Oh, Marina, Marina. It was ever thus. Brainy girl meets hunky boy and, within about ten seconds, is disappointed.'

'Not dis—'

'May I be frank with you?'

'Oh,' she says excitedly. 'Yes. Please.'

'You will be so much happier when adult. You need experience, young Marina, and one day you will have it. I see you with someone older. Don't you?'

Where *is* Marina? This is getting ridiculous. Laura can hardly hang around the school until pub closing time, hoping to bump into her own child. It would look strange. Besides, what if those Vineys turn up again, that cocky son or his thin ethereal somehow old-seeming mother, like a dowager duchess in the body of a twenty-year-old? She has courageous impulses but not the courage to act upon them; at least, not yet.

Then something else occurs to her. For all these weeks Laura has pictured Marina painfully attentive in lessons, or standing on a staircase chatting to friends, as they do in the school prospectus. Until now, sex, hormones, the limitless urges of male adolescents, have rarely crossed her mind. But it is a boys' school, run by men – there does not seem to be a single prominent female teacher – with girls just parachuted in. For all its trumpeting about safety and maturity, does Combe know, or care, what goes on behind the study doors?

Surely anything could happen.

As if a slide has been snapped in place, she sees another image: Marina roaming free. She has given up her A levels without telling them, she has changed everything, lied, pick-pocketed probably, all under the uncertain influence of these awful Vineys. For, even if their unknown crime was decades ago, in Hungarian years it is recent. Forgiveness is out of the question. Laura has to warn Marina about the Viney family;

not just for the sake of Ildi and the others but for Marina too, who may be going wrong just as her mother did before.

Where is she? A little impulse murmurs: *find her*.

But Laura is tired, and familiar with unreliable impulses: pinches of fear on which she usually acts, making everything worse. Resist it, she tells herself. Be strong. Everything is bad enough already.

Besides, if she hurries back now to awful Braegarrold, she might find a pay phone on the way.

She is losing heart. Combe itself is vast and, as Founder's Day has ended for the most part and Marina will have been packed for days, she is not likely to hurry back to West Street, particularly if she is having fun, with friends. She could be. Wandering along Upper Garth Street, Laura assesses the Combe pupils, immediately identifiable among the local teenagers by their pink cheeks and raised voices. They look at her strangely; true Combe mothers are inconspicuous. Could her daughter ever be one of those laughing girls, tossing their curtains of hair?

There is simply no point in hanging round hoping to meet her by chance, she tells herself. Marina's perfectly fine; stop worrying. You might as well just go back to Braegarrold, and wait for morning.

Marina does not want to be rude. Mr Viney, call me Alexander, is just being kind and interested. Hasn't she longed for this? And it is, although it shouldn't be, exciting. It's just that she's not quite sure they ought to be having this conversation, far from school on a bridge, in a wood, at night.

For the first time it occurs to her that there are fields all around: no one in sight, or even earshot. She isn't frightened exactly; he is an adult, and she is actually quite an experienced young woman. Besides, hasn't she loved it so far: being seen in the pub by people who recognized him, talking to someone who is, at last, mature enough to understand her? She has imagined this, and more, when she is alone: so much more, some of it in this very car. Something in his voice tells her he understands.

With a click and a zipping sound he undoes his seatbelt and flings it back across his chest. He stretches his arms out. 'Free at last. You know,' he says, looking out over the lights. 'The odd thing is that I feel terribly youthful.'

'Yes?'

'Entirely. As young as you. If we were . . . If I were closer to your age, and all things were equal, which of course they're not—'

'So true,' says Marina wisely.

'I can imagine great things for us. Great things.'

'How, how do you mean?'

He turns to her: head, then shoulders. 'You in that little school shirt of yours, like a village maiden,' he says. The strangest thought pops into her head: somehow all this talking means that he is going to kiss me. Shouldn't I stop him? Those lips have kissed Mrs Viney. She thinks: I don't know what I want.

But it seems that Alexander Viney does.

37

Ildi's voice in the quiet night: 'Something bothers you?'

Laura gives a little jump. She has lain in her nylon bed, she thought silently, for hours, has rolled around and sighed and probably muttered to herself like a loon, thinking that Ildi was asleep.

'Oh God,' she says. 'Sorry. Did I— I woke you, didn't I?'

'No. I am awake.' Then Ildi says, 'So, it is worse than we think.'

'Sorry, what is?' says Laura tentatively, although of course she knows.

'You take from Marina the book?'

'You, you mean—'

'By the man. You take the book?'

'Well,' says Laura. 'I did try. I'm sorry. We, we argued. But anyway it seems . . . '

'Yes,' Ildi says. 'Well, now I tell you, and it will stop.'

Laura opens her mouth, then closes it. The silence booms. 'About the author? Alexander Viney?' she asks. 'But, you see . . . well, I think I understand.'

'I do not think,' says Ildi, firmly, 'that you do. Only we with Rozsi and Zsuzsi know some things about that family. Now I tell you, too.'

*

'Why not?'

Something has gone wrong. As Marina had feared, talking to Mr Viney has turned into being kissed. She did not mean this, at all. Or did she? Her body seems to feel differently. 'Sorry, I—'

'Why?'

'I'm shy,' she says, to salve his feelings.

'You're not shy! After what you told me, about you girls at school, who gets up to what. It's not exactly chaste, is it.'

'But I didn't . . . I hadn't . . . someone might see.'

'A passing farmer? Who cares? Haven't you heard of animal husbandry? Goes on all the time.'

So, imagining horses, she lets his hand stay on her tights leg, and the other up her blouse. His hand is cold, or her skin is burning, which is worse because then he will know that she is excited. Oddly, she preferred the talking before the kissing, when her two lives, real and imaginary, seemed to be merging like spots of coloured light. But now the tingling excitement in her brain and skin and so forth have been transformed into nervousness, which is ridiculous; he is a man, a father. A husband. Famous. Nothing bad could happen, whatever that means.

She feels she should remind him about Mrs Viney. But Mrs Viney is crushed between them, like the scar in *Thérèse Raquin*: under his fingertips, on his mouth.

'Come on,' he says, and bends over her again. It is interesting (they could discuss this, were he not preoccupied) how being desired, pressingly, urgently, had always been the greatest excitement she could invent, yet in real life it feels quite different: more frightening. Distantly she spies another gap in her knowledge. Is it possible that, for Mr Viney, kissing might not be an end to itself but, via some as yet unrevealed route, lead to sex?

'You silly little girl,' he says. 'Come here.'

But can he be stopped? It seems that she has accidentally given him permission, and she can't offend him by taking it back. When his hand slides up and then down into her tights, she gasps; she can't help it.

'Hello,' he says. 'Someone is pleased.'

'Please, I . . . hang on,' she says uncomfortably. She is expected to lift her bottom a little, to let him pull her knickers down to the top of her thighs; she averts her eyes from the sight. Her breathing is jerky. 'I'm not sure . . .'

'Don't be coy,' he says. 'I know what I know.'

'No,' she says. 'But—'

'You've just been telling me,' he says, 'about your constant visits to the New Street—'

'West Street.'

'Wherever, the girls' bathroom. Unmitigated filth. You can't deny your intentions, surely.'

'What intentions?'

Together they look down at his corduroy lap: trousers in unexpectedly new navy needlecord, in which there is a definite bulge. He's right. It is completely her fault. And isn't it the greatest compliment: a bodily reaction to, presumably, her beauty, her intelligence, her sensitivity? It confirms her; she is viable.

Gingerly she puts her hand there, in homage to the

honour it has done her, but she cannot help starting away almost immediately when his big hand approaches her skirt once more.

This time he ignores her reaction completely. Her face is being squashed into her seatbelt, which is still done up; it crosses her chest between her breasts, pushing one towards him. It is like being murdered; he is looming over her, pressed against her leg, and the susurrations of the moving corduroy and the thickness of his breathing as his fingers push in and up . . . she bites the inside of her lip. It hurts, and she is frightened, and suddenly very very sorry that she made him feel this way.

'Come *on*,' he says in a clotted voice. He is fumbling at his lap, but she pretends to them both not to notice; she moves her bare legs infinitesimally closer together and looks out of the window, into the darkness. 'Christ,' he says. 'Move over, can't you?'

'I'm a bit . . . wedged,' she says.

Then she feels it against her leg, like a dog's nose; hot and faintly sticky. There is that hot smell again, like, like . . . She catches her breath; she closes her eyes and a tear rolls beneath her eyelashes and splashes off her nose.

'Sorry,' she says.

'For God's sake!' he says. 'What is it now?'

'I'm sorry.'

'What?'

'I can't.'

'What do you mean? What the hell do you think you're doing?'

'Nothing.' She thinks: if he's expecting it, I probably have to let him. But he looks disgusted. 'I just—'

'Christ,' he says. 'Don't cry *now*.'

There is a pause. She keeps her eyes closed. Then she hears him exhale sharply, angrily, and a rustling sound as he tucks it into his trousers. He throws himself back in the seat. She keeps herself rigid, closed up like a seashell, until his breathing has slowed. 'Sorry,' she says again. 'I . . . I didn't realize—'

'Now you do,' he snaps, and starts the car.

38

Thursday, 16 March

Founder's Day Week

10 a.m. Combined Cadet Force display, Memorial Quad, free

11 a.m. Champagne reception, to the foot-tapping sounds of Mr Daventry's Barber Shop Quartet – Founder's Court marquee, free

12 a.m. Prize-Giving featuring Tim Pirrey, Commonwealth champion rower and OC, Divinity Hall, free

On Thursday morning, the climax of Founder's Day, Rozsi and Ildi and Zsuzsi and Laura sit at breakfast in Braegarrold, ingesting mixed-fruit jam and battery eggs. Their bags are packed; Mrs Cousins had already stripped the beds, revealing mattresses which might have been better hidden. In the gap between the historical pageant and the pre-Prize-Giving champagne reception, Laura will be alone with Marina. It is all going to have to come out.

So, while the others discuss their charming hosts in

Hungarian and silently rock with laughter, Laura tries to prepare her material.

One: the best friend, Tibor Szőllőssy, essentially robbed Zoltan of everything: the estate, his former girlfriend, his father's love, all of it. This is the story Peter told her, now, with Ildi's accent and place names, given flesh.

Two: but Zoltan forgave him. At least, he carried on seeing Tibor Szőllőssy, and the divorced-woman-now-wife, once they reached England. But why? The Farkases and Károlyis are not like that; they will strike someone from their lives for a funny look outside a newsagent. It makes no sense.

Wait. Didn't someone, Peter maybe, say that the divorced woman, who was poor Zoltan's girlfriend, and then Tibor's, also knew Rozsi? That she was a college friend, a fellow girl-undergraduate pioneer? Might this be the reason?

Three: in any case, Tibor's son then robbed Zoltan in the mid-Seventies in London; at least, as she understood it from Ildi, he asked to borrow a huge sum of money which, as a fellow countryman of Tibor, honourable Zoltan naturally let him have. And then he failed to repay it, which somehow led to the downfall of Femina, and its sale to Mrs Dobos.

Four: and to Zoltan's death? Can that be right?

Five: Tibor Szőllőssy's son is . . . hang on.

Can Tibor Szőllőssy's son really be that historian? Marina's boyfriend's father: is that who they mean? It seems so unlikely; they must have made a mistake.

Or could the Vineys have planned this all along?

Marina has already told her that Guy's parents live quite close to Combe, near Salisbury just over the Wiltshire border.

It's not so odd if they sent their bloody son to a school like Combe. Combe is the sort of school that kind of person likes. If anything, it is odder that the Farkases sent Marina.

Laura pokes at her watery bacon. Why did we?

Into her mind comes the voice of Mrs Dobos, recommender of Combe. Mrs Dobos will know all the answers; Mrs Dobos who bought Femina . . . hang on. Laura looks up cautiously, to find that Rozsi is looking at her, shaking her head.

'You are not listening one little bit,' says Rozsi. 'But today we leave you with Marinaka, so you wake up now. We, with Ildi and Zsuzsi, leave you in charge.'

Ten past eight, and Marina has not gone to breakfast. She has never broken a school rule like this before; there will be such trouble if she is discovered up here, in the West Street second-floor bathroom, scrubbing at her thighs with a flannel and groaning with self-disgust.

Last night she lay awake until the dawn chorus, listening to seagulls or vultures squawking their mating songs, reminding herself that Mr Viney had done her a great honour and trying not to think of the seatbelt or the car on the bridge, the press of his corduroy. Curiously, although her body feels terrible, her mind, hanging high above thought and feeling, is alert. Her thoughts move in slow motion but with clarity: I made him feel bad. It wasn't *rape*. Maybe I should have done what he expected: an older, a distinguished man. He'd have been gentle. No one will ever volunteer to do that for me again.

Now he never will. Thanks to her frigidity, she was not deflowered. Instead she had stared out of her window while he reversed quickly back along the bridge and then, frowning, drove out to the hill road down to Combe and Melcombe.

'I, I love the country,' she'd said. 'The way the trees, you know, arch over the . . . it's one of my favourite things.'

'How original.'

'What do you mean?'

'Never mind. I'll take you straight back. Kindly keep this to yourself, though. More for your sake than mine.'

'Yes. I mean no. Thanks, thank you.'

He had given a little snort. She wanted to lighten the mood, like a good hostess; make him forget his humiliation and disappointment. To think that she could move a grown man's trousers so. 'Sorry about, er, you know.' There was a pain in her throat. 'Will you be OK? I mean, without . . . relief?'

He ignored her.

She thought of penises, engorged past the point of recovery; alarming stories told in West Street, after dark. She bit her dry lips. 'Your . . . interest. I'm very, well, it's lovely of you. But won't you—'

He turned his head and looked at her. 'I expect I'll get over it,' he'd said.

One day, Laura has always hoped, she will have to punch someone for her daughter. It would be more satisfying to have to lift a bus to save her, or sacrifice a limb, but physical violence would be better than nothing: a way to express the white heat of motherhood, the helpless rage.

Standing now at the War Memorial in the drizzle, watching Combe's young soldiers stamping and shouting and waving presumably plastic bayonets, she can imagine herself grabbing a weapon from a boy and running riot. How dare that man, that family, take advantage of Marina's ignorance? Poor Zoltan cheated, denied of his inheritance and then, and then—

She looks at her daughter, just as Marina turns and stares back. She seems very flushed: tonsillitis, probably, which would explain her oddness yesterday. Maybe the only wise thing I've done so far, she thinks, was not to have told Peter that the Viney son, grandson, is at Combe. I may have made my life as complicated and unmanageable as possible by failing to tell anyone that Pete is alive, but at least he won't be blundering onto the lawn at Combe, drunk and shaven-headed, to accuse the Viney father of embezzlement.

Isn't that Marina's housemaster, bellowing at the little boys? I can't ask Marina about last night, Laura decides; she's barely speaking today. Must I tell her off about going to the pub? I suppose I should, and at least then I can stop wondering who those people at the Crown and Mitre with her were, the man who was standing up, facing the window. He could be any respectable adult – a teacher, a parent – but, still, should Marina have been there, unsupervised, with him?

She tells herself this, but she knows the truth.

*

The last quill-waving Elizabethan poet and bowing courtier and merrie minstrel have passed. The historical pageantry is over, at least for this year. Marina has taken two Pro Plus, which was a mistake on top of instant coffee. Her brain feels tangled up in an enormous knot; her heart is fluttering but the rest of her is still half asleep. Everyone at school now will have heard her family's accents, and seen their shabby suitcases propped beside them while the CCF marched past. When she comes back next term she might have a nickname, a horrible one.

She thinks: how can I come back?

Except of course she can, and will; she has had that thought countless times since starting at Combe, yet here she is, still a coward. Everyone is congregating on the Founder's Lawn, although the champagne reception isn't for a couple of hours, and then it will be Prize-Giving, with A Special Guest. All this time she has not let herself look at Mrs Viney, who is frankly beautiful in a greenish suit with a long straight skirt, but she can resist no longer. Everything about her, her hair, her skin, her figure, her smile, makes Marina want to cry. She should catch Mrs Viney's eye, give her a wave or a smile before she drives off to Stoker, but Mrs Viney does not look at her once.

So Marina kisses Rozsi and the others goodbye; she tells them that she has to go and talk to a master, which even her mother believes. Her legs feel stiff; her bottom lip is trembling. Off she goes.

*

Laura, at the first possible moment, is going to do something about those Vineys. But what? She needs guidance, but no one can give it other than her mother-in-law and the aunts, whom she is escorting towards Garthgate and last night's taxi rank. How can it be so difficult to ask any of them what happened? Laura's mother liked nothing more than an ailment or a crisis, but the in-laws' refusal to discuss painful matters has grown upon Laura like a shell. Upsetting poor Ildi still further, even approaching Rozsi, whom she is hurting so much already, would feel like a criminal act.

'*Dar*-link' she hears behind her and obediently she turns. She is already carrying both big suitcases, but now Zsuzsi is standing in the middle of the pavement, oblivious to passers-by, holding out her handbag for her niece-in-law to take.

'It is *ri*-diculos,' says Zsuzsi. 'I do not lift. I am old lady.' Rozsi and Ildi, crossing Upper Garth Street arm in arm, are talking, their old heads close together. She sees Rozsi shrug. This morning, with her sunglasses and lipstick, Zsuzsi is wearing a short silver-fox jacket borrowed from Perlmutter Sári, her black '*sol*-opette-troo-sair, *vair*-y smart', a silky blooze in silver and black, silver wedge-heeled sling-backs and a great gold 'necklet' like a medal. Her perfume is stunningly powerful. Instead of taking her bag, Laura puts a hand on her arm.

'I need to ask you something,' she says.

39

Marina is tearing in half a term's worth of artistic post-cards. She can't bring them home to Westminster Court, with Combe's polluting address upon them; nor can she throw out all these sweet family messages. This seems the logical solution. What should she do with her uniform? It feels like folding up plague-infested cloth to bring into the flat. She is behind schedule already. West Street girls are supposed to have finished packing last night.

She is just watching Heidi lock her vanity case when someone knocks on the door.

'Hello, Hel, Heidi. Heidi. Marina sweetheart,' says her mother. 'What are you doing?'

'What are *you*?' says Marina. 'You're meant to wait outside. I said. Will we manage all my stuff?' She is sounding unwelcoming; she is past the point of self-control.

'Lovely to see you, Mrs Farkas,' says Heidi, the creep. She starts saying things like 'Could you possibly tell me if my valise is going to close?' and 'I don't know how to get the Blu-Tack off'.

Marina waits for Heidi to go, unable even to look at her any longer. She needs to start touching home-related objects. Her hands twitch with the effort of keeping them to her sides. She pretends to be straightening her mattress; it looks like a hospital bed after somebody has died.

'I must dash,' Heidi says at last. 'My father's here. I heard his Jag pull up.'

Now they are alone, looking at each other. There is a strange warm heavy silence.

Marina says, 'Actually I don't feel very well.'

Her mother sits down on the edge of the mattress of death. She says, 'I need to talk to you,' and Marina falls to the floor.

Laura thinks: she's dead. I have to die.

Then Marina blinks. 'What happened?' She sits up. 'Am I all right?'

'Oh, thank God, I don't know. What did happen? I think you fainted, my poor love. Do you feel bad?'

'Did I?' says Marina. 'Really?'

'Are you feeling sick at all?'

'No. Actually, yes. Well, a bit weird.'

'Look, sit, no, like this, your head . . . that's right.'

'Like in a book,' says Marina, muffled, but it sounds as if she is smiling.

'Haven't you fainted before? I should know that, if you have, but—'

'Never. I'm just tired,' and, briefly, she leans her forehead like a pet against Laura's upper arm. Laura stiffens. Her desire to seize Marina and hold her is so strong but she has learned this, at least, from motherhood: do not react to love, or it will go.

'Are you sure?' she asks in an unnatural voice.

'Sure.' Marina takes her head away, gives a little smile,

brushes her hair from her face. Then she says: 'Mum, I need to— Look. There's a thing.'

So this is it, thinks Laura with the benefit of foresight: she has found out about Peter. I have to confess everything and then we will be permanently estranged.

Tell her, says what remains of her conscience.

Where should she begin? She can't just come out with: 'Your father is alive but maybe not for long and is sorry and wants to see you and by the way I want him all over again.'

'Look, Mum . . .'

But, if she tells Marina, in the crying and blaming which will follow the story about the grandparents, and Mr Viney, will be lost. Isn't that more urgent? What if they bump into each other and have a hideous two-family brawl on bloody Garthgate? Prioritize, Laura tells herself, but she is scared to. She knows that she must tell the old story first but not how to make herself say the words.

'Sweetheart,' she says quietly, 'just let me . . . I need to think.' She grips her left hand with her right: go on, she urges herself, viciously.

'Mum— Mummy. Mum. I—'

And what happens if—

'*Mum.*'

Marina is looking at her: her dear pale face. 'I have something to tell you,' Laura says bravely.

'No,' says Marina. 'There's something I've got to tell *you.*'

Two seconds before, Marina swore herself to secrecy. But Mr Viney keeps bursting into her brain; she hadn't meant to say anything, but now she has begun. This is a desperate situation. Her mother looks worried. What if, thinks Marina, I tell her and she goes on the rampage? Shouts at Mr Viney? *Mrs* Viney? Oh God.

She clears her throat. 'Look, will you concentrate? It's really important. I . . . I can't deal with it by myself. I need you.'

'I'm listening,' says her mother.

'I did a mad thing.'

'How mad? Oh Christ. Marina, not now.'

'What do you mean?'

'What have you done? Hell, no, no, don't cry, my . . . don't use your sleeve, love, hang on, there's one in my bag. But tell me quickly, you know I hate—'

'I . . . I can't be a doctor any more.'

'What? Of course you can.'

Now she has started down the wrong route, how can she go back? 'I . . . I really can't.'

'Why?'

'I can't say.'

'Marina. Don't be silly. Say.'

'I, I dropped chemistry. For history.'

'Hang on,' says her mother. 'I don't . . . you . . . sorry, what?'

'I know,' Marina says, blowing her nose. 'It makes no sense.'

'But how did you, what did you—'

'It was so awful, not telling you. Don't be cross.'

'I'm not cross,' her mother says. 'But . . . I'm completely confused. You can't have. Why?'

'I don't even . . . it's complicated,' Marina says. Then she thinks of something which may help. 'OK. You know that family I know? The, the Vineys?'

'What?'

'Guy's, you know, Guy, my boyfriend, Guy?'

'What about them?'

'It was his father. No, don't be— honestly. He's an expert. He advised me. And I don't even want to go to Cambridge any more. Don't look like that. Please, Mum. Honestly, he's . . .' She has practised this speech so often; never mind that it is nonsense since last night. 'I just want you to understand—'

Her mother reaches out her hand. She takes hold of Marina's shoulder and gives it a little shake.

'Darling,' she says. 'There's something I need you to know.'

Of course Laura has to tell her. The Farkases are right; there are things children should never be told, but an emergency seems to be slowly unfurling. So she tries.

And, naturally, fails. Is this because she is distracted by Peter, or because she is a bad mother? At first Marina is only interested in defending the Viney family: their refinement, their style, their elegance. The way that they never drop their t's.

'*I* don't,' says Laura. 'Do I?'

'All the time,' says Marina crossly. 'I'm always trying to s— to help you remember. People would take you more seriously.'

With a supermaternal effort, Laura manages not to smite her child. She merely says, 'Sweetheart, you've misunderstood. It's because of your grandfather. It's what they did to him.'

Marina looks blank. She knows nothing about this. Laura explains what she can: something financial, not once but twice, to do with the Viney grandparents' business—

'Oh, that's Aston,' Marina says airily. 'They're Aston. They told me. Have you heard of them, they're very—'

'That's the one,' Laura says. 'So you knew all along. I can't get over the idea that good old English Aston, all that Argyle check and leather at Harrods—'

'Oh my God. So did we own it?'

'No. No. We'd hardly . . . anyway, no. Actually, I'm not sure.'

Laboriously she explains what she can about the stolen estate, the friends, a tangle of disloyalty half a century ago, among cornfields and silver birches none of them will ever see. 'I think,' she says, 'because they carried on being friends, even once they'd taken over Zoltan's father's estate and turned it into Aston, you know, made it this famous English name, they needed money again, at some point. In the Seventies.'

'When I was alive?'

In her distress Marina is polishing and polishing her glasses. Laura thinks: I could tell her right now how much her contact-lens losing has cost us. No, of course I can't. Poor child. 'Yes,' she says. 'Very small, but yes.'

'Guy's grandparents, this is?'

'Well, yes. His father too; that's the problem. I think

Zoltan, well, he lent them quite a chunk of money. Not that we want you to worry about money, my love, we're fine, really. Fine. But Femina was doing well, in those days, and they were old friends, and . . .'

'But,' says Marina, '*why* would they carry on being friends, after—'

'I know. I thought that. But, well, it was because of Rozsi. The Viney grandmother, Mag— *Mog*-dolna, Peggy, the founder of Aston, was—'

'English?'

'*No*. She was Rozsi's best friend. So there were best friends, Zoltan and Tibor, hanging out at ski lodges together or something, and they each married woman friends, Rozsi and Mrs . . . this Magdolna. I asked Zsuzsi about this, you see, and she said, "Rozsi loved her," and I said, "Why?" and she said, "Because she was beautiful."'

Marina is frowning. 'Are you sure?'

'I know. But yes. Oh, and hang on, the Vineys were something else then, Sol, Szos . . . Doesn't matter. And something went wrong.'

'What went wrong?'

'Szoll . . . something. I think. She didn't say. Maybe one of Zoltan's brothers—'

'He didn't have any brothers.'

'Yes he did.'

'No he . . . they've never even mentioned them. Oh,' says Marina. 'Oh, God, I see. So when did they— how many?'

'Three, I think. Never mind. Don't think about it now. Anyway, the point is that they, the Vineys, I think, they didn't pay the money back. And so, well, it went wrong for Femina. And . . . and so Mrs Dobos took it over. She was connected too. To all of it, I think. She knew everyone.' She should say about Zoltan's death, the timing, the odd silence; no, not now. Marina looks washed out.

'Hang on,' she says feebly. 'Were they all cousins too?'

'Probably not. No. I think Zsuzsi would have said.'

'Try to remember.' She sits up. 'Oh no. It would mean that we, or I, am related to the Vineys. Wouldn't it?'

'Does it matter, darling?'

Marina looks at her lap. 'Well. Yes.'

'Oh. Oh. I see.'

Together they consider this. When they recover, Marina says, 'I just can't believe it. They insulted my family—'

'Sweetheart,' says her mother, 'it's not . . . it's not about honour. Is it?'

Marina just waves her hand. Only now Laura notices that her eyelids are heavy; she is sitting up but half asleep, like a little child. What did happen last night? When did she go to bed?

Adult life requires the capacity either to endure, or to leap, ask the difficult question, face certain pain. Laura can do neither. So she hesitates.

'I just,' says Marina, curling her legs up on the mattress, 'want to have a little rest.'

'Hang on,' Laura says. 'Wait a minute.' She hurries into the corridor; most of the bedroom doors are open, their contents removed, but she finds a bathroom, a few mean little hand towels over an icy radiator, and she brings them in. 'Sit up,' she says, arranging the towels on the mattress. 'Lie down,' and Marina lies. 'Are you really all right?' Laura asks, covering her daughter's legs with her own coat. This is very strange. She might be concussed. 'We could find a doctor—'

But Marina's eyes are closed.

Poets, male ones, have written about watching children sleep. They have no idea; it is not love you feel, but pain. As she watches her daughter, Laura's heart tightens with the thought of future grief. She could gaze at the curve of her cheek and the length of her lashes for ever but she cannot keep her mind from horror: childhood illness; fevers; death. Bloody Auden.

So she creeps downstairs, a ten pence stolen from her daughter's desk hot in her hand and, although Peter doesn't answer Suze's phone, in fact nobody does, she has the conversation she wants to have with him in her head.

Is the Zoltan mess, the Viney mess, the great dragging weight of ancient rivalries and expectation and grudges, the reason that you left?

And: I love you.

And: Pete, my period is late.

40

When Laura and Marina walk out of West Street a little later, past the Memorial Quad and Garthgate and into Founder's Court, the sun is shining. The old walls of the ruins and the abbey glitter wetly; all the crumbling cement, every patch of lichen, is illuminated, as if for a filmset. There must be birdsong but you cannot hear it over the sound of Combe parents' revelry. All creeping things, the squirrels and mice and the rats in the kitchen bins, have hidden themselves away.

An immense marquee, with vestibule and medieval-style scalloping, dominates the lawn. The masters are all in gowns, their hoods proudly displayed: from the snowy rabbit fur of Pa Willey, Latin ('an exceptionally brilliant junior fellow,' Dr Tree murmurs to the parents, 'of King's College, Oxford, who has changed direction, fortunately for us! Ha ha ha!') to the turquoise satin of Pa 'Fletch' Fletcher, PE (Loughborough, no Honours taken).

Pa Daventry's Barber Shop Quartet has already moved on from 'Chattanooga Choo Choo' to a medley of songs of yesteryear. As Laura and Marina enter the hot grassy shade of the marquee, huge pink-cheeked boys in striped blazers and boaters begin to sing 'Daisy, Daisy' suggestively to the headmaster's wife, who is perching on a wobbling Raleigh Caprice amid the hay bales.

'Champagne?' asks a tall fat young man with a pierced ear, holding a bottle; its label has been covered with a large sticker bearing the Combe coat of arms. Marina holds out her glass.

'I'm seventeen. We're allowed,' she tells her mother and Laura nods gamely. 'That was one of the groundsmen,' Marina whispers when he has gone. 'He's weird.'

Shouldn't the feeling of not knowing anyone, and thinking that everybody else does, have faded by the time one is a parent? Laura finds she recognizes no one whatsoever. At first Marina sticks to Laura's side; she seems to be guiding her towards the back of the marquee, where a group of older earnest-looking boys are talking to Pa Bayham, head of music. Then she stops dead.

'They're there,' she says.

'Who?'

'You know. No! Don't look.'

It is too late. Laura has turned. In the middle of a cluster of parents stand the Vineys: no sign of the mother but there is Guy and a haughty-looking girl and, with his arms around them, Alexander Viney himself.

Only last weekend, on leafing through *The Times*, she had wondered how it would feel to be the person who spots a former war criminal, living it up in a café in Belgrade or Buenos Aires. Alexander Viney is talking, laughing, as if he has nothing to do with suffering except the historical kind: that of miscellaneous peasants, or men at sea. Laura thinks: what on earth should I do?

'You know what Rozsi would do,' she hears Marina say

beside her. 'Walk up to them and whack them. Him, anyway. You know she once hit a policeman.'

Marina's glass has mysteriously already been refilled, but Laura is too distracted to say anything about it. 'Yes,' she says tiredly. 'I know that story.'

'But we can't.'

'No, we can't.'

Then, in a small sad voice, Marina says, 'I want to.'

Laura looks down at her. She has asked nothing about poor Zoltan's death, but might she have guessed?

'What?' she says. 'Tell me. What?'

'It's OK.'

'What do you mean? I can see it's not. You look— what is it, my love?'

'Too many revelations. I can't cope with more.'

'Neither can I,' her mother says, 'but, my darling, if something has happened . . .'

'No,' says Marina. 'It hasn't. Really, nothing. Never mind.'

And that might have been it. Marina could have stopped drinking, and she and Laura could have sat through Prize-Giving, and then they could have gone home.

'Hi,' says Hannah North from West Street as if, although she is an Upper, they are old friends. She's my height too, thinks Marina, unlike all those other giants, and not even very thin.

'I've lost my rellies,' Hannah says. 'Where are yours?'

Marina's mother, making elaborate 'I won't disturb you' gestures, starts wandering off towards the parents' toilets.

'Around,' says Marina, looking over Hannah's shoulder for Simon Flowers's family.

'Not the old ladies?'

'What?' says Marina, frowning at her. 'So you know about them?'

'It's not . . . don't look like that. Mine are Irish, my father anyway, so Daventry calls me the Publican's Child. Hilarious.'

'That's terrible. That's . . . racist. God. Don't you mind?'

'Used to it. Look, there's a bottle going round. Grab it.'

Giles Yeo has his hand on Victoria Porritt's lower back; they are chatting to his red-faced father like adults at a cocktail party. 'How long does this last?' asks Marina.

Hannah North moves her face closer as she pours.

'Are you OK?' she says.

'Why?'

'You're not, are you?'

'Why?'

'It's obvious. Always is with you. You look all . . . frozen.'

'No, I don't.' Marina's sinuses are stinging. Shut up, she tells herself. 'I'm fine.'

'You're homesick, aren't you? I could tell you are. I was, I used to vomit. I thought you were, since you arrived. It's obvious. You could have come to me.'

'How? How could I know?'

'Well . . .' says Hannah North vaguely.

'You can't say that now. It's too late.'

'Don't be melodramatic. Anyway, are you going to tell

me what's happened? You look even more miserable than normal. Something's got to be up.'

Why not? thinks Marina suddenly. She leaves out some of the details but she tells her the rest: sitting in the front seat of a nameless friend's father's big silver car, being . . . being . . .

'Oh God,' says Hannah North, but resignedly, almost casually, as if it happens all the time. Marina rests her head against the marquee post behind her. 'Not everything?'

'No!' says Marina. 'No. Definitely not. But a lot. And the thing is—'

'It was unfamiliar,' says Hannah North, after a pause.

'Yes. No. Yes.' She closes her eyes again and tries to explain how what happened in the car is her fault. 'I mean, it's not the olden days. I, I shouldn't mind, I know I shouldn't. Really it was my fault. In fact, I've thought that maybe I should apologize— I can't believe I'm telling you all this. Don't you have, you know, people to see?'

'Yes. But, look—'

'Well you should.'

'But, poor you.'

'Don't be mad.' She tips her head back: don't sodding cry.

'I mean it. Of course poor you, you dope.'

'The thing is,' says Marina in a rush, 'I know it's stupid, but I just don't know what I should be thinking. How, how to feel.'

'Angry.'

'That's ridiculous.' And just like that, Marina's embryonic liking for Hannah North evaporates.

Because Hannah North is wrong. Marina listens to Pa Daventry's boys singing 'Goodbye, My Coney Island Baby', tapping her foot awkwardly just out of time to the music; she shakes her head when her mother, back from the loo, asks if she wants orange juice. Instead she marches up to Bill Wallis in his novelty shirt sleeves, who has commandeered two bottles just for his family; she holds out her glass. Angry? What rubbish. Hannah North, although older, just doesn't understand.

Ten minutes later, during 'Wedding Bells Are Breaking Up That Old Gang of Mine', it hits her. Hannah North is right.

After that, it is as if she is being powered by fury, at all of them. Vengeance, she thinks, with expansive mental hand gestures, will be mine. Ours. Should be. How dare you? she imagines saying to Alexander Viney, pushing him off her. How dare you?

She is possibly a bit drunk now, but everyone is: except, obviously, her mother, which would be disgusting.

'There aren't any sandwiches here or anything, are there?' her mother says, though anyone could hear her.

'No,' says Marina. 'Of course not. We're not meant—'

'Come on, love.' Her mother gives her a look. 'We could go over the road quickly and get you something to eat.'

'We can't leave,' says Marina impatiently. 'It's not allowed.' I *am* so angry, she thinks experimentally but already the guilt is bubbling through to the surface. She needs Hannah North to tell her again what to feel.

'Anyway, soon it's the, the . . . you know.'

'Prize-Giving.'

'Yes,' says Marina quietly. 'I hate him.'

'I know,' says her mother. 'So do I.'

Where is Alexander Viney now? Mrs Viney has gone back to Stoker and her herb garden. Guy catches Marina's eye and mouths something unreadable but she doesn't care, not if she never sees him again, because now when she looks at his father, the giver of prizes, the jewel in Dr Tree's crown, she feels sick. What was he doing, driving her half-drunk to a bridge? He is a married man. Mrs Viney should have stopped him. She thinks confusedly of feet of clay, of statues on columns, of, primarily, the bulge in his too-new needlecord trousers: the lap not of a gentleman but a pretender. 'I don't want to go to the stupid Prize-Giving,' she says.

'Don't be silly, sweetheart. We just have to sit there, and then it's home. Lovely home. You need a rest.'

Marina bites her lip: so sore that it makes her wince. She is wearing ten separate items of Combe uniform, including shoes, ceinture and hairband but leaving out her watch. She sees now that what happened with Mr Viney, in this very uniform, has intensified the contamination: the danger to her family, the betrayal. Even apart from her stupid hugging of them all this morning, isn't her mother being infected right now, inhabiting the same cuboid of air? And then it will be concentrated by the treacherous act of sitting in Divvers, listening, clapping when he gives his spontaneous amazing Prize-Giving speech.

The very thought makes her feel sicker. After all that her

brave family has done for her, this is how Marina will repay them: by bringing everything Mr Viney stands for straight back to Westminster Court.

There is no time to plan. Pa Daventry is at the marquee flap, summoning them all and, although it seems fantastically important that they should be early, to choose the best seats, somehow Marina and her mother hesitate until they are trapped at the back, and reach Divvers last.

41

Marina, her mother has realized, is possibly slightly drunk. So is Laura; her capacity is pitiful. As a Non-Prizewinning Pupil + Parent (1), they are supposed to sit in the body of the hall but, by the time they fight their way in, there are apparently no seats left anywhere.

'What about those?' she says to Marina, nodding at a row of chairs on a long thin platform, running along the right-hand wall. They seem less popular; despite being up a couple of steps, their view is partially blocked by the maroon barley-sugar columns which feature repeatedly in the prospectus. Because of this, presumably, several seats are left.

'We can't,' says Marina. 'They're for Sirs.'

'What? Well, we can today, other people are sitting there. I think the teachers, er, Sirs, prefects anyway, they're all on the stage. And look, there's a couple left near the front.'

If you sit forward you can see quite well around your column: not, as Laura had assumed, ugly marble but merely plaster, painted an unpleasant chicken-liver colour with darker menstrual clots. Or, rather, you can see the audience; not most of the staff nor, thankfully, Alexander Viney himself, who must be beside the headmaster on the stage. Laura rests her forearms on the low rail which divides them from the rest of the school; she resists the urge to lean her forehead on it too, just in time. Marina is protesting about sitting up here; frankly, enough is enough. Laura has a headache and several enormous problems, and it would be good just to rest here quietly, thinking, before they have to catch the train. Alexander Viney may be a bad person but he's still an intellectual, prize-winning, televised, and poor Zoltan is dead. They will just listen to him, clap politely, and leave.

Marina looks out across the audience. Sitting up here, raised only slightly but at right angles to the other rows, against the grain, is like watching television. She has nothing to do with these people. Her ceinture is hurting and her heart feels tight; she can't see Guy, or Simon Flowers, or anyone she cares about at all. Even Mr Viney is out of sight, although soon he will begin his speech. The Prize-Giving is scheduled to start in six minutes, and Dr Tree is very keen on promptness. She feels suddenly rather sick.

Thanks to her Divvers adventures with Guy, she knows that at the end of this platform there is a way into the backstage area, near a little toilet. 'I'll be quick,' she says.

Her mind is moving sluggishly; even her blinks feel slow. She sits down on the toilet seat and has the brilliant idea of removing her tights to allow cool air on her skin, then her ceinture. She is still too hot; she can hear her pulse in the quiet, and another sound, like roaring water. Swiftly, with the expertise of a reluctant room-sharer, she unhooks her bra beneath her blouse, unbuttons the blouse itself and pulls both elastic and cotton out through the head-hole of her voluminous black V-neck. The clothes sit in her hands like entrails; she is panting slightly. She thinks: if I get rid of them now, they can't infect. Her bare feet are resting on her slip-ons. She pulls off her knickers, holds her breath, removes the cover for the sanitary-towel disposal unit to stuff her underwear and blouse inside, and shoves the lid back on.

Then, gingerly, she stands. It is so much cooler in only her jumper and skirt; why do people not, she wonders distantly, as if contemplating the ways of mortals from above, dress like this all the time? She can barely hear her feet on the dusty steps back through the wings, so great is the roar of Combe bonhomie. She gives her mother a smile and sits back down beside her.

'Were you sick?'

'No,' says Marina, scandalized. 'Of course not. Actually I'd quite like another drink! Are you shocked?'

'Well, no,' says her mother, although clearly she is. 'I don't think we should be staggering round drunk just yet, though,' she says. 'We don't want to burn *all* our bridges.'

'What do you mean?'

Dr Tree is standing. 'Shh,' says her mother. 'It's about to start.'

During the headmaster's speech, Laura quite suddenly makes her decision. She will bring Marina home and, when they are all sitting nicely in the living room at Westminster Court, she will tell them everything she knows, the good and the bad. Love is pain; there is no point pretending otherwise, or trying to protect anyone any longer. I have been mad, she thinks, trapped in a teenage bubble of misery and now I am going to be a grown-up. Definitely.

When Alexander Viney takes the stage, she bravely resists clapping. Until now she has only seen glimpses of him, the sleeve of his suit, his clever aggressive profile, and there is a thrill, undeniably, in being so close to a famous man. Do you know, Laura asks him silently, that because of whatever you did, not a dramatic wartime betrayal but a grubby act of dishonesty, a business was lost? A good man gave up on life. Would you care?

If she tells Peter, he will go after him, probably drunk, certainly reckless, and be sued, or end up in prison. What would be the good in that?

Marina is trying not to listen to Mr Viney. Her skin feels cold under the lambswool; her body is ashamed. It is not only what he did but the fact that she is still sitting here which proves her rubbishness. If she were as brave as Rozsi, wouldn't she do something for poor Zoltan's sake?

After the speech, she thinks, I could go up and hit him. She clenches her fist and inspects the muscles: indelicate, yet puny. No use to anyone. Still: I ought to kill him, if I have the chance.

The audience is tilting at an interesting angle. Observing this, she notices in passing that Giles Yeo, quite close by at the end of a row, is smiling at her. She glances away, then back; he hasn't looked away. Giles Yeo, who ignores her. He is only one away from Bill Wallis; he taps him on the arm and whispers in his ear, and then they both stare at Marina, grinning. Smirking. What has she done? Tentatively, she smiles back. She pats her lap. Reflexively, she feels to make sure that the buttons of her school blouse have not come open.

Then she looks down.

At the V of her jumper, where her collar and one or two buttons are usually visible, is skin: an expanse of skin. Thanks to her brilliant blouse-removal decision, the lambswool has slipped, unobstructed by cotton. The V is enormous. Most of both of her breasts are on display.

Her heart forgets to beat.

Then it starts again. She is still alive, unfortunately. Half-naked. Laughed at. She pulls up the V and plucks at her back and collar as if she is being bitten. An inch of cleavage still remains. She crosses her arms, holds her shoulders; she can't catch her breath. Her mother hasn't even noticed. Think, you stupid fuck, think. But her brain won't move. All that works is her eyes: faces of people she doesn't know turning to look at her and, worse, Bill Wallis, Giles Yeo, all their friends and cronies. So she takes off her glasses; they are useless anyway when you cry. Now she can't see but she can still feel them, their delight. Alexander Viney talks on and on.

Marina stands.

'What are you doing?' whispers her mother. 'Don't—'

Marina closes her ears. Not at all cautiously, welcoming the pain that chair legs and railings will cause her, she starts to hurry along the platform, down the long length of Divinity Hall. She is gripping the wool of her jumper collar to conceal her flesh, like an effigy with its wrists crossed on its chest, yet people will still be looking at her, and laughing. She can hear whispering, although Mr Viney's voice keeps on.

Someone grabs her arm. She pulls away, stretching the sleeve, and it seems easier to slip her own arm away into the jumper, hot against her flesh and then, with one quick and graceful movement, to pull the whole thing off. She starts running. By a miracle, she doesn't fall.

There are gasps, noise, outraged shouts; possibly cheering. Nothing to hold back now, she thinks as she stumbles, then runs, on towards the end of the platform. Have a look, then, Giles bloody Yeo, Bill bloody Wallis, Mr fucking fucking Viney. If you're so sodding interested, have a big fat look.

She unbuttons her skirt, undoes the zip and lets it fall. Oh, the feeling of air on her poor hidden skin. Out of the vestibule, down the steps, outside, and she is free.

42

'I shouldn't laugh,' says Laura to her daughter.

For a woman prone to embarrassment, she has very rapidly learned to endure. First there was the hurried gathering up of Marina's jumper and box-pleated skirt and her own coat and bag, then following, blushing, in her wake as she bounded off the platform and made for the doors. Behind them, Alexander Viney said, 'My work has had some extreme reactions, but that—' and his audience laughed sycophantically, then with relief as he just carried on. Towards the back people were standing up, meaning to catch her naked daughter. Laura did not look back, even when she heard an official voice saying, 'Mrs Farkas!' as if she was the one who had erred.

Of course, she has. Clutching her child's garments, she burst out of the doors and found her just outside, shivering on the bottom step.

'Marina!'

'Thank you,' said her daughter.

Then it was a matter of hasty dressing, watched by a handful of spectators at the top of the steps. Marina was quiet: could this be shock? And, after that, who could blame her?

'Mrs Farkas,' said the voice again, now at her shoulder: a fat little man with many chins. 'I must insist—'

'God,' said Marina quietly.

'You're Marina's housemaster, aren't you?' says Laura.

'We have met,' he says. 'I—'

'The person responsible for her pastoral care? I'm sure we were told that when she first arrived.'

'Well, yes. And as Dr Tree's deputy vice-master I must ask you—'

It came from nowhere; Laura, the weakling, was suddenly strong. She held up her hand to stop him, palm outward and he, just as surprised as she was, fell silent. She swallowed hard.

'I think,' she found herself saying, 'that anyone with the least understanding of pastoral care would see that now is not the time.'

Marina gave a tiny whimper.

'I,' Laura announced, 'am taking my daughter home. We will make arrangements for her things.' And, with one arm around Marina's shoulders, without the faintest idea what these arrangements will be, she led her past Divinity Hall and across the Memorial Quad to Garthgate, to the taxi rank, then the station and, eventually, the London train.

To fill the cold anxious wait at Combe Station, Laura bought them coffee, salt and vinegar crisps and a tangerine. They have finished them already. Marina, buttoned up in Laura's coat, says nothing. They sit next to each other in backwards facing seats, in a smoking carriage filled with what seem to be Germans. Laura, thoughtfully licking salt off her fingers, is beginning to realize that, unless she broaches the subject, they will reach London and still Marina will not have spoken. She is also terribly afraid that she may laugh.

'My love,' she says. Her voice sounds crushed. She puts her arm back around Marina's shoulders, leans her cheek against the top of her head and the warmth of her skull, the unwashed familiar smell of her hair, catches her throat.

'Oh God,' says Marina softly. 'I can't believe—'

It would be lovely if the small movements of her head and chest, the snuffling noises, were laughter; of course they are not.

'I can't believe I did that,' she mutters.

'It's OK,' says Laura, wiping her own face with her other arm. She glances down.

Marina is pressing her lips together bravely, but her body shakes with little spasms. Tears drip on her hands. 'I . . . oh, God.'

'Oh God.'

'What will Rozsi say?'

Laura opens her mouth; no platitude comes, only the thought of Rozsi, say, tomorrow morning, when Laura gives them all bigger news than this. She shrugs. 'It will be all right,' she says. 'I'll, well, I'll handle it.'

'Mum, you can't.'

'It's all right. The thing is, love, I'm . . . how . . . it's going to be difficult next term, if you wanted to go back there.'

'I'm not going back,' says Marina simply.

'Aren't you?'

'No.'

'OK. I see. After that I don't really see, anyway, how . . . OK. Fine,' she says.

The train races past a ploughed field and another. If spring is coming out here, there is no sign. Marina is shaking again. 'Shh,' says Laura, stroking her daughter's hair, wiping the tears away, running her fingertips over Marina's cheekbones, her lashes, her mouth, her eyelids. At last she feels her grow calmer.

'You were very brave,' she tells her.

Under her fingers, Marina gives a little smile. 'Do you think so?'

Laura looks down, into her hazelnutty eyes. She knows them like a lover's. 'I do, my love,' she says. 'I do.'

Epilogue

There must be, thinks Laura, sitting in uncomfortable state on the green sofa, an easier way. Running barefoot down a mountainside, for example, bearing stone tablets. Dragging a banner up to the roof of St Paul's: anything to avoid telling her in-laws everything, now, face to face.

She has already informed them that Marina will not be going back to Combe. Their response, by Farkas standards, was curiously muted; partly because Marina herself was there, at Laura's insistence. Perhaps they also sensed further storms ahead.

'*Tair*-ible' they say, and, 'But *vy?*' and, '*Megmondhatjuk Dobos neninek?*' Laura imagines saying, 'Because I've decided and I'm her mother,' but would that make any difference?

'Hang on,' she half-shouts eventually. 'I, I need—' Ildi, thank God, is nearest; Laura glances frantically in her direction and receives what she can only hope is an encouraging smile. 'There are, well, a, a couple of other things we, I—'

'Couple?' asks Rozsi.

'*Leljesen hülye,*' says Zsuzsi. 'Mad.'

'Mum—'

'No, let me,' says Laura, and Marina blinks. 'I . . . well, luckily she can go back to Ealing Girls'.'

Consternation.

'I made a phone call,' she says.

'Mum!' says Marina. 'How could—'

But by now there is so much uproar that Laura can safely ignore her. Surely, she thinks, I could just leave the A-level change for another time? But even she, coward that she is, knows the answer: all or nothing. Slash and burn. 'It's very good news,' she says. 'We're very lucky. They want to have her—'

'*Vell*, of course,' says Zsuzsi indignantly. 'They are lucky. But all those sad old *vom*-ans—'

'There is,' Laura says, 'just one m—' Marina is crying and trying to interrupt. 'Darling, let me. Well, it's good, in a way. They want her to do history again.'

And she sits back, felled by the force of her lie.

In the outrage which follows, she realizes that Marina, whom she had not forewarned, may weaken. While Laura is busy explaining that apparently history is a better choice for Cambridge where, she has been told – by whom? By herself – that medicine isn't even very good, she hears Marina say to Rozsi, 'But if you really want me to I don't m—'

'Sweetheart,' says Laura, 'it's decided.'

She puts out her hand to grab Marina's; she squeezes it hard, to comfort one of them.

'*Tair*-ible,' Zsuzsi says, lighting another cigarette.

'*Von*-darefool,' says Ildi, and smiles. But Laura by now is almost past the point of fear, as though she is leaping boulders, ready to snatch Marina from a lion's jaws, or a woman willing to resist oblivion, the strongest temptation of all, for the sake of her daughter.

'And tonight,' says Laura, 'all of you . . . there's one more thing. Something good, or bad. Well, both, I suppose. You're having a visitor.'

Author's Note

As the grandchild of TransCarpathian-Ruthenian former subjects of the Austro-Hungarian Empire, who were born in what is now the Ukraine, learned their sums in Russian, spoke Hungarian together yet considered themselves Czech, I grew up knowing only the smallest and most confused details about where my maternal grandparents came from, or the language they spoke to each other. I inherited most of their dictionaries, including László Országh's *A Concise Hungarian–English Dictionary* (Akadémiai Kiadó, Budapest, 1967) and *English–Hungarian Dictionary* (Akadémiai Kiadó, Budapest, 1955), both carefully wrapped in plastic and smelling of their flat, from which I discovered that the very few words I thought I knew (dressing gown, central heating) were spelled rather differently from how I had assumed.

It was only when I began to write this novel that I realized how very little I knew about the history of Hungary and the Carpathian mountains. Slowly, painfully, I saw that knowledge was not the point; it was the lives of central Europeans in England, and their silence about the past, which interested me. Consequently – what a wonderful excuse – my research was dominated by one of my and my grandparents' main interests: food. I particularly recommend:

Maria Floris, *Cooking for Love* (Putnam, London, 1959), for its old-fashioned intimacy, Anglophilia and wit; it could have been written by Mrs Dobos.

Károly Gundel, *Hungarian Cookery Book* (Corvina Press, Budapest, 1974).

Erzsébet Hunyady, *A jó Házi Konyha* (Singer & Wolfner, Budapest, early 20th century).

George Lang, *The Cuisine of Hungary* (Penguin, London, 1985), which has all the recipes for Witches' Froth, Eggs Metternich, Transdanubian Corn Cake, Wild Duck with Quinces and *Hortobágyi reszelt tészta tüdővel* (grated noodles with calf's lung filling as in Hortobágy) that one could wish for.

József Venesz, *Hungarian Cuisine* (Corvina Press, Budapest, 1963), chiefly for its startling photographs.

However, certain other books were also helpful for atmosphere, and a little detail, particularly:

Péter Baki/Colin Ford/George Szirtes, *Eyewitness: Hungarian Photography in the Twentieth Century* (Royal Academy of Arts, London, 2011).

Adam Biro, *One Must Also Be Hungarian* (University of Chicago Press, Chicago, 2006).

Edita Katona, *Code-Name Marianne* (Fontana, London, 1977).

Sándor Márai, *Embers* (Viking, London, 2002).

George Mikes, *How to Be an Alien* (Penguin, London, 1966) which, more than anything else, captures the character of the Hungarians I knew; it could have been entitled *How to Handle a Hungarian*.

G. Pálóczy-Horváth, *In Darkest Hungary* (Gollancz, London, 1944).

Jan Pieńkowski, *The Fairy Tales* (Puffin, London, 2005).

Daniel Snowman, *The Hitler Emigrés* (Pimlico, London, 2003).

Bram Stoker, *Dracula* (Penguin, London, 1994).

And lastly:

Ann Barr and Peter York, *The Official Sloane Ranger Handbook* (Ebury, London, 1982) and *The Official Sloane Ranger Diary* (Ebury, London, 1983).

Glossary and Pronunciation

In Hungarian, the emphasis is always on the first syllable. This makes the pronunciation of many English words and phrases rather distinctive:

Don't be funny – *Donnt*-be-fanee
Never mind – *Nair*-vairmind
Wonderful – *Von*-darefool
Terrible – *Tair*-ible
Attila – *Ott*-illó
Waterloo – *Vort*-aloo
Westminster Court – *Vest*-minstaircourt
Rozsi – *Roe*-ji
Zsuzsi – *Ju*-ji
Marinaka – *Mor*-inókó

Hungarians will tell you proudly that their language is phonetic. However, learning how to pronounce each letter takes a little time:

Á or *a* like the English 'ó' as in 'Pot'
C like the English 'ts' as in 'Volts'
Gy like the English 'dy' as in 'D'ye know where the bus is?'
I like the English 'ee' as in 'Flee'
Lj like the English 'ly' as in 'Lure'
Ö like the English 'er' as in 'Her'
S like the English 'sh' as in 'Shame'

Sz like the English 's' as in 'Sausage'
Ü like the English 'oo' as in 'Look'
Zs like the French 'j' as in 'Je'

This is how the following Hungarian words and phrases are pronounced, or at least were pronounced by my grandparents, and what, roughly, they mean in English:

Igen – *ee*-gen (Yes)
Köszönöm – *kus*-unum (Thank you)
Boldog születésnap – *bull*-dog *soo*-lertaishnop
    (Happy birthday)
Hogy vagy – *hodge vodge* (How are you?)
Szervusz – *sare*-vus (I am at your service)
Kezét csókolom – *ke*-zet *choc*-olom (I kiss your hand)
Kedves egészségére! – *ked*-vesh *egg*-ayshaygaydre! (Cheers, i.e. to
    your house)
Krumplisaláta – *krum*-plysólótó (Potato salad)
Paprikás krumpli – *pó*-prikoshkrumply (Potatoes with
    paprika)
Körözött – *ker*-erzert (Liptauer-style cream cheese spread with
    caraway and paprika)
Egyszersmind – *edj*-sairshmeend (At the same time)
Összehasonlíthatatlan – *ursh*-sehóshernleehótótlón
    (Incomparable)
Hanyszor fogsz felkelni ma éjjel? – *Hony*-sore forgs *fel*-kelnee
    ma *ay*-el? (How many times will you get up tonight?)
Ahányszor kell – *O*-hawnysore kell (As often as
    I need to)
Édes Zsuzsi, Virág virágnak – *Ey*-desh *Ju*-ji, *vee*-rog *vee*-rognok
    (Sweet Zsuzsi, flower to flower)

Huszonnyolc – *huss*-onyoltz (Twenty-eight)

Üdvözöljük – Ood-verzerlynook (You are welcome)

Nez – *nayz* (Look)

Nem – *nem* (No)

Nem tu dom – *nem*-tudom (I don't know); 'nemtudom' plums are really called this

Hihetetlen – *hi*-hetetlen (Unbelievable)

Em érted – *em air*-ted (You don't understand)

Viszontlatasra – *viss*-ontlaataashró (Goodbye)

Madártej – *mod*-arté (Floating islands)

Dios torta – *dee*-oshtortó (Walnut cake)

Mákos – *mark*-osh (Poppy seed)

Palacsinta – *pol*-oshintó (Pancake)

Kukorica – *koo*-koritsó (Corn)

Pongyola – *pon*-dyuló (Dressing gown)

Kavitchka – *kaa*-vitchkó (Little coffee)

Szívesen – *See*-vershen (You're welcome)

Buta – *boo*-tó (Stupid)

Csúnya – *choon*-yó (Ugly)

Popsi – *pop*-shi (Bum) also *popó* – *pó*-po

Nagyon szép ház – *nodg*-on sep hoss (A beautiful house)

Kivel beszél – *kee*-vel *bess*-el (Who is she talking to?)

Yoy de édes – *Yoy* de *ai*-desh (Oh, so sweet!)

Nagyon édes – *nodg*-on *ay*-desh (Very sweet)

Teljesen hülye – *tel*-yesen *hoo*-ye (Completely bonkers)

Megmondhatjuk Dobos neninek? – *Meg*-mondhotyook *Dob*-osh *nay*-ninek? (How do I tell Mrs Dobos?)

Acknowledgements

Thank you to:
Marta Buszewicz, Tina Cotzias,
Jane Craig, Marion Donaldson, Lucia Grun,
Mary-Anne Harrington, Pat Kavanagh, Martha Lane Fox,
Jean MacDonald, Kati Mendelson, Max Mendelson,
Rachel Mendelson, Jane Morpeth, Elaine O'Dwyer,
Tamara Oppenheimer, Nicola Roche, Kate Saunders,
Helen Simpson, Caroline Stofer
. . . they know why.

To:
Claire Baldwin, Lynne Drew, Judit Katona-Apte,
Hannah Robson, Àgnes Szervànszky,
Valerie Thomas, Jon Woolcott
. . . for linguistic and other help.

And to all at Rogers, Coleridge and White,
especially Gill Coleridge;
to all at Mantle and Picador,
especially Maria Rejt and Camilla Elworthy;

and to Joanna Briscoe, above all.